Rum 'n' Coke

Roger Smith

First published in the UK by Print2Demand in conjunction with
The Tap Publishing,
Suite 24, Parker House,
Mansfield Road, Derby DE21 4SZ.
enquiries@thetap-publishing.com

This novel is entirely a work of fiction. Any similarity to names or characters,
living or dead, events or localities is entirely coincidental.

ISBN 978-1-910693-82-7

Rum 'n' Coke

Songs of Change

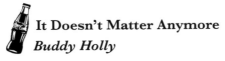

It Doesn't Matter Anymore
Buddy Holly

This'll be the day that I die, he thought. He was falling, trapped in metal. Yet it'd become strangely quiet, almost serene. The lights below started to gather speed and race towards him. He was frightened and helpless.

Looking for hope or comfort, he glanced over at the slightly older man in the Stetson hat who was wrestling in vain to control their fate, but he was preoccupied, swiping wildly at the condensation gathering on the inside of the small windscreen. The man's wide eyes were staring dead ahead, transfixed by the inevitable events that were unfolding right in front of them. His white knuckles were drained of blood; his hands gripped the controls but there was nowhere to go.

His passenger's knuckles were also white, but from gripping the contours of a coke bottle. The contents of which, it seemed to him, he had started in another time and place. The speeding lights, bigger and brighter now, were almost upon them. He could see the ground - a field, fences, shrubs. He closed his eyes submitting to his fate; thinking of his family and the girl, who he suddenly realised, would have had his love forever. But forever was nearly over.

Minutes, seconds, or milli-seconds passed. Nothing had happened. The younger man opened his eyes but they were slammed shut by an unimaginable, violent and irresistible force.

Eventually he opened them again, slowly waking from the dreadful nightmare. But he wasn't staring at the cracks in his bedroom ceiling. There were stars above and in his head. A yellow cloud passed over the moon. He felt as if his body was separated from his head. He looked down and pain shot down through his back. He looked to the right and from the corner of his eye he saw a pile of twisted metal, hissing and heaving like an ugly monster in its death throes. He could see part of a broken wing sticking out of the ground, next to it a crumpled Stetson hat. Beyond that was a body which appeared to be sleeping peacefully except that one leg was twisted up towards the night sky at a hideous angle.

He began to come to his other senses. There were noises like wailing sirens. Another gaseous cloud, green this time, passed above the bizarre montage of broken images. He wondered where he was, what had happened and whether he was still alive. He was sure that the strange, surreal landscape wasn't heaven.

I Hear A New World
The Blue Men

I woke to a new decade. The Sixties. A decade without Buddy Holly. The Sixties. It sounded modern and new but everything around me looked the same.

Fortunately the exciting new age started on a weekend – no school. As usual on a Saturday morning I caught the bus into town with my mate, Whippet, real name David Willis, who lived down the road in Borrowash. The village, just five miles from town, had become a virtual suburb following the post-war council estate building boom. We walked down the same fifties style road where and caught an old fifties style Trent bus. From the back seat, the passengers didn't look different either - flat caps, school caps (even on a Saturday), headscarves and trilbies. No sign of the sixties so far.

Once in town, Whippet had to help his dad at his stall on the open market for an hour so I went onto Cock Pit Hill to watch my favourite street trader - Mad Harry. The icy wind was whipping through the makeshift market stalls and I could still see frost between the cobbles. I loved watching Mad Harry though. Just as he was about to offer a fist full of cheap toiletries to the bargain hunters he'd stop, hesitate for effect, and then make his trademark announcement at the top of his voice.

'Tell you what I'll do, I'll throw these in as well.'

'And I don't even want six shillings; I don't want five and six.'

'They're yours for five bob the lot.'

'Lady over there Bill', he shouted to his assistant.

'Another lady there ...'

When I looked around there wasn't a lady over there. Unless it was the old biddy I'd often seen helping to pack away at the end of the day. But it was still entertaining and almost as good as watching TV.

When Whippet had finished, we did what we do every Saturday when the Rams weren't at home. We went to Alf James's joke shop. I bought some floating sugar lumps and a joke fag. Whippet got a Bird Warbler - a little device that you put at the back of your throat. I was afraid that he'd swallow it but Whippet mastered it within minutes.

I managed to persuade Whippet not to buy any stink bombs – I couldn't stand the smell. And in any case, this routine suddenly seemed a bit childish and not something that belonged in the shiny new sixties. Nevertheless we carried on round town, Whippet warbling away and me with a joke fag hanging out the corner of my mouth. But no one gave me a second look. We were definitely too old for this.

Before catching the bus back to Borrowash we had a coke in the Snackery opposite the bus station. They hadn't mended the 'S' on the neon sign which still read 'nackery'.

We saw Eileen Cole from school on the bus. But she looked very different. Not just because she wasn't in her school uniform. She'd suddenly developed tits. Two pointy cones sticking out of her jumper. She offered her fare to the cheeky Barton bus conductor.

'Don't you point those things at me duck', he said. Eileen blushed but seemed pleased that he'd noticed.

I'm sure she didn't have tits at school yesterday. Perhaps the sixties *will* look different and that's what happens to all sixteen year old girls at the turn of a decade. I decided to conduct a survey at school next week, the start of my final term at school. My last few weeks as a child.

On the second day of the Sixties there was still no sign of this shiny new decade. Everything looked the same. Mind you, Sundays never seemed modern and new. There was never anything to do or anywhere to go.

I got my old fashioned 1950s rusty pushbike out and went down to the playing fields. The park had a small brook running through it and the entire recreation area was known locally as Down Brook. I hated my bike. You never saw anyone under thirty riding a sit-up-and-beg bike. They were designed to transport middle aged men to work; either to the Celanese chemical factory in Spondon or the Railway Works in town, snap bags over their shoulders as they rode.

It was freezing on the playing fields but at least Down Brook was somewhere to hang out and get away from stuffy Sundays at home. Away from the boring *Billy Cotton Band Show* and *Sing Something Simple* on the radio, and the smell of roast meat and gravy (Why couldn't we have chips with Sunday dinner?)

I played football for a bit with the mob. It was too cold to play cards. A new kid with an Everley Brothers haircut came down showing off the new Mercian racing bike he'd had for Christmas. When it started to get dark I picked up my rusty bike and went home for a Sunday tea as unappetising as dinner - corned beef sandwiches, tinned fruit and Carnation milk (yuk!). And nothing but religious programmes on TV.

To relieve the boredom I tried my floating sugar lumps but fooled nobody. As my older brother pointed out, we'd probably never had a sugar lump in the house before.

The third day of the 60s was spent at school. I started my

survey on the anatomy of sixteen-year-old girls and dared the lads to touch Eileen Cole's tits. At morning break we hung around in a huddle and then one of us would rush forward and try to make contact with them. Robin Woolley was the only one that penetrated the circle of girls that tried to protect her like clucking mother hens. But when he touched one of the cone shaped points it just collapsed. What a disappointment.

The day ended with dreaded double maths but I noticed that John Wilkins had started wearing really cool clothes with his school uniform. He looked American with his black suede shoes, white socks and a really great cut-away collar shirt with little shiny flecks in the fabric. Perhaps that was why all the girls fancy him. I decided that I looked really old fashioned and scruffy and that if the 60s wouldn't come to me then I should go out and do something about it. It was time to wake up, wise up and grow up.

It was the first week of the new decade and I had to work twice as hard as I had in the fifties. To cover for a kid who had caught Asian flu I was doing the morning paper round as well as my usual evening route. But I was grateful for the extra money and had decided to buy a pair of black Jeans from the market.

I woke up to the sight of my own breath and frosty swirls on the inside of the window. It must have been the coldest night in history. I had slept with a football shirt and socks under my pyjamas and dreamt I was playing for Derby County on a snow covered Baseball Ground.

As I lay in the warmth of my football kit willing myself to brave the frosty air, I decided to make some more changes to my imaginary room. Nobody was allowed in this room and I went there whenever I needed to escape from the real world. I added big modern radiators painted the same red as the Coca-Cola chiller cabinet that sat in the corner. The room was accessed from a secret door behind my wardrobe. It had plush, wall-to-wall carpet, no lino in sight, and a leopard skin studio couch. A Bal-Ami Juke Box had all the records from the current Hit Parade as well as every Buddy Holly release. The windows had modern venetian blinds and one wall was completely covered in Bamboo with a neon sign reminding me that I was in *The Sunset Lounge.*

I dragged myself out of the room and out of bed by counting down from ten but it took about eight attempts. At least when you're late you have to move fast which keeps you warm.

 ## Tribute to Buddy Holly
Mike Berry

February 3rd 1960. One month into the new decade and at last there was something new to do. An organised wake Down Brook. It was one year since Buddy Holly was killed when the plane carrying him, The Big Bopper and Richie Valens crashed onto a frozen field in Minnesota, USA.

The event had been organised by Bill Sutcliffe, Sooty as we called him, who must have been the late, great's most ardent fan. Thanks to Sooty most of our mob idolised Buddy. To be accepted as a credible teenager in the village, you had to declare allegiance to either Elvis Presley or Buddy Holly. Buddy was our chosen one. We knew the titles of all of his songs and the lyrics to most of them. It was as if we knew him and he knew us, his memory belonged to our little crowd.

Sooty and his younger brother were brought up by their Auntie and Uncle after both parents had been killed in a car crash when their Standard Vanguard was crushed by a lorry on the A52. Sooty left school early, aged fourteen, to carry on his father's market gardening business and had harboured a morbid fascination for death ever since. At nineteen, a few years older than the rest of us, he was the only one in the crowd who could drive.

In 1958 Sooty had seen Buddy Holly and the Crickets on stage at the Theatre Royal in Nottingham and on summer nights Down Brook he liked to tell stories of the night our hero performed less than twelve miles away. He'd tell us how the amplifiers were larger than the bonnet of his Bedford Dormobile van and how the sound from the electric guitars was deafening. But our favourite story related to the Stetson hat that Sooty always wore. He claimed that he caught it after it was thrown from the stage following the rousing encore. Sooty was convinced that it belonged to Buddy Holly himself and when Buddy died in the plane crash a year later he saw it as a sign from his dead parents. After that Sooty worshiped the memory of Buddy Holly to the point of religious fervour.

Although we had all agreed to turn up wearing nothing but black, some of us were obviously compromised by limited wardrobes. I wore my new black jeans and a navy jumper under the old grey duffel coat I wore for school. Little Jimmy Sutcliffe arrived late wearing his uncle's black leather motorbike suit and boots which were about ten sizes too big for him. We saw him trudging down the hill in the gathering gloom like the Monster from the Black Lagoon. His little pin head stretching up above the collar every now and again so that he could see where he was going. When he got closer we noticed that his normally blond hair was black. He had rubbed shoe polish into his scalp which made him smell like the cobbler's shop in the village. As the night wore on and the drizzle increased the shoe polish started to run down his face. We all ended up in the bus shelter singing Buddy's songs to Tony Tolley's guitar but with little Jimmy Sutcliffe looking more like one of the Black and White Minstrels than a devotee of a Rock 'n' Roll legend.

It was getting colder as we huddled together in the gloom and Julia Woodhouse asked if she could cuddle inside my duffel coat. Her warm body next to mine felt great and she smelled so wonderful. Better still I was sure that, now and then, she pressed hard against me. Maybe it was just because she was so cold. Or perhaps she was teasing and actually fancied me. Thinking these irreverent thoughts on the anniversary of Buddy's death made me feel guilty. Like when you got the giggles in church. But I had discovered a new powerful sensation that kept me awake that night.

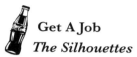

Get A Job
The Silhouettes

Valentine's Day was a special day for me, but not for the obvious reasons. It was the day of my first job interview for the position of apprentice compositor in the printing department of the local weekly newspaper, The Derbyshire Advertiser.

When my mum woke me she presented me with a pink envelope. That was when I found out that it was possible to feel sick with embarrassment and excited at the same time. There it was. Addressed to me – Joseph Maxwell King. My first Valentine's card. But when my mum teased me about it I was overcome with panic and couldn't eat my breakfast. I suggested that one of the boys at school must have sent it to me as a joke.

I felt really grown-up as I waited for the bus into town with all the office workers. The interview was the first time I'd done anything important without my mum or dad, but I was nervous about the interview. What if I suddenly developed a stutter or was unable to remember really basic things like my name and address. But the thought of getting a job, giving up the paper round and having money to spend on records and clothes helped steady my nerves. I wondered what my hero, Kookie from TV's 77 Sunset Strip, would do in this situation. He'd probably breeze in, slide into the chair, put his feet up on the desk then slip a comb from his back pocket to give his quiff a quick tease. He'd perhaps start the interview by announcing

'Hey man, I hear you need to be clued-up on the King's jive to do this number.' (I understand you need to be good at English to get this job). I decided to think of Kookie if my nerves got the better of me.

My interview was with the Managing Director, a Mr William Blake. Although he sounded stuffy and the offices were a bit like something out of Dickens, the ordeal was quite painless. To my complete surprise I was offered the job straight after the interview. And that was despite the answer I gave when asked what I thought of the two pounds, ten shillings and sixpence per week starting wages.

'That's cool with me', I said. 'The bread isn't as important as a steady job.'

On the Fourteenth of April I would start a six-year apprenticeship to become a Compositor. But Kookie nearly cost me the job. It was time to leave him behind.

Back at school I had spent the rest of the afternoon in a state of anticipation wondering who could have sent the Valentines card. Could it have been the beautiful Anthea Knight? Or her ugly friend? Perhaps one of my mates did send it as a joke. But then surely they wouldn't waste their money. What if my mum had sent it to protect me from feeling insecure? But then she'd have sent my brother one as well.

I did my paper round after school but instead of keeping my uniform on I changed into my new black jeans. The Evening Telegraphs were thicker that day and the strap on the bag nearly broke my neck. At least with every paper delivered the bag got lighter. On the front page there was a picture of some bloke holding a copy of the controversial new paperback *Lady Chatterley's Lover* and a report that Clulows book shop in town had sold out by mid-day. Apparently the book was full of sex and Whippet had suggested our gang chip-in towards the three shillings and six pence to buy a copy.

As I rounded into Charnwood Avenue I discovered another Valentine's card suspect - the girl at the end house who always came to the window when I delivered their paper. She wasn't bad but she couldn't have been any older than fourteen. She came out of the house and pretended to be looking for someone in the street. I was glad I was wearing my new jeans.

When I'd finished I went Down Brook to meet the mob. But it was too cold to hang around so we went to the chip shop in the village. I just had enough money for six penn'orth of chips and a small bottle of pop. When I asked for some fish bits the old woman behind the counter gave me a wink and a big toothless smile and said 'Bein' as it's you, ya can mi duck'. Perhaps she'd sent the Valentine's card. I went home feeling slightly deflated except for the fact that the next day would be my last day at School.

School Is Out
Gary US Bonds

When I wiped the sleep from my eyes and realised what day it was I expelled a huge sigh of relief. That special day had finally arrived but I hadn't been looking forward to it with the same excitement as Christmas. It was more like waiting for freedom and independence and the chance to do grown-up things.

I caught the school bus for the last time and ran to the XL Chewing Gum machine for the last time. And yes! The arrow on the knob you turn after putting your penny in was pointing towards me which meant I got two packets instead of one. Some kids can afford to put more than one penny in if the knob isn't on the fourth turn. I never could, so then I knew it was going to be a great day.

Besides being the last day for the final year kids like me and some of the teachers, it was the last day for the whole school at its present site. It was moving from the ancient clutter of

Victorian buildings and prefabs into a new custom-built metal and glass structure down the road. So it was the end of an era for every pupil and every teacher.

All day there was an atmosphere of subdued revelry and rebellion. It was as if at any minute some kid would crack, pull out a machine gun and spray the staff room with bullets while the teachers sipped their mid-morning coffee. We wondered if big Barry Bostock would do what he had threatened and throw every prefect down the air raid shelter.

But it wasn't a happy day for everyone. Some of the girls huddled in little groups crying while prefects hurried around looking nervously over their shoulders.

By lunchtime though, the only sign of anarchy was the chanting of 'No more school, no more books, no more teachers' dirty looks.' Then, just as we were due to file back into class following afternoon break, it happened. Miss Bretles, the highly-strung R.E. teacher, suddenly appeared on the school steps. But she was completely naked except for a red ribbon round her neck attached to a P.E. whistle which dangled provocatively between her breasts. She stood there shaking for a while then delivered the speech which she'd probably rehearsed while she had been off school with a suspected nervous breakdown.

'You little scabby shits! I'm free from you at last!' She shrieked from the steps. 'Shits! Shits! Shits!' She pointed an accusing finger in turn at the groups of kids in the playground who were frozen like statues in open mouthed amazement. Eventually Mr Davies came to her rescue and pushed through the burgeoning crowd of gaping kids. After covering her nakedness with his jacket, he led the blubbering Miss Bretles back into school.

Songs of the Morning

First Date, First Love, First Kiss
Sonny James

The first time I ever kissed a girl was unremarkable. I was eleven and Peter Davis's sister, who was two years older than me, made me kiss her in a phone box while all the other kids from the street pressed their snotty noses up to the small windows. As I recall, I didn't feel anything other than the physical sensation of lips on lips.

After further experiments with willing volunteers I eventually discovered that this simple, physical interaction could produce a sublime feeling that passes through your whole body like a gentle wave of pleasure. And I eventually learnt that a kiss is the gateway to other much more exciting pleasures of the flesh.

I'd been trying to engineer an opportunity to get Julia Woodhouse alone for weeks. Today, after Youth Club, my chance arrived. We were all hanging round the chip shop in the village when Julia announced that she had to go home. Although panic set in for a moment I managed to sound reasonably casual when I said.

'I'm off too, I'll walk with you.'

As we crossed the playing field Down Brook I knew that this was my chance to let her know that I fancied her. While she chatted happily about everything and nothing – my new job, her new shoes, her mates, Bobby Vee, the new banana flavoured ice-lolly from Walls - I was trying to pluck up the courage to kiss her. But I couldn't work out how to interrupt her and make the approach. I knew I couldn't ask her if I could kiss her and eventually realised that it would have to involve some initial physical contact from me. But each step we took was taking the opportunity further away. Then, on the metal bridge over the brook, I pounced. At first she seemed frightened as I grabbed her shoulders and turned her towards me. But then she relaxed as if she knew what was coming and, as she looked up towards me, her beautiful long black eyelashes managed a little provocative flutter.

She smelled so warm and feminine, like the cosmetic department in Boots. Then it was happening. And although I wasn't quite sure how long to continue each kiss I'm sure she was as excited as I was. She started to breathe heavily and pressed her body against mine. I knew that the memory of that first experience of nervous excitement deep in my stomach would stay with me forever.

We walked up the hill and into the estate in silence. I didn't know what to say to her. It didn't seem right to talk about everyday things after we'd been so intimate. Then, at her garden gate she spoke.

'You got my card then?' she said with a cheeky smile. And then ran off up her path.

Later, as I lay in bed staring at the ceiling, trying to relive every millisecond of that first real kiss, I decided that Julia Woodhouse would be allowed into my imaginary room, *The Sunset Lounge*.

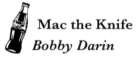 ## Mac the Knife
Bobby Darin

As the Guild Hall clock struck nine, I entered the adult world.

Today was my first day at work and, just as she did for my dad, my mum had packed me up with a mountain of cheese sandwiches wrapped in the red and white striped greaseproof paper that the bread had come in.

The Derbyshire Advertiser was housed in a four storey, Georgian building on the south side of the Market Place. I was excited about working right in the centre of town with the hustle and bustle of the shops, coffee bars and pubs. Some of the kids who left school with me got jobs at the massive Rolls-

Royce or Railway works. But that would have felt too much like school to me, having to serve time away from the real world.

I had arrived fifteen minutes early so I walked round town and through the Market Hall and watched the traders stacking their fruit and veg and preparing for the day. Then I loitered outside the Advertiser window looking at the photographs that captured the dramatic local events of the previous week. There were stunning shots of businessmen cutting ribbons outside new buildings, a large group of smiling workers dressed in their Sunday best standing in front of an excursion bus, dozens of beaming newly weds, and then - the obvious scoop of the week - an enormous Shire Horse with massive bollocks and a rosette pinned to its arse. I knew then that my decision to take a job at the cutting edge of newspaper production was the right one for me. So on the ninth bong from the clock that towered above the market place I walked into a brand new world.

After waiting awkwardly in the reception area I was collected by the foreman, Walter Wrigley, who led me up three flights of rickety wooden stairs to the Composing department. There he introduced me to another new apprentice who was starting at the same time as me and one of the senior journeymen, Eric Champion, who was put in charge of us. Eric was a well built bloke in his late twenties who also assisted the newspaper's photographer during busy times. He was really kind and sympathetic to the traumas of starting work with strange people in a strange environment. The fact that I wasn't not the only new boy also made me feel a little less awkward.

The other kid's name was Ken Mackenzie but he insisted that everyone should call him Mac. Although he was the same age as me he looked much older and more hip. His jet-black hair was shiny with Brylcreem and swept back at the sides then over the top so that a large quiff hung over his forehead - a sharp contrast to my short back and sides with parting. Next to Mac I still looked like a schoolboy. His clothes were different too. He wore large *brothel creeper* suede shoes that stuck out from his black, twelve inch bottomed, cavalry twill trousers like boats. He didn't wear a tie like me. His shirt was open at the neck revealing a crisp, white cotton tee shirt underneath. But it was the final touch that did it – his shirt collar was turned up at the back.

Mac was Derby's answer to my hero from 77 Sunset Strip. Although he looked a bit like Kookie, he wasn't as light-hearted and friendly. In fact he seemed to have a dark and dangerous side. Even on the first day of his new job he exuded a natural confidence that some would interpret as cockiness. He displayed an obvious reluctance to do anything he was told and before long he was swaggering around with a permanent sneer on his face. Nevertheless, Mac fascinated me and immediately became my role model. At lunchtime, in front of the mirror in the toilet, I practised curling one side of my upper lip. But both sides kept curling up together. Then I tried combing my hair up at the sides but it was too short.

The *Stone Room* where Mac and I worked was on the third floor at the rear of the building. This was where the metal lines of type from the Linotype machines, and the half-tone photographic plates were made up into pages. The compositor's job was to place the type in columns around the pre-set advertisements and have the news headlines set according to house-style, position and column width. Besides us and Eric Champion three other men worked in the *Stone Room*, standing all day, making up the pages on large metal surfaces called *Stones*. The room was small and narrow with windows down one side. At the far end, on the left, was a small, hand operated lift, more like a dumb waiter. After publication this was used to send the discarded type down to the machine room to be melted down and recycled. In the other corner, next to a window was a large copper, gas urn that looked like an antique from a Turkish bazaar. In between the two, on the far wall was an old-fashioned ornate domestic gas fire, the only source of heat in the room.

Like all the departments at the Advertiser, the *Stone Room* had a unique atmosphere along with its own distinctive smell. In this case, a mixture of machine oil, molten lead, gas from the leaking urn and the delicious aroma of freshly ground coffee which wafted in through the window from Kardoma Café round the corner.

As apprentices, Mac and I also had to make the tea and fetch chips and cigarettes for the men in the *Stone Room* and *Linotype Room*. As we busied ourselves round the tea urn, Mac suggested I should have a cool nickname like his. As we were thinking of suitable names he suddenly shouted out.

'You must be joking.'

I explained that I hadn't said a word.

'No, you must be Joking. Joseph King – Joking,' He repeated.

I couldn't believe that in more than sixteen years no one else had spotted that one, or what my parents were thinking when they christened me. I didn't fancy going through the rest of my life with people coming up to me and saying 'You must be joking' so Mac suggested *Ginner* to reflect the colour of my hair and as a tribute to one of Derby's most notorious ginger haired Teddy Boys who was also dubbed *Ginner*.

At the end of my first day at work, I was emotionally and physically knackered. There had been so many people to meet, new images to take in and things I had to remember. But I was happy to be part of the adult world at last.

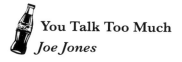 **You Talk Too Much**
Joe Jones

The first month at work went like a flash. My body had adjusted to the increase in physical activity and my hair had grown enough for me to lose my parting, with the aid of a small pot of Brylcreem. I still couldn't turn my lip up like Mac though.

Today I received my first bollocking from Walter Wrigley the foreman, or Wally, as we called him behind his back. I had overslept and missed the bus and as I was standing by the bus stop working out my excuses, Malcolm Bramley pulled-up in his funny little bubble car and offered me a lift. I walked into the road and climbed in through the single glass door which opened to expose the entire front of the car. I sat on the thinly, upholstered seat that must have been less than three inches from the road, he pulled the door towards him and we trundled off towards town.

Malcolm, who lived in one of the private semi-detached houses on Nottingham Road, was the brother of Julia's best friend Cathy. He was eighteen and worked at a solicitor's office. Like his little sister, Malcolm was a bit of a part-time Beatnik. He looked like the archetypal college boy, with his hair cut into a *short back and sides*, his brown corduroy jacket and striped scarf tied loosely round his neck. But although he was a bit posh and really confident he was a friendly bloke and not at all snobbish.

As we bumped our way to town, I wished that I could be that self-assured. But Malcolm drove with a bit too much confidence for my liking and as we dodged in and out between the cars and buses, our arses inches from the road, I began to fear for my life. Not just because I could imagine our goldfish bowl on wheels disappearing under a lorry, but because Malcolm started to talk enthusiastically about Trad Jazz – Chris Barber, Kenny Ball, Acker Bilk and the like, the music I hated most.

It was seventeen minutes past nine when I flew up the narrow flights of wooden stairs to the *Stone Room*. I was met at the top by Wally, his face flushed and arms folded in that manner that says 'What time do you call this?' I could see Mac over his shoulder, giving me one of his evil, sneering grins. I lied and told Wally that Malcolm's bubble car had collided with a trolley bus in Chaddesden and I had to give a statement to the police. He didn't seem to believe my story and asked if I remembered the name of the policeman. Desperate to make him believe me I said the first name that came into my head.

'Er... it was PC... er... Acker Bilk,' I blurted, regretting my answer before the last syllable had left my lips. To my surprise he accepted my explanation and I thanked God that Wally wasn't into Trad Jazz either.

The irony was that I had managed to get him, of all people, to believe me. Wally, who had a hint of a cultured Scottish accent, was about forty-five and a bachelor who lived alone. As far as we could tell, he had no friends and his only social life was the time he spent at work. At the Advertiser, Wally was famous for his tall stories. He would corner people and tell them the most incredible tales about his life. He once told Eric that while he was cleaning his teeth, a jackdaw had flown-in through the open bathroom window and pecked the gold from a filling in his tooth.

Later that day, Wally cornered me as I was proof-reading the columns of type that had been set for the Fatstock Prices at Bakewell Cattle Market. He had obviously forgiven me and wanted to trump my bubble car story. I was grateful for the break from checking the boring columns of 6-point type and managed an expression of expectant interest. He leaned back against the proofing press, hooked his thumbs into his waistcoat, took a puff of his pipe, and started with the phrase that he always used to introduce one of his stories.

'Well old man, when I...'

He proceeded to tell me that he was a part-time member of the MI5 and that they often called on him for assistance at the weekends. Apparently, last Sunday he had chased a group of bank robbers across a field in his Wolsey Hornet and because it has special suspension and a super-charged overdrive button, he caught up with them and trapped them against a farm gate until the police arrived.

Everyone at work despised Wally but I felt quite sorry for him. He must have thought that the only way he could get people to listen to him was to make his life sound more interesting. The truth was we all indulged him with our mock gestures of surprise and wonderment because he was the Foreman and because it gave us a legitimate break from our labours. This was fine during working hours, but as the clock on the *Stone Room* wall moved closer towards five thirty, I found it difficult to concentrate on Wally's ramblings. With the nights getting lighter, there was still life after work and I couldn't wait to get home and join the mob Down Brook.

Eventually, Wally had either noticed that I was edging myself closer to the door or his story-line had dried up.

'... and that was when they sent the army in,' he continued.

I had one hand on the door and shot another glance at the clock.

'But, you'd better get off now old man,' he said to my relief.

I made a dash for freedom, looking forward to a summer night with my friends. And the prospect of walking Julia home again.

Summertime
Ricky Nelson

Not so many kids went Down Brook during the winter months. But in the warm summer evenings it came alive. To us the playing fields were the centre of our social life with an exciting choice of entertainment options.

There was the *Men Only Club* where the hard gamblers sat in a huddle on the grass playing Brag or Poker with a maximum stake of threepence. Then the *Sporting Club*, just lads again, kicking a football around or playing cricket until the ball floated away down the brook. And my favourite, the *Cabaret Club* because it included girls.

The *Cabaret Club* was centred around Tony Tolley and his guitar. He knew the chords to every Buddy Holly song and learned new ones from the hit parade. Tolley would sit on the steps of the children's slide as if it was a stage while anyone interested gathered below and joined in when they knew the words. Today we were singing Eddie Cochran's *Weekend* which captured the excitement of being a teenager on summer nights.

Julia usually came Down Brook around seven o'clock with Cathy, her best friend. Cathy wasn't pretty like Julia. She was small and mouse-like but did what she could to make up for it by dressing as outrageously as possible. Cathy was the village Beatnik, influenced by her brother Malcolm. She wore his old baggy jumpers most of the time with the obligatory branding of the Beatnik – a CND *Ban the Bomb* badge.

Earlier I had decided to ask Julia out on Saturday to see Cliff Richard in *Espresso Bongo* at the Essoldo cinema. Mac told me they had double seats on the back row where he had once been thrown out for going too far with a girl.

By nine o'clock dusk was descending but there was still no sign of Julia or Cathy. I didn't have the nerve to go to call for her and I thought that I might have missed my chance. Then, just as the mob was beginning to disperse, Julia came over the footbridge where we first kissed. She was on her own and looked upset so I ran to meet her. As I approached she burst into tears and turned away towards the brook. She was sobbing uncontrollably and as I put my arms round her I could feel her whole body shaking. When I asked what was wrong she couldn't speak. Then, through the tears, she managed to tell me.

'It's Uncle Sam,' she sobbed.

'What about him?' I asked while she caught her breath.

'He's... he's dead,' she finally blurted, before giving way to more tears.

I didn't know her Uncle Sam but I could see that he meant the world to her. We sat on the bank of the brook and as I held her close the sound of Tolley's guitar drifted over the playing fields on the summer breeze. They were singing Eddie Cochran's *Three Steps To Heaven* which made Julia sob even louder. I wondered if her Uncle Sam had been killed in a car crash like Eddie had last month.

Julia was inconsolable so I decided to take her home. As we walked up the hill I told her I had been planning to ask her out on Saturday but that I understood if she didn't want to go. To my surprise, she seemed to perk up a little.

'I'd love to go,' she said, giving me a peck on the cheek.

I took her to the door where her mum was waiting anxiously and she thanked me for bringing Julia home. I fumbled with my condolences and managed to mumble that I was sorry about Uncle Sam. But again, to my surprise, her mum just shrugged her shoulders.

'Yes' she said. 'Fred's just scraped him up off the road.'

She sensed that I was confused. 'He's burying him right now in the back garden.'

I walked home still slightly confused. Uncle Sam! What an unusual name for a cat, I thought. Perhaps it was American.

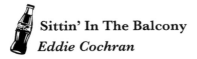 **Sittin' In The Balcony**
Eddie Cochran

What a great day. My first date and my first erotic encounter. The prospect of getting Julia on the double seats at the Essoldo occupied my thoughts all day. I had a bath, cut my nails and Brylcreemed my hair back. I tried to tease the sides over the top of my head into the hint of a quiff but my hair still wasn't long enough. In the end I just turned the collar of my shirt up - my only successful attempt at cool.

Julia looked great when I met her in the village. She had pink lipstick on and wore a white skirt with about six underskirts underneath which made her look like a flirtatious fairy.

While we were waiting for the bus in the village some of the kids from Down Brook saw us. They all started wolf whistling except for one poor, forlorn character dressed in black. It was Sooty who was no longer in mourning for Buddy Holly and had turned his attentions to the late Eddie Cochran. He'd somehow managed to change the hand-painted 'Buddy' on the back of his black zip-up jacket to 'Eddie' but you could still see where he'd extended the 'BU' to make an 'E'. He still wore the Buddy Holly Stetson hat though. I wondered if it was Sooty who was somehow shaping the fate of all these pop stars just to feed his morbid obsession.

I felt so proud to be with Julia as I walked her from the bus stop in Chaddesden to the Essoldo Cinema. I was trying to act as gentlemanly as possible, staying on the road side of the pavement to protect her from the traffic.

At the cinema, flush with my two pounds ten shillings and six pence wages, it was money-no-object. I bought hot dogs and Paynes Poppets, and in the interval Julia had a tub of Neapolitan ice cream and I had an orange ice-lolly.

When the main film started I got closer to Julia on the double seat and slid my arm around her shoulders. It was so hot in the cinema that my lolly was melting faster than I could eat it. And just as Julia nuzzled up to me the rest of the frozen orange separated from its stick and plopped into the lap. Julia squealed and as I frantically fumbled for my clean white handkerchief it was as if the whole cinema had turned round to see what was going on. An usherette briefly shone a torch in our direction. When they all settled down and returned their attentions back to Cliff, I tried to mop the orange from Julia's legs. Then, to my absolute delight, she helped me by slowly pulling the dress over her thighs. I couldn't believe my eyes. The image was so clear, even in the semi-darkness. I was looking at one of the most erotic of sights known to man - stocking tops held up with suspenders which I had only ever seen in a 'Spick'n'Span' Magazine and the pages of Freeman's Catalogue.

As I shakily dabbed the top of her thigh I noticed a cute little mole on the inside of her right thigh. She put her hand over mine, looked up beneath her beautiful long eyelashes and ran her tongue over her full, pink lips.

Julia didn't want dabbing, she wanted to be kissed. Or was it more than that?

Songs of Summer

Summer Holiday
Cliff Richard

The only thing I missed about school was the long summer holidays. At work I only got two weeks off but at least it had come round at last.

Today, the whole family set off for a holiday in Wales. Although I was now officially an adult and I would be leaving Julia and my friends Down Brook, the magic of the family holiday was still there. The excitement of the journey, the discovery of new and strange surroundings, and one whole week away from it all with the focus on fun.

We must have looked like a group of refugees as we struggled up Siddals Road to the railway station with our belongings. Grandma marching out in front, hat clutched to her head while she waved her umbrella to spur us on. She was convinced we would miss the train. Mum carrying baby sister as well as two large bags. My younger brother and I squabbling about which one of us should wheel the pushchair with one of the cases strapped to it and who should lug the other one. Dad, his Trilby hat set at a jaunty angle and a Park Drive stuck in the corner of his mouth. Behind him, my newly-wed, sister, arm-in-arm with my brother-in-law who must have wondered what he had let himself in for. Finally, several paces behind, my older Beatnik brother in his sandals and duffle coat, carrying his book of poetry and trying to pretend that he wasn't with us.

Dad looked longingly as we passed the Alexandra Pub but Grandma waved him on with her umbrella. We didn't miss the train and there was time to buy newspapers, comics and sweets from W H Smith's. I felt really cool buying the New Musical Express and made sure that the title was showing when it was tucked under my arm.

The train was packed with holidaymakers like us and we couldn't find an empty compartment to take us all. So Dad, the master con man, came up with one of his schemes. He took my younger brother and I into a compartment occupied by a middle aged couple and a businessman, brief case on lap. The rest of our party were ordered to wait with our luggage further down the corridor. As soon as the train puffed out of the station my dad put his plan into action. He started to chat with the couple in the corner, just small talk about the weather and where we were heading. Then he presented the poetry book that he had borrowed from my older brother and placed it reverently on his lap.

'So have either of you ever had the calling of our Lord?' He announced in a pompous voice.

There was a silence that seemed to last forever during which I had to bury my head in the NME to hide my laughter. Then, pretending to cough from a blast of coal smoke that had drifted in through the open window, the man finally managed a reply.

'Well, we do go to church on special occasions,' he said, apologetically. 'Weddings, funerals and the like.' He turned to his wife for support. 'Don't we dear?'

At that point I noticed that the businessman had quietly folded his paper and was making a swift exit into the corridor. My dad flicked through the pages of the book, relentless in his assault.

'You see, it's written that we all have the calling deep within us. Maybe I could read this particular extract to you?' He continued.

That was enough for the woman and she prodded her husband in the ribs.

'Come on George, it's our stop next,' she said, rising from the seat.

They left the compartment in a fluster and my brother and I collapsed across the long bench seats, letting out the laughter we had been stifling.

My dad, puffed-up with his success, called the rest of the family into our own private compartment and we continued our journey in comfort. I looked for the poor unfortunate couple when we stopped at Burton-upon-Trent, but of course, they hadn't got off.

Summertime Blues
Eddie Cochran

Although it was great to be by the sea and not to have to go to work, there was not a lot for red blooded teenagers to do in Aberdovey. It was a small seaside town without a funfair or amusements other than crazy golf, tennis courts and a bowling green. There were three licensed hotels, two banks and one pub. I was twelve when we first came here and at that time it seemed like a magical place. My brothers and I were happy to spend days burying each other in the sand dunes, collecting shells and playing crazy golf. And at night, the whole family would play rummy or whist for wine gums and liquorice allsorts which we'd wash down with dandelion and burdock or ginger beer.

Now, every day in Aberdovey seemed like a Sunday. I missed the company of other teenagers, the atmosphere of a busy town centre and, most of all, my new passions in life – girls and pop music.

On Thursday I did manage to find a hint of civilisation. We all caught the train to Towyn, the next town up the coast, and I managed to find a café which served frothy coffee from an Italian espresso machine. But most importantly it had a wonderful Bal-Ami jukebox on the far wall which dominated proceedings like a huge robot. I could have stayed by that jukebox all day, just inhaling the smell of dusty, warm vinyl, waiting in anticipation as its mechanism clicked on to the next selection and feeling the bass notes resound deep in my chest.

When we got off the train back in Aberdovey we were treated to a demonstration of the sheer strength and resolve of the British Army. My older sister was wearing her new spotted bikini which had already raised a few Welsh eyebrows to say nothing of temperatures. As we walked out of the booking hall and into the car park at the rear of the station we were faced with an entire regiment of Welsh Guards. They were standing to attention in full uniform, waiting to board their train. But as soon as they set eyes on my sister, and despite the efforts of the sergeant major, the neat ranks of Khaki disintegrated into a wolf whistling rabble.

As we rushed away from the station with my dad covering up my blushing sister with a beach towel I reflected on how effective it would be to employ these tactics during a war. With the right girls in the right uniforms entire armies could be brought to their knees.

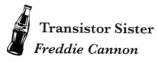 ### Transistor Sister
Freddie Cannon

While we were on the beach today I noticed a girl of about sixteen with her family who were occupying the sand dune next to ours. She was quite tall for her age and not particularly pretty but her brief, white bikini focused my attention on her perfectly formed body. I was captivated by her curves and found it hard to think about much else all day.

To take my mind off her I decided to focus on my other pre-occupation – pop music. My older sister agreed to lend me her Bush transistor radio and although the landlady, Mrs Jones, had strict rules that music must not be played in the rooms, my younger brother and I smuggled it up to our attic bedroom. After nearly a week in Wales on a diet of the Light Programme, the Home Service and Welsh hymns, I was developing withdrawal symptoms. The Jukebox in Towyn had whetted my appetite and I was desperate for a good fix of American pop music which I knew I could find on Radio Luxembourg after dark.

It was nearly midnight before we managed to pick up the signal. Bob Luman was doing his best to reach us over the undulating phasing of the radio waves but now and again a foreign voice would join in.

'Let's think about livin' ... des plateaux ... *about life' ... Let's forget about the* ... minimisent les risques...*and the fellow with the switch blade knife'.*

I rushed to the open attic window to try to improve the reception and placed the radio on the sill. It worked. Maurice Williams and the Zodiacs managed an almost crystal clear rendition of 'Stay'. But in my excitement and an attempt to reduce the volume, tragedy struck. The Radio fell off the windowsill and slid agonisingly slowly down the roof before disappearing over the gutter. Mercifully, the sound of a Bush transistor radio smashing into little pieces on Welsh slate paving didn't materialise. It had found a soft landing.

Although it was after curfew and Mrs Jones would have locked and chained all the doors I knew I had to retrieve my sister's radio. While my brother kept a lookout, I tiptoed down the creaking stairs, undid the front door and slipped into the night. As I found my way to the back of the house and while I was working out where the radio would have landed, help came my way. Deep inside a large bramble bush Sam Cooke was calling to me.

'That's the sound of the men, working on the Chain... Ga-a-ang'.

With blood streaming down my arms from the thorns in the bush, I eventually managed to recover the radio. Sam Cooke had left and as I made for the front door Ricky Nelson was telling all about *Mary Lou*. But the door was locked and must have closed behind me on the latch.

Back at the rear of the house there was no sign of my brother at the window and I knew I couldn't shout him without raising everyone else. I realised there was only one thing for it - the drainpipe. With the radio strap over my bleeding arm and the volume down low, I started my ascent. I made the first floor without any problems. But the drainpipe ended at the gutter and I needed to pull myself onto the roof. Just as I was wondering whether the idea was too risky, Radio Luxembourg once again had a hand in directing events. My free arm had brushed against the volume knob and suddenly Buddy Knox was blasting out his message to the whole of Aberdovey.

'I think I'm gonna kill myself.'

I briefly reflected on the prophetic song title but while contemplating my next move further tragedy befell me. The window right next to me flew open and I was faced with a horror-struck Mrs Jones screaming blue murder. I was screaming too, and so was Buddy Knox. But it was the sight of Mrs Jones that spooked me. Her bulky form was bursting out of a hideous, pink baby doll nightie, the plunging neckline of which was only just managing to contain her heaving bust.

Later, when the household had returned to normal and I had endured almighty bollockings from everyone except my little sister, I lay in bed and reflected on the amazing difference in the half naked images of the female form I had witnessed that day. If the scary encounter with Mrs Jones had served any useful purpose it was probably that it intensified my desire for the girl in the white bikini.

Itsy Bitsy Teenie Weenie Yellow Polkadot Bikini

Bryan Hyland

Today was the sunniest and hottest day so far. As we trouped down to the beach in the usual order, armed with towels, beach balls and picnic basket, and Grandma leading the way waving her trusty umbrella, I decided to try to find my dream girl in the white bikini.

I caught up with Grandma who always chose the sand dune that was to becomes our camp for that day. I deliberately diverted her from her mission by chatting about crown green bowling. Then, as we passed the second sand dune, I saw the white bikini ... then her face. Better still, she saw me and smiled in a way that seemed to promise so much.

That was it. The next sand dune was ours despite a slight protest from Grandma about the amount of spiky grass. We laid our towels out, found some shade for the picnic basket and lit the Primus stove. Grandma's body couldn't function for more than 30 minutes unless it had been revived with a cup of Ty-Phoo tea. I had often wondered if that was the liquid that was fed intravenously to old people in hospital.

Everyone stripped off to their bathing costumes and swimming trunks except me. I hated exposing my body. It looked so puny and you just can't look cool without some form of fashionable attire. So I kept all my clothes on - my jeans, white cut-away collared shirt and the coolest thing I had − my big floppy, powder blue, v-neck jumper. My dad and big brother were threatening to rip my clothes off unless I did it myself so I decided it was time to go for a walk and find the white bikini.

I left our sand dune and started to stroll casually back down the beach. I had to make an impression and imagined what Mac, the master of seduction, would have done. With my collar turned-up and my poor excuse for a quiff teased into place I approached the next sand dune and there she was, playing ball with her little brother. Our eyes met and she smiled that smile again. But I didn't know how to respond other than with another soppy grin.

Before I could think of what to say I had passed the sand dune so I stopped walking. How could I start a conversation? What should I say? What would Mac do? Should I smile or sneer? The sun was pounding down on the back of my jumper and sweat was breaking out on my forehead. How could I look cool when my body was about to self-combust?

Then suddenly a beach ball was heading straight towards me with the bikini in pursuit. This was my chance. But my response was anything but cool. 'Is this your ball?' I stuttered. Her reply was instant.

'Yes, but I'm fed-up playing with my silly little brother. Do you fancy going for a walk?'

Result! I thought it must have been the turned-up collar that did it.

Her name was Pauline and she turned out to be the most forward girl I had ever met. Her confidence was probably due to the fact that she was from Croydon which she told me was not far from London. We walked along the beach back into town and had a milk shake in the Dovey Dairy snack bar.

Pauline was really friendly and easy to talk to, but as she chatted away I was plotting how I could get her alone somewhere. If only I could have just transported her to my imaginary *Sunset Lounge* for a few hours.

We agreed to get together later that evening and take her transistor radio onto the beach. We met at seven o'clock and, even without her white bikini, Pauline looked just as good in pale blue pedal pushers and pink gypsy blouse. She had make-up on, pale pink lipstick and her hair was backcombed into a beehive. It all combined beautifully to make her look older, more sophisticated and even sexier.

Most people had left the beach for the day and we found a secluded sand dune. Pauline had brought a beach towel, her transistor radio and two bottles of Coke. I opened the bottles with my teeth, a cool trick that Mac had taught me, and we lay on the sand listening to Luxembourg. As the sun went down we snuggled closer and closer. Then we kissed. It was amazing. Not like when Julia and I kissed. Her tongue was everywhere, which at first seemed strange, but then I was carried away on a cloud of ecstasy and the fragrance of her perfume.

'You haven't French kissed before, have you?' She said as we broke for air.

But before I could answer, she sat up.

'I thought not, so I'm going to teach you,' she announced, pulling me up to a sitting position.

She started to unbutton my shirt, and then to my delight, began to undo her blouse. She pushed me over onto my back and slowly lowered herself on top of me. I could feel her beautifully formed tits against my skin. She felt and smelt wonderful and I just wanted to stay in that position forever. Then she told me what to do with my tongue and because each move was slow and exaggerated it intensified the excitement.

The sun sank over the sand dune and, in the twilight, we kissed until we couldn't kiss any more. But as we lay looking up at the stars and listening to the waves she broke the magic of the moment and told me she was going home first thing in the morning.

I was devastated, wanting more of this and couldn't believe that someone could come into my life, have such a dramatic effect on my senses, then disappear so quickly and probably forever. On the steps of her guesthouse we kissed goodbye, exchanged addresses and promised to write.

Later, as I lay in bed, I relived every moment of our encounter; every step, every word spoken, every smell, every touch. I even recalled each song that was playing on the radio as if it was background music to a Hollywood movie. But although I knew I would never see Pauline again, I knew that my life would never quite be the same.

Songs of Vision

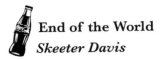

End of the World
Skeeter Davis

Going back to work wasn't as bad as I'd thought. In a way I'd missed Down Brook, the Advertiser and all the characters I worked with. While Mac and I were performing the tedious task of parcelling-up last week's typed-up editorial copy I told him of my French kissing experience. At first he seemed quite proud of me as if I was his protegé.

'You won't be that bad looking when you grow up Ginner, despite the colour of ya hair.' Which was as close you'd get to a compliment from Mac.

But he was disappointed that I hadn't got any further, so he stopped work, lit a cigarette and proceeded to tell me what he would have done, what I should have done and how I should have done it.

The way Mac smoked his cigarettes fascinated me. As he lectured me on the art of seduction, I wondered if I should start smoking to enhance my image. When Mac had lit a cigarette he didn't blow the match out. He flicked the end of the stick with his thumbnail and the flame just disappeared. As he drew in the smoke from his cigarette he'd screw his eyes up as if in pain. Sometimes he'd blow the smoke straight out of his mouth and suck it up through his nose before inhaling. Now and again, he'd spit out bits of stray tobacco from his mouth. But his most amazing trick was when he was trying to impress the girls or assert his hardness in front of his peers. He would take out a cigarette, throw it into the air and catch it between his lips. This he could do in daylight, twilight, while he was walking, while he was talking, even in mid sentence. I wouldn't be surprised if he could do it with his eyes closed.

It was the day before press day and we were working until eight, but by the time Mac had finished his lecherous lecture our shift was nearly over. Despite the late hour, the day was still hot. Britain was in the middle of a heat wave and it always seemed hotter and more humid in the town centre. Even up on the fourth floor of the Derbyshire Advertiser building I could smell tar as if all the streets below were melting. And in the *Linotype room* where the operators set the galleys of type for that week's paper, the molten metal added to the temperature. As the clock moved slowly towards the hour all I could think about was a nice, ice cold bottle of coke.

The morning's national newspapers reported that the leader of a religious sect had predicted that the world would end that day. He had taken his followers 7000 feet up Mont Blanc in France to avoid obliteration. The increasing temperatures seemed to give credibility to his claim.

As I finished my work I promised myself that, providing the world didn't end in the next fifteen minutes, I would drag my hot and weary body round the corner to the Wardwick Café. It was the only place in town where they kept the Coca-Cola bottles just below freezing point.

The Wardwick Café had a long bar down the entire right hand side with high, American style, soda shop stools. Inside the café I headed for a vacant stool and watched with increasing anticipation as the waitress reached into the large red Coca-Cola cooler cabinet for one of the beautifully shaped little bottles. She clipped open the bottle which was still smoking from evaporating ice, inserted a couple of straws and asked me for sixpence.

I sat watching the condensation drip down the sides for quite a while, occasionally running my fingers down its frosty curves. I was teasing myself. I knew that as soon as my raging thirst was quenched, my desire would evaporate as quickly as the condensation on the bottle. I wondered if sex was like that.

Having satisfied my thirst I caught the bus back home. It was too late to go Down Brook so I decided to work on my image. I spent forty minutes in front of the mirror with a packet of my dad's Park Drives practising Mac's aerial fag feat. Most landed on the floor, I nearly swallowed one and they all ended up wet and soggy with much of the tobacco missing, so I threw them all away.

I went off to bed, disappointed, but at least the world didn't end.

Life's Too Short
The Lafayettes

The morning rush hour at home was bedlam today. Everyone was late. My older brother was going back to teachers' training college and couldn't find his scarf. My younger brother needed dinner money and no one had change. I overslept. Mum was frantically trying to make three lots of sandwiches from half a loaf and a bit of cheese. And my dad was flying around in a foul mood because he couldn't find the packet of Park Drives he'd left on the kitchen table last night. Little sister just sat in the middle of the floor with a slice of toast in her mouth while we all flapped around her in a mad panic.

I got to work ten minutes late but fortunately Wally was in a Union meeting in the Machine Room. When he did return, he was red faced and furious. He'd found out that Albert Fletcher, a mere machine minder, had bought one of the sensational new Austin Minis. Wally, owner of a Burgundy Wolsey with walnut dash, had been the only print employee at the Advertiser with a car. He saw owning a car as a status symbol which reinforced his position as Foreman.

After dishing out a few bollockings he calmed down a bit and cornered Mac and I.

'Anyway lads....' he started, and we knew what was coming.

He paused to stuff some St Bruno into his pipe, lit a Swan Vesta match and puffed away until the tobacco glowed red.

'...I've just put my order in for the new Rover 75. Mind you, my little Wolsey can motor a bit. Last weekend when I was passing Burnaston airport I saw a light aircraft that was out of control on the runway.'

You could see that Wally was making this up as he went along because now and again he would pause and look up at the ceiling for inspiration.

'You see the pilot had had a heart attack,' he continued slowly to increase the drama.

'I sensed what had happened and drove onto the runway, caught up with the aircraft, and managed to climb out of my car onto the wing of the plane and into the cockpit...'

Fortunately the internal phone rang in his little cubby-hole of an office and we were spared the rest of his tall story which was incredibly similar to the latest James Bond book.

When Wally returned from his phone call he was ashen. He started running around like a headless chicken, first towards the stairs, then back to his office, then towards the *Linotype Room*. He was shouting something about Jack, one of the older machine minders. In his apparent state of shock his Scottish accent was exaggerated making it almost unintelligible.

'Its Jack! He's trapped! Oh my god! What should...the machine started! Quick!'

He finally disappeared down the stairs, everyone else in pursuit. It sounded as if the building was collapsing as we thundered down the three flights of narrow wooden stairs. In the *Machine Room* at the rear of the ground floor, Albert Fletcher and the other machine minders were right inside the huge Hoe and Crabtree rotary press that printed the Advertiser every Thursday night. A single inspection light bulb in its wire holder was clipped to the machine bathing them in an eerie light. It was unnaturally quiet and Albert was cradling Jack's head which was face down between two huge cylinders, his body twisted unnaturally to one side.

Then I saw Jack's bloodstained arm which didn't seem to be part of the same body. It was twisted at an unnatural angle, pointing bizarrely upwards towards the long ribbons of plain white paper that stretched to the top of the press. But the paper wasn't just white, it was splattered with crimson blood like a huge, surreal Frances Bacon canvas that I'd seen in one of my brother's books. Jack's arm was trapped inside the rollers of the big machine and there was nothing anyone could do.

Eventually an ambulance arrived along with the Fire Brigade. While I watched the firemen and medics free Jack, I was overcome with a sense of vulnerability. I reflected on the fact that Jack had just survived a near-death experience and yet he had woken that morning, just as I had, totally unaware of his fate. My conclusion from this brief, philosophical moment was that life was too short not to live each day to the full, a belief that Mac had been preaching ever since the day I met him.

Jack was eventually freed. He had been conscious throughout and managed a brave smile as they carried his stretcher past us and down the narrow alley to the waiting ambulance in the Market Place.

Wally wasn't quite so brave. He was sitting on the floor in the corner of the *Machine Room* sobbing like a baby. I wondered what the MI5 would think if they saw him.

 ## Standing On The Corner
The Four Lads

I woke with that wonderful Friday feeling - pay-day and the start of the weekend. I arrived at work early for a change to find Mac standing in his usual posing place in the Advertiser doorway. It was a great spot to watch all the office girls and shop assistants as they hurried to work. It was like a beauty parade. They would all trip by trying to stay upright on their winkle-picker, high-heel shoes. They were always beautifully made-up - red lips, pink lips, mat lips, glossy lips. Blue eyes, brown eyes, green eyes - all enhanced by the magic of mascara. Most had beehive hair do's of varying heights, like candyfloss, stiff and sticky with hair spray. Occasionally you would see a girl with curlers still in her hair, held in place with a giant chiffon scarf.

Mac taught me to 'clock their faces first' as they walked toward us, and if they were worth it, check out their legs as they walked away. Mac's main objective was to get eye contact and he was a master at this. He would adopt a cool stance, leaning against the wall with his shirt collar tuned up and a cigarette in the corner of his mouth. Then, if he did get eye contact, he'd raise his eyebrows very slightly. But his moody expression stayed intact. If the response was a smile or a flutter of dark eyelashes he'd store the information away in his head for future reference. Then if he got the same reaction two days running he'd 'go in for the kill'. He would leave his 'perch' and swoop like a vulture. After he'd caught up with his prey he would start his chat-up lines and try to arrange a date.

His success rate was high and most times he returned to the doorway with a smug grin on his face to announce the results of his conquest. 'Seven o'clock outside the Guildhall clock' or 'Saturday afternoon on Markeaton Park'. But despite all his efforts, Mac usually ended up standing them up. He must have done it for the challenge or to relieve some deep seated insecurity.

I tried to implement my mentor's methods and after a few promising eye contacts a really pretty girl came towards us. She was more fashionable than the average 'contestant', wearing an Italian style suit with a short pencil slim skirt. She had dark brown hair cut into a fringe at the front and flicked up at the back and sides. Our eyes met but I found it hard to look sultry like Mac so I just smiled and winked. I didn't notice at first but she was accompanied by a really dapper bloke with waxed moustache and yellow bow tie who must have been her father. As they walked by and my eyes fell towards the back of her shapely legs I did achieve eye contact, but not with the girl, with her father.

He stopped and walked back towards us. He was red with rage and threatened to report me to the police for accosting his daughter. I was just about to apologise when Mac replied for me.

'Fuck off grandad or I'll fill you in', he shouted.

Father and daughter disappeared swiftly into the commuting crowds and I realised that I would never ever be as cool and cocky as Mac and I probably didn't want to be.

Upstairs in the *Stone Room*, Wally had assembled all the workers to announce that the doctors had not managed to save Jack's arm and that it had been amputated just above the elbow.

Later Mac told me of a mate of his called Jim who had lost a leg in a motorcycle accident.

'I wouldn't mind losing a limb', he admitted.

'Jim's got a tin leg which he has to strap on every morning.' He paused to throw a fag up in the air, catching it expertly between his teeth. 'He got nearly a grand in compensation and has no problem getting girls into bed.' He lit his cigarette and extinguished the match with a flick of his fingers before continuing. 'Some think it's romantic, others feel sorry for him and the rest are just curious.'

I was still wrestling with the image of this bloke unstrapping his tin leg at the end of a bed and hopping over to an expectant female when Wally came back into the *Stone Room* waving an envelope.

'It's for you Joe,' he shouted, sounding slightly annoyed that I was using the Advertiser as a post office box.

Since the embarrassment of getting my first Valentine's card I had decided not to give girls my home address. Seeing my name on the envelope written in an unknown hand gave me the strange feeling I had experienced on Valentine's day. It was a combination of excitement and anticipation which created an empty sensation deep in the pit of my stomach.

Even before opening the envelope, I could tell the letter was from Pauline by the Croydon postmark. The handwriting was flowery and feminine and the pages of the letter actually smelt of her. Even before I'd read a word, I was overcome with a yearning to be with her.

In her letter, Pauline asked me if I had practised my French kissing on anyone else. She said she missed me and would never forget that last night in the sand dunes of Aberdovey. The rest of her letter spoke of her everyday life in Croydon and she asked me to write back soon. I didn't want to write back, I wanted to drop everything and hitchhike to Croydon.

After finishing work at eight o'clock – the late shift when the news from the Women's Institutes and cattle markets of Derbyshire began to hot up - I decided to call in Down Brook to see if anyone was around. The clocks had gone back and it was already dark. As I approached the swings and slide I could see some of the crowd huddled together in the gloom and I could hear the clear notes of *Apache* by the Shadows drifting over the playing field. As I got closer I could see that Tony Tolley wasn't playing his guitar on his own and that he was accompanied by John Beniston, the new kid they called Benno who looked like one of the Everly Brothers. He was playing Rhythm guitar and they sounded great together. As I stood there, taking it all in, a shiver went down my spine.

The assembled kids, which included Julia, were just as impressed and I thought how great it must feel to be a professional performer. After they'd played a few Duane Eddy numbers and the usual Buddy songs the crowd began to disperse. I was mesmerised though, and stayed rooted to the spot. There and then I decided that I would do anything to learn to play the guitar.

Tolley could see that I was hooked and invited me round to his garage the following night to see the electric guitar that he had made himself. Apparently he and Benno practised there together now that the nights were drawing in.

Julia was still there and she asked me to walk her home. I hadn't seen as much of her since Aberdovey and I thought that she could sense that I might be losing interest. We would normally kiss on the bridge over the brook so I took the opportunity to practise my French kissing. Although a bit taken aback, Julia responded well to my new technique. Her breath quickened and I could feel her heart beating faster and faster. It was great for me too, but in the dark I couldn't help imagining that I was in the arms of my beautiful, passionate Pauline from Croydon.

Apache
The Shadows

It was Thursday - press day. I left work at 7.30 on the dot, eager to pursue my ambition to become a Rock'n'roll star. The mighty Hoe and Crabtree rotary press was thundering away like a giant stationary steam engine, churning out Friday's edition at the rate of ninety copies a minute. Once up to full speed it created a deep, percussive rhythm that reverberated throughout the old four-storey building. Some of the men called it the heartbeat of the Advertiser. Window frames rattled, dust was shaken off cabinets, floor boards creaked and sighed.

The machine room and distribution staff would be there until midnight. Some of the compositors and Linotype operators worked overtime on Thursdays too, packing the bundles of newspapers and wrapping the copies that went out in the midnight post. Although I'd done a couple of late night stints I didn't really like giving up my precious social time. But there was a real buzz of excitement around the place on press night. Half way through the evening Ben Kellett, one of the machine minders, cooked chips for everyone on a portable gas ring in the corner of the Machine Room. Strong, sweet tea flowed all night. The editor, Mr Bradley, and sub-editor, Edward Ellis, popped in and out between snatched sessions in The Bell Hotel on Sadler Gate.

Brad, as everyone called him, was a small, jolly, portly man in complete contrast to Edward Ellis who was tall, thin and deadly serious. They flapped around, stinking of Bass Bitter and getting in everyone's way until they were finally able to examine the first copies off the machine. At the end of the shift there was a real sense of satisfaction all round. It was the conclusion of the whole working week from a close knit body of professionals and tradesmen which included journalists, sub editors, photographers, lithographers, advertising reps, secretaries, clerks, compositors, Linotype operators, stereotype foundry men, machine minders, and finally, the distribution staff.

It was the day that Jack had started back to work, minus most of his left arm. After negotiations with the union, the management had created a sort of administration role for him. As I passed through the machine room on my way out I caught a glimpse of him, his one good hand wrestling with the pan of bubbling chip fat.

I ran for the 7.38 bus which got me into the village at eight. I couldn't wait to see Tolley's electric guitar and hear him play with Benno again. I walked briskly from the bus stop and as I turned into the road where Tolley lived I could hear it. The sharp, metallic notes from an electric guitar which seemed to cut through the cold night air like a steel knife. So different from the way his acoustic guitar would waft over the playing field, phasing in and out at the mercy of the wind. I stood outside

Tolley's garage for a while as if I knew that moment would have a significant influence on the rest of my life. Unable to wait any longer, I pulled open the garage doors and the volume increased even further.

Inside, Tolley and Benno were sitting on stools underneath a single light bulb playing *Walk Don't Run*. They didn't acknowledge me until they'd finished. Then Tolley showed me his guitar. He'd used his woodworking skills to shape the body just like the Fender Stratocaster that Hank Marvin played - and Buddy used to. He'd sprayed the body with bright red cellulose paint, laminated the fret board with wood effect Formica and added fret wire, keys and strings he had purchased from Derwent Music Store in town. At the electric fire factory where he worked he'd even managed to weld together his own version of a tremolo arm and a shiny chrome cover to hide the string ends. His masterpiece was finished off with a white Formica scratch plate in the distinctive Fender shape. But it was the sound that was special and when they burst into *Apache* the hairs on the back of my neck stood up as if I had been plugged into the home made amplifier along with the guitars. It was a modern, new sound that belonged to the young and I wanted to be part of it.

After they had finished Tolley asked me if I wanted to try playing his guitar. I felt a thrill as he placed it round my neck and showed me how to hold it. But I was so awkward, all fingers and thumbs, and the only way I could raise a note was to lay the guitar on my lap like a zither. I almost gave up on my dream but Tolley was patient and showed me a simple riff. After a few reasonable attempts he took the guitar off me.

'Look, Benno and I have been talking', he said. 'Why don't you learn to play bass and we'll start a group?'

My initial excitement turned to gloom. 'But I was useless just then.' I said, despairingly.

'That's how everyone starts, and I'll be able to teach you the basics,' Tolley continued encouragingly.

Benno joined the assault. 'Why don't you come to town with us tomorrow and buy a tutorial from Derwent Music Store?'

Tolley sensed that my spirits were being lifted again and moved in for the kill. He picked his old acoustic guitar up and handed it to me. 'Here, take my guitar home and practice. I don't play it much now I've got my electric one.'

Like a little kid on Christmas day I took hold of the instrument. I couldn't believe that Tony Tolley had enough faith in me to lend me his treasured guitar and was surprised by his kindness. Despite enjoying popularity from his guitar playing and football skills, he had a reputation as a bit of a bully and was always ready to take the piss. Tolley also had to be the best at everything he did and set himself the highest standards. But today I saw him in a new light. Underneath his hard exterior there seemed to exist an almost fatherly kindness. I ran all the way home and practised the bass riff until my fingers were too sore to carry on.

Songs of Learning

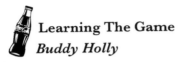# Learning The Game
Buddy Holly

After practising into the early hours of Saturday morning I found it hard to sleep. As I lay in bed, the adrenalin was still pumping through my veins leaving me wide eyed and staring at the ceiling in the darkness. To get off to sleep I visited the warmth and comfort of *The Sunset Lounge*. I moved the leopard skin studio couch away from the wall to a new position under the window. Then I placed three electric guitars on stands underneath the neon sign - two Stratocasters and a bright red Fender Precision Bass. I finally drifted off to sleep and dreamt of Jet Harris.

In the morning, while listening to Saturday Club on the radio, I turned the tone control on the radiogram to full bass and found myself searching out the bass guitar part of each record. I realised then that I was in danger of this group thing taking over my life and tried to remember when I last thought about sex.

After Brian Matthews had said: 'That's the lot for this week, see you again next week,' I left the house to meet Tolley and Benno in the village as arranged.

On the way I bumped into Julia. She was walking arm in arm with a spotty kid from the next village. When she saw me her demeanour changed. She snuggled closer to her new mate and raised her nose in the air as if she was about to walk past a big pile of dog shit. When I said 'hi' she just turned her head away and dragged the unsuspecting youth past me. As I turned to watch them walk away it hit me. I had arranged to walk her home from Youth Club last night and in my excitement I'd forgotten all about it. I'd ran home with another shapely object of desire – a guitar. Perhaps I really was becoming obsessed.

Although I had neglected Julia recently, I still felt betrayed. I experienced, for the first time, the bitter and useless emotion they called jealousy. That had obviously been Julia's intention which made it a bit easier to bear, and when I saw Tolley and Benno waiting at the bus stop I soon forgot about Julia.

When we got off the bus, town was buzzing. I loved the centre of town on a Saturday when it seemed to come alive. It had an atmosphere that was more exciting than any other day of the week. There was more traffic, more noise and the shops and cafes were full of happy people.

We crossed the road from the bus station and had a quick look at the ties on Cockpit Hill market. Benno, who had recently left Grammar School for an apprenticeship at Rolls-Royce, always seemed to have money. He didn't have to pay his mum any board while I had to hand over a third of my meagre weekly wage. He bought a thin red tie which looked as if it was straight out of the Everly Brothers' wardrobe.

We then cut through Boots the Chemist because Tolley liked to look at the cosmetic girls. He said they were all like china dolls, so delicate, carefully made-up and expertly coiffured. He pointed out that when they moved they did so in a deliberate and controlled manner. They didn't bend down, they slowly bobbed. If they had to move their heads they did so stiff-necked in unison with the rest of their bodies. It was as if any sudden movement would shake off a bit of face powder or disturb a strand of hair. One girl, who Tolley idolised, had the largest eyelashes I'd ever seen. She fluttered them almost constantly, especially when she knew she'd been observed. Another had the most perfectly shaped, glossy lips and when she knew she was attracting attention she pouted, making her lips even more desirable. But she never ever smiled.

When it came to girls, Tolley adopted the same high standard of excellence that he applied to his football and music. He also saw the aloofness of the cosmetic girls as a challenge and always tried to make eye contact, the ultimate aim being to raise a smile. But his latest attempt didn't even manage to encourage the slightest twitch of a lip or a single crack in the foundation.

Leaving the store through the rotating doors, we were propelled back into the throng of shoppers and continued up the main street to Derwent Music Store, the main purpose of our trip to town.

The music store was double-fronted with one window displaying traditional and classical musical instruments and a huge white grand piano as the centre-piece. The shop had only recently given in to the demands of the rock'n'roll revolution and had devoted the other window to electric guitars, amplifiers and a modern drum kit. Inside, at the back of the store, there was a long, glass counter that displayed smaller musical items – harmonicas, plectrums and guitar pick-ups.

Tolley and Benno soon engaged in an impromptu jam session which was what all budding local group members did every Saturday. As they burst into *Walk Don't Run* I wandered over to the sheet music displays to look for a bass guitar tutorial.

'Can I be of any assistance sir?'

The voice from behind me was formal and polite. I turned to answer.

'I'm looking for…' and froze in mid sentence.

I turned and faced a really dapper man in his fifties. I knew I'd seen him before but couldn't think where. Then I remembered the waxed moustache and the yellow bow tie. It was the father of the girl I'd ogled outside the Advertiser and who Mac had threatened to 'fill-in'. I gathered myself quickly.

'Er… just looking…. er, for a bass guitar tutorial,' I stammered.

He reached over to another display and then handed me a copy of *Learning to Play the Bass Guitar* by Chas McDevitt and Shirley Douglas.

'I think you'll find that this will get you started, sir'. His tone was still polite but with a hint of sarcasm. Perhaps he hadn't recognised me and must see hundreds of different people every week. I agreed to the purchase, more as a means of getting out of the shop than buying what I'd come in for.

'Take it to the assistant over there,' he said, pointing towards the glass counter.

I thanked him as politely as I could and walked over to the assistant - a young girl with dark brown, flicked-up hair, who I immediately recognised as the man's daughter. Things were going from bad to worse. Under the watchful eye of her father, I tried to conclude the purchase without looking at a single part of her anatomy. But when I had to make contact with her beautiful, big dark eyes, she gave me a shy but inviting smile.

'My name's Sheila Forsythe and that'll be three and six please,' she said in one breath.

She spoke in a slow, sexy drawl as if she was undoing her blouse instead of wrapping my purchase. I couldn't get out of the shop fast enough but Sheila's father stopped me at the door.

'It's good to see young men like you taking up something worthwhile,' he said, holding the door open for me. 'It'll probably keep sir off the streets in future,' he added with a wry smile. He had recognised me all along.

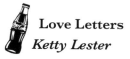

Love Letters
Ketty Lester

I spent most of the next day learning the rudiments of music and practising basic bass guitar riffs with the help of my new book. But judging by the photograph on the cover of the tutorial, Shirley Douglas and Chas McDevitt looked more like Jehovah's Witnesses than rock stars. It didn't sound quite right using the first four strings of an acoustic guitar, but I realised that the basics were the same and made good progress. On the way back from town the previous day Tolley had offered to make me a bass guitar if I bought the materials and this inspired me to work even harder. I didn't find it hard to concentrate either; it was a typical boring Sunday, nothing decent on the radio, no shops open and too cold and windy for anyone to be Down Brook.

On a Sunday at home you could set your watch by the different smells that permeated the household and each distinctive aroma was paired with an equally distinctive sound. First it was furniture polish with the congregation of St. Stephen's Church, Sidmouth on the radio, trying to be heard above the roar of the Hoover. Then the smell of roast meat and Brussel sprouts as Jean Metcalf on *Family Favourites* was dedicating music to servicemen all over the world. And finally, the *Billy Cotton Band Show* which always reminded me of custard, his plaintive cry of 'Wakey Wakey' almost timed to the second with when pudding would be served.

In the afternoon I took a break from my practising and replied to Pauline's letter. I had been having lots of erotic thoughts about her and was sure it was hearing from her that spoilt things with Julia. But I was confused and also fancied Sheila, the girl in Derwent Music Store. Perhaps you can't find everything you want in one girl. Each of the three girls in my life was young, pretty and desirable, but also appealed to me in different ways.

I really liked Julia, but more as a friend. She was warm and comfortable like a favourite old jumper. And I really did feel jealous when I saw her with that spotty kid from the next village.

New girl Sheila was smart and sophisticated. I'd love to be seen with her around town, hanging on my arm in the Boccaccio or jiving with me at the Locarno. And from our brief encounter I could imagine that she'd make me laugh, and better still, that I'd be able to make her laugh.

Then, as I sat with pen in hand, I tried to express my real feelings for Pauline. But I had to admit to myself that it was nothing more than pure sex. It was lust, desire, and a deep craving, all the wicked emotions that I couldn't possibly share with anyone else but her.

So having recognised the truth, I started to write to Pauline.

My Passionate Pauline, I want to tell you how the thought of your wonderful naked body is taking over my mind. I want to lock you away in my secret room where no one can find us. I want to see how the subdued light from the jukebox forms a halo around your perfect silhouette. I want to run an ice cold coke bottle all over your body. I want to carefully pour its contents over your beautifully arched back and watch the liquid fizz over every contour. I want to watch as the little droplets of amber liquid settle on your skin and shimmer in the light.

"On mother Kelly's Doorstep, down Paradise way …"

Someone had turned the radio on in the other room. The Mike Sammes Singers on *Sing Something Simple* brought me crashing back into Sunday.

I read my letter to Pauline once more, but it was no good. The moment had gone. I screwed it up and started again.

Dear Pauline, I want to … thank you for your letter. It was so good to hear from you again ….how have you been?…

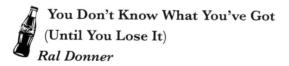

You Don't Know What You've Got (Until You Lose It)
Ral Donner

With my new purpose in life, even starting another working week at the Advertiser seemed bearable. Things were looking up for me at work as well. The Printing unions had just negotiated another pay rise which I would get in my pay packet on Friday. That would be the second rise since I started in March and it amazed me that I didn't even have to ask for more money.

Wages were just calculated according to your age and the union agreement, irrespective of skill, dedication or aptitude. The unions seemed to have so much power and I wondered who I was really working for, especially when I attended the union meetings called by Albert Fletcher from the Machine Room who held the reverential position of *The Father of the Chapel*. At those meetings the *Journeymen* talked in hushed tones about the directors of the Advertiser as if they were the enemy.

Mac was particularly pleased about the pay rise and I don't think I'd ever seen him smile so much in one day. Instead of his usual packet of ten, he bought twenty Players Navy Cut from the cigarette kiosk in the Market Place.

'I'm gettin' a fuckin' bike on the drip now,' he said, blowing the smoke that he had just sucked up his nose straight into my face. 'I'm off down to Bob Minion's at dinner time to see what they've got.'

He stopped placing the columns of type into the sports page and gazed longingly out of the window. 'I want leathers and all the gear just like Marlon Brando in *The Wild Ones.*'

He then flung the window open and shouted down into the Market Place three floors below. 'I'll be free at last and I can leave this poxy town behind whenever I want'. Eric came over with a new galley of type and slammed the window shut.

I decided to tell them both about my dream and the session in Tolley's garage. Mac was impressed. 'Great for pulling birds,' he rasped between drags of his fag. After passing smoke from his mouth, up his nose and exhaling, he continued.

'They'll come running knickers in hand if you pull this off Ginner'.

I was encouraged that he considered there was a way of attracting the opposite sex that didn't involve the loss of a limb. Eric was more impressed with the opportunity I had to play music and offered to bring his bongos along to one of our practice sessions. Eric preferred Latin American music and to relieve his boredom while working in the Composing Room he would spasmodically break into a Latin percussion rhythm by beating the sides and tops of the type cabinets. He'd even clamped a cow bell to the sides of his wooden composing frame. Eric also offered to take photographs of the group for consideration in *The Young Ones* page of the Advertiser.

We returned to our duties and worked in silence for a while, but Mac was restless. Although his mean and moody exterior rarely cracked there was a lighter side to his personality and he liked to play practical jokes when he was in the mood. But they did tend to have a cruel side to them.

Flushed with the news of his improved financial situation, he prowled around like a tiger looking for his prey. He looked over towards where Fred Fawcett, one of the older compositors, was sleeping off his lunchtime pints. Each day, Fred would sleep for as long as he could get away with. The only thing that would rouse him was the sound of Wally's distinctive footsteps clomping up the stairs.

Mac considered the slumbering old man for a few moments, and then carefully painted a moustache of printing ink above his lip. Fred flicked at his face as if being disturbed by a fly, but didn't wake. Mac admired his handy work with a smirk, threw another cigarette into his mouth and left to fetch the chips for the Linotype operators.

Half way through the afternoon Mac came bounding up the stairs and over to the tea table where I was proof-reading. I was right in the middle of a report from Fritchley Women's Institute where Mrs Bradbury had won the competition to see how many articles members could get into a match box. Mac's excitement managed to divert me from my riveting task.

'Quick Ginner, quick! Look what I've got under my jacket,' he blurted.

After checking that no one else was near, he opened his coat slowly to reveal what at first looked like a limb from a tailor's dummy. But it had an almost lifelike hand with all its digits and fingernails too. Then I realised what it was. It was Jack's false arm.

'But where's Jack' I said, knowing that it wasn't the kind of loss that would go undetected for long.

'He's in the wash room getting ready to knock off,' he explained, glancing over his shoulder. 'He always leaves it outside on top of his locker,' he continued, tying a large ball of twine to the end of the prosthesis as he spoke.

'What the hell are you going to do with it?' I asked, nervously looking towards the staircase leading back down to the Machine Room. Mac didn't answer. He just opened the window and started to lower the false arm down the side of the building.

One floor below the *Stone Room* was the Editorial Department where the reporters and sub-editor would be tapping away on their typewriters. I began to see what Mac was up to and could just imagine the reaction from the journalists as the plastic hand began to tap against the window. I couldn't resist and joined Mac in his brilliant prank.

I leaned out of the window and began a bloodcurdling wail to make sure that everyone below experienced the gruesome apparition at the same time. The result was bedlam. First there were screams from the women's page editor and Lynne, the junior reporter, then the sound of windows opening from below. And finally, another bloodcurdling scream, but not from me this time. Down below, at the side of the building stood Jack waving his one good fist up at us. But as Mac and I dodged back in from the window, matters got worse. Mac pulled the string a bit too quickly and the arm fell towards its enraged owner.

We found out later that the arm had hit poor Jack on the

head as he frantically tried to catch it.

Although there was no real damage done, Mac and I were in deep shit. First Wally had us in his tiny little hutch of an office where there was just enough room for the three of us. While Wally dished out the bollocking at full volume I could see Mac getting angrier and angrier. He hated being told what to do, let alone told off. His affected false sneer slowly turned into a real scowl and he started to shake. Fortunately, Wally finished his lecture before it took Mac beyond his tolerance level when I'm sure he would have hit him.

Then we were marched down to the Managing Director's office where we also had to face the victim of our prank. Jack, his repatriated arm folded angrily with his real arm, looked daggers at us as we entered the room. I noticed that there was a bruise on the top of his head where he had been clubbed by his own arm.

The Managing Director, William Blake, was normally quite a friendly, gentle sort of bloke and looked more embarrassed than angry. Wally stood to attention behind us like a sergeant major accompanying a couple of soldiers up for a Court Martial and Albert Fletcher had to be there as our Union representative.

Mr Blake dished out the obligatory warning but I could tell he was trying to get the matter over with as quickly as possible.

'We won't take this any further boys, but a repeat of this kind of behaviour won't be tolerated.'

As Mr Blake moved to open the door Albert Fletcher decided that he should offer some kind of defence on our behalf. 'I'm sure it was meant as a bit of 'armless fun,' he offered.

We all stood there in silence considering Albert's words. Then, one by one, the assembled company started to snigger, then giggle, then laugh out loud. All except Jack who didn't seem to make the connection.

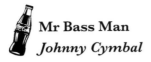 **Mr Bass Man**
Johnny Cymbal

It was the morning of November the fifth and as I lay in bed I reflected on the differences in my life compared with just a few months ago. I realised that the changes to a teenager's body and mind happen at an alarming rate and were totally beyond control. Even simple things like Guy Fawkes Night. At the same time the previous year I would have been beside myself with excitement. But as I lay in bed reviewing the prospect of the day, my all-consuming thoughts were not of bonfires and bangers, but of Sheila and my new bass guitar which Tolley was handing over to me that night. A simple uncomplicated innocence was being replaced by a roller coaster of sensations and emotions. I couldn't wait to get my hands on my very own electric bass guitar, and on Sheila.

Wednesday, the day before press day, was the longest shift at the Advertiser. Fortunately, being busy made the time go quickly. And the countless recalls of the 'armless Jack incident lightened the toil.

As usual, when I had worked late, my dinner was on a plate which Mum would warm up for me. It seemed to take for ages and I needed to get to Tolley's garage fast. While I wolfed my meal I watched the first episode of Britain's first American style soap opera 'Coronation Street'. Everyone had been talking about it and the press had really hyped it up. I was not impressed. It was the exact opposite to anything American. The characters weren't glamorous - they were just ordinary working class people with northern accents. The setting wasn't exotic - it all took place around a row of modest terraced houses and a dowdy old pub. No flashy cars, cool clothes, neon signs or ice-cold bottles of coke - just flat caps, hairnets and pints of mild. No diners, hot dogs or ice cream sundaes - just pies, mushy peas and barm cakes, whatever they were. And worse still, the theme tune was played by a brass band which struck up just as I rushed out the back door. Coronation Street would never catch on, I concluded, as I leapt over next door's cat.

I ran all the way to Tolley's clutching his acoustic guitar and my Shirley Douglas and Chas McDevitt tutor. As I dashed past the swings and slides Down Brook, a cheeky kid shouted 'Give us a tune mate'. But I ignored him. I was on a mission.

I stopped dead outside the front gate of Tolley's house. Seductive, powerful, electric bass notes were emanating from the garage. Certain notes would rattle the doors and windows. I'd fallen in love.

Inside the garage, Tolley was perched on his stool putting his masterpiece through its paces. The guitar was as beautiful as it sounded. The lacquered finish and the chrome on the pick-ups glistened in the light from the single light bulb which hung above Tolley's head. As soon as he saw me he stood up and handed it to me in a ceremonial manner without saying a word. I put the acoustic guitar down, picked up the electric bass and instinctively played the introduction to *Walk Don't Run*. Tolley picked up his lead guitar and joined in. It sounded fantastic. The guitar sounded fantastic. I felt fantastic. Benno soon joined us and we played until midnight when Mrs Tolley appeared at the garage door in her dressing gown and curlers. 'You'll have to pack that bloody row up,' she yelled. 'The neighbours are banging on the wall.'

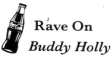 **Rave On**
Buddy Holly

Every day - a new experience. The one today would stay with me forever and would leave me with an incurable addiction. It was seductive, satisfying and exciting, and when the adrenalin had stopped pumping through my veins it left me completely spent, yet craving for more. And it didn't involve any contact with the opposite sex. It was my first performance to a live, appreciative audience.

From the day I had taken possession of my bass guitar it was round my neck at every available moment. Either playing along to records on the radiogram at home or huddled round the paraffin heater in Tolley's garage. The fingers on my left hand had developed hard calluses from the incessant pressing of the thick wire strings against the fret board. We had been practising almost non-stop for our first public engagement at Borrowash Youth Club.

Friday night was Youth Club night in the village. Although it wasn't really cool for teenagers to frequent a Methodist Church Hall it was warmer than congregating Down Brook. And kids brought their latest 45's to play on the little Dansette record player.

We met in Tolley's garage at six thirty and carried our home-made instruments and amplifiers to the hall. We stopped at the chippy for a sixpenny mix and a bottle of coke; the high life was obviously going to our heads. Some of the other kids had begun to gather outside and showed great interest in our guitars. I started to develop butterflies in my stomach. Or was it the effects of the sixpenny mix? Then, as we sat on the wall outside eating our chips, Benno seemed to choke on a fish bit.

'What are we called?' he spluttered. 'We haven't got a name. We can't just be introduced as a group.'

We agreed and frantically tried to think of a cool name that hadn't been used before. First of all we went through the names with obvious influences – The Adventurers (Ventures), The Silhouettes (Shadows), The Hollys (Buddy Holly).

Then Sooty joined us.

'What about The Beechcrafts after the plane Buddy died in?' he suggested. 'Or The Consuls after the car Eddie died in?'

'Why not just call ourselves the Multiple Injuries,' Benno

added sarcastically.

We all agreed that to get Sooty to name the group would be the kiss of death. But time was ticking away towards our first performance and we still couldn't agree on a name. Then, as I started to screw up my empty chip wrapper, Tolley snatched the newspaper out of my hand.

'Here it is,' he said excitedly, pointing to a headline that read 'TWO DIE SHOOTING THE RAPIDS'.

'What, *Two Die?*' queried Sooty.

'No, you twat The Rapids, Tolley shouted. 'It's short, easy to remember and has an element of excitement about it.'

Benno and I agreed and The Rapids were born.

We entered the dusty hall and set the amplifiers up on the small stage as the youth club kids started to filter in. Some went to play table tennis and a couple of kids sorted through the scratched 45s. One or two, including Whippet from down the road, shuffled up to see what was happening on the stage.

We started to tune-up, and one girl, thinking that this process was part of our performance, started a sympathetic or sarcastic round of applause. Then we were ready and Tolley barked a few last minute instructions. 'Don't forget to repeat the riff at the end of *Riders In The Sky*', he warned.

The butterflies were multiplying. I felt sick with nerves. I thought, what if my fingers froze-up? What if I forgot the middle bit of *Walk Don't Run?* What if I threw-up on stage?

Then I saw Mr Barron, the Methodist lay-preacher who looked after the youth club. He was striding down the middle of the hall with a benevolent beam on his face. As he passed the record player he snatched at the pick-up arm, cutting Roy Orbison off in mid-sentence. He mounted the stage and clapped his hands to gain attention.

'Quiet, girls and boys!' he shouted.

He started to deliver his introduction, making it sound more like a sermon than the prelude to an electrifying performance from an exciting, up and coming Rock'n'roll band.

'Some of our members, have got together and formed a …er…'

He turned towards us with a quizzical look. 'Is it a skiffle group?' he asked. Tolley put him right and he continued.

'… a beat group, and they are going to play for you tonight, so give a big round of applause for The …er…' He glanced at me for more help. With my nerves getting the better of me I could only manage to whisper 'The Rapids'.

Turning to the front again, Mr. Barron brought his pathetic announcement to its climax. 'Let's hear it for The Rabbits!' he shouted.

After gathering himself from the shock of the sudden name change, Benno started the chord sequence for the introduction to *Walk Don't Run*. I managed to join in on cue at the second round. Then Tolley cut in with the melody and we were away - the first public appearance from The Rapids. But to be absolutely accurate, The Rabbits.

 Let There Be Drums
Sandy Nelson

The next day, being a Saturday, I was able to lie in bed to bask in the glory of the night before. Despite being billed as a group of soft and cuddly, furry animals, our début had been a huge success. One girl actually screamed when we kicked our legs during the stage routine for *Gypsy Beat*. Julia was really impressed and dumped her spotty new boyfriend to walk home with me. I remembered Mac's response when I told him I was joining a group. 'They'll come running knickers in hand'.

During our performance of *Apache*, Whippet, from down the road joined in playing the drum part on an upturned cardboard box and it was obvious that we needed a drummer.

Whippet was good at everything. He seemed to glide effortlessly through his studies at Long Eaton Grammar and he was better than average at all sports, especially football and cricket. His nickname, Whippet, emanated from his ability to run faster than any kid in the village. As if all that wasn't enough, he was also blessed with good looks and a great sense of humour. All the girls Down Brook fancied him and had been known to queue up to run their hands through his dark wavy hair.

Like everything else, Whippet had a natural ability for music and at Christmas I marvelled at the way he had mastered his new mouth organ by Boxing Day. To say nothing of his virtuoso skills with the *Bird Warbler* from Alf James' joke shop.

After his impromptu performance at the youth club we approached Whippet about joining The Rapids. He agreed and told us that his uncle played a drum in the British Legion band and that he would be able to borrow a few items of kit for a practice session. So, after my usual lazy Saturday morning with Saturday Club and a nice greasy bacon sandwich, I left for Tolley's garage and our first practice session with a drummer.

Whippet's dad had brought him down in his cherished Ford Zephyr which he usually only brought out on a Sunday to polish. We watched in anticipation as they unloaded the kit. The first item out was a useful looking snare drum, then a little side drum that wouldn't have look out of place around the neck of a Confederate soldier. Finally, after a good deal of manoeuvring, out came the largest bass drum I'd ever seen. And to top it all the skin on the bass drum was adorned with eight inch black and gold lettering declaring the name of its owners – *Borrowash British Legion.*

Still, it was better than an upturned cardboard box and once we'd set the kit up and covered the bass drum skin with a bath towel, it looked alright. Better still, it sounded fantastic.

Whippet was a natural and soon slotted into our repertoire of instrumentals and he looked the part too. Perhaps there would be stiff competition for the "nickers in hand", but the sound, line-up and look of the Rapids was complete.

Songs of Innocence

 **Mecca**
Gene Pitney

Another weekend over, another Monday and five working days ahead of me. Sometimes the prospect of having to get through just seven or eight hours of hard graft in a day was too much to bear, let alone a whole week. So I turned to my oasis in the arid desert of duties to get me through the day. In my lunch break I turned towards Mecca.

But this particular Mecca wasn't toward the east. It was due south of the main shopping street. The Mecca Locarno ballroom.

Since Mac had introduced me to the Locarno lunchtime sessions the previous month, it had become a sort of religion to me. At one o'clock on the dot I made my pilgrimage up the main street of town. A right turn by Barrett's shoe shop and my church was in sight.

The building, once The Grand Theatre, even looked like a place of worship. I paid my dues at the door – nine pence. A quick adjustment of the quiff upstairs in the gent's cloakroom then a push on the double doors that led onto the balcony and I was lost for an hour in over a hundred decibels of sound. The Locarno was a large ballroom with a dance floor half the size of a football pitch. The ornate ceiling, from which hung an array of coloured spot-lights, was higher than a house. In the centre of the ceiling was an enormous mirrored globe which slowly rotated sending spots of reflected light dancing around the floor and walls like thousands of shooting stars. The balcony ran round three sides of the dance hall and was furnished with small cabaret style tables, each with its own Tiffany lamp. The front of the dance hall was dominated by a magnificent circular, revolving stage, framed either side by floor-to-ceiling theatrical drapes. On *Over-21 Nights*, Wednesdays and Saturdays, the stage revolved between sets to alternately present the resident

Ray McVay Dance Band and a disc jockey. At the end of his set the disc jockey signed off with his final record and was smoothly transported behind the scenes while it was still playing. Then, as the record faded, the sound of the band slowly filled the ballroom as they emerged. It was just like *Sunday Night At The London Palladium*.

During lunchtime sessions I positioned myself on the balcony at the side of the stage by one of the massive speaker cabinets that were built into the wall. The sound pumped through with incredible volume and clarity. I could feel the booming bass notes deep inside my chest as they thundered along with a resonance that visibly shook the sides of the cabinets and all around them.

In my church the *preacher* never uttered a word; the sound was incessant and uninterrupted. It emanated from flat, circular objects, seven inches in diameter and manufactured from a very sacred and precious material - Vinyl.

These revered discs were decorated with mystical markings and script, the mere sight of which conjured up anticipation and excitement; *London American, London Atlantic, Mercury, RCA Victor, MGM, Top Rank, Coral, Brunswick, Stateside, Warner Brothers.*

Some of the sounds were new releases and some already in the charts. There would be the odd classic from a previous year and nearly all were by American artists. The *preacher* just kept the music flowing, fading one record into another. Now and then he would spin a really obscure disc and if I liked it I would approach the hallowed *altar* below, and with all due reverence, ask for more information about artist and label. These often turned out to be the B-sides of current hits. Like *Cincinnati Fireball* which was on the flip-side of Johnny Burnette's *Dreamin'* or *Fortune Teller* on the reverse of *Lipstick Traces* by Benny Spellmen. Sometimes they were just obscure new releases that for some reason never got played on the radio and didn't make it into the charts in the UK, like *Some Other Guy* by Ritchie Barrett or *Life's Too Short* by the Lafayettes.

Those Locarno lunchtime sessions, with the anticipation of hearing new sounds and seeing new people, got me through the drudgery of the working day. The Locarno was my church, the disc jockey the preacher and the records he played my hymns.

Sheila
Tommy Roe

Although I had been seeing Julia again since the group's Youth Club début I still thought about Pauline a lot. Usually at night while I was trying to get off to sleep and would take her through to *The Sunset Lounge* for a few minutes of erotic pleasure.

I was also determined to take advantage of the come-on I got from Sheila Forsythe. So I sought advice from my work mates about asking Sheila for a date. Eric suggested that I should wait outside her shop for her to finish work and then present her with a single red rose.

'Girls can't resist flowers,' he advised. Eric even offered to buy the rose for me. Mac sneered at this suggestion, pretended to throw-up and then offered his own piece of advice.

'Just go into her shop, tell her to be under the Guildhall clock at seven and not to be fuckin' late,' he insisted.

Eric, a true romantic, but extremely shy with the opposite sex, met his fiancée by waving to her from the window of the *Linotype room* on the third floor. His girlfriend, Pam, worked on the third floor of the insurance company on the other side of the Market Place. They spent three months just waving and blowing kisses to each other until he finally plucked up the courage to wait outside her office with a single red rose. Mac was horrified by this admission.

'How do you know it's got form without seein' the pins on it? He had asked.

Even I thought it was a bit risky to commit himself to someone he'd only seen from a distance of 250 yards and then only her head and shoulders. As it turned out, Pam was worth it. She had all her limbs and a great figure. They got engaged after half a dozen Wednesday dates at the Locarno Ballroom's *Over Twenty-One Night*.

In the end I decided to ask Sheila out in my own way, even though I didn't really have a way, except awkward. I decided to go into Derwent Music Store on the pretext of purchasing sheet music and casually slip it in to the conversation.

As I stood rooted to my usual spot at the Locarno gazing down at the girls jiving on the dance floor, I nervously rehearsed what I might say to Sheila. But then my thoughts were interrupted by the output from the giant speaker inches from my right ear. It was a new yet familiar sound.

The Disc Jockey was playing a record that I was convinced was a previously unreleased Buddy Holly track. The same hiccuppy phrasing "Ahoo, ahoo, ahoo". Typical Buddy Holly lyrics "*Hey Maybe, Pretty Bay-e-bee*". The unmistakable accompaniment of a Fender Stratocaster guitar. And surely it was the Crickets rendering the vocal backing. I had to find out more from downstairs, but when the Disc Jockey shouted out the artist to me and showed me the label I was both surprised and disappointed. *My Baby Doll* by Mike Berry? And horrors of horrors, it was on *Decca*, one of the labels that only released British artists. Who the hell was Mike Berry anyway? I thought. But I just loved the song and the sound. Could it be that my prejudice against British music was coming to an end? I decided to forgo my principles and buy my first ever British vocal record, although it would go against the beliefs of my religion.

I left the Locarno early on my mission to date the delectable Shelia and walked past the shop window twice to make sure she was there. I saw her and my heart flipped, more from the fear of rejection than any real feelings I had for her. The butterflies from the Rapids début were there once more and I walked past the shop again. And again. I finally decided to just buy the sheet music to *Wheels* by the Stringalongs and forget about the date.

Inside the shop I flicked through the rack of music until Sheila came over to offer help.

'Hi again, I hope my father wasn't too hard on you last Saturday,' she said with a cheeky smile.

'Oh …er… no,' I stuttered.

'So how can I help you?' A thousand thoughts went through my mind before I managed to answer.

'Have you got *Wheels?*'

'No, but I've got nice legs,' she replied, stroking her thigh with her hand. And that was it. Sheila ended up asking me out. Better still, to her house in the posh suburb of Allestree. She made it so simple with her easy-going personality and cheeky wit. The butterflies flew away and, elated from my success, I ran all the way back to work, skilfully dodging the shoppers, trolley buses and cars along the main street.

 ## Stairway to Heaven
Neil Sedaka

I planned to go up to Sheila's house after finishing the late pre-press shift at 7.30. I'd taken a change of shirt to work and my bottle of Brylcreme. At last, my hair style was getting better. The back had grown so that I could comb it into a D.A. (duck's arse) and both sides were long enough to be combed up to create a small quiff that fell over my forehead.

Mac even commented on my hair as we made our way down the narrow wooden stairs. 'Ya' hairs lookin' almost acceptable now Ginner,' he said.

'I wouldn't mind bein' seen out with you if you got yourself some decent clothes.' He added sarcastically.

Before we reached the ground floor the giant press started to roll, slowly at first, as if struggling to move all its cylinders and to turn the giant rolls of paper. Then, as we entered the alley that led onto the Market Place, it found its pace and the whole building started to shake and rattle heralding another stunning edition of *The Derbyshire Advertiser*.

I left Mac in the Market Place and caught a trolley bus to Allestree. Sheila lived in a big detached house in one of most affluent suburbs of town. I was a bit nervous about going round to her large, posh house and seeing her snooty dad on his own territory. After all, I was just a relatively poor kid from a council house in Borrowash.

The Forsythe's house was called *The Laurels*. It was double fronted with black and white gables and an in-and-out drive. A Bentley Continental was parked outside the detached double garage. I hadn't been this close to such a grand house before, let alone inside one. As I made my way to the large, oak front door, which had stained glass window either side, a few butterflies started to stir.

Mercifully, Sheila answered the door and not a butler. She looked so different in her casual clothes. She wore jodhpurs which emphasised her shapely legs and a starched white shirt with the top two buttons undone and the collar turned up. She wore very little make-up, just a little pink lipstick and a small amount of mascara which accentuated her beautiful big dark eyes. Her shoulder length dark brown hair was flicked-up at the ends as usual. She looked really classy yet she still had that permanent cheeky expression on her face which seemed to send out a seductive message like "I'm fun to be with". As I stepped over the threshold to another world I wondered if I'd find out.

Sheila took me straight into a large room to the left of the oak panelled hall which she called the drawing room.

'This is where I hang out until my parents finish dinner,' she said, leading the way.

The room was furnished in a style I had only seen during reluctant trips to stately homes and on TV. Slightly faded tapestry upholstery, large oriental rugs covering polished wood flooring and a fireplace you could walk into. In one corner was a large, dark oak cocktail bar complete with cut glass decanters and exotic looking liqueur bottles. In the bay window stood a large, white grand piano similar to the one in Sheila's father's store. I wondered what I was doing with this girl from such a privileged home and such a different background to mine, and if I'd make a fool of myself.

On a rug in front of the log fire was Sheila's portable record player and a pile of singles. She chatted about her day and we selected a few records which we loaded onto the multi-play changer. Seeing familiar names like Johnny Burnette, Billy Fury and Del Shannon made me feel a little more comfortable, and when I heard them sing, it was as if they were there to help me through my terrible ordeal.

Sheila asked me if I wanted something to drink and as we went through to the kitchen there was still no sign of Sheila's parents. The kitchen was equipped with the kind of labour saving appliances you only saw on American TV programmes. Sheila took two coke bottles from an enormous fridge and we returned to the drawing room. As we walked back in I was faced with Sheila's parents.

'Ah, Bunty, there you are,' said the slim, horsey-looking woman. At first I wondered who Bunty was.

'...and this must be the friend you told me about.' She placed emphasis on the word 'friend' as if warning us both that the relationship must not progress to anything more than that.

'Yes Mummy, this is Joe. Joe, this is my Mother. And of

course, you met my father in the store.'

I managed to stumble through the pleasantries and a couple of awkward hand shakes while Sheila explained that Bunty was the family nickname she had been given soon after birth. I thought better of announcing that my nickname at work was Ginner. What was I doing here? I thought to myself.

Just then the door opened and a girl of about nineteen entered the room with none other than Malcolm Bramley, the Beatnik with the bubble car who lived down the road from me. Malcolm looked surprised and a little worried about seeing me there.

The girl was Sheila's older sister, Elizabeth, who unbeknown to me, had been going out with Malcolm. Elizabeth, or 'Lizzy' as her mother called her, was a pretty girl with a round, jolly face. Although she was slightly smaller than Sheila she was just as curvaceous and wore a tight sweater which showed off her two most obvious assets.

Mr Forsythe, who had poured himself a large glass of brandy from one of the decanters on the bar, offered everyone a drink. But I stuck to the comfort of my coke. Then, to my horror, Mrs. Forsythe suggested we carry on with the party atmosphere and play 'Country, County, Town', which she explained was the girls' favourite party game.

Again, I asked myself what was I doing there? I just wanted to be alone with Sheila.

I knew the game. Each player has a list of subjects, a letter is chosen and the players have to write down an example of each subject starting with the chosen letter. I began to panic. As if I wasn't already feeling like some poor wretched urchin from the ghetto, the game was sure to expose my limited education. Besides Country, County, Town the list included Poet, Author and Politician. If there had been Pop Star, Record Label or Footballer, I might have stood a chance.

I thought about pretending to be ill. But before I had chance to think of an ailment the game had started. The letter was M and we had ten minutes. Then I really did begin to feel ill. I started to sweat but tried to focus on the task at hand rather than my own insecurities.

County?

Messapetainia ... but how do you spell it?

Or Mongolia ... is it a country or a disease?

I thought of when I used to go trainspotting and the Jubilee class engines named after British colonies. Ah yes! Malta GC.

County?

Somewhere beginning with M and ending in shire?

Manchestershire ... no.

Mansfieldshire ... no.

The time was ticking away.

I decided to go back to that one later.

I managed Fruit, Flower, Vegetable and Film Star. Drew a blank on Politician, Poet and Author and went back to County. If the categories had been kinder, I could have had The Marcels, Clyde McPhatter, Gary Mills or Hank Marvin.

'Thirty seconds to go,' announced Mrs. Forsythe. Thirty seconds to total humiliation and the worst moment of my life. My mind went blank.

When the time was up, the answer sheets were passed to the person on the left. Mine went to Sheila. She would be the first to find out what a dunce I was. In turn, we each read out the answers for the first category. I just wanted to be whisked away from the moment and transported into the security of *The Sunset Lounge.*

Country? It went round the table. Mexico. Mexico. Morocco. Mauritius. I read out Lizzie's who also had Morocco. Sheila read out my Malta. So far so good.

Now for County. This is where it would all go wrong. I

hadn't put anything. Middlesex. Monmouthshire. Middlesex. Middlesex. Middlesex … I looked at Sheila who was about to reveal my blank space.

'And Joe also has Monmouthshire,' she announced.

I couldn't believe it. Sheila had lied for me. We went through the rest of the answers and she bailed me out on Poet, Politician and Author. She left in my Mountains of the Moon which they didn't allow but at least it raised a smile. I came second to last ahead of Lizzy.

Sheila had obviously sensed my fear, and probably my shortcomings, saving my embarrassment. At that moment I really loved her. What a kind thing to do. I just wanted to reach over and hug her. Although it was only a silly game, if I had been humiliated my already well developed inferiority complex would have deepened and I would have been scarred by the episode for the rest of my life.

After the game Mr Forsythe quizzed me on what school I went to before I worked for the Advertiser. He must have been impressed with my ill-gained score.

'Were you at Repton with Malcolm?' he asked.

I was confused. Malcolm used to go to Spondon Park Grammar School and now worked as a clerk in a solicitor's office. Then I realised why Malcolm had looked so uncomfortable when he arrived. He too must suffer from an inferiority complex and feels uncomfortable about socialising above his station.

Later, small talk revealed that the Forsythes believed that Malcolm lived in a large detached house in the posh part of our village and not the modest semi on the main road. I wondered how much of his contrived background Lizzy was aware of.

Mrs Forsythe started clearing glasses away and plumping up the velvet cushions to signal that she'd had enough socialising for one evening.

'Can I show Joe my room and my gymkhana rosettes before he goes mummy? Sheila asked.

'Yes, but don't be long Bunty,' her mother answered, suspiciously.

She shouted after us as we climbed the opulent, sweeping staircase. 'And don't forget you've got your horse to see to before you turn-in darling.'

As soon as we were in Sheila's bedroom we started snogging. I pushed her against the closed door and we were lost in a passionate frenzy of activity. The frustration of being in each other's company, and yet unable to touch, had heightened our feelings. And Sheila's emotional rescue during County, County, Town had increased my desire. In between our short breaks for air I breathlessly tried to thank her for helping me out earlier. She answered by putting her fingers on my lips and unzipping my jeans. We were lost in total abandonment and Sheila dragged me further into the bedroom. We fell against her dressing table knocking over framed photos of a sweet and innocent young girl in a riding hat. I tried not to look at them and went for the clasp on her bra. I fiddled around awkwardly for a moment and just as the strap parted revealing Sheila's nakedness a voice boomed out from the bottom of the stairs. It was Mr Forsythe, and his voice was getting louder. He was obviously coming up the stairs.

'Come along now Bunty, Malcolm is going to give Joe a lift home and he's ready to leave.'

We both stopped our frantic fondling and stared at each other, frozen in horror. Then we sprung into action and hurriedly adjusted our clothing, Sheila returning her breasts to the confinement of her bra.

'Coming Daddy. I'm just putting my rosettes away'. She answered with a cheeky smile.

It was another narrow escape from total humiliation. I

didn't think my heart could stand any more. One moment it was pounding away from sexual stimulation, then jerked into fear mode. It couldn't be good for me, I thought.

Malcolm and I said very little while we were bouncing our way home in his bubble car. I was lost in my thoughts about Sheila and feeling the frustration of unfulfilled passion. And he was probably too embarrassed at having been revealed as a social fraud. The only time he did speak was when we arrived home and he opened up the front of his bubble to let me out.

'By the way Joe, you've got pink lipstick all over your face, your flies are undone and there's a rosette stuck to your arse. See you around.'

 ## Let's Have A Party
Brenda Lee

I couldn't wait for the weekend to come round. Friday night was the Derbyshire Advertiser Christmas dinner at the Irongates Hotel in town and the next day was The Rapids first paid-for performance at the Borrowash Ex-Servicemen's club. Not quite the Ritz and the London Palladium but both events were new, exciting experiences for me.

It was strange seeing all the Advertiser staff in their best clothes. The older Linotype operators and machine room workers looking awkward in shirts and ties under their double-breasted de-mob suits, the women from accounts and reception in big, chocolate box dresses, the two office girls in pencil slim skirts and chiffon blouses, their beehive hair-do's even higher than normal. A couple of the more sophisticated women journalists were dressed in twin-set and pearls but their male colleagues, not renowned as followers of fashion, wore their usual tweedy stuff – crumpled, baggy suits, sports jackets with leather arm patches and corduroy trousers. The only exceptions were the corpulent Brad and lofty Edward

Ellis who for some reason had donned dinner suits and black bow ties. They looked like guests at the Mad Hatter's tea party. Wally was wearing a really smart pinstriped, three-piece suit and a military tie. He explained to everyone that the suit had been made in Savile Row and the tie was standard issue for the MI5. Mac was remaining faithful to his Teddy Boy roots and sporting his hardest look – powder blue drape jacket, black Bedford cord drainpipe trousers with twelve inch bottoms and a white cut-away collar shirt with a lariat tie. And to finish off his ensemble, a pair of black suede loafers with crepe soles.

It occurred to me that we all unconsciously wore uniforms according to our class, status, age and profession. Our clothes made a definite statement and confirmed our place in society. This must have provided the wearer with comfort and security if they felt awkward at such occasions. And even people who didn't want to conform, like Mac, made statements about themselves. In his case his clothes were a sneer at society - the uniform of the rebel.

And what about me? If the event had been two weeks earlier I would have probably been wearing jeans but mum had lent me the money for my first ever suit. Although it was only off-the-peg' from C&A it was in the latest Italian style with a subtle check, cloth covered buttons and short bum-freezer jacket. Earlier, after getting paid at lunchtime, I ran up to Dolcis and bought a pair of the latest in footwear fashion – a pair of chisel-toe shoes. So my statement was that I wanted to be modern, fashionable and part of this exciting new decade *The Sixties*. I thought I was the bees-knees as I hobbled into the Irongates Hotel.

The dinner was traditional Christmas fare but it was the first time I'd tasted turkey. The Advertiser staff were on their best behaviour, sitting-up straight and trying to use all the correct cutlery. Poor Jack was still tackling his turkey single handed when they bought in the Christmas pudding. We all pulled crackers and most wore the paper hats. But Mac and I both agreed that, besides looking decidedly 'square', the hats would mess up our carefully coiffured hair.

Although wine was served, Mac and I stuck to Black Velvets. This was the first time I'd consumed alcohol in any real quantity. Mac had told me about the cider and Mackeson mix which, besides tasting better than bitter or mild, introduced me to the delightful initial effects of consuming excessive quantities of alcohol.

Despite the fact that partners were invited, Mac and I couldn't raise the extra one pound, ten shillings and sixpence to take a guest. If I had, I would have probably asked Julia rather than Sheila. But I couldn't explain why, other than I would have felt more comfortable with her. So Mac and I amused ourselves by ogling the younger waitresses and chatting up the two office girls. But as usual, Mac the master of chat, left me standing. He even applied his mean and moody version of charm on Eric's fiancée Pam. Although she was six years older than him and engaged to Eric, he really fancied his chances. He did his best to impress her and sat with one arm around her waist as he delivered his best chat-up lines. Every now and then he would flick a cigarette into his mouth with his free hand. Then, with the same hand, manage to extract a match from its box and ignite it in the same, smooth, single-handed motion. I thought then that it would have been more useful if he had left Pam alone and taught Jack a few of his tricks.

As the night wore on Mac went onto Barley Wine which he explained was what serious drinkers do after six or seven pints. I continued with Back Velvet but it began to have a strange effect on me. It took my mind and body through a rapid series of new experiences. First I was feeling really good and laughing uncontrollably. Then I was pissing a lot. Next, egged on by

Mac, I took the suit jacket off the back of Wally's chair and turned it inside out to reveal the label of its maker - 'Burton's the Tailors' with no mention of Savile Row. And finally, I threw-up in the back yard just as snooty Mrs. Chalfont from accounts was walking by. As I cleaned myself up I heard the Guild Hall clock strike ten. I couldn't believe it. The events of the entire evening had seemed to happen in the space of about ten minutes. That was the last thought I remember having for quite a while.

The next thing I knew I was waking up in the field near the bus stop in Borrowash. It was midnight and freezing. I had a paper hat on and was clutching a Barton bus ticket. The stars above me were swirling around like luminous tadpoles. What happened in the intervening two hours was a complete mystery.

 ## Entry Of The Gladiators
Nero and the Gladiators

New experiences were coming into my life thick and fast. On the day after the Advertiser dinner I didn't have to wait long for the next one. I just opened my eyes and it was there - a hangover. But I wasn't that excited about my latest discovery. My head was aching in a new kind of way, as if my brain was loose inside my skull. Any slight movement increased the intensity of the pain and sent signals to my stomach to release another sensation – nausea.

It was midday before I could drag myself out of bed. Fortunately dad was at work otherwise he would have been sure to add to the pain.

Although this was a very special day, being the first professional engagement for the Rapids, I knew I had to shake off the hangover before any excitement would surface. As I stumbled into the bathroom I wondered if the resounding sound of my own bass guitar would make matters worse. Then an unfamiliar face stared back at me from the mirror, a puffy white face framing blood-shot eyes.

By one o'clock, little waves of feeling good were coming over me which was so welcome it almost made the whole sickly experience worthwhile.

I moved as fast as I could to get to Tolley's garage for our final practice before the night's big event but arrived ten minutes late. The boys were already there with Sooty, our self-appointed manager. He'd managed to talk the secretary of the Borrowash Ex-Servicemen's Club into giving us the engagement for the princely sum of seven pounds, ten shillings. So now Sooty thought he owned the group. Tolley looked at me in amazement as I stumbled into the garage.

'Fuckin' hell, what happened to you last night?' he blurted. And without another word, he burst into *Shazam* which sent needles of pain dancing round my head.

The rest of us joined in and Sooty stalked around the garage like a frustrated orchestra conductor, seriously considering every note and every drum beat. As he whirled around I noticed that he'd painted the back of his black zip-up jacket again. Sure enough, like Buddy before him, poor Eddie had been relegated and replaced with 'Rapids'. With traces of the hangover still evident, I had an uncomfortable premonition about being the latest doomed subject of Sooty's morbid obsession.

After running through our limited repertoire of beat instrumentals Sooty took off his Stetson hat, sat on a stool and lectured us on the forthcoming performance.

'Now make sure you look smart,' he started. 'Wear clean shirts and ties like the Shadows.'

He fired a glance in my direction with an obvious reference to my crumpled appearance and blood-shot eyes.

'And let's practice that walk again,' he continued. 'You

don't seem to be swinging your guitars in unison.' He whirled round and thrust a finger in the air in a theatrical gesture. 'And please, please remember the kick in Gypsy Beat'.

Sooty took it so seriously but we let him babble on. Although we didn't take much notice of him, we appreciated his concern and silently indulged his devotion to our cause.

After going home to get changed we all met at the Ex-Servicemen's Club at seven to set up the equipment in readiness for our big début performance. By then I was mercifully back to normal although the nausea in my stomach had been replaced with my little friends, the butterflies.

I'd never been inside a social club before. It didn't look like a pub but it smelt like one - stale beer and second hand cigarette smoke. The club was for members only and although quite basic in its décor it had an atmosphere of secrecy and exclusivity about it. The single, long rectangular room had spindly tables and chairs down each side in front of flowery curtained windows. The walls and ceiling were festooned with cheap Christmas decorations and balloons. At one end near the entrance porch was a bar equipped to dispense every kind of alcohol known to man. Just the sight of it brought back twinges of nausea. At the other end of the room was the stage - a real stage with velvet curtains and a single spot light. This was the big time.

As we set up our equipment behind the curtains, Sooty's head would periodically appear between the gap as he reported on the activity out front.

'There's about thirty in.' Then, a few minutes later, 'There's more than fifty now.' And finally, several octaves higher, 'There must be nearly two hundred in.'

We took turns to peek through the curtains. A blue haze of cigarette smoke hovered above the crowd at the bar and every table and chair was occupied. We were due on at eight and right on cue the club secretary appeared behind the curtain.

'Right lads, are you ready?' he shouted. 'I've got a few announcements to make and then I'll introduce you.' He glanced at his notes. 'What are you called again?'

We all answered emphatically. 'The Rapids.'

The secretary disappeared to the front of the stage and, after testing the mic with a few one two's, he started his echoed introduction.

'Laidiesagenermen... Laidiesagenermen...'

Then after a few more unintelligible ramblings, he raised his voice and we heard our cue. 'Let's hear it for The Rapids!'

Whippet started the tom-tom introduction to *Apache* and as Benno and I hit the first chord, Sooty opened the curtains and Tolley powered in with the opening phrase. We were off, but as I looked around the room people were still talking. Round the bar, they were still trying to catch the attention of the barmaids. Those seated were more interested in the Kershaw's man as he wound his way between the tables with his wicker basket full of seafood. A group of trilby-hatted men round the entrance were still laughing at unheard jokes. Were they deaf? Were we invisible?

While concentrating on the choreography of our simple stage walk I desperately tried to make eye contact with our indifferent audience. Then I saw Julia sitting at a table half way down the room with her parents and they were clapping along to the beat, totally absorbed with what was happening on stage. I smiled at Julia and forgot to raise my guitar to the heavens at the end of the middle eight.

Julia waved back but Tolley scowled at me. I recovered and noticed that more of the audience had started to clap along. People at the bar were turning round to face us. The men near the entrance had stopped talking to each other and were watching us enthusiastically. As we went straight out of *Apache* and into *Riders In the Sky* the audience was captivated. Some even moved to the front of the stage and the white-coated Kershaw's man gave up trying to sell his whelks. Even a little old lady with a hearing aid was clapping along. We were a success.

The first set ended with genuine applause and as I glanced round at the enthusiastic audience I knew I was hooked. I realised then that I hadn't really done anything in my life that had resulted in this kind of appreciation or respect. Even from a single individual, let alone a crowd of two hundred. I fell in love with that feeling there and then and knew I would always crave adoration.

In the break we drank coke, the club had to be strict on underage drinking, but we were all high on adrenalin. Then the Secretary announced that it was time for Tom Bola which I naively thought was the name of another performer. As he dragged a strange, wooden cylinder full of balls onto the stage I went over to Julia's table. She was as excited as I was and I realised once more that she really did care for me.

Then Sooty appeared at the table. 'Tolley says you've got to stop chatting to your fan club and get back on stage.'

I returned and we started our second set with *Taboo*, our own arrangement of a Latin American record that Eric had lent me. Besides an odd request from the old lady with the hearing aid to 'turn it down a bit', the audience's response to the second set was even better than the first. Although this was probably due to the general increase in the consumption of alcohol, the applause at the end of each number was almost ecstatic. A sea of appreciative revellers faced the stage throughout the set and the people at the back were even standing on chairs.

We ended with a rip-roaring version of *Peter Gun* to a standing ovation and shouts for more. But as Sooty started to close the curtains, we could see the Secretary pushing his way through the crowd. He looked worried and was shouting something to us. We couldn't hear him over the cheers but as he got nearer his words became clearer.

'The Queen, the Queen...' he yelled.

We glanced at each other in confusion.

'The Queen, the Queen...' he continued as he mounted the stage.

Sooty quickly took off his Stetson hat and I could see from his expression that he genuinely thought Her Majesty Queen Elizabeth was about to enter Borrowash Ex-Servicemen's Club, but then the Secretary elaborated.

'You have to play the Queen at the end of every performance. It's the law.'

We exchanged worried glances and Tolley attempted to pick out the notes of the National Anthem. Benno and I joined in and Whippet managed to cover up the bum notes with military style percussion.

Despite the pedestrian ending, our first paid-for performance had been a huge success. While we were packing away our equipment, a big affluent-looking bloke in a fur collared overcoat approached us. He introduced himself as the landlord of the infamous Crown Hotel in the Derby suburb of Allenton. In between puffs on his large cigar he offered us ten pounds to play at the Crown a fortnight on Sunday.

That was it. We were truly in the entertainment business.

Songs of Life

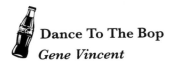

Dance To The Bop
Gene Vincent

After the excitement of our début at the Ex-Servicemen's club
it was hard to face a Monday morning and five whole days
before another weekend. It was even harder to get out of bed.
It was cold, dark and I could see my own breath. I counted
down from ten several times before finally making a dash for
the bathroom.

On the smoky, crowded top deck of the Barton bus with
its long, cosy bench seats I began to thaw out. At the next stop
more workers boarded the bus and one bloke with a flat cap
and snap bag did a double take after seeing me.

'You were in that group that played at the club last
Saturday,' he told me, before giving me his opinion. 'You were
great lad, but you should get a singer.' I thanked him for his
compliment and advice and then reflected on the encounter. I
was recognised. I was famous.

At work in the *Stone Room*, huddled round the gas fire
with Mac and Eric, we laughed about the high points of the
Advertiser Christmas party. Mac explained that he had put me
on the last bus from town after I tried to pick a fight with an
ageing Teddy Boy who took the piss out of my Italian suit.
Apparently he was twice my age and twice my size but, with
my Black Velvet induced courage, I threatened to stamp on his
brothel creepers.

Wally arrived while I was telling them about the Rapids
performance and my new found fame. Although we continued
to talk, we moved from the fire and went into work mode.
Wally caught the gist of our conversation and as he unravelled
his scarf he delivered the immortal words that always herald
the start to one of his famous tales. 'That reminds me of the
time when I...'

We moved back towards the fire, happy in the knowledge

that a story from Wally, while mind numbingly boring and totally incredible, was a good excuse to delay the toils of the day.

He went on to tell us about the time he was at The Royal Albert Hall for the Last Night of the Proms. Apparently, half way through the penultimate number, the orchestra conductor was taken ill. 'He just turned round to the audience with a surprised look on his face, his baton raised but motionless, and keeled over into the Timpani section.'

Wally paused to relight his pipe and turned to Eric. 'Well old man, the place was in turmoil. People rushing about in total confusion and they hadn't even played *Land of Hope and Glory.*'

Eric's eyelids began to droop so Wally addressed the next part of his story towards Mac who immediately adopted his sneering expression. Nevertheless, Wally continued: 'Then the pianist rose from his stool and asked the audience if there was a conductor in the house.'

At this point, forgetting for a moment that this would be pure fiction, I nearly asked Wally why they hadn't asked if there was a doctor in the house.

Wally continued, moving his attention to me. 'So having studied music at Norwich University after the war, I volunteered and led the orchestra into *Land of Hope and Glory.* The place erupted and I was bombarded with flowers.'

As he reached the climax of his story Wally was in a fantasy world of his own, almost oblivious to all around him. 'A bouquet was even thrown from the royal box which I caught with my free hand,' Wally continued, looking directly at me.

I tried desperately to adopt an expression of awe and wonderment, mouth ajar, as Wally concluded his story. 'So I can understand how you must have felt last Saturday night, old man.'

A flash-back of Sooty's face came to mind and I was tempted to give Wally a taste of his own medicine and tell him that The Queen had come to see us at Borrowash Ex-Servicemen's. But I thought better of it.

Wally left us and we started work. I was making-up one of the early news pages which would have been written at the end of the previous week. Mac was working on a farming feature page. My lead story didn't help lift the Monday morning gloom. I read the typed copy paper and the headline which I had set by hand in larger single characters of metal type. 'Lord Ives dies in DRI'. I didn't know who Lord Ives was but it still depressed me. I started to lift the columns of Linotype slugs from the galley into the heavy metal frame that would eventually contain the whole page. Reading from left to right, but upside down as compositors have to, I read the introduction. It reported that Lord Ives was a member of the Derbyshire gentry and a Second World War hero who lived at Ilam Hall. He had apparently led a small party of men behind enemy lines and rescued the crew of a spitfire which had crash landed. I was arranging the introduction into three columns under the headline when Brad, the Editor, came bursting into the *Stone Room* waving a sheet of Telex paper.

'Who's got the Lord Ives obituary?' he shouted.

'I have,' I said.

'Well put it back on a galley and shelve it.' He ordered. 'These war heroes are tough old sods and he's made a miraculous recovery. But don't scrap it just in case he takes a turn for the worse.' He added before dashing back out of the room.

I loaded the type onto a galley and slid it into a rack of pending articles. As I did, I couldn't help wondering what Lord Ives would have thought if he knew that his whole life was set in metal with reference to him in the past tense, just waiting for him to finally croak it. Mac interrupted my thoughts by offering to go to the Derbyshire Royal Infirmary to 'finish the old bastard off' and then reminded me it was nearly one o'clock and time for us to check-out the birds at the Locarno.

On the way Mac told me about his new motor bike which he had picked up at the weekend.

'It's only a 250 Beezer but when I took it down the county lanes on Sunday I felt free for the first time in my fuckin' life,' he said with an uncharacteristic tranquil smile on his face.

He was lost in thought as we dodged the traffic and pedestrians and I had to pull him back from the path of a trolley bus. This bought him back down to earth and into character.

'But I'm fucked if I'm wearing a skid lid.' He shouted at the green and cream monster as it swished silently by. 'There're for fuckin' queers and old farts.' He sneered, taking a swing at the back of the bus.

Mac was still ranting on about his new bike as we made our entrance at the Locarno.

It was only the blokes and birds that were fortunate enough to work in the centre of town that were able to frequent the lunchtime sessions. But it was quite full for a Monday. At lunchtime the Locarno opened between 12.30 and 2.30 except for Wednesdays which was half-day closing when all the shop girls could dance for an extra hour. The girls outnumbered the boys by about three to one and most jived with each other. Mac preferred to call it 'bopping', another sign of his Teddy Boy influences. I didn't dance very often and preferred to take my usual position on the balcony by one of the huge speakers where I could get the full benefit of the beautiful sounds. Mac would stand with me for a while just watching the girls dancing below, his head darting around like an eagle eyeing up its prey. Then suddenly he'd swoop and disappear down the stairs without a word, pulling his shirt collar up higher and adjusting his quiff as he went. Then I'd see him move in for the kill. He'd swagger onto the dance floor, homing in on his victim. The girl he was after would already be dancing with a mate. Mac would just split them up and the mate would retreat to the side of the dance floor while Mac demonstrated his bopping skills with the chosen one. Occasionally they didn't want to be split up and Mac would end up taking them both on - the ultimate skill level for bopping males. Very rarely did Mac get turned down, and when he did, it didn't bother him. He'd just sneer and shrug his shoulders as if to say 'It's your loss baby'. If I was turned down on the dance floor it took me a month to regain enough confidence to try again.

On the way back to work, late as usual, I told Mac about the booking at the Crown the following Sunday. He said he'd probably come to see us but warned me about the venue.

'The Crown's a right fuckin' dive,' he said. 'The hardest blokes in town drink there.' He went on to tell me that his cousin was 'glassed' in there just for looking at someone.

As we quickly shot across the busy main street between two Corporation buses, an omen to this kind of impending doom manifested itself. A flashy, two-tone pink and cream Vauxhall Cresta, which had been overtaking the buses at speed, passed within a whisker of my winkle picker shoes. As the car brushed by me I caught a brief glimpse of a face in the passenger window. It was the most evil face I had ever seen which was set with a twisted, half smile. It was a face I hoped I'd never see again.

'That's one way to get another pair of chisel toe shoes, Ginner,' Mac shouted as he pulled me to safety on the other side of the road.

When I'd recovered I had visions of lying in the next bed to Lord Ives at the Infirmary. But despite my fame within Borrowash Ex-Servicemen's Club, I couldn't see my obituary making even three lines of 7 point, let alone a whole galley of type.

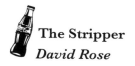

The Stripper
David Rose

The group's début performance was quickly followed by appearances at the Moon Hotel in Spondon and a youth club on the other side of town. But the only gig Sooty could get for this weekend was a Sunday lunchtime session in the small Derbyshire town of Ripley.

Benno moaned all the way about having to get up at the crack of dawn and we couldn't understand why anyone would want to hear live music on a Sunday lunchtime.

'Are you sure you've got the fuckin' details right, Sooty?' Tolley asked.

'Yes, I've got it in writing you ungrateful sods.' Sooty countered. 'You've got to take what you can get if you're going to get on in this business,' he scolded as he pulled up onto the pavement outside the pub.

We all saw the poster on the pub window at the same time. Sunday Strip at the Cock.

'I thought you'd fucked the date up you twat,' Tolley yelled at Sooty.

Sooty just sat in the driving seat staring in disbelief at the poster, then at the letter of confirmation in his hand. Eventually he jumped out of the van.

'I'll go and sort it out,' he said, and disappeared inside the pub.

After a few minutes he returned, still clutching his letter, but with a puzzled expression and a hint of a smile. 'It's ok, everything's in order, I've been to see the landlady.'

But Sooty was obviously finding it difficult to tell us something.

'It's… it's just that we've been booked to back the strippers during their act.'

There was silence while the information sunk in. Then

Whippet and Benno whooped with enthusiasm.

Tolley was less impressed. 'What a fuckin' come down. I'm not going to prostitute my musical genius by providing elevator music for a bunch of tarts.'

'Well, as Sooty said, we've got to take what we can get,' I offered, secretly looking forward to the experience.

In the end, Tolley agreed to forego his high principles and we unloaded the van. As we set the equipment up on a small stage in the empty lounge a couple of large breasted, tarty looking women entered. They were carrying vanity cases and made their way past us, disappearing through a door at the back of the stage.

'You don't get many of them to the pound,' commented Whippet.

A few eager customers started to filter into the lounge. Then a young girl of about nineteen walked in and nervously made her way to the door at the back of the stage. She was slimmer than her colleagues and wore a large white cowboy hat with rhinestones encrusted round the rim. Although quite pretty, she wore butterfly winged, horn rimmed glasses which made her look like 'cowboy's dream girl' meets 'sexy secretary.' She flicked self-consciously at her long, blond hair as she tried to pass Sooty. But he had become rooted to the spot, frozen in the act of lifting one of the amplifiers on stage. It was love at first sight.

The lounge soon filled to standing room only. All but half a dozen were blokes, mainly miners straight from their shift down the nearby pits. And one still had his lamp helmet on.

'It's for when the bottles start flying,' suggested Benno.

Then the landlady, Mavis Brown, pushed her way to the front of the stage. She was a brassy looking, middle-aged woman who gave off an air of total authority. She walked towards us with arms folded across her breasts which were just

104

as large as the two first two strippers.

'The first gal, Fifi, is on in ten minutes. Do you know what to do lads?' she asked.

When we told her we hadn't backed strippers before she just shrugged. 'Oh well, there's nothing to it. Who's the drummer?'

'I… I… I am,' Whippet answered nervously with his hand held high as if he was at school.

'Well duck', continued Mavis. 'Just keep playing until the girl turns and winks at you. Then you'll do a drum roll, and she'll whip her knickers off.'

Then she turned to me and quickly looked me up and down. 'Now son, you can introduce the gals.' She handed me a list of three names scribbled on the back of a beer mat.

'Oh, and try to keep the tempo slow and seductive lads', she added. 'The last lot we had played Hava Nagila and one of the gals broke her collar bone trying to get out of her bra.

Then she winked at me - without removing her knickers - and pushed her way back to the bar. We nervously tuned our guitars and discussed the play list.

'I'm scared', admitted Benno. 'I've never been this close to an exposed tit before.'

'Ya standing next to one now,' suggested Tolley, nodding at Sooty, who was still wandering around in a trance.

There were a few choruses of *Why are we waiting?* before Mavis Brown eventually paused between pouring a pint and waved for us to start.

I blew into the microphone at the front of the stage.

'One, two. One two. 'Ladies and Gentlemen, … '

A heckler interrupted me, claiming that there hadn't been any of them in the place since 1946.

I tried to continue. '… we're The Rapids and please welcome…' I glanced down at the beer mat in my right hand before raising my voice for effect. 'Fifi La Rou!'

Whippet counted us into Duane Eddy's *Three Thirty Blues* and a cheer rang out from the randy miners as the stripper emerged from the door behind us. She slithered into position in front of Whippet, and between Benno and I at the front of the stage. The stage was so small that we had to stand sideways to avoid colliding with the buxom performer. Fifi writhed around on the spot, occasionally facing us and bending over to show her bum to the crowd. Each time she did, her tits spilled out of her skimpy top and she had to quickly stuff them back in before turning to face the audience again. I was finding it hard to concentrate on my playing.

Eventually, to the delight of the audience, Fifi faced the front and removed her top completely. Dozens of tattooed arms thumped the air and shouted for more.

We were nearing the end of the number when, as planned, Fifi turned and shimmied closer to Whippet. A drum roll suddenly interrupted the beat. She'd obviously winked. We all looked over towards Fifi in anticipation. The crowd fell silent and took a few paces forwards. The drum roll continued and necks craned for a better view. Fifi, back to the audience, was so close to Whippet that she was nearly straddling his snare drum.

Then off they came! But the revelation was too much for Whippet. His trembling hands lost their grip, the drum roll collapsed and his sticks shot in the air. That was the end of Fifi's act, but the brief glimpse of bushy pubic hair was enough to send the patrons of the Cock Inn into raptures. Before Whippet had time to retrieve his sticks, Fifi was off the stage and had disappeared through the door behind him.

We played a couple of lively instrumentals while I waited for the signal to introduce the next girl. Mavis obviously wanted to sell as much beer as possible before losing her clientele to the lure of naked flesh. She was pulling pints with both hands when she nodded towards me. After consulting the beer mat I introduced the second older stripper as Diana Draws whose act was a virtual carbon copy of the first. Except this time Whippet managed to hold onto his drums sticks. And although she had platinum blond, bouffant hair, her bush was as black as night. The clever heckler by the bar suggested that she supported Derby County but probably scored more frequently.

After a couple of instrumentals that sent the miners scurrying back to the bar it was time for me to introduce the final act. Sooty would normally stand at the back when we performed but I noticed that he had made his way to the front of the stage. I started the last of my introductions which had become more polished as the show went on.

'Now's the moment you've all been waiting for... will you give a big Cock welcome to... the delightful, the delectable... '

Tolley shot me a look of disapproval for building up my part.

'... the one and only.' I raised my voice to a crescendo looking down at the beer mat but had to do a double take before continuing.

'... Marlene Crabtree!'

Despite the anti-climatic name check the crowd cheered heartily. But the door at the back of the stage didn't budge. I repeated my introduction.

'Let's hear it for the incomparable Marlene Crabtree!'

Then, ever so slowly, the door opened and Marlene made her way nervously to the front of the stage. She was wearing a skimpy, cowgirl outfit with braid around a low-cut white top and the hem of a short white leatherette skirt. Marlene's slim waist was fully exposed displaying a large crimson jewel which covered her belly button and matched the rhinestones round her large, white Stetson.

Despite her lack of confidence she looked stunning and an expectant hush fell upon the patrons, but she just stood there, frozen in front of her audience. The clever heckler by the bar, a tall, greasy looking, middle aged man with a thin moustache, seemed to know her.

'Come on duck, get on with it. I've been waitin' for month's to see what you've got under there', he shouted.

I gave Marlene a smile of encouragement and Whippet started the tom-tom introduction to Apache. Marlene took her cue, pushed her glasses towards the bridge of her nose, and started to gyrate, flicking her long blond hair from side to side. Sooty was mesmerised. He removed his own Stetson in reverence and clutched it to his heart as he stared, open-mouthed, up at the stage.

Marlene's confidence grew as the number progressed. She fiddled briefly with her waist band and then whipped off her skirt at the second attempt. Then she removed her top to reveal long tassels covering each nipple, held in place with a string-like bra. Her youthful body had the audience breathing down Sooty's neck and when we hit the 'F' chord/tom-tom piece at the end of the second verse Marlene swung her tits round sending the tassels spinning like Catherine wheels.

The crowd went wild and when she repeated the trick she turned slightly side-ways towards me to ensure that the whole audience could see. That's when disaster struck. Marlene had stepped too close to me and one of her whirling tassels caught in the strings at the top of my guitar neck. The tassel was totally snagged and her right nipple was stuck between my A and E string. We both froze, stuck together like two mating dogs, and I had to stop playing. At first Whippet and Benno remained professional and continued playing without me. But Tolley had given up and was clutching his stomach with laughter at the side of the stage.

Marlene tried to free herself from my strings and I attempted to assist, my hands shaking as I fumbled with the tassel, trying not to make contact with her breast. The audience egged me on seeing it as a light-hearted, brief interruption before the acts final revelation. Eventually Whippet and Benno gave up playing and watched with delight as I tentatively teased with the tassel as if defusing an unexploded bomb.

Then, without warning, Marlene suddenly burst into floods of tears and surely would have run from the stage had she not been tethered to my bass guitar. Like a flash, Sooty bound onto the stage and draped his jacket round Marlene's shoulders to hide her from further humiliation. She smiled through her tears at his kindness and when she finally freed herself, Sooty whisked her away through the door behind us.

That was when trouble nearly started. The audience, cheated out of seeing Marlene in the raw and spurred on by the slimy heckler, began to boo and slow-handclap. We gamely continued to play and thanks to a watchful eye of warning from the formidable Mavis Brown the crowd soon quietened, finished their pints, and began to drift away.

When the lounge was all but empty Sooty emerged from the back holding Marlene by the hand. Like a knight in shining armour, he proudly led his rescued maiden to a table and sat her down. We stopped packing our equipment away and joined them, which was when we heard the sad story of Marlene Crabtree's short life.

It transpired that this had been her début as a stripper which didn't surprise us that much. She worked part-time shifts at the pit boot factory in Alfreton but was attempting to earn extra money to help support her mother and two younger brothers. Her father, a pit worker and avid Country and Western fan, had been tragically killed in a mining accident eighteen months earlier. The white Stetson hat she wore had been his treasured possession and had been crudely altered to fit her.

Marlene spoke in a soft, but slightly gruff voice with a strong, North Derbyshire accent. 'He always wanted me to be on't stage,' she told us with a mournful look as if she had just blown her one and only chance.'

While she spoke Sooty fingered the rim of his own Stetson hat as if deep in thought. I marvelled at the co-coincidence of the cowboy hats, the tragically killed parents and the rock'n'roll star. Perhaps this was a romance made in heaven.

'The people at work will think I'm a scarlaton for strippin,' Marlene explained during her story. 'But I don't expect I'll get the chance to do it again now anyhow.'

Marlene had an endearing way of making up words she didn't know or couldn't remember. Sometimes they would be an amalgam of two or three words. Scarlaton was obviously a cross between scarlet woman, harlot and charlatan. Sooty stopped playing with his hat and placed a caring hand on Marlene's knee.

'Well you don't have to now Marlene,' Sooty suddenly announced. 'You can come and work part-time for me. I need someone to schedule my work and organise my paperwork and you can also follow-up booking enquiries for the group,' he added with the finality of a done deal.

Marlene gave Sooty another grateful smile and squeezed his hand. The two new lovebirds were gazing into each other's eyes and even Tolley watched, dewy-eyed. But the romantic moment was soon interrupted by a red faced Mavis Brown who was striding purposefully from the bar towards us. As she pushed tables and chairs from her path we could tell she wasn't pleased with our performance.

'Well, what a shambles,' she started. 'I'll be the laughing stock of the Licensed Victuallers.'

She pushed her tightly folded arms even higher beneath her breasts in a gesture of total disgust while we glanced sheepishly at each other like naughty school children. Marlene let go of Sooty's hand and bowed her head. I thought about claiming that it was my fault but was afraid to interrupt Mavis in the full flow of her anger.

'Never in my twenty years as a landlady have I seen such an amateurish performance.'

She fell silent for a moment, gathering more venom. Then, after looking at us all in turn, shaking her head scornfully, she delivered her final verbal assault which demolished us all.

'I've had the Cock Inn longer than anyone else!'

At first we all remained stony faced not daring to look at each other. Whippet took a gulp of his beer in an effort to control his facial muscles. Then he made the mistake of glancing at Tolley who looked in pain as he wrestled to stifle his laughter. It was all too much for Whippet. He looked as if he was about to explode then projected a mouthful of beer in a fine spray that totally engulfed the livid landlady.

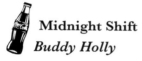

Midnight Shift
Buddy Holly

It was press day and I was working right through from eight thirty in the morning until seven thirty in the evening doing my normal work in the Composing Room. After that I worked overtime through the rest of the evening putting postage labels around the subscription copies of The Derbyshire Advertiser. I didn't mind doing this job because as well as the extra money I loved the atmosphere on press night; the smell of newsprint; the noise of the mighty press; the sense of urgency which consumed the whole team.

On our early evening break, before the press had started running, Mac and I decided to go next door into the Market Place to take a look at the recently refurbished Boccaccio Coffee Bar, but just as we started to leave Wally popped his head out of his little office.

'Hey you two!' he shouted. 'No break until you've finished

that page.' Mac cursed under his breath and started fetching galleys of type for me to fill the last gaps in my page. I quickly justified the columns, placed the final headline and ran off a page proof for Brad to check. This he would do with expert speed before adjourning to the Bell for a few pints of Bass.

The Boccaccio, originally the haunt of Beatniks and Teddy Boys when it opened in the fifties, had been re-fitted in a vain effort to deter the teenagers who lingered for hours over a single coke and made the place look untidy. The idea was to appeal to the more mature customer who spent less time in there but more money. However, the younger element of its clientele was concerned about the refurbishment of one of its bastions. Although the owner would disagree, there was no doubt that the heart and soul of the Boccaccio belonged to the young. Mac and I were on a mission to check the 'damage.' Inside it had been decorated in a Mediterranean villa style with fake windows and black wrought iron grilles which were illuminated from behind frosted glass and set in roughly plastered, white-washed walls. A brand new giant Gaggia Espresso coffee machine, all black and chrome like a new Buick Riviera, hissed and gurgled away at the far end. In front of this, a huge glass counter displayed an assortment of elaborately decorated cakes. I quickly scanned the interior for a juke box fearing the worse but there was no sign of one. Then Mac pointed to strange, small, dome-topped appliances which were fixed to the walls adjacent to each table.

'They're the latest Juke Boxes', he said. 'You make your selection at your table and the actual records and machinery are somewhere in a back room', he explained.

I reflected on the effect these new juke boxes would have on youth culture. It would be the end of leaning moodily against a Juke Box in an effort to look cool; of impressing the assembled company with your selection; and having the opportunity to start a conversation with a pretty girl while she decided what to play. I wasn't impressed. It was the beginning of the end of one of the most prolific teenage icons of the time.

We ordered coffee which was served in Pyrex glass cups and saucers and topped in an inch of white froth. Although I thought that drinking cappuccino was quite sophisticated I knew it wouldn't feel as cool as when there was a Coke bottle in my hand.

I flipped through the framed pages of one of the juke box selectors and chose *Cincinnati Fireball* which was on the flip-side of Johnny Burnette's *Dreamin'*. I always felt it was a sort of duty to introduce the public to undiscovered B-sides and got great satisfaction from noticing any positive reaction. It was like my own private *Juke Box Jury* but Mac voted my selection a 'Miss' by wiping a white moustache of foam from above his curled-up lip and sneering in the general direction of the juke box speakers. Then something else caught his eye.

'Hey, isn't that the posh bird you're knockin' off Ginner?' said Mac, nodding towards the counter.

Sure enough, there stood Sheila and her sister Lizzy. It was the first time I'd seen Sheila since the 'Country, County, Town' evening when I had scurried away from her house with pink lipstick all over my face and my jeans undone. Sheila saw me and waved, giving me one of her provocative smiles. Although it was time to get back to work we went over to her on our way out.

'Hi' I said, in my usual semi-embarrassed way.

'Hi', she replied. 'You're not leaving are you?'

I shrugged my shoulders. 'Got to get back to work. The paper's about to go to press,' I explained.

'Well, Mr King, I think we've got some unfinished business to attend to don't you?' I couldn't believe how confident and forward she was and even Mac looked a bit taken aback. Sheila reached over and put her hand on mine.

'No, seriously Joe, would you like to come round to my house tomorrow night?' she said with a smile. 'My parents are out and we could have the place to ourselves. Bring some records if you like.'

The memory of that frenzied session in her bedroom sent the butterflies in my stomach whizzing round in excited anticipation. Trying not to sound too eager, I agreed and told her I'd be there at about eight. As we hurried through the heavy glass door and into the Market Place, Mac took a backward look.

'You're in there Ginner.'

Back next door I made my way to one of the empty editorial offices where I worked alone gluing the pre-typed address labels round copies of the Advertiser before placing them in a mail sack. The office was immediately above the giant rotary printing press which was already thundering away, shaking the floor beneath my feet and sending vibrations deep into my chest. The combined noise of the machine and the rattling old building created a percussive rhythm that caught my imagination. I joined in by using one of the old wooden desks as a drum kit.

Jack had already dropped off a stack of hot-off-the-press Advertisers so I stopped drumming and glanced through a copy before starting work. Not that I expected to be interested in its contents, but I did like to check on my own handiwork.

I started work, looking forward to when Jack would return with a portion of his famous chips and a mug of hot, sweet tea. He managed to carry these with his one hand on a type galley which he used as a make-shift tray.

Later, after my supper break, and while I was on the last leg of my manual chore, Brad breezed into the office, his little round cheeks flushed from the cold night air and several pints of Bass.

'I see Lord Ives didn't make it then, Mr Bradley!' I said, making polite conversation. I pointed to the back page of the Advertiser on the desk. At first Brad looked puzzled. Then his eyes began to bulge as he stared in amazement at the headline on the back page.

Lord Ives Dies in DRI.

The colour drained from Brad's flushed cheeks and his jaw dropped as if he was in deep shock. His little fists were shaking as they tightly gripped each side of the paper. He tried to speak. 'Is this s-s-s-some k-k-k-kind of joke? he spluttered.

'What do you mean?' I asked.

'L-L-L-Lord Ives! Lord Ives! He's recovered.' Brad finally managed to explain. 'They discharged him this morning!'

 Problems
The Everly Brothers

The next day was the blackest day I'd ever experienced since starting at the Advertiser. No one was laughing, no one was smiling and anyone who spoke did so in hushed tones. It was as if the whole place was in mourning. But not for Lord Ives, who was apparently healthy enough to be tucking into a hearty English breakfast when he read about his demise. Although I did hear that he nearly choked to death on his kedgeree.

Unfortunately, most of the copies of the newspaper had been distributed around the county before Brad spotted the error. The misplaced story had stunned the offices of the Advertiser. The phone didn't stop ringing all morning and Lord Ives was threatening to sue. An internal inquest was underway headed by the Managing Director, William Blake, and the Editor in Chief, Lord Hobson, who happened to be a lifelong friend of Lord Ives. He came up from his London residence on an early train from St Pancras to deal with the crisis in person. And of course, the big question was – who put the article on the back page? The page that Wally insisted had to be finished before I nipped round to the Boccaccio with Mac. It was me. In our hurry to get out of the door Mac must have retrieved the Lord Ives obituary from the racks and I must have placed it on the back page.

Before I was summoned to the Board Room I was briefed by the Union representative, Albert Fletcher. His lofty position with the Union carried the title *Father of the Chapel* which suited him down to the ground. He spoke to me in a manner that was a cross between a Methodist minister and a defence attorney on Death Row.

'Now then lad, admit nothing,' he preached. 'You're not responsible for the fact that the story was written and set in type', he continued. But he looked worried and suddenly started to frantically flick through the pages of the union rule book.

'What's all the fuss about?' I said. 'I would have thought Lord Ives would have been delighted to have the chance to read his own obituary.'

'Now don't get cocky Joe. This is still a very serious matter,' Albert scolded, now adopting the manner of a school master. 'Half the villagers in Ilam still think he's dead and are in mourning.' he said, as he scrutinised the index of his little book. 'They've even closed the local pub as a mark of respect'.

Albert gave up on his Union rule book and continued his lecture.

'Now, I'll be with you at the inquest lad, but whatever happens don't admit anything and don't implicate any of your brothers,' he warned.

At first I was puzzled as to how my brothers could have possibly been involved. Then I realised he was back using his best Trade Union language and I began to realise the seriousness of the situation.

In the boardroom the atmosphere resembled a military Court Martial. Lord Hobson, William Blake, Brad and Wally sat stony faced at one end of the large, oak table while Albert and I stood to attention at the other. Albert was clutching his Union rule book as if it was the Holy Bible and he was about to bless the condemned prisoner before his execution.

For the first time I was afraid. What if I got the sack? What if Lord Ives did sue? I just wanted to be whisked away from the terrifying ordeal and from all the officious people. I wanted to get away from everyone. I just wanted to be alone in the warmth, comfort and safety of *The Sunset Lounge*. I drifted off there, noting the Gaggia coffee machine which I had installed the night before while I was trying to sleep.

'So how did it happen lad? William Blake's harsh tones dragged me from the sanctuary of *The Sunset Lounge* and into the reality of the situation.

I couldn't speak. I realised the answer to the question would have implicated Mac who had lifted the last galleys of type from the pending rack and had placed them on the stone next to where I had been making up the back page. I remembered what Albert had said about implicating a 'brother'. Union solidarity aside, the last thing I wanted to do was to drag Mac into the shit. Or lay the blame on Brad by pointing out that he had chance to see a proof of the back page before he had shot off to the Bell.

Fortunately, Albert broke the silence which gave me more time to think.

'I just want to point out that under Rule 26, subsection 5, of the agreement between the Typographical Association and The Newspaper Society, no apprentice is obliged to answer any allegations appertaining to negligence or misconduct, vis-à-vis the execution of his duties during the time served for his master unless 24 hours notice has been given in writing to both the said apprentice and the Union representative.' Albert was breathless but had a smug, smile of satisfaction on his face.

Brilliant, I thought. More time to think.

The assembled company were staring blankly at each other totally bewildered by Albert's statement. Brad, wiping the sweat from under his collar, looked particularly relieved. I started to speak but Albert, brandishing the open rule book with one hand, pressed the index finger of the other to his lips.

Eventually, Lord Hobson spoke.

'Well Blake, I think you better do as Mr. Fletcher says and follow the correct procedure,' he said in a tone that confirmed his frustration. 'Meeting adjourned until Monday afternoon.' He started to rise and the hearing was over. At least until after the weekend.

Outside the door I thanked Albert and complimented him on his knowledge of the Union rules. 'Nonsense lad,' he said. 'I made it up as I went along.'

Songs of Love

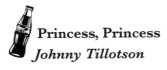

Princess, Princess
Johnny Tillotson

Although the Lord Ives inquest was still hanging over my head, I was able to put it behind me after work. After all, it was Friday night and the start of the weekend. 'Live for the moment and die young,' Mac always said. And I decided that I was going to live for the moment and try to go all the way with Sheila, even if I died in her arms during the attempt.

At home, as I was getting ready, I found it hard to contain my excitement at the prospect of being alone with Sheila. Every time I thought of her, it triggered a delightful sensation that engulfed the pit of my stomach. I couldn't even eat my fish fingers and chips.

I pictured Sheila at home getting ready and wondered if she was feeling like me. Was she too nervous to eat? Although instead of fish fingers it would probably be Dover Sole with croquette potatoes and petit pois, eaten with proper fish knives and forks between sips of chilled Chablis.

When I left the table to carefully iron my shirt and jeans for the second time, the rest of the family noticed that I wasn't myself.

'Are you meeting that nice Julia tonight?' Mum said.

'Er, no. I'm just going into town to meet Mac', I replied.

I was too embarrassed to tell the truth in case she would then see into that wicked part of my mind where I had already undressed Sheila down to her underwear.

On the top deck of the trolley bus to Allestree, I ran through my plan to seduce Sheila. Although the signs pointed to the possibility that she would probably seduce me, I wondered if my total lack of sexual experience would show. Would I make a fool of myself? Would I be too excited and nervous to perform?

As I approached The Laurels I noticed that the Bentley Continental wasn't in the drive which ignited another flutter of excitement in the pit of my stomach. I pulled on the wrought iron door bell and wondered what Sheila would be wearing. Perhaps a 'Baby Doll' negligée or just a towel. Knowing Sheila, it wouldn't have surprised me if she greeted me totally naked.

Getting no reply, I pulled the bell again. The butterflies were beside themselves with anticipation. Eventually Sheila opened the door.

She was wearing dirty jodhpurs, an old duffel coat and Wellington boots, and she was carrying a muddy black bucket. I tried to hide my disappointment.

'Hi' I said. 'You look... horsey', regretting the word as soon as it left my lips.

'Hi, come in. I was just feeding Princess', Sheila said, turning back along the hall. 'The bell also rings outside so I can hear it from the stables.'

'You'll have to introduce me to Princess,' I said, sounding a little jealous.

'Yes I will later but I must go up and change first. You must think I look a total mess', she said, showing me into the drawing room.

I realised then that Sheila wouldn't have been the slightest bit nervous about our date, and that, unlike me, she wouldn't have been pre-occupied by the prospect of a steamy sexual encounter. She wouldn't have imagined every delightful move towards sexual fulfilment. And she certainly hadn't agonised over what to wear. She'd probably even had a second helping of Crepe Suzette after her Dover Sole.

She ran up the wide oak staircase leaving me holding the dirty bucket and wishing that I could be that cool and self-assured. 'Put some records on,' she shouted back.

Just as the automatic changer on the Dansette Record player dropped the fifth single onto the turntable, Sheila reappeared. She paused in the doorway for effect as Johnny

Tillotson spoke the first words of his introduction.

'*When I see my baby, what do I see…*'

Sheila did look like poetry in motion. She was wearing a figure-hugging, emerald green, oriental style dress that emphasised her tiny little waist and every voluptuous curve of her body. Although the dress was buttoned right up to her slender neck, it accentuated the contours of her magnificent tits. A split up the side of her dress revealed a provocative glimpse of thigh which promised further hidden delights.

She dropped her head to one side. 'Now do I look horsey?' she said with a smile.

I stood up but was totally speechless.

'Well, what do you think?' she prompted.

I managed to persuade my mouth to move from its gaping position. 'I think… I think… I think you are the most beautiful girl I've ever seen', I whispered.

Sheila, satisfied with my stuttering reply, slowly walked over to me. We were suddenly lost in a long, passionate kiss. We dropped to the floor knocking the Dansette and cutting Gene Pitney off mid-sentence. '*What a town without pity…*'

We rolled around on the floor as I fumbled for the zip at the back of her dress. She tugged at the belt on my jeans. We were totally engulfed in a frenzy of total lust, hungry for each other. But then, she suddenly stopped, gently bringing my hand away from her thigh.

'Not here.' She whispered breathlessly. 'Let's go out to the stable just in case my parents come back', she continued, while pulling her dress back down over her stocking tops.

I wiped some of her pink lipstick from my mouth and nodded in silent reply, unable to fit words between my gasps for breath. We moved quickly, as if the magical feeling of desire would melt away if our beating hearts were to regain their natural rhythm.

It was cold outside but I was still burning up. Sheila gently led me by the hand into the dark of a small stable behind the garage. She shut the bottom half of the stable door behind us and turned towards me, her back against a metal grille. For a few seconds we stared at each other in the half-light, giving time for the level of desire to return to overload. Sheila's big dark eyes gazed sleepily up at me and she ran her tongue over her full pink lips. Then we were suddenly lost again, our kisses becoming even more frantic. I managed to find the zip at the back of her dress and she helped me by pulling it down to reveal her large, beautifully formed tits. I was in heaven.

I moved her silky, dark brown hair away from her shoulder, kissing the side of her neck, her shoulder and down towards her heaving breasts. Sheila's hands were under my shirt and with each kiss she gently dug her nails into my back thrusting herself against me at the same time. Her tongue was in my ear. I thought I was going to explode.

Despite the feeling of total abandonment, I was still conscious of my inexperience. I tried to arrest my excitement and prevent this wonderful moment coming to its inevitable climax too soon. I remembered the advice that Mac had once given me. Advice I thought I would never need. 'Think of anything other than sex - your guitar, football or even work.' Lord Ives immediately sprang to mind and my heart stopped trying to beat its way out of my chest.

The bottom half of Sheila's tight dress had worked its way to her waist and I found myself caressing that delightful area of naked thigh between stocking-top and panties. It felt soft, warm and velvety. My hand inched upwards and Sheila moved her bum away form the metal grille in an obvious invitation for me to remove her panties. As I slowly slid them down over her thighs, she whispered in my ear.

'Don't let them fall on the floor. They'll get dirty.'

Just her choice of words sent my excitement level soaring and I had to think of Lord Ives again. She stepped out of the tiny, tantalising triangle of white lace which I quickly stuffed into the pocket of my jeans.

We continued to kiss while Sheila undid my jeans which slid down to my ankles, but the mud was the last thing on my mind. We moved closer together and I felt her nakedness next to mine. Our hearts were pounding and Sheila began to moan. Lord Ives came to the rescue once again.

Her tongue was in my mouth and in my right ear. But at the same time. How does she manage that? I thought. I froze.

My head shot to the right and I was face to face with a monster, its huge thick tongue protruding between a giant set of teeth. The tongue came towards me again. I stumbled backwards, my jeans still round my ankles, and fell headlong into the straw and mud. Sheila was laughing uncontrollably and the monster was licking her face.

'Its only Princess', she laughed. 'She likes to join in. Don't you girl?'

I was just wondering how many other threesomes had taken place in Sheila's stable when a beam of light shot across the darkness.

'It's my parents!' Sheila shouted in panic while pulling down the skirt of her dress. The Bentley Continental had purred into the drive without us hearing a thing.

We dressed as quickly and silently as we could and Princess's head retreated back into the gloom. This couldn't be happening again, I thought as I buttoned up my shirt. I considered suggesting that we continue with our love-making and sod the consequences, but the moment had gone again, and Sheila's mood had shifted from passion to panic.

'Quick! Do I look a mess? Are you decent?' She whispered harshly.

Then another voice. 'Bunty. Are you out there?' It was Mrs. Forsythe.

'Yes, mummy. Just coming.'

Sheila gave me a sympathetic smile and led me out of the stables. Although it was cold, I still felt hot and sweaty and wondered if it would be noticed. We entered the kitchen by the back door where Mrs. Forsythe was making coffee in a silver percolator. Sheila spoke first.

'You're back early, mummy. I was just introducing Joe to Princess.'

Mrs Forsythe acknowledged me briefly before answering. 'Oh hello, Joe. Yes darling, Lord Ives is still not himself and gets tired easily.'

Did she say Lord Ives? I thought. The co-coincidence was too much for me and my temperature rose even higher. I was wiping the perspiration from my forehead with my handkerchief just as Mr. Forsythe entered the kitchen. He began to speak but stopped and stared curiously in my direction. Then I noticed that Sheila and was staring too, and so was Mrs Forsythe who had become frozen in the act of pouring coffee from the percolator. What were they looking at? I wondered. Mrs Forsythe broke the silence.

'That's an unusual handkerchief Joe.'

I stopped mopping my brow and looked down at my right hand. I was holding Sheila's white lace panties.

Coming Home Baby
Mel Torme

The first thought I had when I woke was a happy one. 'It's Saturday!' But then my brain began to process the events of the previous day and before I had time to enjoy even a full minute of the Saturday feeling, depression kicked in. How could so much go wrong in one day? The Lord Ives inquest was hanging over my head, I'd once again failed to go all the way with Sheila and her parents had banned me from ever seeing her again. I decided I was destined to become a lonely, jobless virgin.

After Sheila had snatched her panties from my hand her mother sent her to her room. I was left facing the furious Forsythes who obviously thought that their little Sheila was the innocent victim of a sex-crazed young thug from the wrong side of town. Mr Forsythe even brought Lord Ives into his verbal assault.

'That rag of a newspaper you work for is becoming the bane of my life', he shouted, shaking a finger at me. 'First they try to prematurely bury one of my oldest friends. Then one of their employees tries to rob my daughter of her innocence.'

I was tempted to protest that Princess could perhaps help acquit me of the second charge but thought better of it. He then promptly saw me off the premises and threatened me with the police if I ever tried to contact Sheila again.

I wondered if Lord Ives would find out about this latest incident before the inquest on Monday. If he did my goose would surely be cooked. I decided that the best thing would be to play it cool with Sheila for a while and not to phone as promised. So I got out of bed in the depths of despair and switched the radio on. Even Brian Matthews and Saturday Club couldn't raise my spirits. At least, when he played *Perfidia* by the Ventures it reminded me that I had The Rapids performance at The Crown Hotel to look forward to. Then I became depressed again because Sheila had planned to come and see the group for the first time, but I knew she wouldn't be allowed anywhere near the place. I'd probably only ever see her again on the other side of the counter at the music store.

In the afternoon I wandered Down Brook. I hoped that the trivial banter of the Mob would help lift the gloom. On the playing fields next to the brook, Borrowash Victoria football team were at home to Mickleover British Legion. It was a real needle match between two teams near the top of the Derbyshire Senior League and the spectators were two deep in places.

I chattered with Sooty on the touch-line about the arrangements for Sunday's booking. Besides being the Rapids self-appointed manager and roadie, he also helped the Vics out as a sort of unqualified physio. It just meant that every now and then he'd have to rush onto the pitch with his sponge and bucket of freezing cold water to see to any injuries.

The match was tough and Sooty was on the pitch almost as much as the players, but he was in his element. The pitch resembled a First World War battlefield and as well as a morbid fascination for dead pop stars, Sooty was also turned on by footballers with broken limbs. He was a real mother hen with a heart gold who would help anybody in trouble, but if blood was in evidence, so much the better.

So I started to pour out my troubles to Sooty and it seemed to cheer us both up. I was just in the middle of telling him about the threat from Sheila's father when I noticed that Julia and Marlene had joined us. Fortunately I had to stop talking because Sooty had rushed onto the pitch again, sponge in hand and bloody, muddy water slopping from his bucket.

'Talking about your new posh girlfriend were you?' Julia said.

'Which one?' I replied, matching her sarcasm.

'Cathy tells me you're seeing a lot of this rich girl from Allestree.'

I remembered then that Julia's best friend, Cathy, was Malcolm Bramley's sister. With Malcolm going out with Lizzy Forsythe, these details had obviously found their way back to Borrowash. I wasn't sure whether Julia knew about the previous night though. 'Oh you mean Sheila.' I replied nonchalantly.

We looked towards the pitch and silently watched Sooty attending to one of the wounded. Marlene was smiling with pride as Sooty mopped blood from an open wound.

'We're just good friends really. I know her from her father's music store, that's all.'

My denials of any romantic association surprised me and I realised that, despite my lust for other girls, I really needed Julia to be there for me when things went wrong. Right then things couldn't get much worse and I had a sudden desire to hold her really close to me, as if by doing so all my troubles would just melt away.

I decided to play the sympathy card and proceeded to tell Julia and Marlene about the trouble I was in over the premature announcement of the death of Lord Ives and how he had made a swift recovery in a private ward at the DRI. Marlene looked puzzled.

'Was he in a private ward because he's a Lord? Or did he have one of the ostentatious diseases?

Fortunately, Sooty returned from the battleground and she quickly forgot her query. Julia's initial frostiness thawed a bit and she asked how things were going with the Rapids. I gestured towards the football pitch where Tolley had just completed one of his famous scissor-kicks. There was an 'oooooh' from the crowd as the ball skimmed the bar.

'Providing our lead guitarist isn't in traction, we're playing at the Crown at Allenton tomorrow night. Why don't you come?' I found myself saying. 'Sooty's taking Marlene and I'm sure we could give you a lift in the van. Couldn't we, Sooty?'

'It's OK by me,' he replied, more interested in the ambulance that was making its way towards the pitch.

'Yes, please come,' chirped Marlene.

'Ok,' Julia replied, shivering from either the cold or the sight of the broken bone that was sticking out of the Mickleover left winger's right leg.

I slipped my arm around Julia's shoulders and drew her

close. She gazed up at me from under her beautiful, long black eyelashes and put her arm round my waist. A familiar, warm feeling passed into my body. She smelt of Palmolive soap and it felt like coming home to a cosy house on a cold winter's night. Or was it like being comforted by my mum when I'd fallen over as a little boy?

Julia reached up and kissed me on the end of my nose and my troubles just melted away.

 Rumble
Link Wray

It was a cold, crisp, clear sunny Sunday. But as I basked in the luxury of a lie-in, my mind was no where near as clear as the day. Confusion had set in. I had realised that I needed Julia in a spiritual sort of way. But my sexual desire for her wasn't as strong as it was for Sheila, or Pauline, when I fantasised about steamy sessions with her in my *Sunset Lounge*. Although Julia was very pretty and physically attractive, my feelings went much deeper than that. Perhaps this was love or were we just good friends?

Maybe it was normal not to have erotic thoughts about the person you love. Maybe men do have different needs to women. I also felt unsure about getting too involved with Julia. Was I too young to go steady with so many sexy girls out there? I needed Julia more than wanted her, but was sure I couldn't get away with having the best of both worlds. I wouldn't want to hurt Julia anyway, nor lose her altogether. Maybe if I explained my feelings she would understand and agree to me having a string of girls for sex only. But I instinctively knew that relationships didn't work that way, at least not in the civilised western world of the new sixties.

Although it was a boring Sunday, I was excited about our booking at the Crown. I wiled away the hours at home trying everything to subdue the Sunday feeling. As soon as dad sloped off to the Nag's Head for his pre-lunch pints of Marston's Pedigree I switched off the familiar Sunday sound of *Round The Horn* which was on the radio and spun a few discs. Ricky Nelson's *Hello Mary Lou* always worked a treat. It sounded so American and reminded me of the Boccaccio. The next thing I did was to try to make a cappuccino. Although we only had instant Maxwell House, I discovered that by heating the milk in a saucepan and whisking it continuously, right up to boiling point, you could produce a mass of creamy, white froth. My little sister thought it was great fun, especially when I dabbed a blob of froth on the end of her nose and did my impression of a Gaggia Coffee machine. Finally, to totally eradicate the Sunday feeling, I persuaded my mum to cook me chips and Heinz baked beans to go with my roast beef instead of the usual Brussels sprouts, carrots, roast potatoes and gravy.

Eventually, it was time to grab my bass guitar and walk over to Tolley's where we carried the equipment to the side of the road to wait for Sooty and his van. He was late. Then, with a screech of tyres, the Bedford Dormobile swung round the corner and ground to a halt just an inch away from scattering Whippet's new drum kit all over the road. Sooty slid open the door, leapt out of the driver's seat and waved his Stetson hat in the air.

'Whoopee! What do you think?' he said, pointing to the side of the immaculately clean vehicle.

In each of the side windows was a hand-painted poster announcing 'The Fabulous Rapids'. We all cheered and I felt both excited and proud. I was now part of a proper group. But would the villains, ex-convicts and ageing Teddy Boys at the Crown agree with Sooty's typographical claim?

We set off in high spirits, beeping the horn at everyone we passed. Julia and Marlene were waiting for us in the village, but with the van packed to the roof with equipment, they only just managed to fit in. We sped round the ring road like a giant can of sardines on wheels, guitar necks sticking out of windows and Sooty driving as if he was on a mission to add to his list of deceased rock'n'roll heroes.

We arrived at the Crown well before opening time and the cigar smoking landlord showed us into the lounge. The setting winter sun, that had managed to infiltrate the murky interior, sent beams of dust and cigar smoke across the room. The pub had the same distinctive smell as the empty Ex-Servicemen's club. It was a mixture of stale beer, disinfectant, furniture polish and stale cigarette smoke.

The landlord pointed with his cigar to a small stage in the corner. 'That's where you'll be playing lads. Start at eight, have a fifteen minute break at nine and finish after I flash the lights for last orders at ten thirty.'

He started to walk away but then stopped and took the cigar out of his mouth. 'Oh yes, and if there's any trouble, just keep playing.' We looked at each other apprehensively.

I remembered what Mac had said about the Crown and warned the lads as we started to set the equipment up. 'Mac said that his cousin was glassed in here for just looking at someone.'

This prompted a hasty review of our play list. 'We'll start with *Mac the Knife* followed by *Peter Gunn*,' Benno suggested.

'Yea! Then we'll end with the Platters' ballad *Glass gets in your eyes,*' Whippet added.

Tolley started to swing his guitar around above his head. 'If any bastard comes near this beauty he'll get it straight in the teeth.'

We finished setting up and ran through a couple of numbers. Sooty went off to each corner of the room and considered the sound ballance. He stopped near the entrance door, bent his ear towards the stage and with a studious frown shouted his instructions.

'Can't hear Benno.' He walked towards the bar. 'The bass is rattling the glasses behind the bar.'

Great, I thought, just what it should be doing.

We stopped playing as Julia and Marlene returned from fetching the drinks and crisps and the first customers started to filter in. Most would have been drawing their pension, or about to be, and there were a few middle-aged couples dressed in their Sunday best. I began to feel a little easier about the audience, except for the fact that they were unlikely to be impressed by our music. Then Elvis walked in.

He was bigger than the real thing but his facial features were almost identical; the slightly flattened nose, high cheek bones, square jaw-line and heavy, dark brows set over steel-blue eyes. His hair was a masterpiece in Brylcreme with the front slightly forward in the trade-mark quiff. He was wearing a big white jacket and an open-necked black shirt, but it was the permanent, Presley sneer that really carried it off. It was really mean and made Mac's sneer look like a nervous twitch. Of course, as we saw on TV that weekend when he was released from his spell in the army, the real Elvis now had a short crew cut. Other than that, and the worrying scar down the left-hand side of his face, this could have been Elvis on a secret trip to Derby.

We started promptly at eight and by then the average age of the audience had thankfully dropped below sixty-five. A group of youths dressed in Italian-style suits and winkle pickers had congregated round the bar. A few older blokes in drape suits and brothel creepers began to drift in. Now, in the twilight years for Teds, most of them had partners and looked less menacing. However, this couldn't be said of two really dangerous looking characters who loitered moodily near the exit.

One was short but really thick-set. His eyes were

permanently half-closed in a deliberate attempt to look threatening. He peered suspiciously through narrowed slits as if challenging anyone to dare to make eye contact. His sidekick looked just as mean; he was slightly taller, thin and wiry. I had an uncomfortable feeling that I had seen him somewhere before. His short cropped hair had no particular style as if he had recently been de-mobbed from the army or released from prison, but it was his general demeanour that looked dangerous. He had a slightly deranged expression and his mouth was twisted into a half-smile as he nervously scanned the assembled company like a cornered rat.

We kicked off with *Perfidia* and then a couple of Shadows numbers which went down really well. By the time we were on Rhet Stoller's *Chariot* the place was packed. Then someone in the crowd of youths around the bar shouted.

'Can't any of yer sing?'

At this, Elvis rose from his seat near the stage and almost took the table with him. He sort of stumbled sideways towards the stage like a pissed Robert Mitchum, pint still in hand. 'Play *Hound Dawg*,' he ordered in his best mid-Atlantic accent.

Tolley took instant control of the situation and barked his instructions.

'It's just a twelve bar blues. Do it in A.'

We didn't argue and just started to play. Elvis started to sing and he was good. The crowd went wild and, although he was obviously a regular in the Crown, it was apparent that he didn't often have the luxury of a full, beat group backing. A few of the old Teddy Boys started jiving with their partners between the tables and the youths in Italian style suits moved forward away from the bar. At the end of the number Elvis acknowledged the applause.

'Ank-u-erry-mush. Per-ree-ciate it, per-ree-ciate it.'

Then he held one hand in the air and turned to us with the

mic pressed to his lips.

'It's a one for the money...' And we found our way into Blue Suede Shoes.

By this time the enthusiasm of the crowd had rubbed off on us and we were fully into it. Tolley even delivered a guitar solo while lying on his back. In front of the small stage, a sea of bodies was bopping and jiving. Pints were being held aloft, drinks were being spilt, the place was jumping. Elvis finished to a standing ovation and we took our break.

'How we gonna follow that?' Benno asked, wiping the sweat from his forehead.

'We need a vocalist', I replied, not really answering his question.

As the place began to settle down Whippet and I went to sit with Julia and Marlene. I fought my way to the bar and bought Julia her first ever alcoholic drink – a Babycham.

'I feel so sophisticated.' she said, with an excited sparkle in her eyes that matched the liquid she was sipping.

She drained the rest, bit the cherry from the stick and snuggled closer to me. 'I'll have another of those, but I'll pay this time.'

I began to fight my way to the bar but was stopped in my tracks. I was faced with a beautiful, but angry-looking girl with dark brown flicked-up hair. It was Sheila. Lizzy and Malcolm were behind her.

She had what looked like a glass of cider in her hand and seemed quite unsteady on her stiletto heels. 'So Joe King, you think you're a big pop star now, do you?' she sneered. 'And I suppose that is one of your fans, is it?' she continued, pointing at Julia.

I started to speak, but before I could Sheila hurled the contents of her glass towards me. I ducked. The amber liquid flew over my shoulder and hit the back of a white jacket that was being worn by a bulky figure sat on the table behind us.

It was Elvis. At first he didn't move a muscle and the place went quiet. The only thing that moved was the cider which was dripping off the back of his heavily greased hair and onto the turned-up collar of his black shirt. Everyone around just watched open mouthed.

Then Elvis's thick neck twitched once. Then, as if in slow motion, his head started to twist as he rose from the table. This time the table did come with him, sending glasses and ash-trays to the floor. He lurched towards Malcolm who had gallantly moved in front of Sheila. Then, the whole place came alive. Fists were flying, more tables were knocked-over and chairs raised aloft. First to respond to the violence were the thick set and skinny thugs who both rushed from their position near the door with expressions of glee, obviously excited at the excuse to beat the shit out of anyone that moved. The ageing Teddy Boys waded in against the slick boys in the Italian suits. Even handbag wielding women joined in. It was as if the whole place had been waiting for an excuse to fight.

I grabbed Julia and moved towards the stage where we were met by a frantic, but strangely excited, Sooty. 'Quick, get back on stage and play,' he ordered. 'I'll look after the girls.'

The rest of the lads were already there and Benno was into the first chord sequence of *Walk Don't Run* by the time I picked up my bass. The brawl carried on out front and Tolley had to duck as a velvet upholstered stool crashed onto the stage. Sooty was crammed under a table near the front of the stage with Julia and Marlene, his hat pulled down over his eyes. He stared out at us like a prompt in a theatre and waved his hands around in silent instruction for us to keep playing. Although I think he would have preferred to have been rushing out into the fray with a bucket of bloody water and a sponge.

The thick and thin thugs were back to back in the middle

of the mayhem and they didn't seem to be selective about who they punched and nutted. A small youth in an Italian bum freezer jacket was out cold on the floor. A big flabby Teddy Boy was slumped in a chair mopping blood from his nose. From our vantage-point on the stage it was like watching a movie. The audience had turned performers as we watched the events unfold. Fortunately there was no sign of Sheila, Lizzy or Malcolm and we moved into the Ventures *No Trespassing* without missing a beat.

Then, an amazing sight - the Kershaw's man had entered the lounge and, as if oblivious to the mayhem, he was moving between the upturned tables, stepping over bodies, while selling his seafood. One middle-aged bloke in a drape jacket was just about to deliver the killer punch to a youth with a blond crew cut when he noticed the Kershaw's man. Without letting go of his victim's neck, he quickly unfurled his fist and rummaged in his pocket for loose change. Then, he nonchalantly peered into the white-coated vendor's basket and coolly purchased a packet of cockles which he stuffed inside his long jacket before continuing his assault.

There didn't seem to be any let-up and the violence continued. Then, Tolley shouted '*Exodus.*' He didn't want us to vacate the stage. It was instructions for us to play our slow, melancholy version of Ferrante and Teicher's theme from the film of the same name.

It worked and the violence gradually abated. Tables and chairs were righted, the bloke in the drape jacket sat down and opened his blood-stained packet of cockles and the injured were helped to the toilets. I noticed 'Thick and Thin' slip shiftily out of the door, apparently unscathed and satisfied by the amount of blood they had spilt. Elvis took one last look around the place, flexed his shoulders, twitched, and sat down as if nothing had happened. The haunting melody, which came to its climax with a dramatic *pasadoble* beat, did more than just calm the rioting throng. The whelk-munching thug had adopted a soppy toothless smile and was waltzing round the floor with his dazed victim in a mock, romantic gesture before leaving him to stumble off. The thug then sat down with his mates and retrieved a full set of dentures from his pocket which he quickly rinsed in his pint of beer and slipped back over his gums.

As we ended the number to rousing applause, I realised just how powerful music could be. And that it was not just capable of stirring an individual soul, but the collective soul of a whole gathering. Perhaps, I thought, they should have used it as a secret weapon in the war and wondered if it would have helped the crews of the Lancaster bombers if they could have had the *Dambusters March* piped into their headsets.

We finished our set when the landlord flashed for last orders and the place began to clear.

'Well that's it,' Sooty said, surveying the damage. 'We'll never be able to play here again.'

The lounge of the Crown looked like a battlefield, a window in one of the rear doors was smashed, there were chairs with legs missing and broken glass littered the beer-soaked floor. We began to pack away the equipment in silence.

'We need a vocalist,' I repeated, reflecting on our performance.

'Let's see what Elvis is doing next week,' suggested Benno sarcastically.

Then Sooty assumed his managerial role and began to lecture us. 'Let's be serious lads. It's no good having a vocalist if we get a reputation for inciting riots.' He looked at me as if I were totally responsible for the events of the evening.

Tolley joined in. 'Girls and groups don't mix,' he suggested, looking towards the table where Julia and Marlene were waiting.

Julia avoided eye contact when I glanced towards her and I sensed that she, too, wasn't happy about the scene with Sheila which sparked off the whole chain of events.

Tolley continued. 'Girls have split some of the best beat groups around. We must be totally focused and dedicated to our music,' he added.

The discussion ended abruptly as the red-faced landlord began to make his way towards us, puffing more excitedly than ever on his King Edward.

'This is it,' Sooty warned as the landlord took the cigar from his mouth and surveyed the scene. 'Well lads, what a night. WHAT A NIGHT!'

Sooty took off his Stetson in a gesture of apology and began to speak. 'We're so sorry about…'

'No, you don't understand! You were great. It's the best night we've had for months. My punters love a good rumble and my takings are up nearly fifty per cent.'

He pulled a wad of notes from his inside pocket. 'Here's your money and a fiver extra. I want to book you for every other Sunday for the next twelve months.'

 **Saved**
LaVern Baker

Monday mornings were always hard to wake up to, but this particular Monday morning couldn't have looked bleaker. As I lay there trying to will myself to face the day, I reviewed my current state of affairs.

1. In three hours time I would have to face an inquest that could end in unemployment.

2. The chance of my experiencing sex with the girl that has been the main object of my desire had disappeared.

3. The girl I thought I might love; the one I wanted to spend most of my time with and who made me feel safe and secure,

didn't trust me.

4. The leader of the beat group, which was now my main interest in life, didn't agree that we should also pursue a healthy interest in girls.

5. My sideboards weren't growing.

6. In America, Coca-Cola had developed a tin can that could eventually replace the famous contour bottle.

But much, much worse than all of that.

7. Petula Clark was top of the charts.

In an attempt to lift the gloom, I let my mind take me into *The Sunset Lounge* which was my sanctuary. I shut the imaginary door behind me and surveyed the scene. The welcoming red and blue glow of the neon sign reflected in the glass of the Bal-Ami juke box which was crammed with all my favourite sounds from the USA. I padded over the white, shag pile carpet, took an ice cold coke from the red chiller cabinet and reclined on the leopard skin studio couch. My latest addition, the Gaggia coffee machine, gently hissed away in front of the bamboo wall. I reached over and took the bright red Fender Precision Bass from its stand and began plucking its thick, wire strings. Boom, boom, boom…

Boom, boom, boom. 'Joe! Joe! It's ten past eight and you can't be late today of all days.'

Boom, boom, boom. It was my dad banging on my real bedroom door and I was dragged, kicking and screaming into the cold, cruel, real world.

Despite the extended session in *The Sunset Lounge* I managed to arrive at work on-time ready to face the music. Albert was waiting for me in the *Stone Room*, union rule book in hand. We were due in the board room at ten o'clock for the re-convened inquest into the Lord Ives fiasco. Mac was hovering around, obviously anxious about whether or not I was going to implicate him.

'Well Joe,' Albert started. 'I've consulted the head office of the Typographical Association and the area representative of the TUC and under Rule 24 subsection 2, it clearly states…"

I interrupted Albert. 'I don't understand rules and subsections, please just cut to the chase. What should I say? What shouldn't I say? What's likely to happen?'

Albert closed his rule book solemnly. 'Alright, as I see it, you've got three options.' He slowly shook his head sympathetically before continuing. 'One: Resign. Two: Accept full responsibility and throw yourself on their mercy. And three: Blame someone else.'

Mac shifted uneasily and Brad had entered the *Stone Room* in the middle of Albert's prognosis. They both started to look concerned about their own fate and glanced at me in silent anticipation. Someone's job was on the line and the outcome would depend on what I was going to say at the inquest. Then Wally joined us and I half expected him to recount a story where he had spent two years in Alcatraz on death row and then escaped on a boat made from matchsticks.

Mac broke the silence. 'So what are you going to say Ginner?'

I felt the pressure build up in my head as Brad joined in. 'What will be your exact version of events Joe?'

I couldn't stand it any longer. I needed to get away. 'Just leave me alone. I need time to think', I shouted as I rushed from the room, leaving everyone looking more concerned than ever.

I made for the stairs that led to the flat roof of the Advertiser building, high above the Market Place. Although it was in the middle of a busy town it was quite tranquil up there. The noise of the traffic was almost a distant hum and the empty rooftops of town provided a solitary setting, somewhere I could think.

Looking to the north, the tower of the Cathedral rose magnificently above the chimney stacks of Iron Gate. Beyond,

I could just see the Chevin Hills on the horizon, the start of the Peak district. To the south, the roofs of the shops and offices in the town centre were tightly packed together. The aroma of freshly ground coffee rose from the back windows of the Kardoma café. To the east, and literally next door, the Guildhall clock was just to the side of my vantage point. Being that close to the clock face I could actually see the minute hand move. But it was moving agonisingly slowly towards the hour of ten o'clock.

What should I say? Whose fault was it? Was it anybody's fault? How could I blame someone else? For a start I couldn't really blame anyone else and if I did I would be labelled a 'grass' by my workmates. But then if I lost my job, how would I be able to afford the HP payment on the Fender precision Bass that I had ordered from Derwent Music Store?

The fact of the matter was that the management and directors needed a scapegoat to appease Lord Ives and avoid making enemies of a very important, influential and extremely wealthy Derbyshire family. The newspaper depended on the support of the rural community and the county landowners. Legal action could threaten the financial stability of the paper at a time when local weekly newspapers were disappearing at the rate of about one a month. This whole episode could see the end of The Derbyshire Advertiser. So, was I prepared to be that scapegoat and sacrifice my own job for the sake of securing forty others and the preservation of a dinosaur of a newspaper?

I still hadn't made my mind up when I entered the boardroom flanked by Albert and Wally. The same people were there. A red nosed Lord Hobson looking as if he'd hit the port rather hard the night before, an embarrassed William Blake who shuffled nervously with his papers and found it hard to look me in the eye. And Brad, who did look at me, his eyes pleading as if to say: 'Please don't mention that I was in the Bell when I should have been checking what was going into that fateful last page'.

Then I noticed that there was a new face sitting at the far end of the boardroom table. It belonged to an old, kind-faced, sickly looking gentleman dressed in a Prince of Wales three-piece suit with a gold fob watch chain hanging from the waist-coat pocket. He looked as if he was shrinking inside his own body. The suit, which may have fitted him once, hung loosely over his bony shoulders and his scrawny neck poked out of his shirt collar which was a couple of sizes too big for him. His wizened face turned towards us like a tortoise peering out of its shell. But despite looking as if he was on his death-bed, he was the only one in the assembled company who looked relaxed.

William Blake spoke first. 'Gentlemen, the meeting of last Friday is now re-convened.'

Albert, Wally and I stood to attention in front of the table. I found my mind drifting towards *The Sunset Lounge* but managed to fight the temptation to flee the scene and remained alert to the proceedings.

'I'd like to introduce you to Lord Ives who has graciously agreed to attend this inquest,' Blake announced, bowing slightly towards the tortoise.

The little old man was Lord Ives. It was getting worse, and I wondered if Sheila's father had told him about me ravishing his youngest daughter. I took my handkerchief from my pocket to wipe the sweat from my brow, checking first that it hadn't mysteriously turned into a pair of lace panties.

'Now King,' Blake continued. 'Would you like to give us your account of how the offending article managed to find its way into last week's paper?'

This was it. The showdown. If I'd have been Kooky I would have said something like: 'Hey man, this is dragsville.

His Lordship's still on the scene so what's the big deal?'

If I'd have been Mac I would have said: 'Ya can stuff your newspaper right up ya fuckin' arses.'

But I was Joe King and I had decided what I was going to do. I was going to bring the pathetic charade to a quick end and just resign. I cleared my throat and started to speak.

'I think that under the circumstances...'

But the croaky, cultured voice of Lord Ives interrupted me.

'Just a minute young man. I'd like to say something first.' He glanced around the table before continuing. 'If that's alright with everyone else, of course?'

'Certainly, my Lord,' replied William Blake with another little bow.

Lord Ives slowly rose to his feet. This was it, he was going to tell the 'court' about my kinky sex session involving his best friend's daughter and a horse.

'Since we met last week something has happened that has put a new perspective on this whole affair,' he announced. I braced myself.

'It appears that very few people in Derbyshire, and indeed, in my own village, really knew much about me.' He cleared his scraggy throat and continued. 'After D-Day in 1945 the British public didn't want to hear about the war. They'd had enough of it. They wanted to get on with rebuilding their lives in the brave new, peaceful world. Consequently, my so-called heroic act, which happened during the latter stages of hostilities, received very little publicity and was quickly forgotten.'

Lord Ives paused, he seemed pained as if his story was opening old, emotional wounds. His kind expression left him for a moment which betrayed a pent-up bitterness, perhaps at not being recognised for his brave deeds. He composed himself and continued.

'The fact of the matter is that very few people knew that I

was a, so-called, war hero. That is, until my obituary appeared in your very fine newspaper.'

I glanced around the room at the others. The fearful expressions had changed to confusion, and then anticipated glee.

'The result is that the villagers of Ilam are throwing a big party in my honour.' His craggy face broke into a broad smile. 'They're going to invite the airmen I helped rescue and their families. So it appears that the unfortunate error has given me a new lease of life and I've finally been recognised.'

He cleared his throat again and managed a croaky chuckle. 'After all, It's no good people getting to know me after I've gone and I can't take my medals with me.' He glanced round the table, fixed his gaze on me, and gave a knowing wink. 'So thank you all, and to show my appreciation I'll be inviting the entire staff of The Derbyshire Advertiser to the party.'

A clearly audible, collective sigh of relief, passed around the room. Everyone stood and it was all smiles and shaking of hands, but no one could have felt as relieved as I did. Albert was the only one who didn't look pleased, not having the opportunity to display his union negotiating skills.

So the drama was over, but just before I was about to leave the board room, Lord Ives placed a skeletal hand on my arm.

'Just a minute Joe,' he said, looking over his shoulder to make sure no one was listening. 'I hear from my friend Aubrey Forsythe that you know his daughter Sheila.'

'Er… yes.' I replied, wondering how much Sheila's father had told him.

He looked over his shoulder again and continued. 'Right little belter, isn't she? If I was fifty years younger I'd show her a thing or too.'

I tried to hide my surprise with a nod and a weak smile.

'But beware lad. She's one of those girls that likes to tease.' His expression became more serious. 'When some young women wake up to their sexuality they like to demonstrate the power they have over us red-blooded males. She just likes the drama of it all and the more dangerous it is, and the more trouble they can get us in, the more they like it.'

He gave me another knowing wink, suggesting that he knew all about the incident in the Forsyth's kitchen and The Crown Hotel, and then continued.

'I sometimes think she even tries it on with me sometimes'. He gazed up at the ceiling. 'She will straighten her stockings in front of me or make sure I can see her cleavage when she bends to pass me a drink or something.' He attempted a raucous laugh. 'It's no wonder I had that funny turn that put me in hospital.'

Lord Ives became serious again. 'But if you really like her don't give up. She'll be at my party so you should take your chance then. Her parents will soon come round.'

Lord Ives turned to rejoin William Blake but he hesitated. His wrinkled turtle-like neck craned towards me again and he came out with a statement that totally floored me.

'As Kookie would say, you only make this scene once man, so grab all the kicks while you can.'

Songs of Passion

Here Comes Summer
Jerry Keller

Following the satisfactory conclusion to the Lord Ives affair there was an air of huge relief at work. The uncertainty of the newspaper's future had been removed and jobs were secure. It was as if Derby County had just avoided relegation. The Linotype operators were whistling more than usual and Eric was continually humming his renditions of Perez Prado Latin tunes while knocking hell out of the cow bell that was clamped to his wooden composing frame.

Within a couple of weeks everything seemed back to normal at the good old Derbyshire Advertiser. As we moved into June my spirits were lifted even higher. The long cold winter and wet spring were behind us and summer was here at last. More time to get out and about to enjoy the three most important things in my life - music, girls and clothes. Furthermore, in a couple of weeks my new Fender Precision Bass would arrive. Everything was right with the world.

The working week seemed to go quicker than usual and before long it was Friday and another wonderful weekend. I had landed a cushy piece of overtime at The Advertiser. On Fridays I had to go in to work at 7 o'clock on my own. My task was to take the papers next door to Poynton's newsagents in the Market Hall which opened at 7.30. Once this was done I could settle down in Fred Forcett's chair and catch up on my sleep before the rest of the men came in at nine. For this I got two hours at time-and-a-half.

Despite the early hour, it was already quite warm by the time I'd finished my chore. It was a beautiful morning and there wasn't a cloud in the sky. I opened the window at the back of the *Stone Room* and was greeted with my favourite town centre smell. Freshly ground coffee was floating on a light breeze from the Kardoma Cafe. I settled down in the chair with the latest copy of the New Musical Express but soon drifted off to sleep. After about half an hour I was woken abruptly, choking on smoke. Mac was standing over me and had just blown a giant cloud of second hand cigarette smoke into my face.

'Your early morning call Sleeping Beauty,' he laughed.

I opened another window and we set about our first task of the day which was to remove the Linotype slugs from the made up pages of the paper which was now on sale all around the county. Since the end of the Lord Ives affair even Mac was back to his mean and menacing self. He flicked another fag into the corner of his mouth and spoke out of the other side.

'I'm bored now the shit's settled,' he said, looking up and down the *Stone Room* for something or someone to relieve the tedium of his task. His eyes fixed on old Fred Fawcett who was taking one of his naps in the chair in the far corner. I could see that Mac's evil mind was hatching out a plan for some cruel practical joke. His face suddenly lit up, replacing the permanent moody expression for just a split-second.

'Quick Ginner, pass me that ball of string,' he whispered excitedly.

Mac started arranging some items on the table next to the old copper tea urn - a tin mug, a couple of spoons, a wooden mallet. Mac securely tied all the objects together on the end of a couple of yards of the string. I couldn't work out what his plan was until he pointed over towards the slumbering Fred Fawcett.

'Come on Ginner, hold these,' he whispered as we approached Fred.

Mac proceeded to attach the end of the string to Fred's outstretched leg while I held the objects that were tethered to the other end. Eric realised what was going on and stopped his Latin ravings to avoid waking the unsuspecting victim. I carefully placed the objects on the floor. Some of the Linotype operators in the adjoining room had got wind of the ruse and had stopped work to observe the proceedings.

'Right Ginner, do your impression of Wally running up the stairs.' Mac whispered.

The idea was brilliant. Although I did feel a bit sorry for what was about to happen to Fred. I went half-way down the stairs, paused briefly, and then started my assent, gradually increased the pace, just as Wally did. I almost reached the top of the stairs and the entrance to the *Stone Room* when I noticed a strange echo to my footsteps. I looked over my shoulders to see Wally running up behind me.

It was too late to abort the prank and I could hear the sound of clanking metal from the floor above. I burst into the *Stone Room* with Wally hot on my heels. We were met by a wild-eyed Fred Fawcett trying to run in two directions at once like a headless chicken. The metal objects were clanking behind him but in his semi-conscious state it took him a while to work out where the noise was coming from.

Wally stood there, hands on hips watching the confused Fred trying to disentangle himself from the string. Then he looked around the *Stone Room* where everyone else had resumed work but finding it hard to stifle their laughter. Poor Fred. Wally had warned him before about sleeping on the job. If Wally realised what had happened, Fred could be in serious trouble.

'What the hell's happening here?' Wally shouted. He looked around the room and at each smirking face in turn.

He was answered by total silence. Fred's confused expression turned to desperation.

'It was me,' I found myself saying. 'It's Fred's fortieth wedding anniversary and while he was working away, I quietly tied the stuff to his leg.' Wally eyed me with suspicion.

'It's an old Derbyshire tradition,' I continued, trying to bring more credibility to my story.

Wally looked around the room for confirmation

of my claim.

'That's right,' said Eric. 'It's like tying stuff to the bumpers of wedding cars.'

After a further pause Wally bought it. He strode over to Fred with his hand outstretched.

'Well, I suppose congratulations are in order, old man,' Wally said, pumping the hand of a relieved, but still bewildered, Fred. 'That's quite a milestone' Wally continued. And it reminds me of the time in the Far East when I was asked to be the best man at Prince Fuk Tu Lo's wedding…'

We could all see what was coming and gradually slipped away to our respective tasks leaving the unfortunate Fred to endure another of Wally's tall stories. Would he stay awake? I thought. And would Wally remember that Fred was a confirmed bachelor?

 ## You Are My One Desire
Buddy Holly

The day I had been looking forward to for weeks finally arrived. When I woke the butterflies started fluttering round my stomach, the same feeling I used to get waking up on Christmas Day when I was little.

It was the day when I was going to collect my brand new Fender Precision Bass which was the same model played by the bass players of nearly every professional British and American beat group. And the same colour as the one played by Jet Harris of the Shadows – Fiesta Red. The HP payments would cost me one pound ten shillings a week, a third of my weekly salary. But I would have swept the streets of town in my spare time to obtain this wonderful object of desire.

At a group meeting following the successful, albeit eventful, début at the Crown Hotel, we had decided to take steps to become more professional. We had agreed that each of us would order Fender guitars and pay for them ourselves out of our meagre apprentice wages. Whippet's parents had already bought him a new Olympus Drum Kit. We also agreed that, out of the proceeds of our bookings, we would purchase two 30 watt Selmer amplifiers and a 50 watt Selmer bass amplifier. Sooty, being of age, had agreed to be guarantor for the HP agreement.

The final decision was just as important if we were to get more bookings and give the other local groups a run for their money - we agreed to advertise for a vocalist. So it was an exciting day for all members of the Rapids and we set off for town in high spirits . Sooty was meeting his new-love Marlene in town so he agreed to collect us and our new guitars from the music store at one o'clock. Our first port of call when we got off the bus was the offices of The Derby Evening Telegraph to place the advertisement. The offices were much larger and grander than those of the less successful Derbyshire Advertiser. Located in the old corn exchange, the Telegraph building had a distinctive, three storey circular frontage with a domed roof painted green. The reception office was more like the entrance to an exclusive hotel than a newspaper office. An ornate, art deco staircase swept down from the floors above to a highly polished, stone floor.

The staff behind the two curved counters that flanked the entrance looked colder and more officious than the friendly faces of their counterparts at the Advertiser. They eyed us suspiciously as we entered. As I worked for a newspaper and understood the jargon, I was delegated to make the arrangements for the advertisement. I approached the youngest and friendliest looking receptionist, a girl in her early twenties, and explained our requirement.

'It'll need to go into the Personal Column,' she advised with a friendly smile.

'Look through some of the back numbers on the rack to get some ideas, if you like,' she added helpfully.

We gathered round the file of newspapers and started to read some of the small ads in hushed tones. Benno was reading one of the For Sale ads with a quizzical expression on his face.

'Do Jamaicans wear different shoes to us?' he asked.

We read the ad.

"BLACK MENS SHOES FOR SALE. SIZE 10. OFFERS. NO TIME WASTERS"

This inspired us to create our own spoof ads. But our giggling was met with scornful, disapproving looks from the snootier, older reception staff.

'Come on. Let's get down to business before we get thrown out,' I warned.

We each took a blank copy form and started to write our own suggestions for the ad. We settled on an amalgam of all five which read –

"SINGER WANTED FOR LOCAL BEAT GROUP. MUST HAVE OWN MICROPHONE AND STAGE SUIT. TELEPHONE BILL SUTCLIFFE ON DERBY 62215."

Tolley passed me the final form and discarded the others.

'Go on then. Take it to your girlfriend,' he said sarcastically. But as I approached the counter the young girl turned to answer the phone. I was confronted by a dragon of a woman who looked down her nose at me in obvious disdain.

'Give me the form,' she barked impatiently.

I could hear the lads laughing in the background which didn't help. The dragon read the copy on the form but I could see that she wasn't impressed with its content.

'Is this some kind of childish prank,' she bellowed, and slammed the form onto the counter top. The eyes of everyone in the reception area fell on me. I didn't understand so I read the words on the piece of paper.

"G-STRING FOR SALE. KEPT IN GOOD NICK. TELEPHONE JOE KING ON DERBY 66715"

The laughter from behind increased and I could feel myself colouring-up. The dragon tossed her head back in a dismissive gesture and turned to the next customer. Fortunately the younger woman had become free and Whippet rescued the situation by thrusting the correct copy form into my sweaty palms. Still blushing from my encounter with the dragon, I handed her the form.

'Er. I'd l-l-like it inserting on three consecutive nights please,' I stammered.

'Wouldn't we all,' she replied, with a knowing wink.

I was too surprised and embarrassed to reply to her innuendo but managed a limp 'thank you' before leaving the counter.

We left with the lads still laughing at my embarrassment and set off for the main event of the day - taking delivery of our gleaming, new Fender guitars from Derwent Music Store.

As we made our way up St. Peter's Street, I wondered if Sheila would be working in the store, and worse still, if her father would be there. Would she still be as angry as when she threw her drink over me at the Crown? And did Malcolm, Lizzy and her manage to get out unscathed?

We were all so excited about getting our hands on the guitars that we didn't even make the usual detour through the Boots cosmetic department. Then we broke into a trot. then a run, weaving in and out of the throngs of Saturday shoppers.

We arrived, breathless, outside Derwent Music Store where Sooty and Marlene were both waiting. We just stood outside peering into the window, enjoying the magic of the moment for as long as possible, like children hesitating at the top of the stairs on Christmas Day. Through the window I could see Sheila at the far end of the store serving a customer.

Fortunately I couldn't see her father. Facing one angry Forsythe would be as much as I could take.

We entered the store and, in mock ceremonial fashion, slowly made our way, single file, to the rear counter area. For some reason, Benno was humming *The Dam Busters March*. Sooty was also trying to apply some reverence to the occasion. He removed his cowboy hat and did the same for Marlene. He then clutched his hat to his chest and made an attempt at the funeral march with a deliberate hesitation in each step.

Sheila stopped serving a kid with a broken recorder and turned to us.

'Well, if it isn't the Shadows,' she said, sarcastically. 'Come for your new guitars, I suppose?'

She finished serving the kid and Sooty introduced her to Marlene with pride. Sheila then disappeared into the back and returned with one of the male assistants and three guitar cases each adorned with the famous Fender logo. The cases were laid side by side on the shop floor.

'They look like coffins,' Sooty offered, putting a slight damper on things.

This was the moment we had been waiting for. Whippet started a drum roll on one of the display kits as Tolley, Benno and I moved forwards in unison, bent down and prepared to open the cases to reveal the new objects of our desire. I glanced at Sheila who was watching proceedings from a safe distance with Marlene. But there was a slight suggestion of jealousy in her expression. Could a girl be jealous of a guitar? I wondered. Then I imagined opening the case to find that Sheila had scratched graffiti across its smooth body - "TWO-TIMING BASTARD"

Whippet brought his drum roll to a crescendo and we simultaneously snapped open our cases.

It was a moment I knew I would never forget. My Fiesta

Red Fender Precision Bass stared, seductively up at me from its crushed velvet bed. I ran my hands over the sensuous curves of its distinctively shaped body. The finish was smooth and silky to the touch. The fret board was crafted like the finest piece of antique furniture. I blinked as the store's spotlights sent star bursts reflecting from the huge chrome keys like exotic jewellery on a beautiful Egyptian princess. I gently lifted the guitar from its case and slipped the strap round my neck.

'Hello my beauty,' I whispered.

I glanced at Sheila again, hoping she hadn't heard, but her jealousy was obviously getting too much for her and I caught her undoing the next button of her blouse. Tolley and Benno were equally engrossed in their new acquisitions and a reverential hush descended over the busy music store. Even the kid with broken recorder was watching open mouthed. Then I looked over to Sooty who was still clutching his hat to his chest while wiping a tear from the corner of his eye. Whippet broke the silence.

'Well, are we going to stand here looking at them all day or are we going to make some noise? Let's get out of here!'

Before we left I asked Sheila if they had all got away from the Crown without further incident. She said they had and apologised for starting the trouble in the first place. We laughed about Elvis and she placed her hand over mine.

'Listen Joe, just because we can't meet at my house again doesn't mean we can't see each other elsewhere.' She fluttered her long eyelashes and glanced down provocatively at her exposed cleavage. Then her sultry tone became harsher.

'But you needn't think I'm going to play second fiddle to a bass guitar,' she added, with no pun intended.

We headed back to the van with our new treasured possessions and drove straight to the Blue Peter Hotel in Alvaston where we were booked for the evening. The Blue

Peter was one of three local pubs built in the mid 1930s in Art Deco style. They each had distinctive, curvilinear, white stucco walling, flat roofs and other architectural features reminiscent of ocean-going liners.

We set the equipment up in the empty Lounge which had a small stage in front of a wide curved expanse of metal French windows. Then we played our first ever number with Fender guitars. We blasted into *FBI* and the difference was amazing. Tolley's skilful execution of the middle solo was enhanced by the unmistakable Stratocaster sound, Benno's rhythm accompaniment had a new clean, crispness, and the fuller, rounder tone from my Precision Bass nearly shook the panes from the French windows.

We finished the number with echoes of the final notes bouncing off the ceiling and were breathless from the rush of adrenalin. Then we heard cheers from a dozen little kids outside. They had left the swings in the pub garden and had been watching us, their snotty noses pressed against the windowpanes. Then I noticed that someone else was watching. About three paces behind the kids stood a thin, wiry, menacing looking youth with short, cropped hair. I immediately recognised him as one of the two thugs who had caused the most damage at the Crown Hotel brawl. He caught my glance and moved forwards pushing the kids out of the way. I also recognised his slightly deranged expression. It was as if half of his face was smiling and the other half was full of evil.

I didn't mention him to the others but wondered if we would be in for another blood-bath later. All I could think about was how I was going to protect my beloved new guitar.

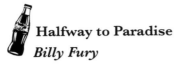

Halfway to Paradise
Billy Fury

The first gig with Fenders had gone brilliantly. The new guitars had given us added confidence and improved our stage presence. The place had been packed, the crowd loved us and the landlord booked us again. Thankfully, the threat of another night of violence didn't materialise. Although half way through our opening set there was trouble at the door. The Thick and Thin thugs were refused entry. Their reputation had obviously preceded them and it took the arrival of two uniformed policemen to persuade them to leave. As they were ushered away from the door, the thicker set of the two gestured toward us. He was pointing his finger menacingly at us while trying to shout something above the roar of our guitars.

We learnt from the landlord that that the two thugs were the notorious McBride brothers who cruise the pubs of town just looking for the opportunity for a rumble. Rumour had it that Tony, the thin wiry one, had a metal plate inserted into his skull after falling through a roof at Bass Brewery where he worked. Apparently he'd never been the same since and was recently released from Leicester prison following a spell for GBH. The landlord also told us that the McBride brothers were convinced that we had tipped him off about their part in the Crown violence and that was why they were refused admission. That would explain the aggressive gestures as the police led them away.

I lay in bed on the quiet Sunday morning processing the events of the previous day and assessing my current situation. I then accepted the fact that when you were young you have to live a roller-coaster life and that if you want the thrilling bits you have to be prepared to put up with the scary bits. In my case, modern clothes, great music, beautiful Fender guitars, pretty girls and ice cold coke have to be balanced by hard work, angry parents protective of the innocence of their young daughters, nagging and demanding bosses and the constant risk of having your face caved-in by a couple of deranged psychopaths.

I spent the rest of the day relaxing Down Brook. Dreaded Sundays weren't quite so boring now that I worked and played so hard. It was good just to slow down a little and recharge the batteries. It was a beautiful sunny summer's day and as I walked down the hill I could see that the playing field was full of kids. The teenage girls in the mob, some in shorts and sun tops, were sunbathing like spokes in a wheel round a pink and white transistor radio. The lads were deeply engrossed in their usual card school. Some of the younger boys had built a rope swing over the brook which broke just as I was walking over the narrow metal footbridge, sending a podgy kid plunging into the sparkling water to the delight of his mates.

I had arranged to meet Julia at two and I could see that she was already there. Seeing her gave me a warm, comfortable feeling and once again I realised that I needed Julia more than I thought. Although the further encouragement I had received from Sheila still gave me a surge of lustful excitement deep down inside. Perhaps if I went all the way with Julia it would remove the urge to have Sheila and every other pretty girl I laid my eyes on. Then my feelings for Julia could be more focused and faithful. At least it would be well worth testing the theory and I was at the age where I was expected to lose my virginity; Mac claimed to have lost his on Markeaton Park at the age of twelve. My body-clock was ticking away towards twenty, counting down the few years I had left as a teenager.

Julia looked as pretty as ever but more sexy than usual. Her crisp, white cotton dress was gathered tightly around her tiny waist by a broad, red, elasticated belt. It had the effect of shortening the hem-line by several inches, exposing more of her shapely legs. She wore short white socks inside her red, flat heeled, winkle picker shoes which seemed to emphasise her bare legs even more.

She ran to meet me and jumped into my arms in her usual 'happy to see you' way. I swung her round and then she kissed me full on the mouth and more passionately than usual. Her French kissing technique had definitely improved and my naturally jealous mind wondered if she'd been practising with someone else.

'So how'd it go at The Blue Peter last night?' she asked as we wandered off hand-in-hand along the side of the brook.

'It was the most, babe,' I replied in my jokey, Kookie voice. 'I just love the sound I get from my new guitar. It's the groovyist.'

'As much as you love me?' she asked.

As it had been with Sheila, I could tell that Julia was jealous of my new guitar. What is it with these girls? I thought. How could they possibly believe that there could be any kind of comparison? Or was it just that there was a natural female instinct to have total exclusivity over a bloke's interests?

I decided to tease her a little.

'Well, let's see now.' I stroked my chin as if seriously considering her question. 'My new guitar is beautiful, so are you.' I slipped my arm round her waist. 'It has sexy curves, and so have you.'

Julia wasn't impressed and pulled away from me, walking ahead in a huff. We had reached the end of the playing field where the brook cut between two fields.

I continued with my analogy nevertheless. 'But more importantly…'

Julia turned, eyebrows raised, waiting for me to redeem myself.

'… it responds to my every touch.'

I then chased her into the long grass and lunged towards her. We fell together, laughing and rolling in the grass. Suddenly

I was on top of her and we were kissing passionately. Although we'd stopped running we both became even more breathless, just like during our first kiss on the bridge last winter. Julia's dress had worked its way up over her waist and my hand slid down over her naked thigh which felt warm and silky. I pressed myself against her and she gasped. I knew from the various Mac lectures that the next step of the seduction process would be one of the most difficult. The point where passion could be killed at a stroke and the moment lost. I had reached the point where I needed to apply the skilful art of removing underwear. Mac had suggested that if girls didn't wear knickers the teenage pregnancy rate would increase ten-fold.

I tried to focus on the task at hand while maintaining the level of desire and rolled Julia over on top of me. Our lips were still engaged in hungry searching kisses. Then the excitement got the better of me, my hands finding the top of Julia's panties. I started to slowly peel them over her writhing buttocks.

Julia froze. 'No!' she whispered.

Her body had become rigid on top of me. The passion had evaporated into the hot summer afternoon. She rolled off me and left me lying in the grass, still breathless from the anticipation and excitement.

Julia snuggled back up to me. 'I'm sorry. It's just that I'm not sixteen yet and I'm frightened of becoming pregnant. My mum would kill me.'

I hadn't thought of any of those things and I realised that the power of lust supersedes all common sense and fear. Julia was still underage and I would have been breaking the law. And what if she had become pregnant? If her mum would kill her, what would her dad do to me? And if I had to get married, how could I afford to keep up the payments on my new guitar. There'd be no more group. Or groupies.

The moment had gone and I was somewhat relieved. I

started thinking about becoming more sensible and the other part of the seduction process that Mac had coached me on – how to remove a Durex from its packet and put it on without your partner knowing. This, he had warned, could be another passion-killing moment. It could also give, who Mac called the 'victim', time to think about what was about to happen and present her with the opportunity to change her mind. For me, the hardest part of all that would be purchasing the Durex in the first place.

Julia could see I was deep in thought. She kissed me lightly on the cheek. 'Don't be sad, It's my birthday in six weeks' time,' she whispered. To me this sounded more like a promise than sympathy.

Wham!
Lonnie Mac

The bookings for The Rapids were increasing week by week. But the more we played the more the working week seemed to drag. This was why practical jokes were such a necessity for Mac and I. Sometimes an unscheduled event or drama would also help lift the monotony.

One such event came along right in the middle of the week. I always found it hard to wake up from my slumbers but on Wednesday I had to do it twice. The first time was at 7.00am staring at the alarm clock, willing myself to get out of bed. The second time was in my lunch break, staring at the low ceiling under the balcony at the Locarno.

Mac was down on the dance floor bopping with two girls when a Locarno lunchtime regular joined me on the balcony. It was Winston Lees, a cool Jamaican lad who worked on the Corporation buses as a conductor. His uncle worked away on the ships out of Liverpool and was able to get his hands on the latest 45s straight from the States. Consequently, Winston ran a thriving underground business supplying enthusiasts with rare American Rock'n'roll, Pop and Rhythm and Blues records. Winston had an unusually high-pitched voice which was able to rise above the full, 120 decibels of sound pumping from the speaker cabinets just above us.

'Hey Man,' he shouted, over the top of Billy Fury's cover of *Bless You*, 'I got de American original of dis if ya wanit.'

'No thanks, Winston, it's not my scene.'

'Well, what about 'dis den?'

He pushed his hand inside a brown paper bag and produced a seven inch single on a strange American label I'd never heard of. I took it from him and read the label - *Shop Around* by the Miracles. The logo read Tamla.

'Come on man, you aint heard any'ting like 'dis. Gimmee four bob.' *

I remembered from the charts in the New Musical Express earlier in the year that this record was Number One in the States for weeks but wasn't released here. Although I'd never heard the track before, the fact that it was on top of the American charts for so long was enough for me. So I knocked him down to half-a-crown and bought it.

'Thanks man,' Winston screeched. 'You won't regret it.'

He turned to continue with his illicit trading then stopped as if remembering something. 'Hey man, how'd ya like to come to a party next week? I'm spinning some platters at my uncle's house party. There'll be lots of great sounds 'dare man,' he hopped about on his toes waiting for an answer.

The thought of more rare American singles was enough for me so I agreed. He said he'd meet me from my late shift at the Advertiser and bounded off. Winston didn't walk, his thin, wiry frame just bounced along as if he had springs on his shoes. As he moved, his head swung from side-to-side taking in all around him, ever alert to the opportunity of making a few bob.

As he stopped at the far end of the balcony I recognised his next prospective customers. They were the notorious McBride brothers who I had last seen trying to get into the Blue Peter. They seemed to quickly dismiss Winston's sales pitch but continued in deep conversation with him, their heads close together trying to hear each other above the pumping music. Tony, the wiry one, pointed towards me and I sensed danger. I remembered his brother's threatening gesture as they were escorted from the pub.

Mac returned but wasn't impressed with my *Miracles* purchase. 'Never heard of them. They must be crap,' he said as we made our way downstairs towards the exit. I remembered later in the day that Mac was ahead of me at that time. I also remembered that as we passed the tables and chairs under the balcony, a heavy hand grabbed my shoulder. It was the hand of Graham McBride and his brother was at his side. Gra McBride spoke first. 'Are you particular about who comes to listen to your crappy group, youth?'

It was over in a flash and I didn't see it coming. I remember turning towards Gra McBride while he spoke and as I did his brother must have hit me.

During the first wisps of returning consciousness, I was lying in my *Sunset Lounge*. But I wasn't there as a result of my vivid imagination. It was as if I was in a dream sequence of a movie, but everything looked so real - the neon sign, juke box, leopard skin studio couch and the red coke cooler. I *was* in *The Sunset Lounge*. It did exist. I stared at the spotlight on the bamboo wall, but it began to fade.

I woke up lying on my back between two tables and upturned chairs under the balcony of the Locarno. The first thing I focused on as I regained consciousness was one of the little gold lampshades with star shapes cut out of them that were set into the low ceiling. As the Manager of the Locarno picked me up there was no sign of the McBrides or Mac. The whole dance hall was empty. I staggered back to work in a daze still clutching my Miracles record. I arrived ten minutes late which must have been the length of time I had been unconscious.

Mac was apparently unaware of my fate and had assumed I had stayed behind to discuss further record deals with Winston. Nevertheless, he was really impressed that I had been 'jobbed' by the McBrides and saw it as a kind of initiation.

'Well, look on the bright side Ginner. You're more of a man now. We just need to work on your virginity.'

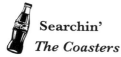

Searchin'
The Coasters

The advertisement for a vocalist brought in over fifteen applications. We sifted through them, rejecting school kids, middle-aged men and mental patients. During this process we agreed that a girl singer wouldn't be right for a beat group either. So there were a couple of rejections there. Although we were tempted to let them come along just to see what they looked like.

We had narrowed it down to five and arranged for auditions at The Crown after we had played at one of the lunchtime sessions. We ordered some drinks and crisps and waited for the regulars to go home to their Sunday lunches.

As we waited for the first applicant to arrive, the lads asked me about the bruise on my chin. It wasn't that noticeable as the inside of my mouth had sustained most of the damage. My teeth had ripped into my cheek on the impact of Tony McBride's fist. I managed to relate the story through the pain of the salty crisps which were attacking my open wounds. Tolley was all for searching the McBrides out and getting revenge. Benno suggested we enlist the services of Elvis who was now a regular part of our act when we played the Crown. I shook my head as I washed away some of the salty crisps with a mouthful of luke-warm coke.

'That would be just the kind of sport the McBrides would be looking for.'

'We'll still have to watch out for the bastards,' Sooty said. 'I have an uncomfortable feeling about them. Like a premonition.'

He started to tell us about a grisly nightmare he had a week ago but his story was interrupted by our first applicant. There came a confident 'Hi!' as he entered the room. Later we christened this candidate *The Teenage Idol*. He was clean-cut, clear skinned and handsome in the style of American singers Bobby Rydell, Fabian, Bobby Vee and the like. His blond hair was cut short at the back and sides but was longer on top and lightly greased back with just the hint of a quiff. I noted his clothes as he made his way through the lingering cigarette smoke towards the stage. He was wearing a powder blue V-neck jumper, a cut-away collar white shirt and a slim, plain yellow tie. He strolled confidently up to the stage with his jacket slung over his shoulder and extended his hand towards Tolley.

'Hi! I'm Ricky Royce,' he said with a strong, confident voice that was almost overpowering.

Ricky Royce and The Rapids, I thought. Sounds great and he looks the part, but let's hear what he sounds like.

We all tried to look surprised when he explained that his real name wasn't Ricky Royce and was in fact Keith Shufflewick. We ran through his repertoire and settled on Del Shannon's *Runaway*. Sooty positioned himself at the back of the room, adopting his usual role as mad musical director. Tolley strummed the introduction and Ricky came in right on cue. He sounded ok right up until the falsetto chorus... *and I wonder, why, why, why, why, wonder...* The *whys* were totally out of tune and resembled a sound I'd heard last year in Aberdovey when a seagull became trapped in a drain pipe. We all cringed and shot awkward glances at each other. Sooty pulled his hat over his ears and turned his back to hide his pained expression. The landlord even poked his head round the door to see what the strange whining noise was. We tried a couple of other numbers but the performance didn't improve and the seagull didn't manage to free itself. Ricky Royce's exit was slightly less confident than his entrance.

The next applicant was already waiting near the door in the gloom, a slight figure dwarfed by the retreating Ricky who was only average height himself. I shouted 'Hello' over the mic and asked him to come forward. As he got closer we could see that he was wearing a Bemrose School blazer and short grey trousers.

Sooty examined his list of candidates. 'Er, I thought you said you were seventeen when you rang?'

'Well, I am next month and I thought that by the time you'd make your mind up I would be,' he replied.

Not a bad answer, I thought.

'What's with the school uniform?' asked Benno.

'I've just come straight from church. I sing in the choir.'

I reflected on the fact that some of the best American Rhythm and Blues singers had started in gospel choirs, but the visual image didn't support my argument. He was white skinned, five foot two and wearing short, grey flannel trousers. We felt obliged to continue with the audition and applicant number two opted for *Stupid Cupid* but although he had a good voice, his pitch was even higher than that of Connie Francis. And when he did *Peggy Sue* it was 'Jimmy Clitheroe meets the Chipmunks.' Tolley mumbled under his breath. 'Thank you. Leave your name and address in the waste paper bin.' and Sooty politely showed the schoolboy out, promising to get in touch within the week.

The next on our list was a Peter Collins. The name didn't

sound all that inspiring but he had to be an improvement on what we'd heard so far. We were just about to think that he wasn't coming when the silhouette of a large, bulky figure filled the distant doorway. The outline looked familiar, turned up collar, quiff, long draped jacket. Then the figure sort of stumbled forward into the light and towards the stage. It was Elvis.

'Good to see you again,' said Sooty politely.

'Likewise I'm sure,' mumbled Elvis.

We all nodded a welcome towards Elvis, each wondering how we were going to turn him down without violent repercussions.

'So what do you want to sing Elv... I mean, er, Peter,' Whippet asked.

'Play *Hound Dawg*,' he ordered, in his half Texan, half Derby, drawl.

Tolley gave him an 'A' chord and he was off.

'You aint nutin' but a hound dawg'

We knew he was good from his various unscheduled appearances with us at The Crown, but he only ever did Elvis numbers. We went through the motions with *Blue Suede Shoes*. Then, during the speaking bit in a dire *Are You Lonesome Tonight*, he fixed his gaze on me. Elvis circled round me, mic in hand.

'Ya know someone once said the world's a stage...'

He sat on the floor of the small stage and tapped the boards, inviting me to join him. Elvis was delivering the heartfelt plea of the lyrics directly to me. I carried on playing but felt compelled to hold his, almost tearful, gaze. Normally, Elvis would find some female in the audience to focus on when he was performing his act. But nevertheless, I found his apparent sincerity extremely uncomfortable as he moved closer to me.

'Honey you lied when you said you loved me...'

I didn't know whether to smile at him, remain serious, wink or what. In the end I settled for a soppy, bashful grin, and

I'm sure I was blushing. The number thankfully came to its mournful conclusion and I was able to look away.

Tolley took the initiative and asked the question we were all frightened to ask. 'That was great Pete, but do you do anything by other artists?' There seemed to be a long moment of silence, just the sound of the amplifiers hissing away like a desert wind. I imagined tumble-weed drifting over the polished wooden floor. A single bell tolled outside.

Elvis eventually broke the silence. 'Ya whaaaaaat?' he yelled at the top of his voice.

We all took a pace backwards and Benno fell into Whippet's cymbals.

'Elvis is The King,' he roared. 'What kinda other numbers are ya referrin' to?'

'Well, like Bobby Vee,' suggested Whippet as he fumbled to reassemble his drum kit.

'Bobby who?' he scowled. 'Elvis's songs are the ONLY songs. I wouldn't be seen dead singing the kinda crap you get in the hit parade now.' He started to mince round the stage with the mic in one hand and the other on his hip.

'*Take good care of my bay-ye-bee,*' he mocked. 'It's crap. It's all crap. And you're crap,' he spat on the stage right in front of Tolley. For a second I thought that Tolley was going to retaliate but he thought better of it.

Elvis calmed down a bit and just let out a big sigh of defeat. 'ank-u-erry-mush, gennermen, but that stuff 'aint for me. Gooday ya'll.' And with that, Elvis lumbered towards the door, knocking a few chairs over as he went in a gesture of contempt.

Things weren't looking good. Not that we would have considered taking Elvis on, but we'd auditioned three of the five without any sign of talent. It didn't get any better. The next applicant had raging acne and a nervous twitch that wrenched his mouth away from the mic at random. His lyrics came and went like the reception on Radio Luxemburg and he was so shy he insisted on singing from the corner of the room while facing the wall.

Then the Landlord appeared round the back of the bar.

'I've just had a phone call from a Del Delaney,' he shouted. 'Says he's not coming, he's joining' the Vibrons.'

That was it. The auditions were over.

We took stock of the situation and reviewed the sum total of the afternoon's performances. A wailing fool, a choirboy, an unpredictable Elvis impersonator and a twitching recluse. We were totally deflated. Sooty tried to look on the bright side and revisited his notes on the applicants we had originally rejected. But it was no good. Tolley punched the off button on his amplifier in a gesture of defeat. At that moment the far door swung open and in waltzed Mac. He swaggered up to the stage with a pint of Black Velvet in his hand.

'Well lads, I've been standin' in the bar for the last hour and I've never heard such a fuckin' row in all my life.'

'Tell us about it,' replied Whippet, who was unscrewing the top of his high-hat.

Mac continued, '... so *I'm* gonna bail you out.'

We all looked at each other in confusion, and then back at Mac.

'I'm gonna sing for you, you prats,' he said, mounting the stage.

'But I didn't know you could sing.'

'You didn't ask, Ginner.' He sneered, warming up the muscles on his upper lip.

When I came to think about it, on the few occasions when Mac was in a reasonably happy mood at work, he would sing his favourite songs. Usually the numbers we'd both just heard at the Locarno lunchtime sessions, and yes, he did have a reasonable voice. But I wouldn't have thought Mac would have the confidence to do it on stage.

'So why didn't you apply to our ad in the Telegraph?' asked Benno.

'Well, I thought I'd check out the competition first,' Mac explained. 'And I tell you what lads! I've got nothin' to worry about.'

He turned to me before continuing.

'Then I started thinking about all those birds milling round the front of the stage at the Locarno. Nickers in hand, eh Ginner?' He took the mic from its stand. 'So come on you prats. Let's do it.'

Tolley shrugged and snapped his amplifier switch back on, Benno picked up his guitar and Whippet quickly reassembled his high-hat. Sooty quickly took up his position at the rear of the room.

Mac started with a version of *Life's Too Short* by the Lafayettes, a medium paced, moody rock'n'roll ballad. His voice sounded great and although he lacked any real stage presence, he looked the part. He was wearing his trademark black cavalry twill, drainpipe trousers with twelve inch bottoms and a white shirt with the collar turned up.

His confidence increased towards the end of the number and he started to move more to the music. After it finished he didn't pause to get our reaction. He shouted to me to start the riff to Ray Charles's *What'd I Say* . The others joined in and Mac delivered a real rip-roaring version of the great Rhythm and Blues standard, albeit more in the vocal style of the Jerry Lee Lewis version. It was explosive and by the second reprise we all had smiles on our faces. Even Sooty was bopping away with an empty chair at the back of the room. While the echoes of the last notes were still bouncing round the room, we had made our minds up. Mac would be the new vocalist with The Rapids and now nothing would stop us.

Songs of Living

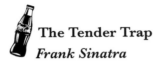

The Tender Trap
Frank Sinatra

Before I left for work the next day I had a phone call from Sheila. A butterfly stirred from within. I'd hoped that she was going to tell me that her parents had relented and allowed her to see me again, but she sounded awkward and worried.

'I can't talk for long Joe, my parents may hear,' she whispered. 'I've got something I need to talk to you about, but it's complicated and... well, rather embarrassing.'

'What's wrong?' I asked.

'I can't tell you now, but can you meet me in the Boccaccio after work?'

I quickly agreed, and on the bus, now late for work again, I tried to imagine what her problem might be and how it could involve me. I knew I couldn't have made her pregnant, which, instead of making me feel relieved, only reminded me that I was still a virgin.

At work I told Mac about the call. 'When a bird asks 'ya that, Ginner, it's usually one of two things. She's either up the duff or she's got a dose,' he advised with his usual bluntness. But although I was relatively naive in such matters I was sure that my brief and scant, sexual contact with Sheila couldn't have resulted in either.

When I walked into the Boccaccio after work I saw Sheila sitting in the far corner, but she wasn't alone. Sooty's Marlene was with her, sipping nervously at her coffee. Sheila smiled at me and waved but when Marlene saw me she seemed to bend her head in shame and I could tell that it was she who had the problem. After we said hello I bought myself a Coke and pulled a stool up close to them.

'So what's wrong?' I asked, glancing between the two of them.

Sheila took Marlene's hand. 'Do you want me to tell

174

him? She asked.

'Yes please,' Marlene answered, and bent her head again.

There was a long pause and I waited, expecting to be told that Sooty required a trip to the VD Clinic or that Marlene was pregnant. But the problem was neither.

'Marlene's being blackmailed,' Sheila finally whispered, looking from side to side to make sure that no one was listening.

Sheila went on to tell me the whole story with occasional embellishments from Marlene and questions from me. It transpired that, before Marlene attempted her part-time career as a striptease artist, she had answered a local newspaper ad for photographer's models and ended up posing nude in a seedy studio in the back streets of Birmingham. She was desperate at the time and needed the money to support her mother and young brothers. When the photographer sent her the train fare she naively believed that the shots would be in the best possible taste.

Marlene plucked up the courage to speak. 'He told me it was art and that I could end up hanging in a famous gallery in London called the Windmill, or somethin.'

'Hanging around, more like,' I commented.

Sheila continued the story and explained that the shots had ended up in a glamour calendar and that Marlene had been recognised by her slimy foreman at the pit boot factory where she worked. He was now threatening that, unless she had sex with him, he would show the calendar to the Personnel Manager and that this could result in her dismissal. She couldn't afford to lose her main job and she knew that Sooty wouldn't be able to afford to employ her full-time. On top of all that, she also knew that Sooty would be very upset if he found out about the photo session. So, in desperation, she went to Sheila for help.

'Sheila's the kindest person I know and she's clever,' Marlene explained. 'I love Sooty so much and I know he would be desecrated if he knew.' Sheila and I gave each other a knowing look to confirm that we understood what she meant.

Then Marlene couldn't contain herself any longer and began to sob uncontrollably. Sheila attempted to comfort her and I tried to think of something constructive to say.

'Er… what were you wearing?' I blurted, unsympathetically. Sheila shot me a disapproving glance.

'Just my white cowboy hat and a bit of rouge on my cheeks,' Marlene explained through her tears. I thought better about asking which cheeks and Marlene continued. 'He wanted to send out for a pair of chaps but nobody else turned up.' Another knowing glance between Sheila and me.

'Oh, and he was wearin' nothin' but one of those silk smerkin' jackets that parted at the front when he bent over his camera,' she added unnecessarily.

'I think Joe was just asking what *you* were wearing,' Sheila explained for me.

'So how do you think I can help?' I asked, trying to shake the images of the photographer from my mind. Sheila spoke first.

'Well I wondered if you could get some of the lads to put the frighteners on him.'

'How big is he?' I found myself saying, looking towards Marlene.

'It was that smarmy bloke that 'eccled me at the Cock Inn when I first met you all.' My memory swiftly delivered an image of the tall, greasy looking, middle aged man with a thin moustache.

'His name is Sidney Slater but we call him Slimy Sid,' Marlene explained. 'He's at it with half the sewin' room,'

And he's got a wife and three kids at home,' interrupted Sheila, folding her arms in a gesture of disgust.

Marlene continued. 'He's got a right Harlem goin' on.

He'll have one in his office every week.

Both girls were waiting for me to speak. 'Well… er… I'll have a quiet word with Tolley and the rest of the lads tomorrow if you like.' Marlene lurched towards me and kissed me on the cheek. 'I knew you'd understand, Joe. You're as kind as Sheila and you two belong together if you ask me 'owt.'

The Guild Hall clock struck six and Marlene suddenly stood up. 'I've got to get the bus,' she announced. 'Mi mams in bed with her leg and her ear and I've got to get tea ready.' I could see that Sheila was wondering about the other leg and ear, so I helped out. 'She's not well then Marlene?' I asked. 'No, she's got an ear inflection and her leg swells to twice its size when she's been on it too long.'

Sheila still looked puzzled as we finished our drinks and left the Boccaccio. I promised to call in to see her at the music store to let her know how I'd got on. Sheila squeezed my hand really tightly and the butterflies took flight.

 Flash Bang Wallop
Tommy Steele

I spent a restless night trying to decide how to help Marlene and get on the good side of Sheila. The lack of sleep worried me because the next day we were meeting Eric Down Brook for the Rapids first photo shoot, complete with our new lead vocalist, Mac. In the morning I looked at the black marks under my eyes and wondered if Jet Harris would have applied make-up under these circumstances.

The shoot didn't go smoothly. We had decided to pose next to the brook at the side of the playing fields, but we hadn't thought that on a sunny Saturday morning half the village and their dogs would be there. Eric had positioned us in a line at the edge of the brook with our guitars by our sides. Whippet had his snare drum under his arm and drumsticks in hand. Sooty wasn't with us because he had promised to take Marlene and her mum, along with her leg and her ear, for a drive around the Peak district. So while Eric busied himself with exposure meters and flash bulbs I told the lads about Marlene's problem. Mac was the first to suggest a solution.

'We'll just pay the slimy sod a visit and persuade him to give us the calendar, or else.'

'Or why not just threaten to tell his wife?' added Whippet.

'No,' I said. 'I've thought of those options but both could get Marlene in further trouble with Slimy Sid.'

'And us,' added Benno, sensibly.

Eric asked us to smile and we all obliged except Mac who adopted his very best sneer. A flash bulb popped.

'Bugger off!' shouted Eric. I looked to my side and saw two snotty nosed kids wedged between Benno and Tolley, grinning like the Bisto kids.

We continued our conversation while Eric mumbled to himself about the cost of film and flash bulbs.

'Why doesn't she go to the police?' asked Benno.

'No, it could get in the papers and then she'd be worse off,' said Whippet.

Eric was ready again. 'Now look moody.' We tried to emulate Mac but it must have looked like an outing from the *Funny Farm*.

'Bugger off!' shouted Eric again. This time a mongrel of a dog was sniffing round my shoes. I gave it a nudge with my foot. The dog looked up, moved a few paces, cocked its leg up and pissed all over Tolley's tremlo arm.

When Tolley returned from chasing the dog round the playing field Eric managed a couple of decent shots. And just as the last bulb popped the idea flashed simultaneously in my head.

'I've got it.' I shouted at the top of my voice. 'We'll give him a taste of his own medicine!' The lads and Eric waited for me to continue. Even the dog and the Bisto kids looked interested. 'He's got a dodgy photo of Marlene so we'll get one of him.' I explained. 'We'll pay him a visit when he's dishing out his weekly bonus to one of his girls and capture it all on camera.'

'Brilliant! We'll have him by the balls,' agreed Tolley.

'But that's blackmail.' Suggested Benno.

'No, its fair exchange and insurance for Marlene.' I said.

I looked towards Eric. 'So will you do it?'

Eric thought for a few moments while packing his equipment away. 'Yes, why not, he said. 'The slimy sod deserves it, let's do it.' And the dog pissed against his tripod to seal the deal.

 **Ambush**
The Outlaws

On Monday lunchtime I called into the music store to tell Sheila about the plan. She loved the idea and threw her arms round my neck kissing me full on the mouth. Two old ladies stopped their browsing and tutted loudly, but fortunately Mr Forsythe wasn't around.

Later that day Sheila got in touch with Marlene and we met in the Boccaccio again. This time Eric came with me and the four of us sat in the darkest corner while we hatched our plot. I put the *James Bond Theme* on the jukebox for effect.

Marlene was to get permission for Eric to photograph the factory for a Derbyshire Advertiser feature on local industry. I would pose as Eric's assistant and, once inside, Marlene would lead us to Slimy Sid's office. We would plan the visit for late Friday afternoon while he was paying the wages from his little office at the end of the factory floor. Marlene assured us that Slimy Sid would end the day by dishing out his special overtime (or undertime) to one of his concubines.

On the Friday lunchtime, with the Advertiser printed and

despatched, Eric and I collected our wages and finished work for the week. We crossed over the Market Place to where Eric's Ford Anglia was parked. I was excited about our secret mission but worried at the same time. What if we didn't manage to get a decent, or indecent, shot and Slimy Sid worked out what we were up to? What if we were escorted off the premises before the evidence was gathered? What if Sid had a break from his philandering and kept his bonus package in his trousers for once?

Eric carefully placed his camera equipment in the boot of his car and we headed north out of town for the twelve mile trip to Alfreton. Marlene was waiting for us by the security hut at the factory gates. She jumped in the back of the car, waved to the uniformed gate man and directed Eric to the perimeter road to the right of the towering mill building.

'I've got butterflies,' she said, prompting one of my own to flutter. 'It'll be fine,' I assured her, without being convinced myself. Eric stayed silent, keeping his eyes on the narrow service road like a man on a mission.

'Here it is, park by the loadin' doors,' Marlene shouted. 'The office is on the right just behin't doors. He'll start calling us for our wages at three o'clock on the dot, but don't come inside till he's in his office.'

She wished us luck and disappeared back inside the factory. It was ten to three and Eric started clicking away at the factory exterior.

'Make sure there's plenty of film left for later,' I warned.

Don't worry, there isn't one in yet,' he replied. 'Do you know the cost of film these day?'

I moved closer to the loading doors leaving Eric clicking away behind me. I could hear the constant clatter of sewing machines punctuated by incessant chatter from their operators as the factory clock counted down to another weekend. At about four minutes to three we heard what sounded like a hand bell coming from just inside the doors.

'Come and get it you lucky girls!' I recognised the sickly voice of Slimy Sid. 'Ya' know ya' want it!'

I peered round the doors to see Slimy Sid slide back into his office. He was early. There was a stampede of excited females, chattering excitedly as they hurried to form a queue outside his office. I beckoned furiously at Eric and we quickly moved inside the factory. A couple of women in the queue wolf whistled in our direction to signal the unusual presence of men on their turf. But most were oblivious to us, desperate for their little brown envelopes and freedom from the sweat shop for another weekend. The queue moved surprisingly quickly and the girls were in and out the office in no time at all. Marlene, who had taken up position near the end of the queue, was suddenly right beside us with a couple of brassy looking middle-aged women.

'Ere, take one of us duck,' shouted one. The two women cackled as they positioned themselves either side of Marlene and pulled their blue stripped work dresses up above their knees.

Eric blushed, clicked his camera and the women moved on with Marlene. Then I saw her. A dark haired girl in her mid-twenties who was standing on her own at the back of the queue and looking rather sheepish. It was obvious to us that she was the one earmarked for Slimy Sid's special bonus. The queue was now down to half a dozen and Marlene was next. She disappeared inside the office but very quickly came running out in obvious distress.

'What's wrong? I said.

'He's not given me my wages. He told me to go to the back of the queue,' she whispered. 'It's me he's planning to have, not her,' Marlene nodded towards the dark haired girl at the back of the queue. 'She had one of her epileptic fits this mornin' and

I bet it's put him off.'

'Yes, and now he's planning to collect his blackmail demand from you,' I suggested.

'What the hell are we going to do now?' said Eric.

We had to think quickly, the queue was down to two women and the dark haired girl. 'I'll just have to go along with it,' announced Marlene.

'You can't,' I protested.

'It's the only way,' She insisted, 'but make sure you catch him before he goes too far.'

There was no time to argue and Marlene joined the dark haired girl who was now on her own outside Sid's office. The girl looked puzzled when she was called into the office first. Then we could hear raised voices from within. The door burst open and the girl rushed passed us in tears, clutching her little brown envelope and obviously disappointed that she hadn't earned overtime. Marlene looked nervously over her shoulder and managed a brave smile. She took a deep breath and disappeared inside the little office.

'Shit!' shouted Eric. 'I haven't put a film in the camera.' He turned and ran back out of the factory towards his car.

It had all gone terribly wrong and now we weren't even there to rescue Marlene from her fate. After what seemed like minutes I looked anxiously over my shoulder for Eric. No sign. The rest of the factory was now empty and silent. I could hear deep murmuring from inside the office. Sid was obviously trying to coax his prey into submission. I knew we would have to move soon. At last I heard footsteps, hoping that Eric was on his way back. I turned to make sure that he was ready for action, but it wasn't Eric's face I met.

'Hi Joe, what are you doing here?' said Sooty looking understandably surprised to see me.

The shock at seeing Sooty and the realisation of what he

was about to witness rendered me speechless. I could still hear the deep, sickly sound of Sid's attempt at seduction from inside the office behind us. Fortunately Eric had now joined us and answered for me. 'We're here taking shots for the newspaper.' He said with false enthusiasm. 'What about you?'

'Oh, I've come to surprise Marlene and give her a lift home,' Sooty explained. 'Have you seen her?'

Sooty glanced curiously over my shoulder towards the little office and the sounds from within. 'Yes, she's finishing off in the leather store,' I said, pointing to the far end of the empty factory floor. Fortunately Sooty accepted my explanation, turned, and made his way between the now silent rows of sewing machines to the back of the factory, whistling as he went. 'See you later,' he shouted happily.

Eric and I sprung into action without a word. We both knew that we had mere seconds to capture our evidence and rescue Marlene before Sooty returned. If he should witness the scene inside Slimy Sid's office it would be far worse than the sight of Marlene in a saucy calendar. We got closer to the office door and I put one hand on the knob. Eric checked his flash holder. Marlene's voice was now clearly audible but she sounded distressed. Sid had obviously gone far enough. It was now or never. Eric's face was inches from mine.

'After four,' I whispered, as if I was counting in one of the Rapids numbers. 'One, two, three...' my hand turned the doorknob. 'Four!' I shouted, and threw open the door.

Eric's camera flashed and bright light filled the dingy little office. The scene that met our eyes was captured by the camera in milliseconds, but the subject matter remained frozen for what seemed like minutes. Sid had his back to us, trousers round his ankles, and his head twisted round towards us with an expression of total horror. The only thing that moved was his eyes which were still blinking from the flash. Marlene was on her knees in front of him, mouth wide open, either from the shock and relief of our entrance, or from the act that she was unwillingly about to perform.

'What the fuck... ' Sid eventually managed to stammer.

'Smile,' answered Eric and his camera flashed again.

The light filled the room and so did a blood-curdling scream. This time the action was frozen with Sid clutching between his legs, his eyes bulging and his mouth twisted into an expression of excruciating pain. Marlene had administered her own revenge. There was another flash that jolted Sid into action and he frantically adjusted his clothing as Marlene scrambled to her feet. At the same time we heard footsteps behind us and I knew that Sooty was returning.

'Oh there you are,' said Sooty as he swung open the office door. 'I've been looking for you everywhere.' No one spoke so he looked at Marlene and continued. 'I thought we'd take Joe and Eric for pint across the road.' Marlene cleared her throat and glanced at the scarlet-faced Sid. 'Ok, I've just been doing a bit of extra piecework but I've finished now,'

As we left the seething Sid in his office, no doubt to inspect the damage, Sooty turned to Marlene with a look of genuine concern. 'I think you work too hard baby, what with working for me, looking after your sickly mum and the boys, and now overtime at the factory for that smarmy Sid.'

'But I need the money,' Marlene protested.

'Well, as long as you haven't bitten off more you can chew,' said Sooty.

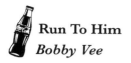

Run To Him
Bobby Vee

On the Monday morning after the stitching up of Sid, Marlene was called in to his office where she was handed a rather dog-eared calendar that she later burnt. Sid didn't mention the compromising photographs of him and obviously realised that they would remain as insurance against any further demands or mistreatment of Marlene. Despite a suggestion from Mac that one of the prints might liven up the window display of the Advertiser office, Eric had assured us that the negatives would remain under lock and key.

Mac was due to make his début with The Rapids on the Saturday at a teenage dance in Belper. Since his appointment we had arranged a number of intensive midweek practice sessions in Tolley's garage. At work, Mac was quite modest about his new role and most of the time assumed his usual mean and moody persona. But now and again his mask would slip and the exciting prospect of performing in front of a room full of teenage girls would get the better of him. Mac would suddenly grab a large screwdriver, and holding it like a microphone, would launch into one of his numbers. The reaction from our work mates was decidedly mixed. It ranged from shouts of derision to impromptu backing vocals. Depending on the choice of number, Eric would sometimes provide percussive accompaniment from the cow bell clamped to his frame and I would beat out a rhythm on the side of one of the wooden type cabinets.

On a hot and sticky afternoon these sessions helped relieve the boredom and would make work more bearable, after which Mac and I would return to working side by side making up the pages of the next edition. I was working on the sports page and Mac was placing galleys of type into one of the farming pages. My lead story brought news that eleven of the Derby

County players had refused the offer of £20 per week plus £5 first-team appearance money now that the minimum wage had been abolished. I briefly imagined what I would do with that kind of money and wondered if I could develop my meagre skills as a right-winger.

Then I noticed that Mac had positioned an engraved half-tone plate across three columns at the top of his farming page. This particular plate would reproduce a photograph of the winner and runners up of the annual Derbyshire Dairy Queen competition. Even viewing it upside down and in its engraved form, I could see that the three bikini-clad beauty queens would introduce a refreshing bit of glamour to the pages of the Derbyshire Advertiser. Then I noticed the headline of the article Mac had decided to position right underneath the photograph. It was reporting on the fat stock prices from Derby cattle market, the headline for which Mac had set in 36 point capital letters which ran directly underneath the beauty queen picture. It read – 'COWS REALISE GOOD TRADE AT BAKEWELL'

I was just about to warn Mac that his little ruse would get us into more deep water when Wally bounded into the *Stone Room*.

'Was that you singing Mac?' he asked cheerfully.

Instead of sounding as if he was about to deliver a bollocking for the disruption, Wally appeared to be impressed by the performance.

We could see it coming. 'It reminded me…' Wally started, and Mac's shoulders dropped.

'… of the time I was asked to sing the National Anthem before the Cup Final between Luton Town and Nottingham Forest.' Mac pretended to spit on the floor. It was a pre-requisite for any self-respecting Rams fan to show disgust at the mere mention of Nottingham Forest.

Wally's mind was in overdrive and he seemed to be

directing the delivery of his fantastic ramblings at me. Mac managed to move behind Wally's back and was moving the fingers and thumbs on both hands like perpetually opening jaws. I was trapped. My eyes were beginning to glaze and my mind started to wander. I wondered why Wally needed these fantasies. Then reflected on the fact that I had my *Sunset Lounge* for when I needed to get away from tricky situations and that Wally needed his fantasies because he was a very lonely man that desperately needed to be noticed.

Wally's voice began to fade as I found myself opening the door to *The Sunset Lounge* but found Wally was in there. He was standing in the middle of my *Sunset Lounge*, his mouth opening and closing but nothing coming out. How did he get in there? No one can enter the shrine without my permission.

More urgency in Wally's voice brought me back to reality. '... and guess what he asked me to do Joe?'

I desperately tried to pick up the thread of Wally's story. 'Who?' I said.

'The Duke of Edinburgh,' Wally tried to remind me.

I was totally lost. 'Er. I don't know.'

'Guess, guess.' Wally insisted, knocking his pipe out into the scrap metal bin.

'Er, play centre forward for Forest?' I heard Mac nearly choke on his cigarette.

'No, no.' Wally was sounding slightly irritated. 'No. The Duke asked me to sing at the Queen's garden party.'

'Wow,' I said, trying to sound impressed. Then the phone rang in Wally's office and I was saved.

Wally rushed off and I returned to my work, but it was nearly five thirty and Mac had already disappeared to wash his hands. I quickly moved Mac's *Cows Realise Good Trade* story away from the beauty queens and joined him.

Mac was coming home with me for tea before his final

practice session, so instead of catching the bus home I rode pillion on his motorbike. As we weaved in and out of the lorries and buses along the A52, I realised why there was a campaign to make the wearing of crash helmets compulsory. Then I remembered Mac's opinion on the subject; 'Skid lids are for fuckin' queers and old farts.'

We got home alive and after a quick meal of beans and chips we set out for Tolley's garage. Thankfully, we left Mac's bike behind. I couldn't ride pillion while carrying my guitar, so we made our way through the council estate, across the playing fields Down Brook and towards Tolley's house on the other side. I noticed that some of the Mob had already started to hang out and Julia was there with her best mate Cathy. She saw us and waved. I quickly explained to Mac that Julia was, sort of, my girlfriend and we went over to say hello.

'So you're the bird that Ginner keeps locked away for himself,' Mac said, turning on the charm and slowly looking her up and down, probably undressing her in his mind. 'I can see why he doesn't bring you into town.'

Julia started to blush and coyly, turned away.

'And this is Cathy,' I said, trying to get Mac's attention away from Julia. Mac took a quick glance towards Cathy in her baggy jumper and ban the bomb badge then returned his attentions to Julia. Jealously began to rise like bile in the pit of my stomach. Especially when Julia fluttered her beautiful long black eyelashes back at Mac. I found myself making excuses that we'd be late for the practice and dragged Mac away.

'How old is it?' Mac asked, glancing over his shoulder at Julia as we walked away.

'It's a she, and only fifteen,' I replied, sounding more like Mac's mum than his cool mate.

'Jail bait,' Mac commented and the subject was closed.

Inside Tolley's garage Whippet was trying to shoe horn his

ever-expanding drum kit into the corner. The smell of dusty, warm amplifier valves enhanced the excitement I always felt just before we played. After a quick, warm-up instrumental, we got down to the business of rehearsing Mac's repertoire. Mac, a once dedicated Elvis fan, had recently changed his allegiance to Chuck Berry. He explained that he'd been particularly impressed by the fact that the little known, black rhythm and blues singer was currently in prison for illegally transporting a fourteen-year old girl across state lines for immoral purposes. I briefly remembered the way Julia had fluttered her eyelashes at Mac and then returned to business.

Mac had brought a scratched 45 of Chuck Berry's *Bye Bye Johnny* which was on my favourite London American label. The familiar black and silver label was a guarantee that the music contained in the grooves would be of the highest quality. We played the record over and over again on the Dansette record player. The lyrics suited Mac down to the ground. All about a rebellious young American kid leaving his home town and family to find fame and fortune. It was written in the traditional twelve-bar blues sequence which only used three chords, so we soon polished it off.

Before we worked on the rest of Mac's repertoire, Tolley raised an important question.

'What are we going to call him?' he said as if Mac wasn't part of the decision. 'Mac and The Rapids don't sound right.'

At first Mac seemed uncomfortable about changing his cool nickname, but then agreed to consider an alternative. We put our instruments down and brain stormed suggestions while Mac scribbled them down on the back of his fag packet. After running out of ideas we reviewed the list which started with the obvious.

Kenneth Mackenzie and The Rapids.
Ken and The Rapids.

Kenny and The Rapids.

Then there was my suggestion, *Randy and The Rapids.*

And finally one from Sooty, *Buddy Cochran and The Rapids.*

Mac wasn't impressed and, after studying the list, ripped the fag packet in two and threw it across the garage. 'I'm not getting up on stage to any of those fuckin' names,' he announced.

Tolley countered with a further suggestion. 'What about *Greasy Bastard and The Rapids.*'

Mac jumped to his feet and lunged towards Tolley.

'I'll wrap that guitar round ya fuckin' neck if ya come out with another quip like that.' he shouted.

Tolley stood up to meet Mac's threat and for a moment it looked like trouble, but Whippet managed to calm them both down and persuaded everyone to think again.

After a few moments Mac broke the silence.

'Right!' he announced. 'What about *Terry Lee Curtis?* Terry after Terry Dene, Lee after Lee Marvin and Curtis after Tony Curtis.' He explained with pride.

They were all cool, Hollywood heroes of Mac's and I liked the American sound to the name. After a few moments discussion during which Sooty expressed his delight at the fact that at least one of the named was dead, we all agreed and the group was renamed *Terry Lee Curtis and The Rapids.*

It was dark when Mac and I made our way back across the playing field and I was pleased to see that Julia had gone home. I was deep in thought and we didn't speak. I was trying to convince myself that I was stupid to be jealous of Mac's apparent interest in Julia and that he'd probably already forgotten that he'd even met her. Then Mac broke the silence.

'So when is *it* sixteen?' He too had been deep in thought and my heart sank.

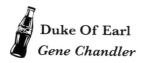

Duke Of Earl
Gene Chandler

As I lay in bed after Mac, aka Terry Lee Curtis, had disappeared into the warm night on his 250 Beezer, I questioned my right to be possessive over Julia. After all, I wasn't prepared to see her that often. I wanted my freedom. And then there was my dalliance with Sheila and the fact that I still wanted her as well as lusting over half the girls in town. But despite my self-reasoning I still despaired at the thought of Julia with someone else.

Mac didn't mention Julia at work the next day. He was too busy rehearsing his repertoire with spasmodic percussive accompaniment from Eric and me. At the Locarno lunchtime session Winston bounded up and reminded me that it was the day of his uncle's house party. He agreed to meet me in the Boccaccio after my late shift.

As the Guild Hall clock struck seven thirty and the presses had begun to roll, I washed, splashed some Max Factor after shave on my face and went next door into the coffee bar. Winston and his family lived in Normanton, a suburb of town that was popular with the West Indian community. We walked from the town centre and down Normanton Road where many of the shops had been taken over by ethnic businesses selling exotic foods and spices and brightly coloured fabrics. As we ventured further into this colourful enclave the night drew-in creating a slightly dangerous, yet exciting, atmosphere. I noticed that, like other parts of the town, this area had its own distinctive smell. It was a combination of spicy cooking, incense and the hops from the nearby Offiler's Brewery.

Winston and I paused outside a small shop crammed with boxes of second-hand, seven-inch singles. Its window was almost completely obscured with record posters and LP sleeves from exotic sounding artists like The Maytells and

Prince Buster.

'Dis is where I distribute all 'de Ska and Reggae platters my dad gets me from Jamaica, man. 'De stuff from the States I sell at the Locarno but 'de Jamaican stuff comes here,' he added.

The glass door of the shop was covered with crude business cards and handwritten advertisements for a variety of local performers, most of whom were billed as MC's. Winston explained that, within the West Indian community, there was very little live music and that the entertainment at most events took the form of vinyl records imported from Jamaica which were played by a disc jockey known as an M.C. or Master of Ceremonies. I read one of the cards on the window.

YOUR WORSHIPFUL HIGHNESS THE DUKE OF ROLO, MC EXTRAORDINAIRE, PRESENTS THE GROOVIEST SOUNDS FROM THE CARRIBEAN. HOUSE PARTIES. WEDDINGS. FUNERALS.

'See those cards at 'de top man?'

Winston pointed to two cards with graduated blue backgrounds and gilt edging. One read KING PLEASURE FOR YOUR PLEASURE and the other SIR LEES DOWNBEAT IV. SPINNING THE PLATTERS THAT MATTER.

'Dey're both me man,' and he let out a high-pitched giggle. 'And I also go out as MR SOULFUL,' he added as he bounded on down the road, flushed with pride after sharing the secret of his aliases.

'So which are you tonight?' I asked, as I caught up with him.

'Don't know yet man,' he shouted, as we turned into a side road. 'I'll decide when I get dare.'

Winston spoke to a couple of pasty-faced white girls who were loitering provocatively on the corner and I realised that he was quite a well known figure in that particular area of town. He suddenly stopped in his tracks and told me to listen. I could hear the deep bass thud of heavily amplified music drifting towards us on the warm summer breeze. The sound increased as we progressed and I wondered what make of amplifier and speakers could pump-out that kind of volume. Winston ushered me down an alley between two run-down, Victorian terraced villas and towards the source of the sound. The alley led into a small backyard where a few West Indian blokes had gathered in the gloom, drinking from beer bottles and paper cups. The window frames above us rattled from the resonance of the bass notes and the sheer volume of the music. Winston opened the back door and led me into a small, brightly-lit kitchen packed with happy smiling people. Everyone seemed to be under the influence of the ear-splitting music rather than the large amount of alcohol that covered the kitchen table. No one was actually dancing but every movement of their bodies seemed to be in rhythm to the music. A big, round faced, West Indian man wearing a parrot print shirt and a small pork-pie hat was jigging around with two black women in brightly patterned summer dresses. Winston shouted above the pulsating music.

'Dat's mi uncle, man. It's his birt'day.'

He shoved a paper cup in my hand and poured me a drink from a coke bottle. He then nodded towards the next room in the house and we squeezed between the gyrating bodies into a large lounge area which was also full of revellers. It was then that I noticed that I was almost the only white face at the party. There were two Chinese men playing cards in the corner and a scrawny young white girl with pale, bare legs. But other than that everyone else was West Indian or African. I nervously took a big swig of my coke. It hit me like a punch in the face. I thought I'd been poisoned.

'What the hell's this?' I shouted to Winston.

His face creased-up with laughter that I couldn't hear.

'Don't worry man. It's only Ready Mix,' he yelled, taking a swig himself. 'It's just Rum and Coke.'

The burning sensation had coursed down my throat and hit my stomach. But it felt good and gave me an instant buzz. Winston poured more and pointed through the swaying bodies to a huge speaker cabinet in the corner of the room.

'What d'ya think of dat man?'

We pushed our way forwards. The cabinet, throbbing away in the corner, was the size of a small wardrobe. The front was covered in black, fabric mesh material, interwoven with gold thread and embedded with small coloured fairy lights that twinkled along with the music. At the side of the speaker was a smaller cabinet which housed a huge industrial amplifier and supported a professional-looking record turntable. More fairy lights on the front of the deck illuminated the elaborately hand-painted name of tonight's M.C., 'COUNT COSTA DUKE OF SOUL. 100 WATTS OF POWER.'

Count Costa was a tall, lanky West Indian, probably in his late twenties. He wore a palm tree print, short-sleeved shirt and tight white jeans and permanently bobbed up and down to the music, thrusting his chin out on the off-beat. He continued to 'bob' even while he was thumbing through his collection of singles or shouting to his friends. His records were housed in an old wooden Schweppes Tonic Water crate which I noticed was just the right width for seven-inch singles. The music that Count Costa was serving up was hypnotic. Every record had a raw and primitive quality with a distinctive emphasis on the off-beat. Most of the sounds were vocals backed by a basic line-up of two electric guitars, bass guitar and drums. Many had further accompaniment from a varying assortment of brass instruments that punctuated the off-beat but sounded slightly out of tune. The rhythm was relentless and the whole party seemed to be under a trance-like spell. I could feel the bass notes deep in my chest and I began to move to the music, albeit self-consciously. Winston pointed to the speaker cabinet.

'I put dat cabinet together man. Eighteen inch bass speaker and two twelve inch for de top end,' he shouted.

I reflected on the fact that my bass amplifier had a single fifteen inch speaker and was powered by a meagre 50 watts. I suddenly felt inadequate, like I had once in the showers at school after cross-country running. Winston broke my train of thought.

'Give me forty quid and I'll make you one as big as Count Coster's man,' he yelled.

When I realised that he was talking about a speaker cabinet and not plastic surgery, I turned my pockets inside out miming my response to his offer.

We made our way back to the kitchen and Winston handed me a coke bottle from a crate under the table.

'Just coke this time eh?' I shouted.

'Try it, man,' Winston answered with a gleam in his eye.

I bit the top off the bottle and took a sip. It was the Rum and Coke Ready Mix again. I inspected the bottle top and noticed that an 'x' had been crudely scratched across the distinctive coke logo.

'Where's this stuff from?' I asked.

Winston just tapped his nose as if to say 'don't ask' and after a few more gulps I couldn't have cared less. The Rum and Coke had got to me. The music had got to me. And the sheer exuberance of the people had got to me. I was in Kingston, Jamaica.

Winston's uncle was now dancing on the kitchen table, skilfully avoiding the bottles and paper cups like an Arabian sword dancer. A large West Indian woman was dishing out dollops of rice and a thick spicy meat stew that Winston told me was Goat Curry. The music seemed to be increasing in volume. 'Madness... madness... they call it madness' came the refrain and a sea of happy black faces sang along. Then I noticed that not all the blokes in the room were black. Skulking by the back door I saw two familiar white faces. And their expressions weren't happy, they were evil and menacing. A wave of fear coursed through my body like an electric shock. I sobered up in an instant. It was the McBride brothers.

My natural instinct was to make sure they didn't see me, but it was hard. I stood out like a sore thumb. A white sore thumb. Tony McBride spotted me first and he nudged his brother who was in the process of placing what looked like a crate of coke bottles on top of the sink drainer. At that moment, Winston, unaware of my fear, grabbed me by the arm and shouted something about me seeing the speakers that were wired up to the other rooms in the house. I let him lead me up the stairs to temporary safety. The two large bedrooms, which were also full of party revellers, had been virtually cleared of furniture. But in the corner of each room were speaker cabinets as large as the ones downstairs which also pumped out Count Costa's magical music.

The small Victorian terraced house was a virtual night club and I made a mental note about an extension to my *Sunset Lounge*. But, despite the idyllic atmosphere and the effects of the Ready Mix, the nagging fear of the McBride brothers was distracting me. Why were they here? I remembered what the landlord of the Blue Peter had told me about them cruising the pubs of town just looking for a rumble, and that Tony McBride had just been released from Leicester prison for GBH and possessing a sawn-off shotgun. Were they planning to finish the job they started at the Locarno and leave me in a pool of blood in the dingy yard below?

I didn't have to wait long to discover my fate. We made our way back down the narrow staircase and there, on the bottom step, sat Tony McBride. The bulky figure of his brother Graham filled the small hallway behind him. Winston, who was unaware of the previous week's events at the Locarno, nodded to them as we tried to squeeze past. My heart was pumping. The hairs on the back of my neck warned me of impending doom. Then a heavy hand grabbed my shoulder.

Graham McBride turned me towards him and spoke.

'You're the bloke our kid jobbed at the Locarno last week, aren't you?'

His words were delivered in a sort of challenge as if to say 'What are you going to do about it?'

But they, and I, knew that I wouldn't do anything about it.

'Er… yes, I'm afraid so.' My weak reply sounded like an apology for getting in the way of his brother's fist.

'You took it well youth,' he said, sticking out a thick hand which I shook limply.

Gra McBride then nodded to his brother to do the same. But as I shook Tony McBride's bony hand, I got the impression from his mocking sneer, a kind of lopsided smile, that he wouldn't have hesitated to repeat his assault if his brother hadn't been there. Nevertheless, I was overcome with relief and actually managed a shrug of my shoulders and a half smile, as if I was finding it hard to recall the event.

Winston became bored and bounced away towards the kitchen.

Gra McBride then thrust his big, mean face closer to mine and whispered in my ear. 'Actually youth, we've got a business proposition for you. 'Aven't we Tone?'

I took a swig of my Rum and Coke but didn't speak. He continued to explain that he and his brother worked in the bottling plant at Bass brewery in Burton-on-Trent and had the opportunity to work overtime at the weekends. He went on to say that there was a backlog of orders and they needed extra labour. He suggested that I also asked Sooty to help because his van would come in handy to supplement the over stretched,

Bass delivery wagons. The promise of cash-in-hand was like music to my ears and I thought of Winston's offer to make me a monster bass speaker cabinet for £40.

I soon agreed to Gra McBride's offer and he lightly punched me on the shoulder in a gesture of comradeship. Then, with one hand round his brother's shoulder and the other round mine he shouted towards Winston who was bouncing back down the corridor.

'He's one of us now Winston.'

But I could tell from the uncharacteristic frown on Winston's forehead that he was less than happy about me getting involved with the notorious McBride brothers. And I still couldn't work out what they were doing at a West Indian house party or why Gra McBride had called me 'one of us' as if it included Winston. I had an uncomfortable feeling that something else was going on, but shrugged it off and rejoined the revellers in the main room. I was soon back under the spell of Count Costa's cocktail of Caribbean sounds and the Ready Mix.

It was time for Winston's spot as MC and Count Costa introduced him as Sir Lees Downbeat IV. The evening then became a bit of a blur. I remember opening another bottle of coke with a cross scratched on the cap. I remember Winston's uncle making me try some Goat Curry. And I remember feeling ill and sitting on one of the barrels marked *Jamaican Rum X* which were outside in the back yard.

The music and laughter merged together into one sound which was swirling around inside my head. The scrawny white girl, who had been flitting in and out all evening, asked me if I was alright. Then she disappeared back into the street when she heard a car coming. The last thing I remember was looking up at the sky and seeing the stars swirling around in time to the pounding bass notes of the music.

Songs of Desire

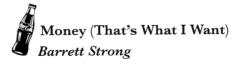

Money (That's What I Want)
Barrett Strong

When I stood on the balcony during the Locarno Lunchtime sessions I could spot when the disc jockey had selected a record on the London American label. Even from up there the distinctive black and silver label was clearly visible. Then I thrilled at the anticipation of the next sound that would boom through the speaker cabinet above my right ear. It could, of course, be a record by one of the more popular artists currently in the charts – Roy Orbison, Del Shannon, Bobby Darin, The Coasters, Bobby Vee, Sandy Nelson or Duane Eddy. On the other hand, it could be a new sound by an obscure artist I'd not yet heard of. Like when I first heard *Fortune Teller* by Benny Spelman, *Some Other Guy* by Richie Barrett and *I Like It Like That* by Chris Kenner. When that happened, and I liked what I heard, I would rush down the stairs to get the details from the disc jockey. If I really liked the record I'd waste no time and on my way back to work I'd call in at Dalton's Record Store and order it for collection on the next pay day. These exciting, rare new sounds were very seldom ordered for stock and were not usually played on Juke Box Jury or even Radio Luxembourg. But that's the way I liked it. They were my discoveries and I wanted to be the one to promote them. It was as if I had been somehow involved in their production and I took great pleasure in introducing these treasured sounds to others. To me it was a religion and I was the disciple responsible for spreading the word to the uninitiated. If the record finally made it into the charts or was covered by a British artist I'd imagine that I would be credited for having found it first. I realised that my own insecurity had resulted in a constant need for respect and credibility amongst my peers. This was one way that helped me achieve it.

Today, on the balcony of the Locarno, my predatory

instincts were somewhat dulled by the hangover of all hangovers. It had been with me all morning, but fortunately, each time I remembered more detail of the West Indian party, the intensity of the hangover went down a notch or two.

From my position, slumped against the balcony rail, and a few yards further away from the booming speakers than usual, I squinted through blood-shot eyes in anticipation of the next record label to hit the turntable. To my surprise, besides searching for the London American label, I found myself looking for another image that had etched itself into my returning consciousness – The Blue Beat label. Much of the Ska music pumped out by Count Costa and Winston the previous night had displayed this marque in silver on a dark blue background.

Being Friday, with the Derbyshire Advertiser on sale, Mac and I finished work at lunchtime. After the Locarno session we cruised round town following our ritualistic route for Friday afternoons that would take in all our favourite spots. This was skilfully devised by Mac and it took us into, and through, several shops and stores. Not for the goods they were retailing, but for the fine displays of available females behind the counters.

As usual we started at Dalton's Record store at the top end of town where our tame shop assistant would let us take more than our fair share of newly released singles into one of the private, soundproof booths. Then, after I purchased *Ooh Poo Pah Doo*, a new rhythm and blues release on London American by a distinctly black but unknown artist called Jessie Hill, we went next door into Derwent Music Store to pay the one pound ten shillings weekly HP instalment for my new guitar.

As we waltzed into the store I could see that Sheila was behind the counter and I felt a flutter in my stomach. Or was it lower down? As usual she seemed pleased to see me. After completing the serious business of depriving me of the best part of my wage packet, Sheila moved into seductive mode. She flicked her dark brown hair and looked up at me from under fluttering eyelashes.

'Hey Joe, when are you going to come up and see Princess again?' she said with a knowing wink. 'She misses you. We both do.' She leaned further over the counter and continued in a slow, sexy whisper. 'My parents are away this weekend.' She glanced at my little record store bag searching for further enticements. 'You could bring that new disc with you, and I've got the latest Cliff Richard LP,' she pleaded.

It was there for the taking and the fluttering in my stomach increased, matching the pace of Sheila's eyelashes. But all I could think about was the high price I'd have to pay for the promise of sex – having to endure both sides of a Cliff Richard LP. And I thought about Julia. Even having thoughts about someone else was starting to make me feel guilty. I half reluctantly made an excuse about playing with the group all weekend and Mac dragged me away.

'Listen Ginner. If you don't see to that, I will,' he scolded, as we made our way out of the shop.

We continued our route down the main street and slipped into Boots cosmetic department. We studied the form while running the gauntlet of dismissive looks and pouting pink lips, then, out the other side and across East Street to the Midland Drapery department store. We started with the Cosmetic department for a quick comparison and Mac nudged me as we weaved our way past the Estée Lauder counter.

'See that?' Mac whispered, pointing to a shapely brunette with a massive bee-hive hair-do. 'I ad that last night.'

I stopped in amazement. She must have been in her mid-thirties and at least fifteen years older than Mac. He pushed me on and continued talking. 'Its husband works nights at Royce's and I give it one now and again.' I looked back over my shoulder. She had obviously seen Mac and was trying to catch his attention as we scurried by, but Mac was playing it cool.

We made our way to the men's counter and Mac dished out his usual cheeky banter to the elderly female assistant and proceeded to shave himself with the Remington electric razor on the demonstration stand. Mac realised that I was still traumatised by his earlier admission.

'Yea, it's no spring chicken but she's bloody grateful.' Mac explained, through the small round mouth he had made while shaving up the other side of his face. Mac finished, passed the razor to me and continued. 'It lives at the house that backs onto ours and when she leaves the kitchen light on with the red curtains closed, that's my signal that the old man's at work, the kids are in bed and she wants it.'

I finished shaving and we doused ourselves in Factor for Men after-shave lotion from the sample bottle. Still pre-occupied by the apparent ease with which Mac obtained sex, I wondered if I should take up Sheila's offer and get this thing out of the way. I followed Mac out of the department store in a cloud of confusion and after-shave.

We always ended our Friday afternoons in the Boccaccio but today we made a detour through the Market Hall because Mac fancied a girl on one of the pet stalls. As we entered the pet section I steeled myself in readiness for the obnoxious smell.

'That's it over there,' he said, pointing to a young girl behind one of the stalls who didn't look like Mac's type at all. She was quite slim, probably about sixteen and wore her hair in a pony-tail. She had a fresh complexion without a trace of make-up except for a hint of pink on her generous lips. Then, as she moved from behind the display of budgie seed I could see the attraction. She had wonderful breasts. They weren't just big, they were enormous. Her nylon overall buttons were strained to the limit of endurance. She had obviously given up on the top buttons which had the effect of pushing her tits higher and accentuating her cleavage. They looked as if they would spill out at any moment.

Mac was coaching me as we approached the counter and explained that it wasn't possible to chat a bird up in a busy environment like this and that the secret was to just 'get yourself noticed'. To demonstrate the point, Mac delivered his well-rehearsed line just as she bent forwards to shovel some dog biscuits into a brown paper bag.

'If ya gonner drown those two puppies, love, I'll 'av the one with the pink nose!'

She blushed and coyly tried to pull the top of her overall together.

We made a quick exit from the Market Hall, giggling like schoolboys. 'Get yourself noticed,' Mac repeated.

The Boccaccio was full of shoppers because most people our age would still have been at work at that time on a Friday afternoon. We ordered a couple of coffees, found a vacant booth and proceeded to choose a few records from one of the small, dome topped, juke box selectors that was fixed to the wall adjacent to our table.

Mac selected a couple of the numbers he would be performing at his début with The Rapids at the Belper Over Sixties Club. I could tell that he was excited about the event but I had to reassure him that, despite the name of the venue, the birds were much younger than sixty. I then told Mac all about the West Indian house party and the offer from the McBride brothers. He wasn't impressed and appeared uncharacteristically concerned about my welfare. He warned me not to have anything to do with them and reminded me of the rumour that Tony McBride has a metal plate in his head and an obsession with sawn-off shotguns.

'That bloke's a psychopath,' he said. 'He's got a real

mean streak and they say that since he had that plate fitted it's taken away his capacity to experience fear.' Mac did seem genuinely concerned.

'But I need the money,' I protested.

Mac took a long drag of his fag and let the smoke exit slowly down his nose for dramatic effect. He finally spoke, looking up at me from under heavy eyebrows. 'You can't spend money in hospital Ginner, or in the morgue.'

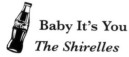

Baby It's You
The Shirelles

Mac wasn't the only one trying to dissuade me from accepting the weekend work from the McBrides.

The next night I took Julia to see Cliff Richard and The Shadows in a pop package tour at the Gaumont Cinema. When Cliff took the stage she screamed along with the rest of the girls. But I couldn't take my eyes of my hero, Jet Harris, and studied every note he played on his beautiful, red Fender Precision bass.

After the show we went to the new Wimpy Bar which had to be one of the best things to hit town since the Locarno Ballroom. The interior was based on the American soda shops and roadside diners I'd seen in movies. The tables and red leatherette upholstered bench seating were fixed to the floor in booth formation and there were matching high stools at the counter. But it was the menu that made it so American. A red and white illuminated panel behind the counter offered all kinds of cool sounding fare based around the classic American hamburger and hot dog. The mouth-watering delights included a *Double Cheeseburger* (two hamburgers either side of a Kraft cheese slice) and a *Bender* (a hot dog sausage, scored along its length and twisted into a ring so that it fitted into a round hamburger bun). We both had Wimpy Cheeseburgers and Julia had a Strawberry *Whipsy* which was a huge, whipped milkshake made with ice cream and served in a sundae glass. I had to make do with a Pepsi because Wimpy obviously had an exclusivity deal with Coca-Cola's arch rival.

I could tell that Julia was excited, yet a bit overawed by the occasion, and she explained that it was the first time a boy had taken her out to a concert and a meal. I wanted to suggest to Julia that there was a first time for everything in life but the time wasn't right.

Although a little self-conscious, Julia was happier than I'd ever seen her. When the straw made a gurgling sound at the bottom of her sundae glass she blushed, put her hand to her mouth and apologised coyly. Then, when she was sure no one else had heard, she giggled and did it again. But when I told Julia about the prospect of working with the McBrides and what Mac had said, her mood changed. She seemed genuinely worried that I would get into some kind of trouble and suggested that I should listen to Mac's advice. I realised then that Julia really did care for me. More than she liked me to believe. I put my hand over hers and tried to reassure her that everything would be all right and that if I was to continue wining and dining her like this, I'd need the extra money.

We caught the bus home and I walked Julia across the playing fields Down Brook. There was a full moon and we stopped on the metal bridge and watched the reflected light dance on the ripples of the water. I pulled Julia towards me and we kissed more passionately than ever before. I wondered whether it would be the perfect end to a perfect date. But once again, Julia stopped me before things went too far. Although I could tell that she was aroused, just at the point of total abandonment she suddenly stiffened. It was as if a little angel in her head was warning her that things were getting out of hand. The little devil in *my* head (looking a bit like Mac with horns) was red in the face and jumping up and down in a blind rage while prodding me in the arse with his fork.

Julia breathlessly reminded me that it was her sixteenth birthday next week and I finally gave up. We walked home hand-in-hand in the moonlight both deep in thought. The time wasn't right and I knew that the place wasn't right either. But where would the place be? Where could we go?

At the end of the night I fell to sleep in Julia's arms. We were lying on the leopard skin studio couch in *The Sunset Lounge*, both naked and totally spent after our first love-making session. The Shirelles, *Baby It's You* was playing on the Juke Box.

Let The Good Times Roll
Shirley and Lee

I woke up back in my own bed with the sunshine streaming through the window and that wonderful realisation that it was Saturday. No work! A lazy morning with Saturday Club on the radio and a big fry-up for breakfast. I had to make the most of this Saturday morning if I was to start working for the McBrides next week.

In the afternoon the group met up at Tolley's garage to load the equipment into Sooty's van. It was the day of the booking at the Over Sixties Club in Belper and Mac's début under his new name, Terry Lee Curtis.

On the way there we met Mac at Jackson's the Tailors in town to be fitted for our new stage suits. The slightly effeminate middle-aged assistant greeted us at the door with his tape measure round his neck. He looked us as if we should have been round the back collecting the dustbins, but Whippet quickly reminded him of our previous visit and our appointment for the fitting. We had chosen an ice blue mohair cloth that had to be specially ordered from the mills in Leeds. And, as the lead singer, we persuaded Mac to have his suit made in red mohair to contrast with the rest of the group. He really wanted his trade mark black but reluctantly agreed in the end.

Once he had accepted us the assistant gushed with enthusiasm and addressed each of us as 'Sir' as he fussed around with the fitting. He started with Benno who was first out of the changing room. The assistant, with his head on one side and hand on hip, looked him up and down.

'Now, which side does sir dress?'

Benno looked puzzled but finally answered. 'Well, usually on the side next to the wardrobe.'

The assistant sighed in exasperation but Tolley came to the rescue. 'He means, which leg do you hang your wedding tackle, you prat.'

Benno provided the information and the assistant turned his attention to Mac. First of all he made the mistake of trying to persuade him to have sixteen, rather than fourteen-inch bottoms.

'Ooh sir! They're not wearing them that tight in London these days. Is sir sure?'

Mac was horrified and answered by giving him a steely look that left the assistant in no doubt. He moved off the subject.

'Now sir, I need to get your leg measurement.' He flipped the tape from around his neck.

Mac looked increasingly more uncomfortable as the assistant ran the tape slowly up the inside of his leg. I could sense danger. On reaching the top of the thigh the assistant's hand jiggled about in a little flourish.

Mac flipped. He jumped back, grabbed the assistant's tape measure, wound it round his neck and pulled it tight. 'Get ya hands off me, you fuckin' queer,' he shouted.

We all ran to rescue the purple-faced tailor who was on his hands and knees looking up at Mac as if begging for his life. After calming Mac down we managed to get him to apologise to the assistant who quickly finished the task without further need for his tape measure.

On the way up to Belper we teased Mac about his experience. 'Oh, sir is a big boy, isn't he?' 'Bottoms are not as tight as this in London sir!'

When the banter ceased I took the opportunity to tell Sooty about the offer of weekend work from the McBrides and asked if he was interested. After telling him as much as I knew, he agreed to give it a whirl.

Temptation
The Everly Brothers

We arrived at Belper in high spirits. Despite its name, the Over Sixties Club was the hub of the teenage social scene in the small Derbyshire town and it presented live local groups most weekends. Despite the average age of the audience being around eighteen, the entertainment was always formally introduced by the club's secretary. The night's event was billed as 'Rock'n'Beat Nite' and even the tickets included a sub-headline stating 'Master of Ceremonies, Mr. Fred Stevenson'.

The Over Sixties Club was just a glorified village hall. The modest, pre-fabricated building was set in landscaped memorial gardens just off the main road in the centre of the town. Its interior was basic and the décor non-existent. At the entrance end there was a kitchen with a large serving hatch where teas, coffees and soft drinks were dispensed. At the other end was a stage which was really just a large, wide plinth about a foot higher than the floor. The rest of the hall was taken up by a magnificent sprung dance floor which probably cost as much as the construction that housed it. There were no theatrical curtains and just two spotlights. The acts just had to wander on stage and wait for Mr Fred Stevenson to introduce them.

As Mac and I were struggling to get the bass speaker cabinet out of the van, we heard guffaws of laughter coming from the entrance of the hall. We looked up to see Tolley and Whippet rolling around the ground with laughter. Tolley was holding his stomach and pointing to the posters that were displayed either side of the double doors. The rest of us rushed over and soon saw what all the excitement was about. Somehow, someone had got Mac's stage name, Terry Lee Curtis, slightly wrong. The posters read –

ROCK'N'BEAT NITE

With the fabulous

TERY-LENE CURTAINS AND THE RAPIDS

Mac was beside himself with rage. 'How the fuck could they get my name wrong?' he yelled, clawing one of the posters from the wall. 'Can't they fuckin' read?'

Sooty was the only one able to control his laughter and speak. 'This was a last minute booking which I took over the phone,' he explained. 'When I come to think of it, it was a bad line. They just couldn't have heard me right.'

'You useless bastard,' Mac shouted, ripping the other poster from the wall. 'That's it, there's no way I'm going on as Terylene Curtains!'

The jokes started.

'Pull yourself together, man,' shouted Benno.

'We'll go on as your new backing group the Pelmets if you like,' added Whippet.

Mac finally calmed down and agreed to perform providing the club's secretary made an apology during his introduction.

After we had set up, tuned up and Sooty had carried out his usual sound test, we had to take Mac next door to the George Hotel for a pint of 'Dutch courage'. Even the cool and confident Mac admitted to being nervous as he gulped down his black velvet, especially after the billing error. He lit another cigarette despite already having one burning away in the ash tray. We ran through the play list and the sequence for his entrance.

We had devised a routine whereby Mac would make a specially choreographed entrance. After the group has played six or seven instrumental numbers, we would start playing the introduction to the Cliff Richard Rock'n'roll standard *Move It* . This was Mac's cue to enter from the wings, leap on the stage, grab the mic off the stand and twist around in front of us before starting the vocals. This was all part of Sooty's efforts to get us to become more professional.

When we returned from the pub the hall was nearly full. Despite his nerves Mac still managed a quick 'Hello darlin, waiting for me?' as we passed a cute little red-head in the queue round the entrance. We got ready in a small room at the side of the stage which had a toilet cubicle, one chair and a bare light bulb hanging from the ceiling. I had to make do with a broken piece of mirror to arrange my quiff which was developing nicely and now flopped down over my forehead.

Mac peeped round the door into the Hall. 'Fuckin hell!' he shouted. 'The birds round the front of the stage are three deep and the rest of the hall is packed.'

The door opened fully from outside and a smartly dressed, bald headed man in his fifties marched in.

'Good evening, gentlemen. I'm Fred Stevenson the club secretary,' he announced in a regimental tone that had obviously been perfected in his war years.

'Are you ready, men?' he asked, looking us up and down as if inspecting his troops.

Sooty nodded and politely explained the mistake over the name while Mac scowled in the corner of the room. Fred Stevenson managed a little chuckle as he led us onto the stage. We left Mac in the dressing room to wait for his big entrance. The club secretary tapped the mic a few times and started his introduction. 'One two, one two! One two, one two, testing! Attention girls and boys, attention!' The mic was feeding back through the amplifiers but he continued. 'Welcome to Belper Over Sixties Club.'

There were a few half-hearted cheers from the audience.

'Settle down, settle down.' He was now in schoolteacher mode, trying to keep his class in order. 'First of all I have an announcement to make. Due to an administrative error we don't have Terrylene Curtains for you tonight.'

Most of the audience just gawked back at him but two middle-aged women with shopping bags stood up from the side of the dance floor, tutted their disapproval, and shuffled off towards the exit. One of them turned back to face the stage.

'We've come all't way from Bull Bridge 'ont bus to buy them curtains,' she shouted back at the secretary.

Fred Stevenson just shrugged an apology and continued with his announcement. 'And now's the moment you've all been waiting for.' He paused slightly, turned towards us and raised his voice to a shout. 'Let's have a big Belper welcome for... TERRY LEE CURTIS AND THE FABULOUS RAPIDS!'

We powered in with the Ventures *Perfidia* and, from the first note, the girls went mad. It was obvious that teenagers in Belper and the surrounding villages didn't get out much. Into the third instrumental I noticed that one of the army of girls packed round the front of the stage gave me a 'come-on' smile that woke my gastric butterflies. My devoted fan was particularly shapely and her curves were accentuated by a short, tight fitting tartan dress that rose to a white lace frill high around the neck. She had full pink lips and her hair was blond, almost white, and piled high in a massive, lacquered beehive.

I wallowed in the attention and Tolley shot me a glance of disapproval as I miss-timed the end note to *Shazam*. We went straight into our forth instrumental number and the excitement of the girls round the stage seemed to be increasing with every number. I wondered what kind of a reception these pubescent Belper maidens would give the mean and moody Mac when it was time for him to make his entrance later in the set. But then, from the corner of my eye, I saw that Mac was already out of the dressing room. He mounted the stage and Benno gave me a puzzled look.

'What the hell's he doing on the stage now? He shouted.

Mac had miss-heard the introduction to our instrumental and had thought it was his cue to come on. The others didn't notice at first and continued playing. Mac grabbed the mic off the stand and started twisting around at the front of the stage.

Tolley then saw what was happening and kicked the back of Mac's leg. 'Not yet, you prat,' he shouted.

Mac was still twisting around in front of the expectant teenagers but when the music didn't stop, and he realised his mistake, a look of horror replaced his Elvis sneer. He was trapped in an instrumental with no way out. We all looked at each other wondering whether we should try to move into Mac's number. But then Mac gave up and twisted off the stage in the manner he'd arrived, but with a good impression of a skulking dog. He mouthed 'you fuckin' bastards' to us as he disappeared back into the changing room.

What a début . The teenagers looked puzzled. Sooty was jumping up and down like an angry orchestra conductor. Even Mr Fred Stevenson looked bewildered. Mac must have been beside himself with this further embarrassment, but we couldn't help seeing the funny side as we struggled to finish our instrumental.

When we eventually started the introduction to *Move It*, Mac's real cue, I wondered if he'd still get back on stage. After twelve bars there was still no sign of Mac and I thought that maybe he'd made a bee-line for the George Hotel to drown his sorrows. The monotony of the repeated introduction was making the crowd restless and a worried Sooty hurried into the changing room. I looked over towards Tolley as if to say 'what do we do now?' but he just shrugged his shoulders. Some of the crowd were beginning to drift away from the front of the stage, so I smiled weakly at my fan in an effort to retain her interest. Then, at last, the dressing room door began to open. At that moment the hall was plunged into total darkness. We continued with our riff and after a few moments of concern and confusion a beam of brilliant light shot down from the single spot above the centre of the stage. Underneath, caught in the light, was Mac. He was motionless; legs apart with his back to the audience, shirt collar turned-up and his right hand outstretched clutching the mic. The crowd was silent, almost stunned. After a few dramatic moments, he suddenly spun round and burst into life.

'Well come on pretty baby, let's a move-it and a groove-it'

The rest of the lights flooded the room and, as if turned-on by the same switch, the crowd were suddenly animated into an excited frenzy. There was a scary rush for the front of the stage and the entire audience jumped, jived and gyrated on the spot. Mac's dramatic, alternative entrance had injected us with an extra shot of adrenalin and the number rocked. Arms reached up from the front of the stage and Mac was an instant star. But I was still pleased to see that my fan still only had eyes for me.

Mac was in his element and went through his repertoire with increasing confidence. In the middle of *I'll Never Find Another You* he reached down and touched the hands of some of his adoring audience. This sent the girls into raptures and nearly created a riot as they each clambered to make contact. We ended the set with a rousing version of *Be Bop A Lula* and the hall went crazy, jumping up and down, shouting for more. After a couple of encores, Mr Fred Stevenson took the mic from Mac and in an effort to restore some order he reassured the crowd that the group would be back next month.

Back in the dressing room, we were all totally spent but high from the overdose of adrenalin. Mac was slumped in a chair, bathed in sweat. He was staring at the ceiling with a dreamy grin on his face as if he'd just returned from a trip to paradise. We were all congratulating Sooty on his quick rearrangement of Mac's introduction sequence when Mr Fred Stevenson entered. Behind him was a sea of expectant female faces and he quickly shut the door behind him.

'You'll have to go back out there to sign some autographs or they'll never leave,' he said, glancing at his watch. 'I've got to lock up in fifteen minutes.'

Mac's ears seemed to prick up, or maybe something else did, and he made a swift recovery. After a few coiffeur adjustments in front of the piece of broken mirror, we went back out to wallow in our first experience of fan worship. The girls clustered round as we each signed on anything they could find, from ticket stubs to fag packets. But the best moment was when one girl of about sixteen insisted that I sign my autograph on the section of thigh between her stocking tops and her knickers. For a moment, I was lost in my own fantasy sequence as she exposed that magical and mysterious area of flesh that every male, from spotty teenager to middle-aged man, dreams of. My hands were shaking as I applied the biro to her soft, pink flesh. She giggled and said that it tickled. Then I noticed that there was already an autograph on the other thigh - a typographic flourish that seemed to go higher than I would never have dared. 'Mac was ere' it read and I was quickly brought back down to earth.

Most of the girls had got what they wanted and were being ushered out by an impatient Fred Stevenson when I noticed that my special fan was standing last in line. Next in the queue was a girl who'd managed to win most of Mac's attention during the signing session. After I'd finished signing an autograph on a crumpled Fry's chocolate wrapper she moved forward and spoke.

'My mate wants you to give her your autograph outside,' she said coyly.

Fred Stevenson had decided that time was up anyway and was waving his hands, shouting for everyone to clear the hall. I quickly agreed to meet her friend outside and they were bundled towards the exit. Mac then told me that he was seeing the other girl outside too. With a twitchy Fred Stevenson standing over us, we cleared the equipment from the hall and into the van in record time. But it was the anticipation of meeting my girl that spurred me on rather than the impatient secretary.

The lads had decided to walk out onto Derby Road to get some chips but Mac and I pretended we weren't hungry and arranged to meet them back at the van in twenty minutes. The girls were waiting in the shadows at the side of the hall. Mac flicked his cigarette butt into a rose bed and led the way. 'I'm on a promise here Ginner, but it'll have to be a quickie,' he said as we approached the girls.

Suddenly, Julia came into my thoughts. A quick pang of guilt tried to drive the lust from my loins but the butterflies had grown horns and were rampant. Mac grabbed his date by the hand and disappeared back towards the van without uttering a word. I was left staring into the eyes of my fan wondering whether to ask her if she'd got a Biro, but she spoke first. 'Should we go in to't' summer house?' she said, pointing towards the landscaped gardens at the rear of the hall. She took my hand and led me into the darkness. As we made our way in silence, I was experiencing a new kind of excitement which was more to do with being desired and seduced by a total stranger than the anticipation of sex. We came to a small, wooden structure with a thatched roof which was more like an ornate bus shelter than a summer house. We stumbled into the darkness and she turned to face me.

Neither of us had anything to say and after a few seconds we fell into a frenzied embrace that seemed to last for minutes. I guessed it was her way of getting to know someone. We stopped briefly for breath and when we continued I let my hands slip towards the hem of her dress. She wriggled a bit to help and I slid her dress high over her thighs. I caressed her silky flesh and she began to breathe really heavily. The frenzy intensified and her hands fumbled around the zip on my jeans. Then, with an expert twist of her wrist, she released me. My hands were now inside her knickers and, although she appeared to be enjoying herself, she began to gasp for breath. I started to worry. She seemed to be having some kind of attack.

'Are you alright?' I whispered, without daring to remove my fingers from their advanced position.

She took a few laboured breaths and replied. 'It's ok... I suffer from ...asthma and... this is what happens when I get... too excited.'

This admission seemed to excite me even more - the fact that my love making skills could actually bring on an asthma attack. 'Yes!' I thought. She recovered a bit, and when I was sure that she wouldn't die on me, we continued. I removed my hand briefly while she slid her knickers down. My jeans and pants were already round my ankles. Our kisses became even more passionate as our tongues seemed to compete to cover every inch of the insides of our mouths. We pressed our nakedness against each other and she opened her legs wider as I tried to enter her. Her breathing was returning to danger level as I eased myself into her. She pulled away from my lips long enough to suck in more oxygen and then sighed as I moved in and out with increasing speed. I was desperately fighting to control myself and delay the inevitable explosion when a raucous voice pierced the passion of the moment.

'Where the fuck are you?' It was Tolley's angry voice. 'We're going without you if you don't fuckin' come now.'

And I did.

Songs of Fear

Workin' For The Man
Roy Orbison

I woke up as a man, the sun streaming through my bedroom window in celebration. At last I'd done it. After months on a roller coaster of emotional turmoil I had managed to lose my virginity. But on reflection it was all a bit of an anti-climax. The build-up to the deed had been wickedly thrilling and, without doubt, the most pleasurable experience imaginable. But I'd thought that the climax to such a momentous event would far exceed the prelude. In the end, it was just the end. A full stop. A release valve that immediately dispelled all the passion and fury of the foreplay along with the rampant butterflies. And when I was left standing with my jeans round my ankles, clinging on to a semi-naked, near stranger whose name I didn't even know, I wondered what all the fuss had been about.

Then there was the guilt. Should I have waited for Julia? How would she feel if she knew? What would she do if she found out? It didn't help by the fact that The Sunday Service was on the radio downstairs. Having these thoughts with the sound of church music in the background made me feel even more unworthy. If Eddy Cochran had been playing, I'm sure I would have been able to gain more satisfaction and pride over my achievement. I eventually managed to justify my infidelity by claiming to myself that it was all carried out in the interests of self-development, and that now I could put it behind me and approach my romantic relationships with more maturity and without the burden of virginity.

As I was still ruminating over the event of the previous night the phone rang downstairs. Mum turned the hymns down and shouted that it was for me. The gruff voice on the other end was Grey McBride's checking that Sooty and I were still up for the part-time work at the brewery in Burton-on-Trent. I agreed that we'd meet at the main gates at one o'clock and quickly rang Sooty with the arrangements.

When we arrived the McBrides were parked outside the main gates in their flashy, two-tone, pink and white Vauxhall Cresta. It was the nearest thing Britain had to the beautiful, sleek, tail-finned vehicles of the USA. Sooty's dream was to own one. He leaped down from his van and started to stroke the shiny body of the car. Tony McBride immediately jumped from the driving seat. 'Keep your greasy mits off the chrome, cowboy,' he yelled as he pushed Sooty away and buffed the top of one of the rear fins with his handkerchief.

Gra McBride got out of the passenger seat, lit a fag, leaned on the car and proceeded to explain what was expected of us.

The McBrides both worked in the bottling plant and this weekend they were working an extra shift on the Coca-Cola line which Bass bottled under licence. That suited me fine, working with the shapely coke bottle that had become my favourite icon of teenage cool. I wondered if I'd be allowed to take free samples home. Our job was at the end of the production line, placing the bottles into small, red wooden crates. Then, after the shift, we were to load Sooty's van and make a couple of special deliveries around town.

Gra McBride went to speak to the gate man and seemed to look nervously over his shoulder as he passed him something. I assumed it was some kind of pass and he waved for us to bring the van into the plant. We slowly followed the pink Cresta around the narrow roadways within the huge brewery complex.

In Burton-on-Trent, there were about four breweries, all situated around the town centre and linked by a network of railway lines which criss-crossed the streets of the small town in a maze of metalwork. Consequently, Burton had more level crossings per square mile than anywhere else in Britain. The whole town smelled of hops and malt, twenty-four hours a day, but inside the Bass plant the smell was noticeably stronger.

We weaved our way round the service roads following the Cresta as it bounced up and down over the railway lines like the big American cars on *Highway Patrol*. We eventually stopped outside a decaying, old factory building that only seemed to be supported by the cloak of cables, pipes and valves that surrounded it. Steam drifted from vents high on the side wall and an eerie light shone behind grimy metal windows.

The McBrides ushered us inside where the production line wound its way round the bottling plant like the big dipper at Skegness amusement park. The empty, green tinted coke bottles were suspended from overhead rails like soldiers waiting to march off to war.

Another shifty looking bloke joined the McBrides and soon afterwards the production line jerked into action. The lines of clean empty bottles passed under a bank of bright, stainless steel filling nozzles which were connected to two flexible pipes. One pumped in carbonated water, the other thick, black syrup. This was the special Coca-Cola cordial produced from a secret recipe and imported under licence from Atlanta, Georgia. The noise from the machinery and clinking of the bottles increased in volume as the production line gathered speed. I reflected on the fact that the whole process was not dissimilar to the printing of The Derbyshire Advertiser on its mighty rotary press. The different sounds – clanks and clinks, whooshes and hisses, bangs and bumps – were galvanised into a percussive rhythm that filled the vast interior of the bottling plant. And, as it was when the Advertiser's press reached its pace, the bricks and mortar, window frames and doors of the whole building began to shudder along in time to the rhythm.

At first, Sooty and I juggled precariously with the full bottles as they collected at the end of the line. Then we managed to find a pace that kept up with the line and were soon loading the bottles into the red crates with mechanical dexterity.

After what seemed like an hour, the machinery mercifully slowed and when it finally ground to a halt, Gra McBride came over to us.

'We're going out for a fag break but first we want you to help us in with some barrels,' he said, already moving towards the loading doors.

We followed him outside where Tony McBride was standing at the rear of the Cresta. He was looking furtively up and down the service road, then whipped open the boot of the car to reveal two wooden barrels.

'Quick lads, get em inside,' ordered Gra McBride with a sense of urgency.

Tony McBride was still keeping a watchful eye on the service road, his scrawny neck craning above the car like a weasel sniffing its prey. Sooty and I looked suspiciously at each other. We lifted the barrels from the boot and rolled them inside the bottling plant. There were two more under blankets on the back seat, and when they were all inside, Tony McBride bolted the door behind us.

'Now lads, grab some more empty crates while we make a few adjustments to the machinery,' ordered Gra McBride.

As we moved the crates, I looked over my shoulder to see the McBrides high up in the assembly line positioning the barrels next to the carbonated water and syrup pipes above the filling nozzles. It all looked a bit suspicious but I couldn't work out why. Then the machinery started to roll again and we assumed our positions at the end of the line. But something was wrong. There was a different smell in the air. Not just the sweet smell of cola and hops from outside, but another familiar smell that reminded me of a recent experience. I stopped work and sniffed the air again. Ska music started to play in my head to the rhythm of the production line. The percussive roar of the machinery was punctuated by a solid off-beat. '*Madness,*

madness, they call it madness.' Winston's face came into mind. Sooty was juggling with the bottles single-handed, puzzled as to why I wasn't helping. Then it hit me. The smell was rum; Jamaican rum. I looked down at the bottles as they shot off the production line into Sooty's fumbling hands, then over my shoulder at Tony McBride who was working behind us. He was bent over, scratching something into the crown caps of the bottles we had loaded into the crates. It was the letter 'X'. We were producing Ready Mix.

Tony McBride looked up from the crates. 'Get back to fuckin' work if ya want payin', he shouted above the din. 'And keep ya eyes on what ya doin.'

I continued with our task but my mind was racing. Then I remembered sitting on a rum barrel in the back yard at the Jamaican house party. The same type of barrel as the ones we had taken from the McBrides car, with a black letter 'X' printed onto the wood.

After the last drop of rum had been drained from the barrels, the production line stopped and we loaded the crates into Sooty's van. Gra McBride stuffed two five pound notes in my hand and told us to take half the crates to Winston's uncle's house and deliver the rest to the landlord of The Crown Hotel next weekend after we have performed there. That meant that Sooty would have half a dozen crates of illicit booze in his van for nearly a week.

So that was it. Winston's uncle didn't just bring rare American and West Indian records into the country. He was smuggling rum and was part of an illegal scam with the McBrides whereby they cleverly distributed their contraband disguised as coke. Only the 'X' scratched in the crown cap identified the illicit contents. Worse still, Sooty and I were now part of this illegal operation; part of the gang, and criminals.

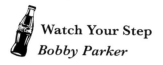# Watch Your Step
Bobby Parker

The realisation of what Sooty and I had become involved in had kept me awake most of the night. Even frequent trips into the sanctuary of *The Sunset Lounge* couldn't stop me worrying about it. If, or rather when, the scam was discovered, the McBrides wouldn't hesitate in taking us down with them despite our innocence.

But was I totally innocent?

Although slightly confused about events, Sooty was oblivious to the details of the illegal operation. As far as he was concerned he had pure Coca-Cola in the back of his van, and I just couldn't bring myself to tell him the obvious truth. I thought it best that he knew as little as possible and that way he would be innocent of any wrong doing. I, on the other hand, had sussed it out. And from the moment we loaded the van and made our deliveries, I had become an accessory; At best guilty of aiding and abetting, at worst guilty of distributing contraband and stolen goods.

I thought about telling Sooty and suggesting we dump the crates into the river Derwent, but then this would implicate him. Not only that, as far as the McBrides were concerned, we'd be dead meat. It would be the same if we grassed on them. I was trapped.

As I lay awake wrestling with my dilemma I wished that I were tough enough to take on the McBrides. Looking under the sheets at my puny body I regretted not responding to the cutting I had taken from the Daily Express earlier in the year. It was an advertisement for the Charles Atlas Dynamic Tension System. I reached for the yellowing newspaper cutting that was tucked in the frame of my mirror and read the advertisement again. It was in the style of a strip cartoon. A spotty, skinny youth was lying on a beach with his girlfriend. Two thugs, not unlike the McBrides, walk by and kick sand in his face. *'Hey, quit kicking sand in my face,'* he shouts from his cartoon bubble, but the thugs just laugh at him. Then the cartoon shows the same youth three months later with bulging muscles and his testimonial –

I was a 7 stone weakling until I discovered 'Dynamic Tension' - the secret method of developing REAL MEN. Send for my free book and details of my 7 day free trial.

It was too late for that now and the McBrides would probably shoot me anyway.

During that long sleepless night I felt desperately lonely and in need of someone to share my burden. If only I could have held Julia in my arms and told her all about it. She'd have listened patiently, perhaps offering a few words of advice, and then given me a kiss on my nose making everything alright. As the sun started to creep through the slats of the venetian blinds in *The Sunset Lounge* I came to the only conclusion I could come to. I just had to see it through on my own and hope that the scam would never come to light.

I got up for work feeling like shit and in the mirror I looked even worse. My face was as white as the shaving soap I brushed over my chin, my eyes were red and even my quiff had given up the ghost and flopped in defeat over my pasty forehead.

At work I began to feel a little better. Problems always seem smaller in the light of day. I realised that my work place, despite the tedium and hard work, was a form of sanctuary for me; another *Sunset Lounge* but real, and set apart from the outside world in its own little universe. Today I took comfort from the comradeship of my work mates - my extended family.

The main topic of conversation throughout the week was the forthcoming party at the stately home of Lord Ives. Following his near-death experience and the premature tribute paid to him in the columns of the Derbyshire Advertiser, he had invited the entire staff to his Eightieth Birthday Ball. And better still he had booked the Rapids to perform. William Blake had arranged for a private Trent bus to transport the whole staff and the men in the machine room had arranged a whip-round to buy a crate of brown ale for the back seat. The more cynical members of staff thought that Lord Ives would croak it before the big night and took bets on how many days Lord Ives would survive. It was a kind of insurance policy against the disappointment of the event being cancelled.

At lunchtime I made my usual trip to the Locarno where Johnny Burnette, Roy Orbison and Chubby Checker also managed to lift my spirits. On the way back to work I called in at Derwent Music Store to buy a new string for my bass guitar. Sheila was behind the counter and her mischievous smile even managed to rouse a couple of butterflies from below - the wicked horned variety. Sheila was still quite cool with me but could never resist the opportunity to exercise her seductive charms or tease me. After I'd asked for a Fender bass 'G' string, she leant forward and slowly licked her full lips before speaking.

'And would sir like me to fit the 'G' string for him?' she whispered seductively.

After having her fun she asked for news of The Rapids. I told her how I was taking on extra work to pay for a new bass speaker cabinet, but when I told her who was giving me the work her mood changed and she, too, seemed genuinely concerned for my safety.

Before I left she told me that she'd be at the Lord Ives party and that he was going round for dinner with her parents that night to discuss the final arrangements.

Back at work I had almost returned to my usual, carefree self. Besides feeling safe and secure in the company of my work mates I also took comfort in the familiar surroundings, sounds and smells of newspaper production. Work started that afternoon with one of the most menial tasks allocated to apprentices. Mac and I had to haul the recycled ingots of metal, called 'pigs' in the trade, from the foundry on the ground floor up to the *Linotype room* on the fourth floor.

There were six Linotype machines at the Advertiser. They were like giant floor-standing typewriters that produced metal slugs of type. Each line of type in each column of the newspaper was made up of single 'slugs' of metal. The Linotype operator sat at a keyboard retyping copy sheets from the editorial department. So the time employed in setting a complete column of text and casting it in metal, line by line, was somewhere akin to the time it took the journalist to write it in the first place. Each machine contained a pot of molten metal set above a gas ring which kept the metal in its liquid state. The pot was replenished by the large 'pig' of metal which was slowly fed into the pot of molten liquid with each rotation of the machine. On a Friday morning, following publication of the latest edition of the newspaper, all the columns of metal type were sent back down to the foundry, melted down and recast into the 'pigs' that Mac and I then had to haul back up to the *Linotype room*. And so the cycle went on. The same metal was used again and again to produce news, articles and advertisements for the next riveting issue of the Derbyshire Advertiser.

Mac always tried to carry more 'pigs' in one trip than I could. I realised that it was just a macho thing and usually let him score the point. As far as I was concerned avoiding a double hernia was more important than feeding my ego. But I was sometimes tempted to secretly subscribe to the Charles Atlas Dynamic Tension System and put Mac in his place.

As we struggled up the four flights of narrow, wooden stairs, Mac raised the subject of our experiences with the groupies after the booking at Belper.

'So did ya manage it Ginner?' he rasped breathlessly, as

he struggled with four 'pigs' of metal. 'Or are ya' still a virgin?'

Although I was still feeling guilty about betraying Julia I was also proud of the fact that I had done it at last. On the landing of the first flight of stairs which served the editorial offices, I put my three 'pigs' down so that I could catch my breath and answer him.

'Course I did, it was great. But I'd like to try it lying down next time, and I wish I knew what her name was.'

Mac put his 'pigs' down. 'That was what ya' call a knee trembler Ginner.' He'd obviously decided that it was time for a little more coaching now that I'd broken my duck.

'And it's best if ya don't know their names. And never give them yours unless ya have to.' Mac was now preaching to me and he raised his voice to give emphasis to his final words of wisdom. 'My advice is to you, Ginner, is to...'

Behind Mac I could see a figure through the frosted glazed door. Someone from the editorial department was just about to push their way into the corridor. The door swung open just as Mac finished his sentence.

'... just fuck em and leave em.'

Mac caught my glance and swung round to face a wide-eyed and startled old lady. It was Rosemary Bagnall, the ageing and extremely posh Women's Page editor who was on her way to the toilet. We quickly lifted our bars of metal and started to ascend the next flight of stairs, leaving the red-faced journalist fumbling in her handbag for smelling salts.

Stopping for another rest on the next landing, Mac flicked a fag into his mouth, lit it, spat out a fragment of tobacco and we continued our conversation. 'So Ginner, are ya gonna break that Julia in now, or what?'

I told him that Julia wasn't yet sixteen but her birthday was the coming Thursday. An evil smile came to Mac's face as he let the smoke drift from his nose. 'She's a nice piece of

stuff Ginner, decent tits and those big, dark come-to-bed eyes.'
He gazed at the ceiling with a wicked smirk on his face and
was obviously mentally undressing *my* Julia. 'Tell ya what,' he
continued. 'If *you* don't want to do it, I'll do it for ya.'

The suggestion filled me with jealously but I didn't want
Mac to know that. He'd have seen it as letting the side down
and a sign of weakness. I quickly changed the subject and
began to tell Mac about the trouble I was in with the McBrides.
He listened silently to my story with the occasional grunt of
concern. But I sensed that my brush with the McBrides and the
law was earning me growing respect in Mac's eyes. However,
the advice which followed was as black and white and as basic
as his recommendations for dealing with young virgins.

'Don't fuck with the McBrides,' he warned, with what
seemed like genuine concern.

The door at the top of the next flight opened. It was
Eric. 'Where are those bloody 'pigs' you skiving little sods?' he
shouted down the stairs. 'The Lino's are running dry and we've
got a fuckin' paper to get out,' he bawled.

Behind us we heard a frightened whimper as Rosemeary
Bagnell returned across the landing. We quickly picked up our
heavy loads and made for the top of the stairs.

 It Keeps Rainin'
Fats Domino

Sometimes, if you put your problems out of your mind for
long enough, they seem to disappear altogether. Since my
sleepless Sunday night and my discussion with Mac about my
being mixed-up with the McBrides, there had been no further
developments. It was almost as if the whole affair was just part
of my vivid imagination and I was almost back to my old self.

I was busy making plans to take Julia out on her birthday
for a really special night. I had decided that we'd start at the

Boccaccio coffee bar, then I'd take her for a Babycham in the Bell and we'd end up at the Locarno. Thursday night was under 21's night with non-stop records. On other nights, the ageing, resident Mecca dance band would try their best to replicate the latest American pop hits, but it never sounded right. Just as the 45's on Woolworths own *Embassy* label didn't sound right. British musicians couldn't capture the slickness, soul and style of the originals from their counterparts across the Atlantic.

I wasn't sure about the conclusion to our big night out. If only it could have the perfect ending spending the whole night together. But we had nowhere to go where we could be alone. And after my experience in the summer house at Belper, I realised that furtive sex *al fresco* had its limitations and certainly couldn't be described as romantic.

At work my mind kept drifting from my task of making up one of the general news pages. I would find myself in *The Sunset Lounge*, now furnished with a king-size, double bed set in the body of a powder blue Buick Riviera which I'd seen in Reveille magazine. A leopard skin covered mattress was set between the wings of the car which gradually inclined into huge shiny tail fins at the foot of the bed. The headboard, which was where the dashboard would have been, was upholstered in luxurious red leather.

In my mind I had placed candles around the perimeter of the bed. I was lying there with just my jeans on. Soon, Julia would open the padded door to *The Sunset Lounge* wearing the baby-doll nightie I'd bought her for her birthday. I nonchalantly lit another Peter Stuyvesant with one of the candles. The door started to open tantalisingly slowly. She was shy and probably very nervous. It opened further. But then the door suddenly swung open with a crash.

I was faced with a hideous sight. It was Wally wearing nothing but a pink, baby-doll nightie. His hairy legs were twitching impatiently as he puffed angrily on his pipe. 'What do you think you're doing?' he shouted. 'We've got a paper to get out!'

I was suddenly sucked back to reality from my fantasy world and facing a fully dressed, red-faced Wally. 'Well, what's the matter lad? Are you ill?'

'Nnn... no,' I replied weakly, not being able to get the image of Wally in a baby-doll nightie out of my mind.

'I... I was just.' I hesitated a bit longer, and then decided to come clean. 'I was just wondering what to buy my girlfriend for her birthday.'

My frankness took the wind out of Wally's sails. He just ordered me to get back to work, shrugged, and wandered off in a cloud of St Bruno.

I returned to my task of arranging the columns of linotype slugs into the chase that would frame the news page of Friday's edition of the Advertiser. But when I reached for the headline to one of the stories I froze.

I re-read the type, which was upside down and back-to-front.

CHADDESDEN MEN QUESTIONED

ON BREWERY THEFTS

And the sub-headline.

POLICE SEARCHING FOR BEDFORD VAN

All the fears and worries I'd had earlier in the week came flooding back. The police were onto the McBrides, and worse still, they were on to Sooty and me. I quickly read the article which reported that stock had been disappearing from the Bass plant over several months. It also suggested that the McBrides were the main suspects and had been suspended by the brewery. The Police had linked the case to a Customs and Excise investigation into barrels of rum which were being smuggled into the country via Liverpool Docks. It gave no further information other than that, following a police investigation, the Chaddesden men had been released due to insufficient evidence. And the only bit of hard evidence they had was the sighting of an unidentified dark blue Bedford Dormobile seen leaving the plant. It concluded with the report that the police were appealing for information.

So Sooty was driving around Derbyshire in his blue Bedford Dormobile van loaded with contraband, totally unaware of his implication. I considered dumping the whole article into the scrap bin where it would be melted down and lost forever in a new 'pig' of metal. But Brad, the editor would be sure to notice and the typed copy would find its way back into the *Linotype Room* to be reset. The article would hit the streets on Friday morning, so I needed to find Sooty and tell about the trouble we were in.

After finishing work at 8pm, I went straight Down Brook to look for him. I also needed to make the final arrangements with Julia for her special birthday night which could be one of our last. In any event, I needed Julia now like I'd never needed her before. I really wanted to tell her all about my problems. She would look up at me, smile, kiss me, and all my troubles would disappear. But if I did it would ruin her birthday.

It was a warm evening and the playing fields were livelier than usual. Kids were playing football and cricket. The card school had more punters than usual and the girls, some in summer tops and shorts, were either huddled around a transistor radio or with the crowd that had gathered around Tolley and his guitar. As I got closer I could see that Sooty's van wasn't parked in its usual spot, but I couldn't decide whether that was a good thing or not. Then I saw Julia with Cathy and a few other girls chatting near the metal bridge. I felt warm inside and wanted to run over, pull her away from her friends and hug her close to me. But that wouldn't be cool in the eyes of the assembled company so I resisted the temptation, slowed my pace, and casually wandered towards her with a half-interested smile on my face.

Then a very strange thing happened. When they saw me coming their chatting became more intense. My smile broadened as Julia looked towards me. But she totally ignored me. She just turned away and hurried off with one of the girls.

I approached Cathy who had turned to meet me with her arms folded menacingly over her sloppy sweater.

'Hi Cathy, where's Julia gone?' I asked, puzzled.

'As far away from you as possible, I hope.'

'Why, what's wrong?' My mind was working overtime.

'We've all been hearing about your escapade at Belper with that tart Susan.' She spat back, raising her folded arms even higher so that her *Ban the Bomb* badge rested under her chin.

'Don't know anyone in Belper called Susan.' I was on the defence and it was an honest reply. But the bad part of my mind made a quick note of my first conquest's name. The good part, realising the shit I was in, was plunged into panic. Cathy continued her attack like a mother hen protecting one of her chicks.

'Don't come that you bastard Joe King. Your group mates told us they had to drag you back to the van with your jeans around your ankles,' she countered, taking a threatening step forward.

I looked over the playing fields. Tolley had stopped playing and was laughing with some of the crowd. He'd shopped me. What a bastard, I thought. This was his way of ensuring that girls wouldn't interfere with his group's success. I walked away from Cathy in defeat. Julia had gone at a time when I needed her most. I wanted to tell her that it didn't mean anything, that it was disappointing anyway and that it was her I really wanted, needed and loved. But I knew that wouldn't have been an acceptable excuse for my indiscretion.

Then I focused on my other problem and frantically asked around for Sooty. I was told that he'd driven to Ripley to see Marlene.

So that was my day. Sooty was driving around Derbyshire with six crates of illegal booze that I'd help bottle and load into his van. The police and Customs and Excise were on our trail. The McBrides would probably put me in hospital if I didn't go through with their demands. And I had lost the girl I thought I loved on the day before her birthday and our special night out. I turned to walk up the hill towards home and placed the right foot of my new, chisel toe, grey suede shoes into a large, fresh, steaming dog turd.

Songs of Sadness

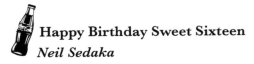

Happy Birthday Sweet Sixteen
Neil Sedaka

Despite my mounting problems and deepening heartache at losing Julia, I slept well. I was tired, physically and emotionally. I was also becoming resigned to my fate. Whichever way it went, things looked bad for me.

At work, Mac was in an unusually happy mood. He was almost joyful which was a state of mind that he either didn't experience very often or he repressed for the sake of his cool image. Today, I was the mean and moody one. Then, while we were making the jugs of tea for the men in the *Linotype room*, Mac revealed the reason for his exuberance. But it pierced my heart like a stiletto.

'So Ginner, you've split up with Julia then?' he started.

'How do you know?' I asked suspiciously.

'She rang me last night which really surprised me,' he answered. 'She seemed upset though.'

I couldn't believe that Julia would phone Mac. I remembered the coy look she had given him when I first introduced them. The jealousy rose within me like a green monster.

Mac sensed my dismay but continued. 'She just wanted to talk. And when she told me it was her sixteenth birthday today, I offered to take her for a coffee in the Boccaccio.'

Mac became more sensitive to my silent reaction.

'I'm meeting her under the Guildhall clock at eight tonight. Ya don't mind do ya, Ginner?'

I remained silent, trying to deal with my emotions. Mac didn't know how much I needed Julia. It was not something blokes told each other, especially Mac, who wouldn't understand the concept while there were so many young girls out there. So I couldn't really blame him. He was only being Mac, but it hurt. He was one of my best friends, but at that moment I hated him.

'Ginner! Ya don't mind, do ya?' he repeated before continuing. 'She's not like the usual birds I knock off. She's sort of pure. I'm looking forward to introducing her to the Mackenzie charm.' Mac was trying to make light of his plans.

'Er… no. No, of course not. She's nothing to do with me now,' I replied trying to sound disinterested as I angrily spooned tea leaves into each jug.

I really wanted to say, 'If you lay just one of your greasy fingers on her I'll kill you.' But I didn't.

As far as Mac was concerned the subject was closed and he was free to pursue another notch for his bed post. As he proceeded to pour boiling into the enamel jugs, he started to sing. His excitement at the prospect of sacrificing yet another young virgin at his altar of sex was evident. Especially when he amended Neil Sedaka's lyrics.

Tra, la la la la, la la la la, Happy Birthday Sweet Sixteen.
Tra, la la la la, la la la la, Happy Birthday Sweet Sixteen.
Tonight's the Night, I've waited for.
Because it's not illegal any more…

I could see it now. Mac would buy Julia a quick cup of cappuccino in the Boc. He'd choose a few romantic Elvis numbers from the juke box selector at the side of their table for two in the corner. Then he'd turn on the charm, flicking his fags into his mouth and blowing the smoke down his nose. His hand would creep over her shoulder and he'd caress her hair as they laughed and joked. Finally, he'd suggest that they went round to his mate's flat on Osmaston Road to listen to some more records. I'd heard the sordid script from his ongoing campaign against virginity so many times.

Mac had a mate called Jack, a bloke in his late twenties who managed H. Samuels the jewellers in the Cornmarket. He had his own flat close to town and Mac used it as a convenient venue for his sexual conquests. How could I prevent Julia from falling prey to Mac's basic animal instincts and from losing her innocence to anyone but me? Even if we did eventually get back together, how could I match the silky, smooth skills of Derby's master of seduction? She'd be spoilt forever.

We dished out the jugs of tea and returned to our real jobs of making-up the pages for tomorrow's edition. The one that would carry the story of the search for the blue Dormobile van. While I was half way through placing the single column cinema ads onto the back page Wally popped his head out of his office with the internal phone in his hand.

'Joe. It's the front office,' he angrily shouted. 'There's an outside phone call for you.'

The Advertiser staffs were only allowed personal phone calls in emergencies. I left my work and made my way down the wooden stairs wondering how much more bad news I could take. Was it the police or Customs and Excise? Was it Sooty ringing from prison? Or was it Julia to say she'd forgiven me and everything would be alright?

When I walked into the front office the snotty receptionist looked me up and down disapprovingly and handed me the phone. The front office staff hated having dirty, ink stained printers on their territory where the general public could see them.

I wiped my ink-stained hand down my cow gown and took the phone.

'Hello.' I said expectantly. There was silence. 'Hello, hello,' I repeated.

A rough, menacing voice finally filled the earpiece. My heart sank. If it was Julia she had a bad case of laryngitis.

'Is that Joe King?'

'Er... yes, who's that?' I replied.

The voice continued, almost in a whisper. 'Do you like hospital food youth? Cause if ya don't make the drop at the Crown on Sunday you'll be eatin' it for months.' It was Tony McBride.

'Ok but… ' I tried to reply by telling him about the search for the van but he cut me short.

'Sunday lunchtime! Not before and not after.'

'But…' I tried again but he wasn't having any of it.

'Just do it or I'll scar your face for life.' And he hung-up.

I just stood there for a few moments, stunned, holding the phone down by my side. The receptionist carefully took the receiver from my hand with two fingers and placed it back on its cradle.

That's It – I Quit – I'm Movin' On
Sam Cooke

Why is it that when you have a sleepless night you finally fall into a deep unconscious state just before you have to wake up? All night I had been tossing and turning. My patchy dreams drifted from being slashed across the face with a razor to watching Mac making love to Julia. At one point I nearly got up to walk round to Julia's house. I wanted to see if her bedroom curtains were open which would have indicated that she hadn't come home and was spending a lustful night somewhere with Mac. Maybe she had told her Mum she was staying at Cathy's house.

The night before I had watched the latest issue of The Derbyshire Advertiser as it came off the press. I stood by the giant press as it thundered away, printing, trimming and folding complete editions of newspaper at the rate of one every two seconds. I watched the stream of white newsprint as it weaved its way in and out of the rotary printing plates. I was focused on the point where the black inked plates of the news page came into contact with the pure, white virgin paper and the sub-headline of the lead story which repeated its message with each rotation - *Police searching for Bedford van. Police searching for*

Bedford van. Police searching for Bedford van.

I knew then that in less than ten hour's time this headline would be read by thirty thousand people throughout Derbyshire.

Mac had left earlier to meet *my* Julia and as the press thundered away I reflected on the probability that he would soon be leaving his own dirty impression on my pure, white virgin. He had said his goodbyes with an evil glint in his eye like a black panther that was about to descend on a young, innocent gazelle. I wanted to leave my work and rush out into the Market Place to save Julia from her fate. But I didn't. Later in the evening when I nipped out to the cigarette kiosk to get the fag order for the machine minders I pressed my nose up against the Boccaccio window. There was no sign of them. Perhaps he had already whisked her away to Jack's flat. I was desperate. Jealousy, anger, and a deep, deep sadness engulfed my mind. I couldn't stop myself imagining every detail of Mac's seduction process.

Now, in the cold light of the following morning, I didn't feel much better. But at least it was Friday and work would be finished at lunchtime. Then I could catch up on my sleep in the afternoon before the big night out at the Lord Ives eightieth birthday bash. So I dragged myself out of bed.

On the way to the bus stop I did a detour past Julia's house. I just needed to be near her. As I rounded the corner into her street and approached her house I could see that her bedroom curtains were drawn. She did spend the night in her own bed. But then quickly reasoned that she could have drawn them before she left to meet Mac. What if, what if, what if? My mind was inventing all kinds of scenarios.

I stood beneath her window for a while just hoping for a sign of life. But then I thought, what if she was at home tucked-up in bed? Mac could have spent the whole evening making love to her and put her on the last bus home. A disturbing vision came into my head. Mac was giving Julia's bum an appreciative pat as she slowly climbed aboard the bus, exhausted but happy.

On the bus ride into town I reflected on my other problems. By the time I got off the bus at the Council House, I had decided what to do. Or more like, what not to do. I knew that Sooty wouldn't be going far in his van because he'd had the day off from work to load the equipment for the Lord Ives gig. So the best policy was to say nothing until after we had made the drop on Sunday. Otherwise Sooty could have panicked and gone to the police or dumped the crates of rum and coke, either of which wouldn't have been healthy for me. And this way Sooty was still innocent.

Mac was late for work which I immediately saw as proof that he'd shagged himself stupid the night before. The jealousy and anger began to rise again. We started breaking down the pages of linotype slugs for melt down. Then we distributed the individual characters of type from the headlines into their respective compartments in the type cases. Mac said nothing about the previous evening. Usually at this stage he'd be telling me about how he had persuaded his prey to lie on the shag-pile rug in front of Jack's open fire. Or how he'd managed to undo her bra with one hand as he flipped through the 45rpm singles that were scattered on the floor by the Dansette record player. And how she'd shuddered with pain and pleasure as he finally 'broke her in'.

But Mac was unusually silent. This was obviously to avoid any aggressive reaction from me rather than a noble effort to spare my feelings. I was desperate to know more and tried to open him up by threatening his pride and massaging his ego. 'So how'd it go last night?' I started.

Mac paused a while before answering. 'OK thanks. She's a nice kid.'

More silence, so I decided to try to make it easier for him.

'I'm glad you've taken her off my hands mate. She'll remain a virgin until she's married that one.' I tried to sound convincing but the words hurt as they came out.

Mac was still silent but started to hum Happy Birthday Sweet Sixteen.

I was getting to him so I continued with my psychological ploy. 'Yea, even the great Mac will never crack that one. Admit it; you've met your match.'

I hated talking about Julia in this way but I had to know. 'I'll bet you didn't even get to first base.' I was bombarding Mac's pride with salvo after salvo.

Mac had stopped humming and was now singing the lyrics. He was ready to crack.

'She'd have kept her legs crossed all night, right?' I was relentless.

Mac suddenly stopped singing and turned slowly towards me. With an evil grin on his face he began to speak. 'Well if she kept her legs crossed with you Ginner, it was probably to hide that cute little mole at the top of her right thigh. And when I…'

My heart sank and I dropped a whole galley of linotype slugs across the floor. Wally came rushing out of his office to see what the commotion was and Mac never completed his sentence. After dishing out a bollocking, Wally ordered Mac to go and help out in the machine room. The chance to find out what had happened had gone. I was left on my hands and knees picking up the pieces of metal along with my shattered emotions.

I finished work at lunchtime after Wally had dispensed the little brown wages envelopes. He loved this part of his job. It was the one moment when he seemed to have lots of friends eager for his attention. He'd dish out the money as if it was his own and he was some great benefactor to mankind.

On the way to the bus station I picked up my copy of the

new Musical Express from Poynton's, the newsagents in the Market Hall. On the bus I read about how many local British beat groups were turning professional and finding work in Germany and Holland. The article explained that groups, from Liverpool in particular, were finding success in the clubs and bars of Hamburg.

That was it. The answer to all my problems. I could escape the police, the Customs and Excise and the McBrides. And now that Mac had stolen the heart and innocence of my girlfriend, I had nothing else to lose. I remembered that The Vibrons, another local group, were thinking of turning pro but their bass player didn't want to give up his apprenticeship at Rolls-Royce. So I decided to mention it to the lads after the session at the Lord Ives party and if they didn't want to come with me, I'd contact The Vibrons.

A Shot Of Rhythm and Blues
Arthur Alexander

After managing a couple of hours sleep at home I got ready for the party and caught the bus back into town. The private coach was picking all the Advertiser staff up in The Market Place. So, Mac and I weren't travelling with the rest of the group in Sooty's van – his blue Dormobile van - the van containing contraband. The van that half the police force of Derbyshire was looking for.

After boarding the coach, William Blake made a little speech saying how proud he was that the Advertiser had been so highly favoured by Derbyshire's greatest war hero. He complimented the staff on how smart they looked (The de-mob suits and chocolate box cocktail dresses had come out of mothballs again). He then explained that the party was being held in a large marquee in the grounds of Ilam Hall, the family residence of Lord Ives. He finished by asking everyone not to let the name of The Derbyshire Advertiser down and to be on their best behaviour. The bus moved off and was filled with excited chatter as the crate of brown ale was passed around.

It was a warm, hot summer night and the coach made its way towards Ashbourne, the gateway to the Peak District and some of the most beautiful countryside in England. I sat next to Mac at the back, but had decided not to return to my abortive attempt to find out how far he'd got with Julia. His knowledge of the mole on her thigh was perhaps all the evidence I needed. Despite the fact that a part of me hated Mac, I still couldn't blame him. He hadn't known how I felt about her and it appeared that she had made the first move in any case. So the subject wasn't mentioned again.

As the crate of brown ale emptied, the noise inside the bus became louder. A bottle of Sherry was passed from seat to seat for the ladies. Jack was opening his bottles of brown ale single-handed with his teeth. Brad and his assistant Edward Ellis, resplendent in their penguin suits, took turns to sip whiskey from a hip flask. And Wally had Eric cornered in his seat and, between puffs of his pipe, was telling the story of when he was invited to spend Christmas with the Duke of Devonshire at Chatsworth House.

Just as the bus started to descend the long steep hill into Ashbourne, Mac nudged me and pointed out of the back window. A blue Dormobile van was right up the backside of the bus. It was Sooty and the rest of the group. But something was wrong. The van was weaving all over the road. I could see Sooty's face peering from behind the steering wheel. He had a stupefied grin on his face and was waving something out of the window. The van suddenly swerved out into the centre of the road to overtake. As it passed, I watched in frozen horror. Tolley and Benno were hanging out of the passenger window, shouting and grinning like fools while waving half empty coke bottles. The van passed, still weaving all over the road as it headed towards the traffic lights at the bottom of the hill. I could see Whippet in the back window saluting us with a coke bottle before taking a long swig.

Most of our fellow passengers waved back enthusiastically. But Mac and I looked at each other in silence, realising that the lads had innocently decided to sample the coke in the back of the van. But of course, it was heavily laced with pure Jamaican Rum. And they must have experienced the same sensation as I had when I took my first swig of Ready Mix at Winston's uncle's party. Worse still, Sooty was driving the van in what appeared to be a state of total inebriation. All we needed now was a sharp eyed policeman from the Ashbourne constabulary and that would be it.

I doubted whether Sooty could even manoeuvre the van through the narrow streets of Ashbourne without hitting something. Mercifully, our convoy made it through the town without incident and we were suddenly off the main road and heading for Dovedale and Ilam. The van continued its mazy course and every now and then an empty coke bottle was hurled towards the leafy hedgerows of the country lanes. The bus rumbled over the cattle grid at the top of the hill to reveal the splendid view of Dovedale beneath us. But Mac and I were oblivious to the beautiful scenery. Mac took a swig from his brown ale bottle, grimaced, and nudged me.

'I wish I was drinking what the lads are drinking. This tastes like piss.'

Mac was the only person who had knowledge of my dilemma and, like me, had soon worked out the consequences of this latest twist. 'What are ya going to do about the missing bottles of Rum and Coke?' he asked.

'I was just wondering about that,' I replied.

We entered the little village of Ilam which was bedecked

with flags and bunting in celebration of the birthday of their famous Lord and master. But Mac wasn't impressed with the sleepy little hamlet. 'It must be like being buried alive livin here,' he sneered. 'I can't even see a pub.'

Ahead of us the Dormobile van was weaving its way towards the entrance to Ilam Hall. Sooty swerved into the tree-lined drive on two wheels as another empty coke bottle flew from the side window scattering a few stray chickens. At this rate I knew that the Rapids would be too pissed to play. I needed to stop the raid on the Ready Mix before things really got out of hand and my debt to the McBrides multiplied.

Mac and I were first off the bus. We ran to the van and I just managed to catch Sooty as he stumbled out from the driving seat, his cowboy hat at a jaunty angle.

'Wooh, what a ride. And what's in this coke Joe, meths?' Sooty slurred.

The other lads, who didn't appear to be as worse for wear as Sooty, gathered round waiting for an answer to his question.

'Listen lads, there's been a big mistake. You weren't meant to drink that coke,' I offered, hoping vainly that my answer would suffice.

'It's hot, it was a long journey and we were thirsty. What do you expect when there are six crates of Coca-Cola in the back of the van,' Benno argued.

'But what the fuck's in it?' demanded Tolley.

'You could have fuckin' poisoned us.' Whippet added, joining the onslaught.

'OK OK, its Rum and Coke. But lads, I'm in deep shit over this and I don't want to involve you.' I explained, having no option but to come clean.

'What are you up to, you twat?' Tolley was angry and wanted to know more.

Before I could continue with my explanation, a tall man

in a tweed suit approached us. He introduced himself as The Estate Manager of Ilam Hall and wanted us to set our equipment up in the marquee before more guests arrived. I welcomed the interruption which gave me time to think how to tell the rest of the group about my problem. Which had just become our problem. 'Listen lads, I'll tell you all about it after we've set up. But we'd better get the gear in now,' I said, pulling my Fender bass case from the back of the van.

The subject was temporarily closed and we quickly unloaded the equipment. The lads reckoned that Sooty must have downed at least six bottles. So we told him to sleep it off in the back of the van. He'd have to sober up if he was going to drive us home after dark.

The marquee at the side of Ilam Hall was magnificent. It was joined to the main building by a wide canvas corridor which was decorated with splendid flower arrangements in wrought iron stands. This opened up into the main marquee which was as big as the Locarno ballroom. The walls and pitched roof were draped with festoons of silky fabrics. An ornate waterfall, complete with mermaid and dolphin statues, gurgled away opposite the entrance. Dozens of huge round tables were laid with colour co-ordinated linen, fine crockery, silver cutlery and elaborate floral centre-pieces. At the far end a wide, tiered stage, complete with spotlights and curtained backdrop faced a specially laid dance floor. I had never seen anything quite as magnificent as these surroundings. It reminded me of the pictures I'd recently seen on television of Princess Margaret's Wedding.

We just stood for a while taking in the splendour of it all. Then Tolley spoke. 'Beats Borrowash Ex-Servicemen's Club,' he said.

'When will the Kershaws Seafood man get here?' added Benno.

We set up in front of the sixteen-piece orchestra which was billed as being 'Resident at the Dorchester Hotel in London'.

People were beginning to enter the marquee where they were offered a glass of sherry. The guests seemed to be a combination of social acquaintances of Lord Ives, civic dignitaries, residents of the village of Ilam, and the staff of the Derbyshire Advertiser. Some were in Evening Dress and there was the odd army uniform worn by wartime comrades of Lord Ives including the soldier whose life he'd saved.

The orchestra began to play, we made our way back out of the marquee to our dressing room in the main hall. As we passed the queue of guests waiting to enter, I notice a stunning looking girl with familiar dark brown, flicked-up hair. I then realised that I'd been subconsciously looking for her ever since we'd arrived. Sheila Forsythe was with her sister Lizzy and their mother and father. Sheila's face lit up when our eyes met and she called me over. Mac, who had clocked the cleavage revealed by Lizzy's cocktail dress, was right by my side.

Despite the circumstances of our last meeting, the Forsythes were extremely civil as we renewed our acquaintances. I introduced Mac who insisted on kissing the hands of Mrs Forsythe and the girls – anything for a closer look at a cleavage. Then Mr Forsythe moved slightly to one side to reveal another guest whose back had been towards us. As he turned, my heart sank and Mac took a sudden step backwards. It was a police inspector of some kind, in full uniform, with a flat hat and a cane under his arm.

'Let me introduce you to a friend of mine,' Forsythe said as the policeman turned to face us.

'Joe, Mac, this is Henry Clements, the Chief Constable of Derbyshire.' Forsythe continued the formalities. 'And he was particularly interested in your van that's parked outside.'

Mac took another step backwards, his eyes now focused on

the exit rather than Lizzy's tits. This was it. The Chief Constable would surely be aware of the search for the blue Dormobile. I tried to prepare myself for the next question. Chief Constable Clements looked stern and took a step towards me.

'Yes, er, Joe, did you know that there appears to be a cowboy asleep in the back of your van and someone has applied graffiti to the side windows?' he announced.

My relief might have been too obvious as I explained how Sooty was our manager and he was making sure that he would be alert enough to drive us back, and how girl fans often wrote messages in lipstick on local groups' vans.

Mrs Forsythe interrupted me. 'Yes. I particularly like the one that says *I've had Mac in the back.*" she said with a distasteful sniff.

Mac was almost at the exit as the Chief Constable ended the conversation.

'Well, my advice would be to remove it lads, especially on the side windows where it will obscure vision.' He turned to accept a glass of sherry and the conversation was over.

 ## Stay
Maurice Williams and The Zodiacs

Despite the police chief's apparent trivial interest in the van, I still had the feeling that matters were closing in on me. It was time to tell the lads all about it. So, before making a swift exit behind Mac, I thanked the police chief for his advice and told Sheila that I'd catch up with her after our set.

Our makeshift dressing room was the drawing room in the main buildings of Ilam Hall. It had a high ceiling with ornate cornice pieces and was furnished with fine antiques, huge gilt framed oil-paintings and a magnificent Bluthner grand piano complete with candelabra.

As we were missing dinner in the marquee the Ilam Hall

staff had organised a buffet for us which was laid out like a banquet on a lacquered dining table. We were being treated like Lords and Whippet assumed the part. He donned a smoking jacket that he found in an cupboard and gracefully reclined in an armchair beside the huge fireplace.

'More caviar, Jeeves! And see if her ladyship has finished dressing for dinner,' he mocked.

We sat formally at the table and tucked into game pie, poached salmon, roast beef and a large bowl of exotic fruit. Despite being alone, the ambience of the room inspired us to apply good manners and be on our best behaviour. Tolley delicately dabbed mayonnaise from the corner of his mouth. 'Exquisite salmon, chaps,' he commented.

'The quails eggs are perhaps slightly overcooked,' added Benno.

Then Mac, choking on his game pie, brought us all back down to earth. 'I could do with summat to wash this fucker down with.' He frowned, looking up and down the table for liquid.

'Why not get some of Joe's fuckin special brew from the van,' offered Tolley, now back to himself.

The lads stopped eating and turned towards me. It was time to tell them all about my problem. At that moment Sooty stumbled into the room, still looking a little groggy but better for his sleep. They all listened silently as I told them every detail including the article in the Advertiser, the telephoned threat from the McBrides and how it seemed that the Customs and Excise had dug their claws into the case and were determined to make an example of all concerned. Then I pointed out the problem of the missing bottles of Ready Mix that would surely be noticed and come to the attention of the McBrides. Sooty listened opened mouthed as he began to realise what he was involved in. I ended by announcing what I intended to do about the sorry mess and ensure that they wouldn't be implicated.

'First of all, I've decided that the best thing is for me to make the drop at the Crown Hotel,' I started. 'I'm going to replace the missing bottles with real Coke from the bar here. Then, tomorrow morning I want Sooty to drive me to The Crown to deliver the crates.' The lads listened in silence as I spoke.

'The McBrides will think that Sooty is unaware of the scam so when they discover the missing bottles, they won't come after him,' I continued.

'But what about you?' interrupted Sooty.

I paused before answering, making sure in my own mind that I wanted to follow my plans through. 'By the time the McBrides find out or the authorities become involved I'll be out of the country and you won't have to worry,' I concluded.

There was silence while it sunk in and then everyone started speaking at once.

'Why? Where are you going? What about the group? What about your job?' And then Mac had the nerve to say 'What about Julia?'

I told them that I planned to escape to Hamburg with The Vibrons.

More silence. And then Tolley stood up and walked over to the fireplace with his hands behind his back like a school teacher. He seemed deep in thought but then turned to face me and started to speak. 'First of all you're going nowhere. There's no way the Rapids are going to lose the best bass guitarist in town,' he announced.

It was uncharacteristic of Tolley to hand out praise and I was genuinely touched.

'Secondly, I'm not scared of the McBrides.' He turned towards the others. 'We are five fit blokes, and if we can't deal with a skinny little psychopath and a short, fat bastard, there's something wrong,' he continued.

The others nodded in agreement as Tolley walked over

towards me. 'And finally, we're not just a group. We're best mates, soul mates and we love you, you twat.' He put his hand around my shoulders and turned to the others. 'We're gonna stand by Joe, aren't we lads?' he concluded.

They all immediately voiced their agreement and my eyes filled up. We all hugged and a lump came to my throat as I struggled to control my emotions.

Mac debunked the situation once again. 'Ginner, just help me get my hands on that Lizzy Forsyth's tits and I'll be your bodyguard twenty-four hours a day,' he said with a lecherous leer.

'What's wrong with mine?' shouted Whippet, stuffing two Jaffa oranges down his shirt.

He was still prancing round with Mac in pursuit when a butler, dressed in morning suit and winged collared shirt, walked into the room with a small crate of Coke. He put it down shakily, placed a hand to his mouth and coughed politely. 'Er, the Coca-Cola you ordered gentlemen,' he spluttered.

Sooty insisted that the butler open a bottle for him to try. He then suspiciously sniffed the amber liquid before nodding for the rest to be poured. When we stopped laughing, we drank the coke and got ready for our performance.

We returned to the marquee in our stage suits where the ball was in full swing. Dinner was over and most of the guests were crowded round the two bar areas where wine flowed freely and beer was dispensed continuously from a row of wooden barrels. The orchestra from the Dorchester had managed to get a few guests onto the dance floor but it was a strange spectacle. There were couples in evening dress doing the tango like contestants in *Come Dancing*, younger couples trying to jive or twist to the orchestra's Latin rendition of *In a Little Spanish Town* and, in the middle of the floor, there was Wally who was leading the Advertiser's Women's Page editor, Rosemary Bagnell, in a cross between the military two-step and a barn dance. But everyone was happy and ready to party.

The orchestra ended its set and, having warmed up the audience, handed over to us. The lights dimmed briefly as we took our positions and then Whippet started the drum beat to *Let's Dance*. A single spotlight picked out Mac and he shouted us into a full-blooded version of the Chris Montez chart-topper.

'*Hey baby won't you take a chance…*'

The rest of the lights flooded the stage and everyone made a rush for the dance floor. Those who didn't dance stood round the front of the stage clapping or moving to the beat. And right at the front were Sheila and Lizzy. Sheila looked up at me with an expression that suggested that she missed me. But the hurt I felt over losing Julia was still subduing my lust. Mac, on the other hand, was totally focused on Lizzy's breasts. His vocal delivery seemed directed at his objects of desire as he peered down from his elevated position.

We finished the number to tremendous applause and Mac swung straight into *Lucille*. More guests crowded onto the dance floor and the whole fabric of the marquee seemed to be moving to the beat.

The bonding session in the dressing room had injected new passion and fury into our performance which, in turn, fuelled the frenzied enthusiasm of the audience. There was even louder applause as the number ended and Mac walked forward. He took his mic from the stand with one hand and gestured for the applause to cease with the other.

'Thanks. Ok! Yea!' He waited for the applause to die down. 'Thanks. What a great crowd!' he shouted.

Then he walked right up to the front and looked directly down at Lizzy. 'Hey love.' He shouted down the mic. 'If you're gonna drown those two puppies luv, I'll have the one with the pink nose!'

Most of the audience got his well-worn joke but there were a few frowns from the Forsyths and their friends. Lizzy blushed as she tried to cover herself up by crossing her hands over her chest. But she did give Mac an encouraging smile which I had seen girls do before. Not just the girl from the pet stall in the Market Hall but Julia, and I knew he was in there with Lizzy.

Mac retreated a little and announced the next number. 'Now folks, here's a number which is a dedication from our bass player, Joe, to the other beautiful girl at the front of the stage.'

Whippet started the Buddy Holly style drumming and Mac came in on cue.

'Sweet little Sheila, you'll know her if you see her…'

Mac was obviously trying to make up for taking Julia away from me. Sheila, flattered and encouraged by the bogus dedication, smiled up at me throughout the song. And for most of the rest of the set.

We finished with the Chan Remero number *Hippy Hippy Shake* to tremendous applause. Even Lord Ives had been jigging around the floor and I wondered if his obituary was still set in type back at the Advertiser.

 ## Under The Moon Of Love
Curtis Lee

Back in the dressing room, after towelling off the sweat, I grabbed a couple of bottles of coke and went to find Sheila. I found her waiting for me by the entrance to the marquee and she ran towards me. We kissed formally.

'Joe, that was great. The Rapids have come on a bit since I last saw you at The Crown,' she said as I took her hand.

'Yea, but I don't know how long it's going to last,' I found myself saying.

'What do you mean?' she asked.

I realised that, now I didn't have Julia, I still needed

someone else to tell me that everything would be alright. Not just someone with common sense or reasoning, but someone warm, soft and feminine who would provide comfort and assurance.

We walked behind the marquee and into the beautifully manicured gardens of Ilam Hall with their exotic plants and flowering shrubs. The light was fading fast but the night was still warm. Sheila held onto my arm as we crossed the lawns in the dusk and made our way down towards the river. The music and merriment from the marquee faded and was replaced with the natural sounds of an English summer evening and the rippling waters of the Manifold. As we walked, I told her everything; about the crates of illicit booze in the back of the van and about the threat from the McBrides. I even told her about Mac taking Julia from me and of my plan to skip the country. We sat on the grassy bank beside the narrow river and watched the reflection of the moon dance on top of the water. I opened the coke bottles with my teeth and passed one to Sheila. She quickly checked to make sure there wasn't a cross scratched onto the cap, then drank from the bottle.

'Well Joe,' she started. 'You've got yourself into a right mess, haven't you?'

There was no kissing my nose and telling me everything would be alright. She just looked up at me sternly and continued her scolding. 'I really think you should go straight to the police and tell them everything before it's too late and they catch up with you. But that's up to you.' She paused before continuing.

Her coolness suddenly seemed to melt away and she looked away. 'And as for Julia, I know you really love her and that she loves you. You'll never think of me that way.'

She became melancholy and fell silent, lost in her own thoughts. After a few moments she looked back up at me.

'I think about you all the time, Joe. But I know it could never happen between us.'

I put my arm round her and pulled her closer to me. Her admission had taken me by surprise and I didn't know how else to respond. Julia had never told me how she felt about me. 'Do you like me as much as your horse?' I said, trying to lighten the situation.

Sheila tried to smile. 'You will always be special to me Joe but you're just messing about. Once you'd had me you'd be looking for another notch on your bass guitar.' She squeezed my hand tightly and retreated back into thought.

'You will always be special to me too,' I replied.

'It still wouldn't work,' she said with a shrug of her shoulders. 'My parents would never approve and you would always feel uncomfortable with my family. That's why Lizzy's Malcolm has to pretend he's something he's not,' she explained. 'No. The only hope would be for us to run away together,'

She hesitated before continuing. 'So just remember, if things don't work out for you tomorrow, I'll come to Germany with you.'

I could tell that she meant it and I was overcome and humbled by her obvious devotion. She was right in everything she had said and perhaps at that moment I had started to really love her. I took her in my arms and we just hugged for a while in the moonlight.

Songs of Danger

 Let The Little Girl Dance
Billy Bland

Sheila and I walked back to the marquee, hand-in-hand but in silence. The noise from the party gradually destroyed the peace and tranquillity.

As we entered the main building we passed the Chief Constable in the hallway who was on the telephone and appeared to be issuing urgent instructions. When he saw me he hesitated briefly, then turned his back on us and continued his conversation in a hushed tone. I was sure he was on to me and wondered if he'd discovered the illicit bottles of Rum and Coke in the back of the van. I thought he could be phoning for assistance and that Ilam Hall would soon be surrounded by policemen with loud hailers and dogs.

Sheila hadn't noticed my concern and interrupted my thoughts. 'Come on Joe, you can take me for the last waltz.'

The party atmosphere had lifted her mood. She took my hand and dragged me down the corridor and into the main marquee. The orchestra leader had announced the last number of the evening and the dance floor was full of revellers. Most were feeling the effects of excessive alcohol. Some glided round the floor with their partners like professional ballroom dancers. Others just clung on for dear life in an effort to stay upright. But everyone was happy and appeared not to have a care in the world. Unlike me with the weight of the Derbyshire Constabulary, Customs and Excise, the notorious McBride brothers, two would-be lovers and the fabulous Rapids, all precariously perched on my wilting shoulders.

Sheila and I danced close together and I felt the comfort of her warm body next to mine. She was still unaware of my latest concern and was determined to teach me how to waltz. 'One two three. One two three. One two three.' she kept repeating as we stumbled round the floor.

But I was preoccupied with other things and was straining to hear the sound of police sirens above the last offering from the orchestra. Sooty suddenly appeared by the side of us. 'Come on Joe. It's time to load the van and get the hell out of here,' he shouted.

Behind Sooty I could see the Chief Constable looking impatiently at his watch. Although I was reluctant to leave Sheila I realised that we had to take ourselves and the blue Dormobile van as far away from Ilam Hall as possible. I made my excuses and we kissed long and hard right in the middle of the dance floor. But I had a strange feeling that I would never see her again.

'Good luck Joe! And promise you'll phone me tomorrow,' she whispered in my ear. 'Remember what I said earlier,' she shouted after me as I rushed off with Sooty.

Outside, the lads were already loading the equipment into the back of the van. I returned to the dressing room with Sooty to collect my bass amplifier and quickly secreted a dozen bottles of pure coke in the back of the speaker cabinet. Back at the van, I searched out the empty slots in the coke crates and replaced the missing bottles of Ready Mix.

I told the lads about the Chief Constable's phone calls and Sooty quickly checked that everything was on board. 'Let's get out of here then!' he shouted, jumping into the driving seat.

It was then that I noticed that someone was missing. 'Where's Mac?' I shouted.

We all saw him at once. He was climbing over a fence between the large, sweeping, in-and-out drive and a field at the side of the Hall. Behind him was Lizzy Forsythe.

Benno and Whippet applauded as he ran towards the van still zipping up his fly. Tolley was less impressed. 'Can't you leave it in ya fuckin' trousers just for once? You're like a rat up a drain.'

I kept quiet because I noticed that Mr and Mrs Forsythe and Sheila were leaving the Hall at that very moment. With them was an agitated police chief who seemed to panic when he saw the headlights hit the gravel and the van move slowly down the drive with Mac in pursuit. Lizzy walked sheepishly over to her speechless parents still adjusting her dress. Mac caught up with us and leapt into the van, sliding the door shut behind him. Sooty put his foot on the gas, spitting gravel in the direction of the gaping onlookers, and we were away.

I looked out of the back window as we sped away. Sheila was waving, Lizzy was waving. Even Mr Forsythe was waving - his fist - while Mrs. Forsythe appeared to be in tears. The red-faced Chief Constable was rushing frantically back towards the Hall, perhaps to the telephone.

 Road Runner
Bo Diddly

As we careered round the wide, sweeping, tree-lined drive towards the main gates, Sooty let out a whoop like a cowboy heading his herd across a prairie. In the back, the lads held onto the equipment as it bounced from one side of the van to the other. I steadied the crates of Ready Mix as they rattled and clinked with every bump.

Just before the gates Sooty braked hard and we all lurched forwards. A black Wolsey police car with its blue light flashing was turning off the road and into the drive towards us. Sooty hesitated for a second then hit the gas pedal. The police car swerved to avoid us and we passed it between the large pillars of the gate with inches to spare.

'That's fuckin done it. If they weren't onto us before they are now,' shouted Tolley as he wrestled with a speaker cabinet.

'They gotta catch us first,' answered Sooty who seemed to be enjoying every moment.

I wondered if Sooty had recognised that this was another golden opportunity to fulfil his rock'n'roll related death wish. We raced through the sleeping village and onto the narrow road to Dovedale. Behind us the police car, its blue light flashing, was only just pulling back out of Ilam Hall to start its pursuit.

'Let's dump the fuckin stuff now,' shouted Benno.

'No, we've got to think this through,' I protested.

'Don't worry guys, I'll lose em,' yelled Sooty, who had suddenly assumed an American accent.

As we approached the small humped-back bridge on the bend at Dovedale, Sooty killed the lights and swung into a small car park frequented by ramblers and hikers, but he didn't stop. He drove the van across the car park, then slowly through a narrow gap in a hedge and onto a footpath at the side of the river. When the van was almost completely covered by overhanging trees he hit the brakes and we skidded to a halt, the back end sliding precariously towards the river.

No one spoke. Our gazes were all fixed on the bridge behind us. Sure enough, the blue lights of the police car briefly illuminated the bridge as it passed over the river and wound its way up the hill towards Thorpe village.

There was a collective sigh of relief. Then we all piled out of the van and watched the police car disappear over the top of the hill. We sat in silence by the edge of the shallow river. Sooty swaggered up to Mac and threw him a cigarette as if he'd just successfully crash-landed a B52 bomber. After the trauma of the chase, everything seemed incredibly peaceful. The full moon hung over the flat top of Thorpe Cloud which towered above us. The riverside was bathed in a beautiful silvery light that reflected on the ripples of the crystal clear, shallow river. It was almost like daylight and we could see fish swimming over the stones on the riverbed.

I thought how romantic the setting was and how it would

have been the perfect place to have brought Julia. But when I imagined turning to kiss her on the stepping stones over the river, it was Sheila's face I saw.

Mac was oblivious to the beauty and was the first to speak. He took a long drag of his cigarette, sucking the smoke back up his nose and out again. 'Well! Come on then! Let's dump the fuckin' crates in the drink and get off home. This place gives me the fuckin creeps,' he shouted, startling a couple of wood pigeons in a nearby tree.

'No', I protested. 'If they find the stuff here, they're sure to link it to us.'

'But I don't think you should wait until tomorrow. Or make the drop at the Crown,' advised Tolley.

'Yea, the feds are onto us now and they'll probably have the Crown staked out tomorrow,' agreed Sooty.

During the chase I had thought that things were becoming too hot and that immediate action was necessary. I decided that it was up to me to take responsibility.

'Ok, this is what's going to happen. Sooty and I will drop you lot off home and then we'll dump the crates in the Derwent down by Spondon power station,' I announced decisively.

'But we've still gotta get back to town unnoticed,' Whippet pointed out with concern.

'A piece of piss,' exclaimed Sooty, sticking his hat back on his head as if it was a flying helmet. 'I'll avoid the main roads and take us back through the country lanes,' he continued, heading back to the van.

'But what happens to you two when the McBrides find out that the drop hasn't been made?' asked Benno.

Tolley stood up slowly. 'We'll deal with those bastards if we have to. Won't we? Are we men or mice?' he asked, challengingly.

We all agreed on the plan and returned to the van.

Sooty drove back to town through narrow country lanes and sleepy villages. The only vehicles we saw were the occasional cars parked in field entrances with the windows steamed-up. Whenever we came across one of these hot beds of passion, Sooty slowed the van right down and we all let out a whoop. Although Mac became increasingly frustrated by the fact that other people in the world were having sex besides him. We slowed down to a crawl as we approached a little red MG Midget parked on the grass verge.

'I wish I was in there instead of being stuck in here with you lot.' Mac complained.

'There's not enough room in there for two, let alone three.' I answered sarcastically.

Tolley joined in the banter. 'Hey! I'm sure that's your missus in there Sooty and she's got nothin on but her cowboy hat!'

Sooty took the bait and slammed on the brakes coming to a stop just ahead of the little sports car. The full moon provided more than adequate light to see two naked bodies thrashing about in a frantic effort to find their clothes.

We all cheered and clapped and when Sooty was satisfied that it wasn't his Marlene, he accelerated away.

Mac had the last word. 'Give it one for me mate,' he shouted from the side window.

We made it to the Ring Road without seeing another vehicle but we knew that this would be the difficult bit. Sooty had decided to proceed through the back streets but as we headed towards town, Benno noticed a black car slip silently out of a garage forecourt behind us.

Sooty peered in the mirror. 'Is it the feds?' he shouted.

We all watched nervously as the black car gathered speed and gained on us. Then, the quiet of the night was shattered by the distinctive be bah, be bah of a police siren. A blue light flashed its warning from the radiator grille of the black Wolsey.

Inside the van it was panic stations.

'Lose em Sooty.'

'No! We'll have to stop.'

'What the fuck are we gonna do?'

'Let's get out and run for it!'

Sooty's instinct was to hit the gas pedal. But ahead of us was a further obstacle. Slewed across the road was another police car, its headlights on full beam, doors open and two uniformed policemen standing at the side of the makeshift road block.

The game was up.

I Fought The Law
The Crickets

Sooty had no choice but to bring the van to a halt. We just sat there in silence and waited for something to happen. I still had one hand on the stack of coke crates but moved in front in an effort to conceal them. The policemen conferred for what seemed liked minutes and finally two of them wandered nonchalantly over to the passenger door of the van. The most senior looking, a big man with sergeant's stripes on his arm, indicated for the door to be opened. Mac demonstrated his hatred for the police by cowering in the far corner and adopting one of his most evil sneers. The rest of us instinctively went for the handle together, then simultaneously backed off. The sergeant became impatient and slid the door back himself with a bang. He took his helmet off and poked his big fat face inside the van.

'Well, well, well lads, and what have we got in here then?' he asked, looking us all up and down in turn.

'We're a beat group and it's our equipment,' replied Sooty nervously.

A skinny policeman with a torch joined the sergeant

and craned his neck into the van. The sergeant turned to address him.

'We've got the bloody Shadows in here Jim,' he said to his partner, sarcastically. 'And which one of you is Stiff Richard?'

His partner, who was more interested in our equipment, shone his torch around the van and rested its beam on the coke crates I was half concealing. His beady eyes found mine.

'Is it thirsty work this Rock'n'roll then?' he asked, pointing at the crates with his torch.

I had to think fast. 'Oh this,' I answered, pushing the crates another inch towards the back of the van. 'We're playing at a sixteenth birthday party tomorrow and we agreed to supply the liquid refreshments,' I lied.

Sooty was quick to latch on.

'Yes, it's only Coke officer, and my mum's making the sausage rolls,' he added, unnecessarily.

The big policeman also became interested in the crates. 'Let's have a look at those bottles, lad,' he said to me.

I hesitated and then slid the crates forward a few inches. The silence inside the van became even more obvious. You could have heard a plectrum drop. I just prayed that the others would stay calm.

Then, the worst thing imaginable happened. The skinny cop removed his helmet and tugged at his tie. 'Phew! It's a warm night, lads. You can spare one of those cokes, can't you?' he asked, licking his lips and reaching further into the van.

Again, I had to think quickly. In the gloom, I scanned the bottle tops in search of the ones without a cross scratched into the metal, crown caps - the ones containing 100% pure Coca-Cola which I had nicked from Ilam Hall. All fingers and thumbs, I passed a bottle to the expectant policeman. He snapped open the top using an opener which was attached to a bunch of keys on his trouser belt. Keys that could be locking us up before long, I reflected. I was sure that these cops knew what they were looking for.

We watched in silence as he sniffed at his drink and to our relief, downed it in one. But worse was to follow. The sergeant, hand outstretched, had been waiting for his subordinate to share the drink.

'Bloody hell Jim, you could have saved some for me!' he exclaimed.

Then, before we knew what was happening, he stretched forwards and dragged the crates towards him. 'You don't mind, do you lads?' the sergeant asked politely.

His fat fingers hovered agonisingly slowly over the crates. His sausage-like thumb and forefinger idly traced the bottle tops. I watched in horror as he paused over one of the bottles of Ready Mix marked with its tell-tail cross. The rest of the lads just gaped, open-mouthed. Mac huddled further into the corner. Sweat was dripping down the back of my neck.

Then I sighed with relief as the sergeant gripped one of the pure Coke bottles. But then he was suddenly distracted as the other policeman offered his bottle opener. The sergeant's hand moved one place along the row of bottles, hovered for a second, and in one swift movement, pulled a bottle of Ready Mix bottle from the crate.

I winced as he held the bottle out for his partner to open. The lads could see from my expression that the shit was about to hit the fan. Eyes shut tight in readiness to accept our fate, I slumped against the inside of the van. It was deathly silent. Almost in slow motion, the bottle opener made contact with the crown cap. This was it.

'Snap, fizz'

Be ba, be bar, be bar.

A police siren shattered the silence. The sergeant spun round in alarm and dropped the coke bottle which smashed, sending shards of glass fizzing across the floor on a river of rum and coke.

One of the policemen from the roadblock car, its siren blaring, poked his head into the van.

'It's the McBrides! They've just done a handbrake turn to avoid us and are heading back out of town,' he shouted breathlessly.

We could see the tail fins of the pink and white Cresta accelerating away in a cloud of dust. Without noticing the distinctive smell of rum, the sergeant shouted fresh instructions to his colleagues.

'Come on, these lads are clean, but it looks as if our friends the McBrides have something to hide.'

And with that, both police cars disappeared up the road. We just sat there for a while, emotionally drained. I needed a drink and instinctively grabbed a bottle from the crate. Biting the silver crossed top off with my teeth, I downed the Rum and Coke in one.

'That's it!' shouted Tolley, as if he'd found the solution to the problem. 'Let's drink the fuckin' evidence.'

And with that the other lads joined me.

 ## The Point Of No Return
Gene McDaniels

It had been a narrow escape and we realised that the sooner Sooty and I dumped the crates in the Derwent the better. After persuading Mac to hand over the bottles of Ready Mix he had stuffed into his pockets, we dropped him off in town where he had parked his motorbike.

We made it back to Borrowash without further incident and, after unloading the equipment into Tolley's garage, we dropped Whippet and Benno off.

It was past 2 am. as we drove back towards Spondon Power

Station and the giant Celanese factory which dominated the skyline. The factory never slept, it just slumbered. Whatever time of day or night, the hum of the processing plant was evident in the sprawling suburb of Spondon. But the cocktail of chemicals it used could be smelt much further afield. The Celanese factory was a town within a town. It had named roads, a railway network, its own shops and even a bank. Thousands of workers toiled round the clock in shifts, deep in the belly of this huge, ugly, smelly monster. Some workers never came out alive, there were frequent stories of horrific accidents involving vats of slimy chemicals. At night, the factory was particularly scary. The plant was dimly lit with an eerie green light. Every now and then coloured clouds of chemicals belched forth from the maze of pipes and chimneys that encased the huge assortment of grimy buildings. And strange, unidentifiable sounds echoed across the night sky as if the monster was crying in pain or getting ready to terminate another of its employees.

We had decided to dump the crates in a stretch of river next to the side of the power station which served the Celanese plant and the surrounding areas. We drove off the main road and into the mile long, isolated service road which led to the three giant cooling towers that were silhouetted against the night sky. As we got closer, the slumbering monster seemed to stir. The hum became a murmur and the acrid smell of chemicals became more intense. As if in warning of imminent danger, a distant siren sounded and a yellow cloud of steam thundered from the side of a huge silo. I began to feel uncomfortable. It was like driving down the road to hell.

'Shit,' Sooty cursed, looking into the rear view mirror. 'We've been spotted'.

About five hundred yards behind us we could see the dim outline of a car, its headlights dipped.

'It's not the police, is it?' I said, trying to identify the shape of the pursuing vehicle.

'Naw, it's probably a security patrol or a courting couple,' he replied, hitting the accelerator.

The car kept pace with us. Then, as the full moon reappeared from behind a passing cloud, I caught a glimpse of the vehicle's two-tone bodywork. Pink and white.

'It's the fuckin McBrides,' I shouted.

'Ya joking! What the fuck are they up to?' replied Sooty.

'They've probably got wind of our plan and want to protect their investment,' I suggested.

The van sped towards the power station, now completely dwarfed by the cooling towers. We were both scared. We knew that the McBrides were capable of anything and would probably be armed with knives or even Tony McBride's famous sawn-off shotgun. Sooty changed down a gear and slammed his foot to the floor in a vain effort to make the Dormobile go faster. We were hurtling towards the foot of one of the giant cooling towers and the McBrides were right behind us. Suddenly, we were driving underneath the massive concrete structure after narrowly missing one of its supporting sections. Water and steam engulfed the van, too much for the little windscreen wipers to cope with. Sooty was driving blind. All we could see ahead of us was total blackness and the torrents of water that crashed against the windscreen. I thought we were going to die.

'Get the fuck out of here!' I yelled.

But Sooty, eyes bulging, stared silently ahead. At nothing.

My brain tried to take me from the danger. I opened the door in my mind to my special room and when I saw the Bal-Ami juke-box in the corner and the red Coke chiller cabinet, I began to feel calmer. Although the black and white leopard skin studio couch seemed to have blood splashed all over it. Once inside the sanctuary of The Sunset Lounge, I slammed the door behind me. But I wasn't safe. As the door banged shut the ceiling caved in. Steam and water cascaded down from above, drenching my prized possessions and destroying the comfort of my little haven.

A bump from underneath the van brought me back to reality. We had hit a ramp and the van was flying out the other side of the cooling tower. But as the wipers finally dealt with the diminishing deluge they gradually revealed a stationary obstacle right in front of us. A two-tone pink and white Vauxhall Cresta.

Sooty slammed on the brakes and we ground to a halt inches from the car. Both McBrides were out of their vehicle, one on either side. The eerie light from the chemical plant silhouetted them with a green halo. They looked even more menacing than usual and we stayed in our seats waiting for something to happen.

Gra McBride took a step forwards. 'Well, I've never seen your crappy little van look so clean,' he shouted. 'And ya were on ya way to dump our stuff, weren't ya?' he continued.

Sooty and I glanced at each other wondering how they knew.

Tony McBride spoke next as if he had read our minds. 'Yes! Your shitty singer told us all about it,' he yelled.

I slid open the passenger door of the van. 'Where is he? What have you done to him?'

'Well, he's probably on his way to hospital if he's lucky,' replied Gra McBride.

'Yes! Had a nasty accident on his bike. Just after our little chat with him,' continued Tony McBride with a sadistic smirk on his face.

I noticed that there was a dent in the front wing of the Cresta. He suddenly stopped smiling, twitched, and looked nervously over his shoulder as a purple cloud of chemicals belched from the monster behind him.

'We gently persuaded him to tell us about your double-crossing plan,' explained Gra McBride.

'Yea, and he won't be shakin' his skinny legs on stage for while,' added Tony McBride, eyes turned towards the night sky as if he was enjoying the recall of his actions.

'Now get out the fuckin' van,' shouted Gra McBride impatiently.

At this, Tony McBride slowly produced something from behind his back. Sooty and I watched in horror as he revealed the unmistakable shape of a sawn-off shotgun.

Fear sent adrenaline coursing through my veins. The hairs on the back of my neck stood to attention. These thugs would obviously stop at nothing to avoid detection. I shot a glance at Sooty who looked as if he was about to slam the van in reverse and attempt a getaway.

'Get out the fuckin van,' yelled Tony McBride, raising his weapon.

I saw Sooty's left hand move for the gear stick and I instinctively pushed it away. I knew it wouldn't be any good. He looked at me and I shook my head. Then we both climbed slowly from the van and stood side-by-side like defeated soldiers ready to face the firing squad.

'There's good news and bad news, lads,' Gra McBride said, pacing up and down in front of the Cresta. The good news is that ya had the right idea, the cops are hot on our trail and we've gotta dump the stuff,' he continued.

'So what's the bad news?' I asked nervously.

He stopped pacing. There was an ominous period of silence as the McBrides looked at each other. Tony McBride twitched and glanced over his shoulder again as a siren wailed somewhere in the distance and a roar from a silo announced the expulsion of another green cloud of chemicals.

Gra McBride eventually spoke. 'You've been involved with our production process. You know all about our operation. And about our distribution network.' He took another few paces in front of the Cresta and then whirled round.

'You even know our source of su-fuckin-ply,' he finished angrily. Then, after hesitating for effect, he lowered his voice. 'You two are a big danger to us.' He shook his head from side to side as if he only had one choice in the matter.

'A big danger,' repeated Tony McBride, while massaging his shotgun.

A flash-back of the blood splattered leopard skin studio couch flashed into my brain.

Sooty finally spoke.

'We're not going to say anything. Are we Joe?' he offered with a nervous smile.

I remained silent, keeping my eyes on the shotgun. I was too busy wondering whether to hit the ground or run if its sights were set in my direction.

'Of course ya not,' Gra McBride answered for me.

'Yea! Just remember, ya the only group in town with a cripple for a singer,' added his brother.

'So this is what ya going to do,' Gra McBride ordered.

I felt a wave of relief at the confirmation that we weren't going to be shot on the spot.

'Ya going to drive the van down to the river and we're going to watch while you smash each and every bottle against the weir.'

'Then what?' I asked defiantly.

'Just get back in the van and drive. We'll be right behind you,' he shouted, turning to get in the Cresta. His deranged brother pointed his gun at us, ushering us into the van.

When the Cresta had moved out of the way, Tony waved us on pointing towards a rough track with his shotgun.

I needed a another drink, Dutch courage, and opened two bottles of Ready Mix with my teeth, passing one to Sooty as he started to inch forwards. The dimly lit track rose to a hill top in the general direction of the river. The Cresta was right behind us with Tony McBride waving his weapon threateningly from the window, urging us forwards. As we reached the top of the hill, a full panoramic view of the Celanese plant unfolded before us. An array of coloured lights popping up over our horizon and twinkling between clouds of drifting steam and smoke. Below us the track dropped steeply for about 500 yards, curving down towards the river and a concrete weir. Sooty slowed to a virtual crawl but the Cresta urged us on. I wondered what the McBrides planned to do with us after we had destroyed the evidence.

Sooty was obviously having the same disturbing thoughts. 'Should we make a dash for it?' Sooty suddenly shouted.

'It's a dead end,' I replied. 'There's no way out'.

I took a swig of Rum and Coke. Then, suddenly, a different sound cut through the industrial hum. It was the distinctive wail of police sirens. I spun round to see blue flashing lights on the power station service road about a mile behind us. The McBrides had heard it too. And that's when all hell broke loose.

The Cresta suddenly smashed into the back of the van, pushing us forwards over the top of the hill. Sooty accelerated to avoid another collision but the car hit us again, forcing the pace. We were now hurtling down the hill towards the river, the car still inches behind. It then became clear to us both; with the police on the scene, the McBrides had now decided that there was a much quicker way to destroy the evidence. And make sure that there was no one left around to grass them up.

The Cresta hit us again. We were now doing over fifty miles an hour.

'They're trying to put us in the river,' shouted Sooty.

For the second time in minutes I prepared myself for the worst. Sooty had to brake to negotiate a bend in the track and the Cresta hit us even harder. The crates crashed against the back doors then slid forwards, smashing against the front seats and sending a fizzing shower of Rum and Coke up our backs.

Sooty wrestled with the steering wheel as the van raced on. 'I can't control it,' he screamed, wiping Ready Mix and sweat from his eyes.

We missed the bend completely and hit a rock at the side of the track. The van was launched into the air. It smashed through a wooden fence at waist height. We were airborne, clipping the tops of small trees and shrubs. I glanced at Sooty who suddenly looked ridiculous in his Stetson hat. In front of us; the spectacular illuminated panoramic view of the Chemical plant; below us, the rough terrain, falling sharply away.

It became quiet, almost serene. We were floating like a satellite in space. But I knew that this window of calm would soon be shattered. And so would I.

This'll be the day that I die.

Songs of Desperation

Falling
Roy Orbison

This'll be the day that I die. We were falling, trapped in metal. Yet it had become strangely quiet. Almost serene. The lights below started to gather speed and race towards us.

I was afraid and sad at the same time. Looking for hope or comfort, I glanced over at the man in the Stetson hat as he wrestled in vain to control our fate. But he was totally preoccupied. He swiped wildly at the condensation that was gathering on the inside of the small windscreen. His wide eyes were staring dead ahead, transfixed by the inevitable events that were unfolding in front of us. His knuckles, white, drained of blood, gripped the controls as he tried to steer. But there was nothing to steer.

My knuckles were white too, from gripping the contours of a coke bottle, the contents of which I had started in what seemed like another time and place.

The speeding lights, bigger and brighter now, were almost upon us. I could see the ground - a field, fences, shrubs. I closed my eyes and thought of my family. And of the girl who, I suddenly realised, would have had my love forever. But forever was nearly over.

Minutes, seconds, or milli-seconds passed. Nothing had happened. So I opened my eyes. Only to have them slammed shut by an unimaginable, violent and totally irresistible force.

Eventually I did open my eyes again, slowly waking from the dreadful nightmare. But I wasn't staring at the cracks in my bedroom ceiling. There were stars above me and in my head. A yellow cloud passed over the moon. I felt numb as if my body was separated from my head and tried to look down to see if it was. Pain shot down my back. I tried looking to my right where, from the corner of my eye, there appeared to be a pile of twisted metal, hissing and heaving like an ugly monster in its death throes. I could see part of a broken wing sticking out of the ground, next to it a crumpled Stetson hat and beyond, a body. The figure looked to be sleeping peacefully except for the fact that one leg was twisted up towards the night sky at a hideous angle.

I began to come to my other senses. There were noises like wailing sirens. A green, gaseous cloud passed above the bizarre montage of broken images. Where was I? What had happened? Was I still alive? This strange, surreal landscape certainly wasn't heaven.

 ## Valley Of Tears
Buddy Holly

A sudden gust of wind lifted Sooty's hat and threw it against the piece of broken front wing that had been ripped from the Dormobile. But there was no movement from the body that lay beyond. My mind quickly engaged. I was still alive, but was Sooty?

I tried to get up to see if I could help my friend. It was then that I noticed that I was still clutching the coke bottle. Despite the carnage that surrounded me, it had survived intact. And thankfully, so had I.

The sirens were louder and right behind me. I managed to get to my knees and turn my head towards the noise to look for help. Silhouetted against the moonlit cooling towers, the distinctive shapes of British bobbies were running in several directions, holding their helmets to their heads like slap stick characters from a silent movie.

They were after the McBrides and a rugby tackle brought the thick figure of Graham McBride to the ground. His more agile, wiry brother lasted longer and led the chase down towards the river. Other truncheon-wielding, uniformed figures were running towards me. I tried to shout, but my throat was full of dust. 'Never mind me. Go and help my mate!' I rasped.

They ignored my pleas and were suddenly upon me. Realising that I wasn't badly hurt, they unceremoniously dumped me face down with my hands behind my back. I felt cold steel against my flesh as a pair of handcuffs gripped my wrists.

'Please, he needs help,' I pleaded.

But other men in blue were already on their way to Sooty's twisted body. Their colleagues had caught up with Tony McBride who had obviously tried to use the river as a means of escape. He was being dragged, wet through like a drowned rat, towards a police van.

There were more sirens and more heavy booted footsteps. I turned my head back towards the crumpled wreckage to see Sooty's body being gently lifted onto a stretcher. A medic picked up the Stetson and carefully laid it on top of his blanket covered body.

I found myself wailing Sooty's name. But the response was from two burly policemen who, satisfied that I wasn't badly hurt, dragged me off towards the waiting van. I was being treated like a hardened criminal and was obviously perceived as being one of the McBrides gang of Rum smugglers.

I was too upset about Sooty to be concerned about my own predicament. 'Is my friend alright?' I said to one of my captors.

'Shut it!' came the reply as I was bundled into the back of the van, 'Just thank your lucky stars you were thrown clear.'

After being wedged between the two burly cops on a bench seat, I found myself facing the handcuffed McBrides. We sat in silence but as we trundled our way back to the main road on our way to town, Gra McBride shot me meaningful, warning glances. I understood and fully interpreted every expression in his mean, menacing eyes - 'Grass us up and you're dead.'

Take A Message To Mary
The Everly Brothers

I'd never been inside Derby Magistrates Court and Police Station before. However, from the top deck of the bus, I'd often seen unsavoury characters leaving after paying their fines, or huddled together in front of the red brick, art deco building while they grabbed a quick fag during a court recess.

Now, I had a much closer view. I knew it was no good protesting my innocence and, in any case, the threat from Gra McBride needed thinking through before I said anything.

After being formally charged with aiding and abetting a smuggling operation I was detained deep in the bowels of the police and court buildings. Despite my recent ordeal, and the fate of my friend, I was being treated like a hardened criminal. Everyone I came into contact with while being processed seemed to look straight through me as if I wasn't there. I tried to ask about Sooty but was totally ignored. I was pushed and prodded from pillar to post, searched so intrusively that a double hernia could have been diagnosed, then handcuffed to a tall Victorian desk at the entrance to the cells. The only acknowledgement of my existence as a human being was when the desk sergeant asked for my name and address. Even then he conducted his enquiries between discussions about cricket.

'They're 230 for 5 overnight… Name?' The sergeant was talking to a plain clothes policeman and me at the same time, his tone changing from human to android for the last bit'

'Joseph King.' I quickly whispered, afraid to interrupt their conversation.

'Sobers could get another century tomorrow if it doesn't rain,' replied the detective.

'Mmm, he's invincible… Address?' continued the sergeant.

With the paperwork complete, he pushed an old black Bakelite phone across the desk towards me. 'Right! You've got one phone call. And make it snappy,' he ordered. 'There's a list of solicitors on the wall if you need one,' he added before returning to his cricket conversation.

In the movies, the accused usually rings a lawyer in this situation. But, besides not accepting the seriousness of my position, and although it was three in the morning, I just wanted to ring home for comfort. Like when I used to fall down and graze my knee as a little boy, I knew my mum would make everything alright. She'd ask me to put the nice policeman on the phone, and then tell him there'd been a terrible mistake, before ordering him to put me on the first bus back to Borrowash. But those innocent childhood days now seemed decades away. At sometime during the last six hours, I'd passed another boundary into manhood and a further chunk of innocence had evaporated into the warm, night air.

I was clinging onto the hope that Sooty had survived the crash and somehow had let Marlene and the lads know about his fate. I dialled home and it rang for ages. Then my mum's sleepy voice answered.

'It's me,' I whispered, not wanting the cops to know that I was ringing my mum.

'What time is it? Where are you?' she asked, irritated by the interruption to her night's sleep.

'Mum, listen carefully, I'm at the police station and I've been arrested,' I explained, slowly and deliberately.

There were a few moments of silence. 'Why? What have you done? Did you get drunk?' she spluttered, suddenly wide awake.

'No, but stay calm while I explain. I've... I've... I've been arrested for smuggling.'

It was as if her brain wouldn't accept that explanation. 'Have you been in a fight?'

'No mum, listen. They think I'm involved with a gang of rum smugglers but I'm innocent so don't worry,' I whispered harshly, desperately trying to make her accept the facts.

'Have you got clean underpants on?' she asked instinctively, her mind still trying to assemble the information.

'Mum, I've not been run over and I'm not in hospital.' I raised my voice in frustration. 'I'm in prison. And yes, I have got clean underpants on.'

The policemen suddenly stopped talking cricket and looked towards me, eyebrows raised.

'Come on, that's enough now, there isn't time to discuss your laundry.' The sergeant moved back towards the desk.

I quickly told my mum about Sooty and asked her to get in touch with his family, Marlene and the lads. The Sergeant snatched the phone from me and slammed it back on its cradle, cutting me off from the outside world.

I was then led down a dingy corridor with two tone walls painted brown and dark green. Two naked light bulbs hung from the low ceiling illuminating the cell doors on the right of the corridor. We passed an empty cell with its door wide open and then a couple that were occupied, perhaps by the McBrides. Then I was marched into another empty cell at the end of the row. Despite the warmth of the night, it felt damp and cold. The smell of urine and bleach invaded my nostrils and the first thing I focused on was a toilet without a seat. It dominated the windowless room as a reminder to occupants of the depths of degradation to which they had fallen. This wasn't a room with a toilet. It was a toilet with a bed.

The sergeant told me that he'd be back for me in the morning, then left the cell, slamming and locking the door behind him. I was suddenly overcome by a wave of claustrophobia and began to hyperventilate. I took deep breaths to calm myself down and tried to reason with myself that they couldn't keep me locked-up like this for long. I needed to get my mind out of the place, if not my body. So I lay on the hard, iron bed and waited to be transported into *The Sunset Lounge*. But I couldn't make it happen. I could see the plush, padded door but I couldn't get it to open. I could see the white venetian blinds at the window but couldn't see through them. I was locked out of *The Sunset Lounge* as securely as I was locked in the cell.

Eventually I gave up trying and realised what had happened to my treasured emotional retreat. First of all, the experiences of the past few hours had hardened me. I'd been pursued by the police, threatened at gunpoint by gangsters, involved in a serious road crash, seen one of my best friends seriously injured – or killed – then searched, arrested, handcuffed and thrown in jail. I had become a man. And real men didn't need somewhere to hide when things got scary. Secondly, the Spartan surroundings of my *real* bedroom, and the rest of that simple place I call home, now seemed better than any other place on earth. How I longed for my little sister to annoy me, mum to nag me, and dad to give me a clip round the ear. How I longed for the familiar smell of Sunday dinner, the signature tune to the *Billy Cotton Band Show* and even *Sing Something Simple*.

Despite the claustrophobic surroundings, the smell, and my deep despair, I managed to drift into a shallow sleep.

 Only The Lonely
Roy Orbison

Disturbing dreams drifted in and out of my brief and fitful slumbers; one where Sooty was standing in a cold and barren landscape, snow flurries flying round his head. He was looking towards two faceless figures on the horizon which were silhouetted against an intense and brilliant light. One had a semi-acoustic guitar slung round his neck. The other was wearing distinctive horn-rimmed glasses. They were beckoning Sooty towards them but he was hesitant, taking a step towards them one moment and stopping in his tracks the next. I was trying in vain to shout for Sooty not to go, my mouth opening wide in soundless screams. And when I tried to walk towards him my legs seemed full of lead, moving slowly but without progress. I reached out, making a desperate lunge, and woke with a start on the cold, blood and urine stained linoleum which covered the cell floor. I had woken into another nightmare. Still locked away from the outside world, desperately alone and afraid.

It must have been morning but I couldn't tell. My watch had been taken from me when I was processed. The only light came from the small square shutter that was cut into the heavy cell door. I slowly got up from the hard, iron bed. Every bone in my body seemed to ache from the effects of the van smash. There was no clue as to the time of day.

I thought about Julia and the warm, comfort of her body next to mine. I wanted her to touch me on the nose and tell me everything would be ok. But, even more, I longed for Sheila's bright, cheeky, sexually charged banter to lift my spirits. I needed her to look at me in that dreamy, intense way that promised excitement, deep love and commitment.

I turned back from the door and faced the ugly toilet pedestal. As an act of futile defiance, I had been resisting the natural urge to use it. As if succumbing to my basic need would be surrendering to the harsh reality that I was in prison. Me, Joe King, in prison? That likeable lad who never did anyone any harm, who was just in love with music, people, clothes and life in general.

I reflected on the fact that all the fond and familiar spots around town were only yards away from me. The Boccaccio, the Locarno, the Market Hall, the Kardoma, Dalton's record shop, Derwent Music Store, Cockpit Hill, Beverley's Men's Wear shop, Boots cosmetic department. And my second home, that housed my second family, the Derbyshire Advertiser. How I needed those friends right then. But under the circumstances all these things could have been on the other side of the world.

Finally, I gave way to the reality and accepted the indignity of having to take a piss in a prison cell. I began to choke inside. I was in prison. I'd lost my girlfriend. I'd lose my job. The group days would be over. I had reached my lowest ebb.

The sound of a key in the lock shook me from my despair. The Sergeant strode into the room carrying a plate of toast and a tin mug of tea on a metal tray. At least it wasn't bread and water, I thought.

'Here, eat this and then you're wanted in the interview room,' he said, without even a 'good morning' or 'did you sleep well?'

'I'll be back in a few minutes.' He grunted, before locking the cell behind him.

As I tucked into my meagre breakfast, it occurred to me that the last food I'd eaten was game pie, poached salmon, roast beef and exotic fruits. But the slice of toast tasted just as good.

Ten minutes later I was escorted back down the corridor and shown into a small interview room furnished with a battered table and half a dozen chairs. The whitewashed walls were bare, save for a calendar open at the month of July which featured a colour photograph of Chatsworth House and the headline *Take a day out in the beautiful Peak District*, a cruel message for visitors to the interview room. But at least it was a room with windows and by the angle of the sunlight I guessed that it was mid morning. This time I wasn't handcuffed and, after placing a large jug of water and glasses onto the table, the sergeant sat with me at the far end of the table.

I wondered if I would be going through the 'nice cop, nasty cop' routine seen in the movies. Mac once told me about one of his mates who had been beaten up by the police in a room like this. But that they had done it in a way that was undetectable on the surface. I heard several footsteps approaching the room.

Surely they didn't need an army to beat the truth out of me.

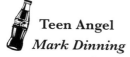

Teen Angel
Mark Dinning

The door swung open and there she stood like an angel, her youthful beauty and sparkling eyes lighting up the room and outshining the sun. It was Sheila. I started to stand but the sergeant gently pushed me back down. Behind Sheila was a plainclothes policeman, another in uniform and an old man with a wrinkled face that I instantly recognised. This kind, wise-looking face was supported by a scraggy neck which poked out of a Burberry shirt that was two sizes too big for him. The face belonged to the frail and slender frame of Lord Ives.

Now I was totally confused. Was Sheila implicated? Had she implicated me? And what the hell was Lord Ives doing here? One of my questions was almost answered without words because both Sheila and Lord Ives were smiling at me. I attempted to smile back and then the plainclothes policeman spoke.

'It seems Mr King, that you have some very influential people on your side, but I'll let Lord Ives fill us all in on the details,' he announced before they all sat down.

Lord Ives thanked the policeman and cleared his scraggy throat as if preparing for a long speech. The story he told was just like one of Wally's fantastic ramblings. Except that this was undoubtedly actual fact. It transpired that, since giving up his military duties, Lord Ives had been working as an undercover officer for the Customs and Excise in London. Being based in Derbyshire, he had been assigned to a case that had been frustrating the department for months. The authorities were aware of the mass distribution of crates of rum mixed with Coca-Cola – the cocktail Winston introduced me to as Ready Mix. And that the illicit booze was cleverly hidden in the glass coke bottles and distributed throughout the Midlands in large quantities. It was explained that the contraband would mainly find its way onto black markets within the West Indian communities of the larger towns and cities, and that in some cases whole kegs of rum changed hands. They also had a good idea that they were being smuggled in from Jamaica on ships that docked in Liverpool. But they couldn't get a lead on where the Ready Mix was being bottled or by whom. That was until Bass Brewery reported to the police that stock was going missing from its Coca-Cola bottling plant in Burton-upon-Trent. From that moment the police suspected the McBrides but had no hard evidence. All they had to go on was that a blue Dormobile van may have recently been involved.

Lord Ives took a sip of water to lubricate his vocal chords. 'That's when young Sheila here unwittingly helped us out,' he said, smiling in her direction.

'It all came about after dinner at Sheila's parent's house,' Lord Ives continued.

The old man went on to explain that after the meal Sheila had sat with him and told him how she loved dancing to live beat music and that she was into the local group scene. She admitted that, despite being under age, she regularly visited the dance halls and pubs around town, but asked Lord Ives not to tell her parents.

The Sergeant shot a disapproving glance towards Sheila before Lord Ives continued.

'I already knew of Sheila's friendship with Joe, here, who I had met previously at the newspaper where he works. Sheila also told me that Joe seemed more interested in his music than in her and that he was even taking on part-time work at Bass Brewery to earn money to buy better music equipment.'

Lord Ives paused for effect before relating the moment when the break-through to his case had materialised.

'But Sheila was most concerned for Joe's safety as he had been commissioned for this work by a couple of well-known thugs.' Lord Ives took another sip of water.

'It was then that I put two and two together.' He beamed with a look of satisfaction that added a hundred more wrinkles to his face.

Lord Ives explained that he'd only met me on a couple of occasions and was left with a dilemma. Priding himself on being an excellent judge of character, he was convinced that I wasn't knowingly involved with the smuggling operation. And, being particularly fond of Sheila and as a family friend, the last thing he wanted to do was betray her trust.

He knew that if he had involved the police at this stage Sooty and I could have become the main suspects and there would be no hard evidence to link the McBrides.

He went on to explain how he then laid his bait to bring the McBrides out into the open. Having established that the contraband was in the Dormobile van when it arrived at his party, he made an anonymous phone call to Graham McBride.

Lord Ives's face lit-up like a mischievous schoolboy as he recalled the conversation.

'I just whispered into the phone – Your crates are being dumped tonight, youth – and then rang off,' he said with delight, obviously proud of his attempt at a local accent.

'I knew that the McBrides would take steps to make sure that this didn't happen and I told the police that if they followed your van they'd catch the real culprits red-handed.'

He turned to me and his face became sombre as he continued. 'What I didn't expect was the intervention of the other patrol car or that the McBrides would be bent on destroying the evidence and you along with it,' he said apologetically.

'Is Sooty alright?' I interrupted, looking round the room.

There was a long period of silence. Everyone just looked at each other hoping the other would answer first.

'Well, is he alright?' I repeated, angrily.

Sheila reached over and took my hand. I could see that she was fighting back tears. 'He's in a bad way Joe, but he's still with us,' she stuttered.

I jumped to my feet. 'So you all just watched while the McBrides tried to kill us both,' I shouted.

Lord Ives tried to calm me down.

'I'm sorry Joe, we didn't expect them to go that far. And it was the only way we were going to catch them and prove your innocence.'

The plainclothes policeman decided to defuse the situation.

'Well Mr King, I think you've got a lot to thank Lord Ives for and you're free to go for a start.' He got to his feet as a sign that the interview was over.

He was right, so I apologised for my outburst and shook the old man's wizened hand, which had a surprisingly firm grip.

'We'll have to stop meeting like this,' he said with a smile.

I took Sheila in my arms and gave her a long hug. She felt so soft and warm. Oh, how I had needed that hug in the night and the sweet, feminine smell of her body to take away the foul odours of the police cell.

We held each other for far too long but I didn't want to stop. I felt so safe in her arms. The Sergeant coughed politely and I finally broke away.

Sheila kept hold of my hand. 'We should go and see how Sooty is,' she whispered.

Songs of Destiny

Poor Boy
Elvis Presley

We were dropped off at the Infirmary by Lord Ives in his chauffeur driven Rolls-Royce. I've always hated the smell of hospitals; ever since I cut my wrists open on a broken milk bottle when I was three. We walked purposefully up the long, central corridor and the smell of ether and boiled fish triggered signals of dread that were buried somewhere deep in my sub-conscious. But my spell in the police cell had inflicted fresh damage on my battered soul and the hospital didn't seem quite so bad.

We were shown to a narrow corridor outside the intensive care unit. There were chairs all down one side and at the far end sat a sad and lonely figure. It was Marlene, head bent, nervously fiddling with the braid around Sooty's Stetson hat which she clutched to her breast. She lifted her head as we approached and managed a weak smile.

'How is he?' I asked, taking her hand.

'I'm not sure. The nurse called for the doctor ten minutes ago and he's with him,' she stuttered, before breaking into tears.

As Sheila comforted her, the swing doors to the main corridor burst open. A stern looking matron, all starch and superiority, strode ahead of a grim looking Tolley, Benno and Whippet. The Matron ushered them towards us.

'Now sit there and don't make any noise,' she ordered. 'And remember, if they do let you see him, it'll be one at a time.' She shook a forefinger like a scolding school mistress.

After looking us all up and down as if she were unsure whether to leave us unattended she sniffed and pushed her way back out of the swing doors.

While we waited for news of Sooty I filled everyone in on events of the previous night. Up until then, all they knew was what my mum had told them on the phone - that Sooty was in intensive care and I was in prison.

'We should have come with you and sorted the fuckin McBrides once and for all,' Tolley shouted, struggling to keep control of his anger.

I told them about seeing Sooty, all bent and twisted and being covered with a blanket before they lifted him into the ambulance.

'If he doesn't make it, at least he'll be with his heroes,' whispered Benno, without much thought.

Marlene heard this and started to sob uncontrollably adding more tears to the soggy Stetson.

'I keep thinkin of how his mum and dad died in that crash with the articulate lorry,' she managed to say through her tears.

We all managed a kind smile despite her reference to a talking vehicle

'He'll be OK, Marlene,' comforted Whippet. 'He's in good hands here, and besides, he wouldn't go anywhere without that hat.'

A nervous laugh punctuated Marlene's sobs as she examined the crumpled hat and bravely tried to regain control.

We eventually ran out of things to say and sat in silence. Nurses came and went, sometimes running, sometimes walking. Each time the doors swung open we half stood in anticipation of news. But the nurses always avoided eye contact. While our eyes were still fixed on the doors to the intensive care ward, there was a noise behind us. We all turned to see the swing doors to the main corridor slowly open. An orthopaedic crutch poked through the gap. Then the shoulder it supported pushed through the doors and in stumbled Mac, a fag with two inches of ash dangling from his sneering mouth. He hopped forwards and I rushed to help him. Mac had his right leg in plaster. But it wasn't white plaster. It had been crudely painted black to match the right leg of his drainpipe trousers that had been cut off just above the cast.

'What the fuck happened to you?' shouted Tolley.

Mac moved forwards slowly on the crutches, the ash finally dropping off his fag and spreading down his black plaster cast. 'Broken ankle. Those fuckin' McBrides,' he explained, balancing on one leg so that he could brush the ash away.

'After you dropped me off they caught up with me at the lights on Friargate and forced me off the road. But I wouldn't tell them where you were going, so as I was lying on the road the bastards reversed their poxy Cresta over my leg.' Mac winced and carefully brushed more ash away.

'Trouble was, I was so pissed off with what they'd done that I told them their precious fuckin' booze would be at the bottom of the Derwent before long,' he explained, with a look of regret.

'Why is your plaster black?' Benno enquired, asking the question that was on all our minds.

'White looked crap so I got my sister to paint it this morning.' he replied with a frown, as if it was a stupid question and the most obvious of explanations.

'I even got the nurse to make the plaster as thin as possible - a sort of drain pipe cast,' he went on, stroking his leg with pride.

Suddenly the door to the intensive care ward opened. This time it was a doctor, stethoscope dangling from his neck and he was heading straight towards us with a sister and nurse on either side.

'Put that thing out immediately.' The sister shouted to Mac before the Doctor had time to speak.

I grabbed the fag from Mac's mouth as he wrestled with his crutches. The doctor was relatively young and I noticed that the collar of his white coat was turned up in an obvious rebellious attempt to kick against the traditions of the medical profession.

'Are any of you related to... er...' the doctor paused to

look at the sister's clipboard, '…William Sutcliffe?'

'No, his parents are dead and he lives with his Auntie,' I explained.

'Yes, she was in earlier this morning,' continued the doctor.

There was another long pause and the doctor appeared uncomfortable and lost for words. Marlene gripped my arm and dug her long red nails into my flesh. We were all anticipating what his next words would be. He took a deep breath before finally continuing.

'Well, I'm afraid to tell you… ' Marlene drew blood… ' that your friend is in a pretty bad way but I think we can save him with your help,' he announced.

 ## Wake Up Little Susie
The Everly Brothers

The relief was evident as we all started speaking at once, asking the doctor about his injuries, his chances, and how could we help with his treatment. Mac asked if he could smoke on the balcony.

The doctor held his hands up.

'One at a time now, please,' he pleaded, before proceeding to give us his prognosis.

He then explained that Sooty hadn't yet regained consciousness. He had broken both legs, punctured a lung and fractured his skull.

'Unless we can bring him round in the next few hours we'll have to take over his bodily functions for him,' explained the doctor.

'What's that mean?' Marlene asked, as she wiped the blood from my arm with her soggy handkerchief.

'It's what we call a life support machine,' the doctor explained. 'We take over his breathing for him and feed his body intravenously. The problem with that is, it could encourage his brain to hand over control too. And that could send him into a deep coma which could make his condition even more serious,' he added.

'So how can we help?' I asked.

The doctor invited us all to sit down and the sister brought him a chair. He positioned the chair in front of us but sat on it backwards which I thought was really cool for a doctor.

'It's a bit of a long shot, but I want each one of you to sit with, er… Sooty for a while and talk to him about anything that would resonate with his subconscious. 'It could be something he loves, something he hates, anything he's passionate about. Even familiar sounds or smells,' he concluded.

I sensed that this treatment wasn't the norm and noticed a sniff of disapproval from the sister. But the cool, young doctor was obviously determined to try something unconventional to help his patient.

We all agreed to take turns to sit with Sooty in an attempt to bring him back from unconsciousness, but we were only allowed in one at a time to minimise the risk of infection.

Marlene went first. After about ten minutes she returned in tears and told us how awful he looked.

'He's just lying there, his mouth wide open, tubes everywhere - down his throat and in his arm,' She explained through her sobs.

Sheila comforted her and asked what she had said to Sooty.

'I just kissed him on the cheek, told him how much I loved him and how he couldn't leave me all on my own,' she explained. 'I tried to remind Sooty about that Last Will and Testamonial that he had insisted we make and that despite being his Power of Eternity, I couldn't manage his affairs without him,' she sobbed.

'You mean Power of Attorney, don't you dear?' interrupted the sister in a condescending manner.

'No, I'm his Power of Eternity,' insisted Marlene, suddenly angry.

I was still thinking about what to say to Sooty so Whippet went next. He took Sooty's hat from Marlene's lap and disappeared through the swing doors. A few minutes later he returned, dejected, still clutching the hat, and told us what had happened.

'I put the hat by Sooty's side and ran his lifeless fingers over the braiding. Then I spoke of the day Buddy threw it to him. But no joy,' Whippet shook his head in defeat.

Benno started to get up, ready to go in and tell Sooty one of his famous jokes. They usually end up being shaggy dog stories that last for hours so we all prepared ourselves for a long wait. But before he could get to his feet, Mac pushed him back down into his seat with one of his crutches.

'Listen Benno, we'll all be dead before you finish one of your bleedin' jokes so let me go next. Anyway, I've got a great idea,' he said, with a mischievous sparkle in his eyes. Without waiting for a reply Mac pushed through the swing doors. The doctor and nursing staff looked uneasily at each other.

A few moments later Mac hobbled back but he had lost his sparkle.

'So what did you do?' Tolley asked for us all.

Mac hesitated and looked in the direction of the equally inquisitive medics. 'I'll tell ya later. It didn't work anyway,' he mumbled.

'Tell us now, you prat, we may want to do the same thing,' insisted Tolley.

'I don't think so, but... ok I'll tell you. I let rip with one of my blockbusters,' Mac announced with pride.

We all stared in amazement.

'Sooty was really sensitive to one of my specials,' he added defensively.

Mac turned to the shocked and now frostier faced sister. 'But I'd give it five minutes before you go back in if I were you duck.'

'What ya trying to do. Finish the poor bastard off?' Benno shouted, still annoyed at Mac's queue jumping.

'It was worth a bloody try and I swear his nose twitched briefly,' Mac argued.

'Well, don't expect me to go in there after you've dropped your guts,' Benno countered.

It was all getting a bit out of hand and could sense that even the liberal young doctor was beginning to doubt the wisdom of his plan. So I quickly volunteered to go next and pushed through the swing doors before the whole exercise was aborted.

I stopped dead in my tracks as I saw the pathetic figure lying there, a single angle poise lamp spotlighting his infirmity. An electrical monitor at the far side of the bed bleeped in time with his heartbeat. A bag of clear liquid was suspended upside down, its contents apparently being dripped into Sooty's arm via a rubber tube. I waved away the lingering evidence of Mac's recent visit and moved to the chair at Sooty's bedside. His pale face was totally expressionless and the only sign of life was the rising and falling of his chest from his shallow breathing.

I took Sooty's hand and began saying the first things that came to mind. I told him what had happened after the crash and that the McBrides were now locked away for good.

Not even a flicker from his closed eyes.

Then for some reason, I started softly reciting the spoken words from Mike Berry's hit *Tribute To Buddy Holly* - one of Sooty's anthems.

Buddy Holly was killed in a plane crash in 1959.

But his songs will always be remembered. Always.

Still no response. But then it came to me.

Three Steps To Heaven
Eddie Cochran

I quickly left Sooty's side in search of the doctor. From the look on my face when I burst back into the corridor they must have all thought that Sooty had come round. So I quickly told them my plan.

'He's not back with us yet but I just know what'll do it,' I announced.

They all stared back at me expectantly.

'*Eddie's Three Steps to Heaven*,' I blurted with excitement. 'It's Sooty's all time favourite and the one he always begs us to sing a cappella style on our way home from gigs,' The doctor looked puzzled.

'Yes, and it's *our* special song,' added Marlene hopefully.

The lads agreed and joined me in trying to persuade the doctor to let us all in at once. Despite the looks of derision from Sister Frosty Face, the young doctor agreed, providing that we all stood as far away from the bed as possible.

Back in the small intensive care ward, Marlene sat by Sooty's side and held his hand while the rest of us gathered at the end of the bed. The doctor stood behind us near the door. To simulate the guitar introduction, Whippet started a soft paradiddle by patting the blankets on the bed. Tolley signalled for Mac to start singing and we answered his refrain.

Now there... (Three steps to heaven)
are three... (Three steps to heaven)
steps to heaven. (Wap, wap, ooh)

Mac continued, getting into character with a sneer and a shaking of his black plaster cast.

Just listen... (Three steps to heaven)
And you will... (Three steps to heaven)
Plainly see.

There was no reaction from Sooty and Marlene started to

cry. But then she took a deep breath, wiped her eyes, stood up and took over at the chorus.

Step One... You find a boy to love.
Step two... He falls in love with you.
Step three... You kiss and hold him tightly.
Yea that sure... seems like heaven... to me.

I'd never heard Marlene sing before and her voice was like an angel's. Crisp, clear and pure. A lump came to my throat as she continued with the second verse. Mac joined us in the backing vocals.

The formula... (Three steps to heaven)
For heaven's... (Three steps to heaven)
Very simple. (Wap, wap, ooh)

Then, suddenly, Sooty's hand twitched. We all watched in amazement but continued with the song. The doctor quickly moved past us towards the bed. When Marlene reached the chorus again, Sooty's arm started to gently move from side to side, in time with the song. He was trying to direct Marlene like an orchestra conductor.

We continued singing but Marlene began to choke on the words with tears of joy and expectation. Sooty's eyes lids flickered. Then, very slowly, his eyes started to open. Marlene kept singing.

Then, suddenly, Sooty's eyes shot open, staring like a wild man. He flung his right arm to the side, sending the intravenous drip stand crashing to the floor which pulled the tubes from his arm.

The doctor pushed Marlene out of the way.

'Sister! Nurse! Get in here quick,' he shouted. 'And you lot, Get out!'

Back in the corridor, we waited in silence, all wondering the same. Had we managed to bring Sooty out of his coma or had he taken a turn for the worse?

These questions were soon answered. The doctor burst through the swing doors, a big smile of satisfaction on his face. 'You did it, he's conscious and he's going to be alright,' He shouted with absolute assurance.

We all hugged and Mac punched the air with one of his crutches. Marlene jumped into the doctor's arms sending his stethoscope flying. A smile even broke out on Sister Frosty Face. Then, Sheila and I kissed passionately, suddenly oblivious to the company we were in and the surroundings. We could finally express the relief from the traumas of the last twelve hours.

The doctor calmed things down. 'Now, he's not out of the woods yet and we've still got a lot of work to do,' he warned. 'But you can all go in and see him, one at a time,' he continued. 'Oh, and by the way,' he added with a smile. 'The first thing he said was "where my bloody hat", so you better take it in Marlene.'

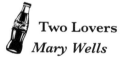 Two Lovers
Mary Wells

Sooty had taken three steps to heaven and four steps back. One month on, he had made good progress except for a mild relapse when Marlene took his Stetson hat to be dry cleaned. He came out of intensive care and into a general ward nine days after regaining consciousness and was waiting to hear when he would be moved to Bretby Convalescent Home.

Meanwhile, with the McBrides and their more illustrious generals in Leicester prison awaiting trial, The Rapids got its act back together. Even without Sooty and the trusty Dormobile, which was now in the scrap yard, we managed to fulfil our bookings. The publicity about our apparent heroics in bringing the smugglers to book, and an appeal in the local press, had resulted in offers from all kinds of would-be roadies.

We travelled to one gig in the back of a painter and

decorator's van until Mac's carelessly flicked nub end set fire to a pile of turpentine-soaked rags. But we managed to beat out the flames and avoid joining Sooty in hospital. Then, a cattle truck was sent to transport us to our engagement at the Derbyshire Young Farmers Ball in Wirksworth. We went on stage smelling of cow shit and even the rural groupies gave us a wide berth. There was even a trip to Borrowash Ex-servicemen's club on the back of a milk float and for a booking at the Moon Hotel in Spondon we had to resort to loading our equipment, drums and all, on to a double-decker Trent bus.

Mac, leg out of plaster, returned to work. We were back to our normal routine at the Derbyshire Advertiser except for fervent activity in helping with a campaign to raise money to replace Sooty's van. With only third party insurance and no chance of claiming from the McBrides, Sooty was without the means of carrying on his horticultural business. Then there was the matter of his loss of earnings until full recovery. We had only managed to raise £34 but the climax to the campaign was a Gala Rock'n'Twist Nite at the Locarno - all proceeds to Sooty's fund. Tickets had sold well and, with all the free publicity, it promised to be a rip-roaring night. Our target was to raise about fifty quid. Enough for a good deposit on a new van.

The events of a month ago had brought Sheila and I really close together. She had been working tirelessly in getting Sooty's appeal together and had turned Derwent Music Store into a virtual campaign headquarters. Her seductive charm, bubbly personality, and bare-faced cheek meant that few customers were able to leave the shop without making a contribution. At first, we were both so busy sorting things out that there was little opportunity to be alone together. Then, to my dismay, she left with the rest of the Forsyths for their annual two-week holiday in the South of France.

I missed Sheila more than I thought I would. When I first

met her, the desire for her company was inspired by pure lust. The memory of her wonderful body and seductive caresses still occupied my thoughts while we were apart. But I now missed her whole being. Sometimes I'd feel an ache deep down inside as if something had been ripped from my soul. Other times, jealousy would raise its ugly head. I'd imagine her beautifully tanned and lying on a beach in San Tropez surrounded by muscle-bound, wealthy French playboys.

I felt abandoned. Surely, if she had the same feelings for me she wouldn't have wanted to go. The Forsythe's holiday in the playground for the rich and famous also illustrated the vast social divide between us. The most I could hope for this year would be a trip to Skeggy with the lads. With each new day without her, I gradually accepted the futility of our relationship. But the desire and sense of loss didn't abate.

When Julia found out that Sheila was away, she saw it as an opportunity for us to get back together. One warm evening, when most of the mob had congregated Down Brook, Cathy told me that Julia still loved me and wanted me back. And then, one day at work, Mac made a confession about the night he went out with Julia. Despite being against Mac's egotistical principles, he told me that he hadn't gone-all-the-way with Julia and that, as far as he knew, she was still "ripe for the plucking." The admission stuck in Mac's throat and I suspected that Julia had persuaded him to come clean to help her win me back.

The longer Sheila was away, the more this made sense to me. Julia was from the same side of the tracks as me, we were old friends, I felt comfortable and safe in her arms, I fancied her, I was lonely and sexually frustrated and her best mate said she loved me.

The arguments and temptation became stronger each day and I hadn't received a single letter or even a postcard from France. Sheila was due back on the day of the *Rock'n'Twist Nite* at the Locarno - the big event.

A couple of nights before that, I bumped into Julia and Kathy in the Boccaccio and ended up taking Julia home. We kissed on the bridge over the brook, just like old times. So that was that.

I slept well that night, bathed in a warm feeling of security. But just before I drifted off to sleep, the door to *The Sunset Lounge* started to open.

I had no need for the sanctuary of what lay behind it, but I couldn't help wondering who was reclining on the leopard skin couch.

Songs of Praise

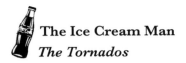

The Ice Cream Man
The Tornados

The next morning, as I lay in bed waiting for Saturday club to start on the radio, I forced myself to stop fantasising about what might have been with Sheila. I finally managed to convince myself that I would be a lot happier with Julia and it would be for the best.

Two hours of the latest pop music from both sides of the Atlantic was the perfect therapy to help me forget my romantic angst. The music inspired me and I started to look forward to the big *Rock'n'Twist Nite*, Sooty's benefit gig. My love affair with music came without emotional complications and I realised then that I was at my happiest and most fulfilled when I was playing my bass guitar. And that the Mecca Locarno, packed with young and beautiful, fashionable people, was the most exciting place in my world. The thrill of performing on the famous revolving stage and sending my bass notes thundering into the chests of an appreciative and adoring audience was like a drug to me.

Later in the day, we all met at Tolley's house to load the equipment into our latest form of temporary transport – Whippet's dad had borrowed an old converted Franco's ice cream van which we had adorned with posters for Sooty's benefit night. The rest of the lads were just as excited as we drove through the centre of town with the ice cream van's chimes playing Oranges and Lemons. Mac made us slow down near a group of girls in the Market Place.

'Fancy a lick girls?' he shouted out of the van's serving hatch window.

'I'll lick yours if you'll lick mine,' came the quick, witty reply from one of the girls and Whippet's dad nearly crashed the van into the war memorial.

After regaining his composure, he drove up the main street

and turned into the narrow alley at the side of the Locarno where we unloaded our equipment. It was the first run-out for my new bass cabinet which Winston had made for me. The solid wood cabinet housed an enormous 18 inch speaker and it took two of us to carry it into the empty ballroom.

The Locarno was a very different place out of hours. Without the lights and the music it looked like the inside of an aircraft hangar. The only sound to be heard in that temple of noise was a deliveryman pushing a squeaky barrow, stacked with coke bottle crates, across the polished dance floor. But as we set up our equipment the ballroom slowly came to life.

First of all the neon signs leading to *The New Yorker Bar* lit. Then we heard the lighting man throw a switch and the stage was flooded with pools of coloured light. The huge, mirror-glass ball high in the ceiling started to revolve sending thousands of bright spots dancing round the ballroom like a swarm of white locusts. Then the resident disc jockey ambled across the floor to test his equipment. His blond quiff was not quite in place yet and his bow tie was hanging, untied, around his neck. He mounted the gold quilted, twin-deck record console on his section of the revolving stage. After shuffling a few 45's he slipped a disc onto one of the turntables and I noticed that it was on the London American label. The silence was suddenly shattered as the drum introduction to Chris Montez's *Let's Dance* blasted from the mammoth speakers and bounced off every wall. The Locarno was awake and ready for the beautiful business of bringing music, fun, love and laughter to hundreds of young revellers.

The Locarno was the largest venue the group had played and Tolley, anticipating a large audience, decided to experiment with the positions of the two AC30 Vox amplifiers. He leaned them back against upturned chairs at an angle that would send the sound over the heads of the audience and up towards the ceiling. When we had set-up, tuned-up and tested the sound levels, the DJ pressed a switch sending our half of the revolving stage behind the scenes and the half with him to the front. There were fifteen minutes to go before the three sets of double doors would be opened for our audience.

Please Mr Postman
The Marvelettes

We sat in the dressing room in silence, our high spirits replaced with pre-stage nerves and for the first time since we started the group, our nervousness didn't just relate to the performance. This time we were the dance promoters as well. Sooty's livelihood and the future of the group would be shaped by the outcome of the event.

I wondered if Sheila had made it back from France in time for the performance as she said she would. Despite my acceptance of the futility of our relationship, I still loved her. And although I was hurt that she hadn't even written, I ached to see her again. If she was back in town, surely she would have come backstage to see me. Especially as she had spent all that time helping to organise the event. I told myself once again that she just didn't feel the same way about me and I should try to put it all behind me. Then I remembered the curt phone call I had received earlier from Julia's best friend Cathy. She said that something had come up and Julia wouldn't be able to make it to the performance. So at a time when I should have been in the highest of spirits I had become morose and depressed and we were due on stage in less than an hour.

Mac broke the silence. 'I bet no fucker turns up,' he mumbled as if he'd been reading my thoughts. 'They all hate me in Derby,' he added.

'Yea, that's because you've pissed-off half the blokes in town by shagging their girlfriends,' suggested Tolley.

'But tickets have sold well,' I offered, trying to raise their spirits, and mine.

'That's just out of sympathy,' Mac sneered.

'Yea, it doesn't mean they're going to turn up on the night,' added Benno.

A knock on the dressing room door interrupted the argument. We were all surprised when Wally Wrigley from the Advertiser poked his head round the door. 'Just popped in to wish you luck, lads,' he said, offering his hand to us all in turn.

'I didn't expect you to come along, Mr Wrigley,' I said as he pumped my hand.

'Oh, my friend Lord Ives asked me to join him. He's out there too,' he answered. 'And of course, we had to support you. After all, you wouldn't be in this mess if you hadn't helped us solve the biggest case we've had for years,' he added.

'The biggest case *we've* had?' repeated Mac.

'Er, yes, I... I suppose I can tell you all now,' he said slowly and deliberately. He stroked his chin in thought and sat on one of the dressing room chairs. Mac and I gave each other a knowing glance and waited for the start of one of Wally's fantastic ramblings.

'The truth of the matter is, lads, I'm an undercover secret service agent and the Customs and Excise department asked me to help Lord Ives with this case,' he announced with pride.

The other lads listened open mouthed. They hadn't been subject to one of Wally's fantasies before and were captivated by his words.

'So when I overheard Joe here, talking about the West Indian party, I put two and two together,' he continued.

Mac and I had heard enough.

'That's fantastic,' I interrupted, with false enthusiasm, 'but we have to get ready to go on stage now.'

I opened the dressing room door and Wally took the hint.

'Of course lads, I understand. But thanks again, and by the length of the queue outside it should be a huge success.'

'Queue?' asked Whippet.

'Yes, it's stretching right down to the bottom of Babington Lane', answered Wally. 'Oh! And I nearly forgot.'

He pushed his hand into the inside pocket of his tweed, three piece suit and produced a crumpled pink envelope.

'You've had another letter Joe. It was delivered to the office on Thursday.'

He handed me the letter and the first thing I noticed was the French postage stamp.

'Sorry I didn't give it to you earlier, but I kept missing you,' he explained with mild apology.

Then I realised what he had said.

'Another letter?' I asked.

'Yes, I gave the other one to that friend of yours, Julia, when she came in for more tickets last week.'

I was silent as the realisation of the situation sunk home. Wally had quite innocently given Sheila's first letter to Julia to pass on to me. And she had deliberately withheld it. She'd probably read the contents and that could be why she wasn't coming.

Wally spoke again. 'You did get the other letter, didn't you?'

'Err... oh yes. Thanks,' I stuttered and shut the door behind him.

I was left holding the letter with both hands but afraid to open it. On the back where the envelope was stuck down were handwritten initials S.W.A.L.K. which I knew was a soppy abbreviation for *Sent With A Loving Kiss*. At the bottom of the envelope there were the initials B.U.R.M.A. which I didn't understand.

I just stood there clutching the envelope. The lads had watched Wally hand me the letter and my stunned reaction.

They started to take the piss.

'Ooh la la! I wonder just who that could be from,' mocked Whippet.

'Leave him, it's the first time he's seen a French letter,' added Mac.

I told them all to get stuffed and left the dressing room to a barrage of cat-calls and wolf whistles. I carefully opened the envelope as I made my way towards the backstage fire doors. But once outside in the alley I hesitated before removing the contents. I'd heard about "Dear John" letters and was preparing for the worse. I finally removed, and slowly unfolded, the single page of pink notepaper.

'Dear Joe,'

Not Dear John, I thought, a good sign. For some reason my hands were shaking and I could hardly focus on the beautifully flowing and distinctly feminine handwriting.

'I hope you are well and that Sooty is making good progress. There's something I didn't tell you in my last letter, but here goes. I miss you more than I thought possible. It's still hot and sunny here and San Tropez is beautiful. But all I do is mope around, thinking of you by day and dreaming of you at night. I'm no company, and my father has threatened to send me back to my Auntie's in London. This is not like me as you know Joe, but I'm lost without you. I just want to be with you and no one else. I hope you are being good and are managing to fight off the groupies. The only good thing about all this is that I'm building up a really good tan and my body has turned a beautiful bronze colour. I can't wait to show it to you when I get home. At night, when it's too hot to sleep, I fantasise about us making love on the beach to the sound of the sea. I love you so much, Joe King. I just hope and pray you feel the same way too. Otherwise this letter is going to seem really pathetic. Well anyway, I've said it now, and providing I have the nerve to finally post this letter, you will soon know how I really feel about you.

All my love, forever, Sheila xxx

PS. Our ferry gets in Saturday lunch-time and all being well I'll be there for the start of Sooty's benefit night.

I took a leap into the middle of the narrow alley and punched at the small patch of blue sky that was just visible between the roof of the Locarno and the block of shops next door.

'Yes! She loves me!' I screamed.

A sudden round of applause interrupted my exuberance as the section of queue passing the end of the alley responded to my announcement.

Embarrassed, but elated, I dashed back inside the dance hall and burst through the dressing room door in mid air.

'The queue is four deep and it's going to be a fabulous, fabulous night,' I shouted.

Mac was pulling on the drainpipe trousers to his red mohair suit. 'On a promise are we Ginner?' he said, pointing at the pink notepaper that was still in my hand.

The rest of the lads were all dressed in their powder blue suits and busy doing their hair.

'Come on Romeo, get ya kit on, we're on in ten minutes,' Tolley warned.

I stuffed the letter into my pocket and started to get changed.

At this point in the proceedings Sooty would normally poke his head round the dressing room door to tell us how big the audience was. We all missed his positive enthusiasm which made us all the more determined to make this performance our best ever.

A lively knock on the door broke my chain of thought and from the expressions on the lads faces I could tell that they were all hoping, beyond reason, that Sooty was on the other side of the door. I, however, was hoping to see Sheila. I quickly zipped my trousers up and opened the door. There stood Winston, bobbing up and down and waving an open bottle of coke in his right hand, his face alight with excitement and enthusiasm.

'Just called back stage to wish you guys luck. 'Dis is your big moment!' He thrust the bottle of coke in my face and laughed.

'Here Joe, have a swig of 'dis before your go on.'

We all reacted at once and playfully pushed him back out the door.

'Hey man! It's 'de real 'ting. 'De source of 'de Ready Mix has mysteriously dried up,' he protested as we slammed the door in his face.

The disc jockey was now well into his first set with a thunderous selection of superb sounds that shook the whole building. Our adrenalin levels began to rise. Whippet and Benno beat the top of the dressing table surface in time to Sandy Nelson's *Let There Be Drums*. I sat on the floor with my back pressed against the wall where I could feel the bass notes course through my body like a second heart beat. Mac bopped around the room practising his pelvic thrust. And Tolley paced up and down, miming to the guitar breaks and nearly wrenching the tremolo arm from his Stratocaster. We were like caged animals waiting to be let loose for the kill.

Let's Go
The Routers

Our animation was interrupted by yet another knock on the dressing room door. I rushed to open it, again, hoping to see Sheila . But this time it was the manager of the Locarno.

'Ok lads! You're on after the next record,' he shouted.

The butterflies went berserk.

'Come on! Let's do it for Sooty,' yelled Tolley.

We were out of the dressing room like greyhounds from a trap. After taking our positions on the rear half of the revolving stage, Tolley switched on the power to our amplifiers.

'*Lucille* in C,' he yelled, and we were ready to go.

Out front, Benny Spellman's *Fortune Teller* began to fade and we heard the muffled voice of the DJ rise to a crescendo as he shouted out the magic words '… the fabulous Rapids.'

The stage jolted into motion throwing me momentarily off balance as Whippet counted us in.

'One, two, a one, two, three, four.'

And we blasted out the introduction riff to *Lucille*.

The stage moved slowly, gradually transporting us round towards our audience. Very soon we would see just how much support we had managed to drum-up. And I wondered if the face of my sweet little Sheila would be there looking up at me.

Half-way round, the blast from our amplifiers hit the side walls of the stage with almost physical force. Part of the dance floor and a section of balcony were now visible. I could see the audience, crowds of young people, four deep on the balconies and as far back as I could see on the dance floor. As the revolving stage brought us further toward the front, our thumping riff burst out into the hall. It was met by an equally powerful sound – thunderous applause. The reception from the crowd almost drowned the noise from our guitars and drums.

A bank of coloured spotlights hit us full-on and Mac had to shield his eyes as he fumbled for the mic switch. We hit G at the conclusion of the intro and Mac, shouting rather than singing, started the show.

'Lucille… you don't do your daddy's will.'

The crowd responded with even more noise. They jumped up and down, clapping, shouting and screaming. Some even hung from the balcony. I hadn't heard or seen anything like it before. The doormen were fighting to keep the kids off the stage, things were thrown in the air, and a pair of frilly knickers hit Mac full in the face as he struggled to be heard above the sound of the crowd.

The reception had an overwhelming effect on us. We responded in kind by performing with a pace and passion that I didn't think we were capable of. Each note and beat was emphasised with exaggerated animation and facial expressions that moved between ecstasy and excruciating pain. Mac gyrated to the front of the stage and thrust his groin towards the audience inciting one girl to grab his ankle and another to fall backwards into a deep faint.

Despite the competition from the audience, the sound we were making on stage was sensational. The angles of the guitar amplifiers sent the clear, crisp notes from the Stratocasters crashing against the ceiling where they exploded into a shimmering rain of sound. The 18 inch speaker in my new cabinet pumped out full, round bass notes that shook the walls and covered the dance floor with a plush, velvety carpet of sound. Bass and treble met in a perfect fusion of sound that was underpinned by the driving beat of precise percussion.

The more we played, the more the excitement increased, both on and off stage. But as I searched the faces of the captivated crowd, there was no sign of Sheila. Oh, how I wanted her to be there to share our moment of glory. My euphoria became tinged with doubt and I wondered if she'd had second thoughts about us. Or if some French hunk had swept her off her feet on the way back from posting my letter. Shaking away the gathering gloom, I allowed the music and atmosphere to carry me back to that wonderful experience of mass adulation.

The temperature inside the packed dance hall increased with every number and the sweat poured off us in buckets. After bringing a rousing version of *What'd I Say* to a close, Mac wiped his forehead on a hand towel and threw it into the crowd where girls fought to catch it. An empty coke bottle followed which smashed against the front of my new bass cabinet as the fever-pitch took on a dangerous dimension. I briefly remembered what Tolley had said about how Mac was so unpopular with the young males of town and hoped that, along with the sweat, there wouldn't be blood and tears.

We finished our electrifying set with *Sweet Little Sixteen* but the crowd wanted us to continue. They stamped on the floor, whistled and chanted for more. We looked over our shoulders at the DJ who was waiting to throw the switch that would bring him forward and take us back behind the scenes, but he gestured for us to play another number.

'Let's do *Sheila*.' shouted Mac, and Whippet started pounding out the introduction on his tom-toms.

The response from the crowd nearly took the roof off. Half way through our encore I noticed that something was happening out on the packed dance floor. Round the front of the stage it was shoulder-to-shoulder bodies, at least twenty deep. Although it was hard to see clearly through the glare of the spotlights, there appeared to be some kind of a commotion at the back of the crowd. I wondered if a fight had finally broken out. I saw that the kids on the balcony were focusing on the back of the crowd and clapping. I shot a questioning glance at Tolley but he was too busy concentrating on our performance and just shrugged.

Then, suddenly, the crowd in front of us slowly parted like a human Red Sea. A path was being made right through the centre of the dance floor. I could just make out the silhouettes of a group of people moving slowly forwards from the back of the hall. But they appeared to be pushing something and the crowd were greeting them as they moved forwards. As they came into clearer view through the halo of light my eyes gradually focused on a figure in a wheelchair wearing a huge Stetson hat.

It was Sooty. He had a broad beam on his face as he acknowledged the crowd. Marlene was pushing him from behind, already in tears. On one side of her was the young doctor from the Infirmary and, a now smiling, Sister Frosty Face. Walking on the other side of them was the most beautiful girl I had ever seen. She was wearing a figure-hugging, emerald green, oriental style dress that emphasised her tiny little waist and every voluptuous curve of her body. Her golden tan toned beautifully with her dark brown, shoulder-length hair that flicked up at the sides. It was Sheila.

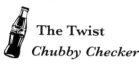

The Twist
Chubby Checker

We had finished our encore to thunderous applause but I was oblivious to the ovation. Then, the shouts and screams turned to warm applause for the unexpected appearance of the beneficiary of the event. But while all eyes were on Sooty, all I could see was Sheila. I needed to touch her, hold her, and kiss her. Our eyes met and Sheila's face lit-up with the loving smile that I had been pining for. She ran towards me and I started to take my guitar off. But I was pulled back from the front of the stage by a frowning Tolley.

'*Three Steps to Heaven* for Sooty,' he yelled.

I hurriedly put the bass back round my neck as Whippet counted us in.

Marlene positioned the wheelchair right in front of the stage and a huge spotlight was trained on Sooty, bathing him in a pool of white light. As Mac started the refrain, Sooty waved his hands at us like an orchestra conductor.

Now there… (Three steps to heaven)
are three… (Three steps to heaven)
steps to heaven. (Wap, wap, ooh)

Although Sooty was beaming with delight, I noticed him wipe a tear from under his Stetson hat.

Just listen… (Three steps to heaven)
And you will… (Three steps to heaven)
Plainly see.

Sooty's anthem continued with backing vocals from the

entire audience who clapped along to the beat. But my eyes were still fixed on Sheila's as we mimed the lyrics to each other.

Step One... You find a boy to love.

Step two... He falls in love with you.

Step three... You kiss and hold him tightly.

Yea that sure... seems like heaven... to me.

I was desperate for the number to end so that I could get to my sweet little Sheila. When the last chord was finally struck the Locarno exploded into applause. Chants of Sooty, Sooty, echoed around the dance hall. Sheila reached up towards me from the front of the stage and I ripped the guitar from my neck. But our hungry passion was thwarted once again.

'Attention everyone, attention!' A frail, croaky voice I recognised was speaking over the p.a. system.

'Stay right there boys,' the voice continued.

And then I saw Lord Ives approaching from the side of the stage with a mic in his trembling hand. He held up his other hand in an attempt to quieten the crowd.

'Quiet please,' Lord Ives repeated, shielding his wrinkled eyes from the glare of the spotlights. He had reached centre stage and the noise from the crowd began to abate.

'Give us a song granddad.' The old man ignored the heckler.

'Ladies and gentlemen, boys and girls,' Lord Ives announced formally.

I looked down at Sheila, wondering how long this speech would delay the moment when I would be able to take her in my arms. She smiled back longingly.

'On behalf of Her Majesty's Customs and Excise Department, I would like to take this opportunity of thanking The Rapids here, and especially Bill Sutcliffe and Joe King for helping us solve one of our most challenging cases.'

Cheers and applause rang out and we all took a bow. Lord Ives held his hand up again and continued.

'I can tell you that, thanks to your support and generosity, the proceeds for the evening have realised ...' He looked down at a scrap of paper in his bony hand and tried to raise his voice. '... one hundred and fifteen pounds.'

The crowd cheered once more.

'But that's not all' Lord Ives was straining his voice to be heard.

I looked down at Sheila again and she blew me a kiss of encouragement. I was now beside myself with frustration. But Lord Ives cleared his throat and continued his long, drawn-out speech.

'What I haven't mentioned yet is that Her Majesty's Government had put up a reward for information that would help solve this case and put those responsible behind bars.'

My frustration suddenly turned into expectation as the old man's words sunk in. We all exchanged quizzical looks and I looked back at Sheila who gave me a knowing wink.

Lord Ives bent down from the front of the stage towards an open-mouthed Sooty and raised his voice as much as he could.

'So it gives me great pleasure in presenting William and the band with this cheque for...'

He paused for effect, glanced down at the piece of paper in his hand and shouted the rest.

'... one thousand pounds.'

We just stared at each other in amazement but the crowd went berserk.

'And that's still not all folks,' the old man yelled, trying to quieten the crowd once again. He turned towards us and ushered us forward. 'Boys! Please take your guitars off and step to the front of the stage.'

We obeyed without question and stumbled forwards like zombies. Our brains were still trying to cope with the shock and delight of the cash reward. As we stepped onto the fixed front edge of the stage, the revolving section jolted into action to take our guitars, drums and amplifiers behind the scenes. We turned to watch our equipment disappear wondering what was going to happen next. I looked at Mac but he seemed as bewildered as the rest of us.

Then we could see it emerging from the dark side of the stage. The silhouette of a large, bulky object was slowly being transported to the front. As the stage inched slowly round, several spotlights hit the mysterious object and we saw it in all its glory.

A brand new, bright red Commer van completed its manoeuvre and came to a halt. The crowd were chanting and cheering once more but we just stared at the shiny vehicle in amazement. It was immaculately finished with white walled tyres and chrome everywhere. I rushed forwards and peered through the windscreen. It was fitted with a small coke chiller and bench seats upholstered in leopard skin. Passenger windows had been cut into the side panels below which *The Rapids Tour Bus* had been beautifully sign written. The ornate type face with shadow effects reminded me of American roadside diners. Then I noticed a discreet Coca-Cola logo painted in the centre of the driver's door. The rest of the lads, who had been rooted to the spot in total disbelief, joined me to inspect this voluptuous vehicle. Tolley sunk to his knees and kissed the front bumper while Mac climbed on the roof to pose for a press photographer.

Walking round the back of the van, I saw that the back doors had been sign written too, displaying the proud announcement –

Joint Tour Sponsors: The Coca-Cola Corporation and William Sutcliffe. Landscape Gardener. Tel: Derby 62215.

I stood back from the van to take in its splendour and nearly fell backwards off the stage. The spotlights reflected in the highly polished chrome adornments to create star-bursts of coloured light. Then I realised what the van reminded me of. It was like a mobile version of my Sunset Lounge. My heart sank.

I wondered if this whole experience – the Locarno, the crowds, the acclaim for our performance, Sheila waiting for me on the dance floor, the money, the van – was all in my imagination too. Was it just a dream? Was I in a giant version of my Sunset Lounge? I pinched myself. The van was still there. I pinched myself again and looked down at Sheila. She was still there, wiping a tear from her eye, and still smiling back at me. Then Lord Ives voice finally ended my fears.

'Yes folks, thanks to the efforts of a certain enterprising young lady, the Coca-Cola Corporation has donated this wonderful vehicle to The Rapids.'

Cheers rang out and he continued. 'She wrote to their head office in Atlanta, Georgia, USA and they agreed that putting an end to the use of their brand name to peddle contraband was worthy of reward too.' The old man walked over to my side of the stage before continuing.

'So please welcome her on stage right now …

'… Miss Sheila Forsythe.'

At first, Sheila refused to move and hid her face in her hands out of sheer embarrassment. But the crowd insisted and she was man-handled onto the stage. I was now closer to her than I'd been all night. It was agony. After learning what she had done for Sooty and the group, I loved and desired her even more. But Lord Ives was waiting for her, arms outstretched and the crowd were chanting her name. As she passed me, we stared into each other's eyes and her hand gently brushed mine. I could feel the love pass between our fingertips like an electric current. She moved under the spotlight and the old man put a bony hand around her shoulders.

'Let's give this remarkable young lady a big hand,' he

shouted, and the Locarno erupted yet again.

Lord Ives voice had now been reduced to a hoarse whisper and the manager of The Locarno took the mic off him.

'Finally, ladies and gentlemen, boys and girls, let's welcome the star of the show....'

He raised his voice to a shout.

'.... the man who bravely endured pain and personal loss through this whole episode....,' he paused for effect. '...let's hear it for William Sutcliffe... or to you...' He raised his voice to a crescendo 'Soot... tee!'

As two, burly Locarno bouncers lifted Sooty and his wheelchair onto the stage, I made way for them by stepping back onto the turntable section. I was now standing behind Sheila, waiting for the opportunity to whisk her away. Sooty was in tears as he waved his acknowledgment to the cheering crowd. Suddenly the stage jolted into motion and I stumbled backwards. When I regained my balance I found myself moving behind the scenes along with our shiny new vehicle as the disc jockey's quilted console moved forward. Sheila quickly ran back from the front and jumped into my arms.

We fell backwards and landed on the moving floor which slowly transported us backstage and then shuddered to a halt. We were completely out of view in the dimly lit back-stage area and alone together at last.

The Night Has A Thousand Eyes
Bobby Vee

Sheila had landed on top of me but I felt no pain. Only the warmth of her body as our hungry lips finally engaged. We writhed together in a frenzy of passion; a passion that had been fuelled by the agonising, almost tortuous, delay in being able to express our emotions. I was kissing her ear, her neck, and almost every exposed area of her body.

Sheila's emerald green dress had worked its way up to her smooth, freshly tanned thighs. She tugged at my shirt and her hands gripped my naked back as we rolled over the stage floor. Our hearts were beating faster and louder than the beat from Johnny Burnette's *Dreamin'* which thumped out at the front of the stage. As I fumbled for the zipper at the back of her dress, Sheila stopped me and pointed to the van.

We didn't need to speak and probably couldn't have. We were still kissing as we climbed inside our precious new passion wagon and fell across the leopard skin bench seat. My shirt was soon off my back. Sheila wriggled out of her dress and then straddled me as I lay back against the upholstery. With uncommon ease I managed to unclip her bra single-handed and felt the soft warmth of her breasts spill against my bare chest. Sheila was naked except for her white, lacy, bikini pants. Our desire for each other knew no bounds and we had reached the point of no return.

On the other side of the stage the party was still in full swing. But Sheila and I were oblivious to the revelry, invisible to the rest of the world and deeply engrossed in our own private party of passion. Sheila frantically tugged at my belt and we stopped kissing just long enough for me to arch upwards and slide my jeans and pants round my ankles. It became hotter and steamier in the van and the music seemed louder as Elvis encouraged us to *Surrender* to each other and indulge in the ultimate expression of our love and desire.

Our frenzy of excitement froze momentarily as I slowly entered Sheila. She threw her head back and dug her nails into my flesh. We just clung to each other, motionless, not wanting the glorious moment to end. I stared into Sheila's dark, dreamy eyes and then the frenzy of passion exploded once more. The van rocked from the motion of our hot, wet bodies. As we moved together, faster and faster, the music seemed to be getting even louder. I wanted to explode.

Suddenly, thousands of bright spots burst in my head like a swarm of white locusts and I floated away into ecstasy. I slowly opened my eyes and sucked in the hot steamy air. But the locusts were still there. We were motionless but the van was still moving. Brilliant shafts of light suddenly shot through the windows of the van. I could hear loud applause which seemed to be right on top of us. Sheila's eyes suddenly opened wide with fright.

The realisation of what had happened came to us simultaneously. We both sat bolt upright and stared in disbelief through the front window of the van. We were no longer in the dimly lit backstage area. We were front of stage, under the spotlights, totally naked and facing over 800 appreciative, if rather shocked, pairs of eyes.

When they realised what they had just witnessed the crowd went wild. The applause turned into cheers and whistles of appreciation for our energetic and extremely animated, climatic performance. We froze like two rabbits caught in the lights of an oncoming car. Two rabbits that had just finished doing what rabbits do best. I caught a glimpse of Mac in the sidelines, hovering over the controls that rotate the stage, his smile of self-satisfaction explaining our fate.

I looked over at Sheila who was holding her crumpled emerald green dress to her chest. She looked radiant. Her face was flushed both from her embarrassment and the recent physical exertion. Her dark, shiny hair, wild and dishevelled, had fallen forwards over her face. We glared at each other in horror, wondering what to do next. But as we gazed into each other's eyes, our love overcame the fear.

My open-mouthed expression of shock turned into a smile and Sheila smiled back. Then we both started to laugh.

The crowd were stamping on the dance floor chanting for

more. Sheila just shrugged her bare shoulders in acceptance of the situation then turned to face the front. She rose slightly from the seat and, still hiding her naked breasts with one hand, started to wave to the crowd. I reached for two cokes, bit off the caps and slid across the seat to get closer. Before checking for the distinctive aroma of rum, we clinked bottles and toasted our very public performance.

'More! More! More!' continued the chanting crowd.

I felt Sheila's hand on my thigh. She looked up at me with those dark dreamy eyes and whispered in my ear.

'So! Can you manage an encore, Joe King?'

Pulling her closer to me, I kissed her gently and we both knew that this would be the longest running show on earth.

THE END

Seventy-Seven Songs

1. It Doesn't Matter Anymore – Buddy Holly (1959)
2. I Hear A New World – The Blue Men (1960)
3. Tribute to Buddy Holly – Mike Berry (1961)
4. Get A Job – The Silhouettes (1958)
5. School Is Out – Gary US Bonds (1961)
6. First Date, First Love, First Kiss – Sonny James (1957)
7. Mac the Knife – Bobby Darin (1959)
8. You Talk Too Much – Joe Jones (1960)
9. Summertime – Ricky Nelson (1962)
10. Sittin' In The Balcony – Eddie Cochran (1957)
11. Summer Holiday – Cliff Richard (1963)
12. Summertime Blues – Eddie Cochran (1958)
13. Transistor Sister – Freddie Cannon (1961)
14. Itsy Bitsy Teenie Weenie Yellow Polkadot Bikini
    – Bryan Hyland (1960)
15. End of the World – Skeeter Davis (1963)
16. Life's Too Short – The Lafayettes (1962)
17. Standing On The Corner – The Four Lads (1956)
18. Apache – The Shadows (1960)
19. Learning The Game – Buddy Holly (1960)
20. Love Letters – Ketty Lester (1962)
21. You Don't Know What You've Got (Until You Lose It)
    – Ral Donner (1961)
22. Mr Bass Man – Johnny Cymbal (1963)
23. Rave On – Buddy Holly (1958)
24. Let There Be Drums – Sandy Nelson (1961)
25. Mecca – Gene Pitney (1963)
26. Sheila – Tommy Roe (1962)
27. Stairway to Heaven – Neil Sedaka (1960)
28. Let's Have A Party – Wanda Jackson (1960)
29. Entry Of The Gladiators – Nero and the Gladiators (1961)
30. Dance To The Bop – Gene Vincent (1958)
31. The Stripper – David Rose (1962)
32. Midnight Shift – Buddy Holly (1959)
33. Problems – The Everly Brothers (1959)
34. Princess, Princess – Johnny Tillotson (1960)
35. Coming Home Baby – Mel Torme (1962)
36. Rumble – Link Wray (1958)
37. Saved – LaVern Baker (1961)

38. Here Comes Summer – Jerry Keller (1959)
39. You Are My One Desire – Buddy Holly (1957)
40. Halfway to Paradise – Billy Fury (1961)
41. Wham! – Lonnie Mac (1963)
42. Searchin' – The Coasters (1957)
43. The Tender Trap – Frank Sinatra (1956)
44. Flash Bang Wallop – Tommy Steele (1963)
45. Ambush – The Outlaws (1961)
46. Run To Him – Bobby Vee (1961)
47. Duke Of Earl – Gene Chandler (1962)
48. Money (That's What I Want) – Barrett Strong (1960)
49. Baby It's You – The Shirelles (1962)
50. Let The Good Times Roll – Shirley and Lee (1956)
51. Temptation – The Everly Brothers (1961)
52. Workin' For The Man – Roy Orbison (1962)
53. Watch Your Step – Bobby Parker (1961)
54. It Keeps Rainin' – Fats Domino (1961)
55. Happy Birthday Sweet Sixteen – Neil Sedaka (1961)
56. That's It – I Quit – I'm Movin' On – Sam Cooke (1961)
57. A Shot Of Rhythm and Blues – Arthur Alexander (1962)
58. Stay – Maurice Williams and The Zodiacs (1961)
59. Under The Moon Of Love – Curtis Lee (1961)
60. Let The Little Girl Dance – Billy Bland (1960)
61. Road Runner – Bo Diddly (1960)
62. I Fought The Law – The Crickets (1961)
63. The Point Of No Return – Gene McDaniels (1962)
64. Falling – Roy Orbison (1963)
65. Valley Of Tears – Buddy Holly (1961)
66. Take A Message To Mary – The Everly Brothers (1959)
67. Only The Lonely – Roy Orbison (1960)
68. Teen Angel – Mark Dinning (1960)
69. Poor Boy – Elvis Presley (1957)
70. Wake Up Little Susie – The Everly Brothers (1957)
71. Three Steps To Heaven – Eddie Cochran (1960)
72. Two Lovers –Mary Wells (1963)
73. The Ice Cream Man – The Tornados (1963)
74. Please Mr Postman – The Marvelettes (1961)
75. Let's Go – The Routers (1962)
76. The Twist - Chubby Checker (1960)
77. The Night Has A Thousand Eyes – Bobby Vee (1963)

About the author

At the 'birth' of British pop, Roger Smith was playing bass guitar in Derby semi-pro groups The Rapids and Godfreys Grit'n'Soul Band. Later in the decade he helped establish Derby's Discovery Discotheque, Clouds, and Shotgun Discotheque. Roger worked at The Derbyshire Advertiser and The Derby Evening Telegraph for many years and in 1975 joined Derby County Football Club, then Football League Champions, as Advertising and Sponsorship Executive. He formed Smith East Associates in 1977, with Trevor East, and created one of the region's leading advertising agencies. He is still working as a marketing consultant, and has lived in Derby all his life.

Also by the author

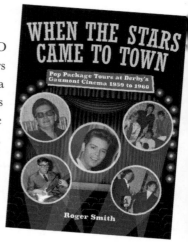

WHEN THE STARS CAME TO TOWN chronicles over forty shows that visited Derby's largest cinema between 1959 and 1966 and shares the memories of people who were there. It also presents a fascinating, previously unpublished, collection of photographs of some of these stars taken while of they were in the city. These shows presented as many as a dozen International pop stars along with up-and-coming British artists - usually lower down on the bill. For example, one of the acts supporting the Everly Brothers, Little Richard and Bo Diddly at Derby's Gaumont cinema on 11 October 1963 was the Rolling Stones who closed the first half.

Thanks

… to the following for the inspiration behind this work of fiction.
Teenage friends from Down Brook in Borrowash – 1959-1964
Colleagues from the Derbyshire Advertiser – 1960 to 1969
Fellow members of the The Rapids beat group – 1961 to 1965
John Pemberton who invented Coca-Cola in 1886

And finally
…to Steve Fox and David Foster (artwork, illustration and
design collaboration) Eric Chapman, Melvyn Lloyd-Smith
and Richard Cox (encouragement, advice and valuable help)